Jo Wats..ove series
and *Love to Hate You* which has sold over 100,000 copies. She's
a .... winner with over 50 million r...
Wat... ....
Depeche Mode devotee. She lives in South Africa with her family.

For more information, visit her website www.jowatsonwrites.co.uk,
follow her on Twitter @JoWatsonWrites and Instagram
@jowatsonwrites and find her on Facebook at
www.facebook.com/jowatsonwrites.

Praise for Jo Watson's hilarious romantic comedies:

'Witty, enjoyable and unique' *Harlequin Junkie*

'Found myself frequently laughing out loud and grinning like a fool!'
BFF Book Blog

'Heart-warming, funny, sweet, romantic and just leaves you feeling
good inside' *Bridger Bitches Book Blog*

'Full of pure-joy romance, laugh-out-loud moments and
tear-jerkers' *Romantic Times*

By Jo Watson

Destination Love Series
Burning Moon
Almost A Bride
Finding You
After the Rain
The Great Ex-Scape

Standalone
Love to Hate You
Love You, Love You Not

Love You, You, Love You Not

JO WATSON

HEADLINE
ETERNAL

First published in Great Britain in 2019
by HEADLINE ETERNAL
An imprint of HEADLINE PUBLISHING GROUP

1

Cataloguing in Publication Data is available from the British Library

ISBN 978 1 4722 6552 4

Typeset in 11.55/16.25 pt Granjon LT Std by Jouve (UK), Milton Keynes

Printed and bound in Great Britain by Clays Ltd, Elcograf S.p.A.

HEADLINE PUBLISHING GROUP
An Hachette UK Company
Carmelite House
50 Victoria Embankment
London EC4Y 0DZ

www.headlineeternal.com
www.headline.co.uk
www.hachette.co.uk

I'm going to have to dedicate this book to all my ROSA ladies, you know who you are. Thank you all for helping me solve this story and make it the best it can be.

CHAPTER ONE

Poppy

Drama!

It always finds me. No matter where I go, or what I do. On some days, I can almost feel it watching me, waiting to pounce, waiting to hand me that one aerosol can that explodes so loudly that the neighbors call the police and they break down my door. Or to hand me that one bottle of defective hair remover cream (too much peroxide) that scalds my vagina and lands me in the ER with a hot doctor. That accidentally locks me in a toilet cubicle in a shopping center overnight, or that causes that freak wave that rips off my bikini bottom on that crowded beach.

Drama. Look it up in the dictionary. If my face is not plastered next to its definition, it should be. In fact, I've often considered sending an email to the good people of the Oxford University Press and suggesting that they include me in its definition somehow.

My mother used to say that drama was my destiny, that it was ingrained in my DNA. After all, that's how I'd come into the world, she'd said. Bursting into it in the hospital parking lot, unable to wait a few more minutes until I made my grand appearance. Maybe that's one of the reasons behind the career path I'd chosen. Maybe that's one of the reasons I was about to make one of the most dramatic and ridiculous decisions of my life . . .

I gazed up at the big, shiny building that towered above me like an intimidating giant made of metal and mirrors. If I walked in and did what I was planning on doing, I'd be breaking the law! Okay, so maybe lying on my CV to get a job wasn't exactly "breaking the law," per se. Maybe it was just twisting it a tiny bit. Not that bad, right?

"If you lie, you become a liar." But I could hear my mother's words echoing in my mind, over and over again. I hung my head and reviewed my options.

One, I could *not* do this and in a month's time would be evicted and blacklisted and living on the streets. Or two, I could do this and potentially save myself from a life of street living.

I took a deep breath and looked up at myself in the rear-view mirror.

Oh God! I looked ridiculous in my short, brown wig and purple cat's eye glasses. Both the wig and glasses had been props from the TV show I'd recently acted in—that is, until my character had met her rather dramatic and untimely demise.

I'd played the part of "Executive Administrative Assistant to the CEO." So when I'd seen that *exact* same job offered in the employment section of the paper just two days ago, I'd taken it as a sign. A light at the end of the dark tunnel of debt I currently found myself wading through.

My debt was mostly due to the fact that I was more of an "out of work" than "in-work" actress. And I couldn't even supplement my income with waitressing work like most other actresses did. My waitressing skills were infamously terrible ... how was I meant to know that Mr. Wong's secret sauce was *that* flammable and that the patron had been wearing a toupee?

It's not like I'd never gotten work as an actress before. In fact, in the last year I'd gotten several roles. I'd played "Scary Witch Five" in a children's pantomime, "Rushed Train Commuter Nine" in an action film, and I'd also gotten an advert for pantyhose. Granted, only my leg had been seen, but the leg had been attached to my body, as my agent had pointed out. But my biggest role to date had happened a few months ago, playing Ramona González, Executive Administrative Assistant to the CEO of an experimental, secretive government laboratory testing facility, on a very low budget telenovela called *Venganza Ignacio* (*Ignacio's Revenge*) that had been shot in South Africa (because it was cheap), dubbed into Spanish and only screened in Paraguay.

The only reason I'd gotten the job was because the original actress playing Ramona had gotten food poisoning on day one and the director had decided that they didn't need all four "Terrified Lab Assistants." And so, I'd landed myself my first speaking role.

The job had lasted exactly two months, before my character had been viciously killed off by the evil twin brother of the CEO, who for years had been presumed dead when his private jet had crashed in the Amazon rainforest. Except he wasn't dead. As it turned out, the brother had been taken in by a wild tribe of cannibals, who'd taught him to be very evil and instructed him in the ancient art of killing people with poisonous darts made from the slimy stuff found on the backs of venomous tree frogs. Exactly how my character had died, btw.

What a pile of crap! At least I'd scored this wig and glasses and some other props from the show, which I was now wearing for my job interview in precisely ten minutes. I guess wearing this disguise made me feel slightly better about lying. It made this feel less like a job interview, and more like an audition for a role.

I climbed out of the car and headed for the building clutching my (fake) CV in my now very shaky hands.

How hard could this be? All I'd done in the show was answer calls, staple papers together, file stuff, shout things like "Shall I get the head of the army on the phone?" and "Put the facility on emergency quarantine lock-down!" and "There's been a breach in the radioactive containment field and the rats have mutated." Not to mention have sex with my hairy boss on his desk. Not that I'd be having sex with *this* CEO; well, I hoped that wasn't part of the job description anyway.

I carried on walking, forcing my head into the air in the hopes that faking confidence might actually help allay my fears somewhat. I was good at faking, I was an actress, after all. Not a great one. I wasn't terrible, but I was no Meryl. But I loved acting. I cursed loudly as I walked. Why couldn't I have loved accounting, or lawyer-ing, or doctor-ing or something sensible like that? Something that ensured my fridge was stocked with more than an old jar of peanut butter and that I didn't need to rent in the most undesirable part of town. "*Undesirable*" you must understand is a polite euphemism for "shittiest shithole in the Southern Hemisphere."

The big shiny building was even more intimidating on the inside. The entrance hall looked like the interior of a modernist museum, complete with very uncomfortable-looking steel chairs that seemed more like sculptural pieces than actual things to put your butt on.

"Hi." I walked over to the terribly busy-looking receptionist. "I'm here for the job interview. Doris Granger." I smiled, trying to hide the embarrassment at the fake name I'd chosen for myself. *What was I thinking?* Doris bloody Granger! But for some reason choosing a fake name had helped add to the illusion that I was assuming a character and playing a role. I'd briefly thought of giving Doris an accent. Something exotic, like Romanian or Czechoslovakian. Thankfully, I'd come to my senses. Besides, Doris did have a certain studious ring to it, certainly more so than Poppy Daisy Peterson. (My mother had been a florist and had named me after her favorite flowers.)

"Have a seat," the receptionist said, pointing at the "chair." I smiled and approached it tentatively. I lowered myself onto the avant-garde metal thing and, yes, it was definitely the most uncomfortable thing I'd ever sat on. I looked around for something to do and grabbed one of the magazines on the table.

Travel and Leisure Now.

Leisure Management.

Leisure in Focus! (I wondered why that one had an exclamation mark?)

It all seemed like quite a bit of leisure overkill. Mind you, this was Stark Leisure Group. I tried to make myself comfortable and flipped through the pages of one of the magazines; beautiful sea-front villas, bushveld lodges and mountain sanctuaries soon filled the glassy pages and I was just about to read an article about the tourist boom in Rwanda when—

"AAARRGGHH!"

A loud noise made me look up as a woman ran through the reception as if she was being chased by a pack of invisible wolves. The harassed-looking woman stopped when she got to the receptionist and pointed a finger at her. I sat up straight and watched the spectacle.

"I have *never* been treated like that in my entire life." She was on the verge of tears. "I don't know how you work for him?" she snapped. "He is the rudest, the . . . the . . ." She stuttered, the words sounded like they were getting stuck in her throat. And then she turned and looked at me. "Are you here for the interview?" she asked, sounding frantic. I nodded. "Well, don't! Just don't," she said and then started marching off. I stared after her in horror as she flung the doors open and threw herself out of the building.

"What the—?" I muttered under my breath.

"Clearly, he's in one of his moods again today," the receptionist said, shaking her head. "Good luck to you," she tutted and looked down again.

"Sorry . . . uh, what do you mean?" I stood up and walked over to the desk.

The receptionist looked around nervously and then leaned in and whispered. "Mr. Stark, well, let's just say he's not exactly easy to get along with."

"Really?" I swallowed hard and clutched my CV even tighter.

The woman nodded. "He's made almost every one of his staff cry at some stage. And you better know how to do your job, he doesn't like inefficient people or take kindly to—"

The phone interrupted her and she answered it at the speed of light. "Yes, sir, Mr. Stark," she said into the phone. She paused and looked up at me. "Yes, there's one more." Another pause as she listened intently on the phone. "No, I'm afraid I can't tell if she's an 'airhead buffoon with no real qualifications other than being the most inarticulate person you've ever met' like the other one." The receptionist widened her eyes at me. "I'll send her up." She put the phone down.

"Um." Nerves gripped me. "Maybe . . ." I started backing away. "Maybe I've made a mistake. Maybe this job isn't really for me after all."

I didn't wait for a reply and ran out the door as fast as my legs would carry me. This Mr. Stark sounded like a monster and even though I was desperate for the money, I didn't want crying to be part of my job description. I cried enough already. I was one of those "nervous crier" types. And if I were truly honest with myself, I was feeling quite relieved that I had an excuse to leave. I mean, what had I been thinking . . . *a disguise, a name change, a fake CV, for heaven's sake*. It sounded like a storyline straight out of the telenovela itself. It was probably one of the most ridiculous things I'd *almost* ever done in my entire life.

But then I saw it and stopped dead in my tracks . . .

"HEY!" I yelled as my car was lifted onto the back of a tow truck. "What are you doing?" I raced over to the traffic officer standing next to it.

"Are you the owner of this vehicle?" The man asked in that firm police tone that is intended to strike terror into your heart. *It did*.

"Why?" I asked cautiously.

"Do you know this is a no-parking zone?" The traffic officer pointed at a sign that was barely readable, due to the layer of rust on it.

"That?" I protested. "But you can't even read it. That should be illegal, having a sign that no one can read. How are people supposed to . . . uh, uh—"

The traffic officer raised an eyebrow at me and pointed down at the road as my car moved off it.

"Oh! That." I swallowed hard.

"Yes, that," the traffic officer answered sarcastically. "That giant red cross through the big yellow word 'parking' is a dead giveaway, don't you think?" He flashed me a patronizing smile.

"I guess I didn't see it." *How the hell hadn't I seen that?* "I'll move my car right now if you stop towing it." I started digging frantically through my bag for the keys.

"Too late for that," he said, sounding way too pleased with himself. He tore a piece of paper off his little notepad and thrust it into my hands. "One thousand rand gets it out. But you'll have to come down to the pound to collect it. Have a nice day . . . *ma'am*." He said that last part with disdain. And then he and my car were gone.

I looked down at the ticket in my hands. Asking me to pay R1,000 was like asking me to pay a million. I just didn't have that kind of cash. Or any cash for that matter. I was down to my last hundred rand and unless I could use my eviction notice to print more money on, I was broke.

I looked at my other hand, the one that was still clutching my CV, and then my eyes slowly drifted back up to the cold steel building in front of me . . .

CHAPTER TWO

～

Ryan

*H*e crunched the CV up and tossed it across the room where it landed in the dustbin. His aim was perfect, but he'd done this quite a few times already. He was frustrated. His entire world was falling apart around him and he didn't like it one little bit.

He felt like he was walking a knife's edge at work; with the current recession business was not great. The number of people taking vacations was down 35 per cent, and this was very bad for their cash flow, since holidays were their business. The shareholders and his board were putting huge pressure on him, and on some days he felt like he was drowning. He was also struggling to balance his business and his personal life, and currently feeling like he was failing at both.

"Dammit," he cursed loudly. He needed an assistant! And he needed one now. And he needed one that didn't cry and break down and go through ten boxes of tissues a day because she was going through a bad break-up. Boo-fucking-hoo. He'd *had to* fire her.

Of course, this had only gone on to cement his reputation even further as a cold-hearted bastard, incapable of any real emotions, and generally a bad, horrible boss! (That's what he'd overheard them say around the proverbial water cooler anyway.)

What they didn't know, *couldn't know*, was that he was very much capable of real feelings. Real pain and anguish and every other negative emotion you could think of. His emotions tended to err on the negative side. In fact, he couldn't really remember the last time he'd felt happy—or laughed, for that matter. All he felt these days was pain. He'd just become very good at hiding it behind a wall of anger. Because anger was so much easier to deal with.

And he had to hide it, because on some days the feelings were so overwhelming that they threatened to knock him off his feet. And if he collapsed, three hundred people would soon find themselves jobless—but they never thought about that, did they? They never thought that their job security relied on him being a "cold, hard bastard," always in perfect control of his emotions. "*Never get distracted. Always stay focused. Never show weakness,*" as his father used to say. He'd let him down once before in this regard; he didn't intend to do it again.

He had one more candidate to interview before the end of the day. He'd promised his niece Emmy that he would be home early tonight. He'd broken so many promises to her lately, and he couldn't face the guilt that came with breaking the heart of the only person in this world that he truly cared about.

He skimmed the next candidate's CV. Doris Granger. She sounded a hundred years old but, according to this, was only twenty-nine. He read over her previous job experience . . .

Executive Assistant to the CEO of a company he'd never heard about in Paraguay. Waitress and perfume salesperson. He sighed.

Her CV didn't exactly gleam and sparkle and inspire him with confidence, but this was the last, *last*, person he could interview.

He'd gone through five assistants in the last two months. Two had quit in tears after their first day and the other three, *yes*, you guessed it, the heartless bastard had fired them. But none of them had been good enough, and now the job recruitment company said they weren't sending anyone else to him. Apparently, he was "insensitive" and "emotionally abusive." This was a job, not a bloody date. What did they expect? Candlelit dinners, roses and walks on the fucking moonlit beach? But now he had been forced to place a job listing in the paper, which had caused all manner of strange people to come crawling out of the woodwork.

Maybe he would need to lower his expectations somewhat? What was he thinking . . . *lower them*? His expectations would need to be somewhere in a gutter to hire someone who'd served burgers, sprayed perfume and did God knows what for some company in, where was it? Paraguay, Papua New Guinea . . . *Whatever!* But what other choice did he have?

He buzzed down to the main reception. "Send Doris Granger up." He paused and listened. "What do you mean she's left?"

"Sorry," Ayanda's voice quivered, as if she was afraid of him. She probably was. They all were. It was better that way: "*Never mix business and your personal life*," he'd learned that the hard way. "Yes, she just seemed to—oh wait, she's back."

"What do you mean she's back?" he asked. Doris was clearly indecisive. He hated indecisiveness.

"Yes, she's back. I'll send her up, Mr. Stark."

"Fine." He hung up the phone and sat back down at his desk.

CHAPTER THREE

~

Poppy

*H*e was certainly *very* attractive, that's for sure. The kind of attractive that steals your breath for a moment and makes your heart beat a little faster. Pitch-black hair, sky-blue eyes, a jaw so masculine and chiseled that it could probably cut glass. Yet, he was unbelievably intimidating at the same time as he sat there and stared at me relentlessly. I hadn't said a word since walking in and sliding my CV across his massive desk. Why was his desk so large? It was unnecessary and seemed more like an intimidation device than anything else. Well, Doris Granger was not one to be intimidated . . . *oh, who was I kidding!?* Both Doris and Poppy were shaking in their bloody seats. I gazed around his office quickly. It was cold, impersonal and had a somewhat dead, morgue-ish feel to it. The only other sign of (almost) life in it was the poor *Chlorophytum comosum*, aka the spider plant, in the corner that looked like it hadn't been watered all year and should not be kept in direct sunlight. "*You can tell a lot about a person by the plants they keep,*" my mother used to say. I wondered what this dead pot plant said about Ryan Stark?

"So?" He finally spoke. His voice was gruff and demanding and it made me feel like I was back in the principal's office, about to get detention.

"Who are you?" he asked.

"Oh . . . sorry, yes." I jumped back up and tried my best to extend my hand across the enormous table. "Doris Granger, pleased to meet y—" my voice trailed off when he made no attempt to shake hands.

"I know your name, Miss Granger. Now please, sit back down." He gestured and I obeyed.

There was another awkward silence, and I suddenly pointed at my CV on his desk.

"My CV," I mumbled.

"I know," he said. "You also emailed it. There was no need to bring a hard copy too."

A pit formed in my stomach. I hadn't even been in his office for a minute and I was already in trouble. He glanced down at the CV on his desk and gave a slow tutting sound before looking up at me again.

"And?" he asked.

"And?" I repeated stupidly, my voice cracking slightly.

He shook his head. He seemed frustrated. "I see you worked as an assistant in Uruguay?"

"Paraguay. The 'guays' can get very confusing." I smiled as widely as I could. Smiling like this would hopefully hide the fact I was a blatant liar. Not that it mattered at this stage, I was clearly *not* going to get this job.

"And how did you land up there?" he asked. "It's a rather unusual place to work."

"Mmmm." My mind raced for an answer. I hadn't given my character a backstory yet. "My uncle," I said, uttering the first thing that popped into my head. "He's South American and he . . ." I tapered off, unable to finish the lie that was about to come pouring out of my mouth. "Uncle," I repeated.

"Don't they speak Spanish there?" he asked.

"¡Sí! ¡Muchas gracias!" I said quickly and immediately regretted it.

"You speak Spanish?" he asked, looking as perplexed as I felt right now.

Don't say it, Poppy, don't bloody say it . . . but I did and I wanted to kick myself the second it came rushing out of my mouth. "Fluent in it!" *Fuck!* Why had I just said that? What was wrong with me?

"Interesting," he said. "Of course, Spanish is of no use here in South Africa. It would be better if you were fluent in isiZulu."

Please don't lie about being fluent in Zulu . . . I mentally begged myself because I seemed to have suddenly lost all control of the things that were flying out of my mouth. I'd always babbled when I was nervous, but this was a new low, even for me. My mouth started to open before I could stop myself. "Nkosi Sikelel' iAfrika," I said quickly.

He looked at me. Strangely. "Miss Granger, I'm fully aware of what our national anthem is."

"Of course you are. Yes, of course you are. I didn't mean to imply you weren't." I looked down at my lap, feeling defeated. Another silence followed.

"This is a job interview, Miss Granger. You're supposed to be selling yourself to me."

"Selling?" I looked up at him again.

"Why should I hire you?" he asked, sounding irritated.

"Uh, um . . . uh?" My mouth wasn't working properly. And neither was my brain. He was so gorgeous and terrifying. It was a deadly combination. I tried to adjust my big glasses that were slipping down my small nose, but it was too late. They dropped to the floor with a loud *thunk*.

"Sorry!" I threw myself onto the floor. *Shit!* My glasses had made their way under his desk. I lay down flat and stuck my arm out, trying to retrieve them. I finally grabbed them, put them back on and shot back up to the chair as quickly as I could. "Sorry about that! Slippery little things." I flashed him another smile but he didn't reciprocate. He pointed at me, deadpan expression etched into his face.

"They're cracked," he said flatly.

"Oh?" I looked down my nose at my glasses; a large crack had indeed appeared in one of the lenses.

"Well?" he asked.

"Well what?" I was swimming in a state of nervous confusion now, more like drowning in it. Nothing was going well. My glasses had cracked and I was on the verge of cracking . . . it was all just too much. *Please don't cry too!*

"Job! Hire you! Why?" He spat the words out.

"Oh. That. Why should you hire me?" I adjusted my glasses again, this time because I needed to give my hands something to do.

"Tick, tick, tick, Miss Granger. I have lots of important things to do, so if you're not going to talk to me, I must insist that this is over." He flashed me a cold, hard look.

"Okey-dokey," I quickly jumped in. "You should employ me

because I am . . . am . . . because . . ." I paused again. *He shouldn't hire me!* At all. I had no qualifications, I had no idea what the hell I would do if I worked here, and I was wearing a stupid disguise. In all honesty, I was the last person on earth he should hire.

"You're not doing yourself any favors here, Miss Granger. Because with every second that passes, I want to hire you less and less." He tapped his foot and it made the desk wobble. "Miss Granger?" he asked again.

But by now, I was beyond forming any kind of coherent thoughts, let alone sentences. And I feared that if I stayed in the room for a second longer, I might find myself with my whole leg in my mouth, not just my foot.

"I'm so sorry!" I shot up out of my chair. "I think there's been some kind of terrible misunderstanding here." I backed away from his massive desk. *Had they used an entire forest to make it?*

"What kind of misunderstanding?" He stood up. God, he was tall. Tall and big in all the right places. And did I mention intimidating as hell? He towered above me like the steel building itself.

"I think I'm in the wrong place." I looked around the room frantically. "Wrong job interview, even. I think, maybe, I'm supposed to be somewhere else . . ." I edged towards the door.

"Somewhere else, where?" He started walking around his desk and I wanted to turn and run.

"Mmmm, where indeed? Now that is a big question, isn't it? Where are any of us meant to be, really?" I said.

He stopped walking and I was sure I could see the slightest smile on his lips. "A philosopher as well as an assistant?" He was mocking me now.

"What can I say, I'm a woman of many talents."

"Really?" He kept approaching me and I wanted to run. I could feel the door behind me and I'd never wanted out of one so badly. Suddenly a scene from the telenovela came to mind.

Oh God, I had to do it. How else was I going to get myself out of this? I looked out the window behind him and feigned dramatic shock. I brought my hand up to my face and gasped. And then slowly, with shaking fingers, I pointed.

"He's returned. He's coming for us. Run!" I said in that voice that Ramona had used so many times before. Low, slow and dragged out for added dramatic effect.

"What?" He swung around suddenly, exactly as I'd hoped. And when he did, I ran. I bolted out the door and straight to the elevator. I'm not proud of it, but that's what I did.

As I climbed into the elevator, I heard laughter. His laughter was so loud that it echoed down the hall. I put my head in my hands. I'd never been more embarrassed in my entire life, and I'd done some pretty embarrassing things before—many of which had been filmed and put on TV. But this was next level.

CHAPTER FOUR

⌐

Ryan

*H*e couldn't remember the last time someone had amused him so much. She was just about the most idiotic thing to have ever set foot in his office and, truth be told, the comic relief had been a rather welcome surprise.

Doris Granger . . . even her name was idiotic. Not to mention those stupid glasses with the cracked lens and that pink dress which was totally inappropriate for a corporate office. *What on earth had possessed her to even come for the job interview?*

He let out another chuckle and called down to the reception. Ayanda answered immediately. "Has Miss Granger left the building?" he asked.

"Yes. I just saw her run past."

"Good. If she ever comes in here again, please make sure security escorts her out. I'm not sure she's entirely stable." He put the phone down and let out another small chuckle. Usually, when someone completely unqualified turned up for a job interview he would be pissed off. But he wasn't.

"Doris Granger from Paraguay," he repeated to himself thoughtfully. Who the hell works there? And who is named Doris in this day and age? It sounded totally made up. It probably was.

He looked at his watch and realized that if he left now, he would make it home just in time to have dinner with Emmy. He packed his laptop and grabbed his car keys out of the drawer. The framed photo of himself in happier times caught his attention. It was the only personal item he kept in his office. He looked at it for a moment and then put it down. On some days it was very hard to look at the photo. Today was one of those days.

He walked through the now empty corridors of the building; it was after five and all his staff had already left. He climbed into the elevator and pressed the ground floor button. As the glass-backed cage sailed down, he looked out at the building.

He'd taken over the business from his father ten years ago after his father had retired. And when he had, Stark Leisure Group had been one of the biggest holiday resort builders in the country. His father had been a real pioneer in the leisure industry, building the biggest resorts in South Africa that were affordable for everyone. He believed that holidays should not only be reserved for the upper class. But in the current financial climate, it was their resorts that were suffering, not the high-end luxury ones that the recession-proof public could afford. Their profits were down, and they were slipping each month. As a result, he'd been pressured into making a business decision that he wasn't sure was the right one. He knew his father would definitely disapprove of it; his father's old business associate Mr. Rautenbach had made that abundantly clear to him. His father, who had passed away four years ago, was probably rolling in his grave right now. He could almost see his face—that gruff, angry, disappointed expression that he'd worn for most of his life. He still felt like a disappointment to his father, even though the man was dead.

The doors opened and he walked into the reception area. It was raining outside and he grabbed an umbrella on the way out. He stepped into the storm and made his way to his car, the last car in the parking lot. It was always the last car in the parking lot. But as he got closer something, *someone*, caught his eye . . .

There, sitting on the pavement, drenched from head to toe was none other than Doris Granger. She was holding her head in her hands and . . . oh God, was she crying? Her shoulders were heaving up and down and her whole body was shaking. He should have known she was a crier. He sighed and carried on walking.

He climbed into his Porsche SUV and was just about to start the car and drive off when he found himself staring at the pathetic figure sitting alone in the rain crying.

God, it was so irritating and infuriating. He didn't want people sitting and crying outside his place of work. That would not be good for business, and it was also—

Also . . . ???

His stomach twisted and suddenly he felt uncomfortable in his seat. He held onto his steering wheel tightly and squeezed. He really wanted to get home, but Doris bloody Granger was sitting on the pavement in the rain crying. And he didn't know why, but it bothered him.

Maybe it was because he found her strangely amusing. He sighed again, grabbed the umbrella once more, and climbed out of his car.

CHAPTER FIVE

∽

Poppy

I saw the feet before I saw him. I recognized them immediately because, half an hour ago, I'd been face-to-face with them under his desk while looking for my glasses.

The sound of his throat clearing was barely audible over the rain which was coming down in buckets now. But I didn't want to look up. I didn't want to look into those big blue eyes and make an idiot of myself once again ... mind you, I was sitting on a pavement in the rain crying like a baby!

"Miss Granger?"

I cringed at the sound of that name. Why hadn't I chosen a better name for this character?

"Miss Granger?" he said, louder this time.

I forced my eyes up. He was towering directly above me, blocking some of the rain with his umbrella.

"Hello, Mr. Stark," I managed through the water that was cascading down my face.

"What are you doing in the rain?" His tone was stern.

"I'm sitting." It was all I could think of to say back.

"I can see that. But the question is . . . why?"

"Because I don't have a lift home," I whispered feebly. *And I can't afford a taxi*, I thought.

"I didn't hear that," he boomed.

"I can't get home," I said again, not that much louder than before.

"God, could you speak up . . . never mind." In one swift movement, he was crouching in front of me. His sudden proximity caught me off guard and I gasped.

"Repeat!" he commanded.

"I can't get home!" I half shouted back in fright.

"Don't you have a car?" he asked, looking around.

"It was parked in a no-parking zone and got towed away."

"Well, that was rather stupid," he said coldly.

"I didn't see it," I wailed. "I was so nervous for the interview. Oh God, I shouldn't have come here in the first place." Another long, loud sob escaped my lips. I went with it. I didn't care about holding the tears back anymore. It's not like I was ever going to see this guy again.

Another sudden throat clearing made me look up.

"Where do you live?" he asked through what was clearly a very tightly clenched jaw.

"In West Parks." The rain was coming down even harder now.

He let out another massive sigh. I'd never heard such a loud, long, exasperated sigh before. "Come." He stood up and started walking back to his car. I was so shocked I wasn't even sure I'd heard him correctly until he looked over his shoulder and yelled at me.

"Are you waiting for Christmas?" He rolled his eyes.

I jumped up and ran through the rain. I opened the passenger door and climbed in. I was dripping wet and immediately, inadvertently, splashed water across his polished dashboard.

"Sorry," I said when I saw his disapproving look. He was obviously irritated and wanted to take me home as much as someone wants a plantar wart on their toe. But I had no other choice right now and I wasn't going to turn down a lift, even if it was from *him*.

"Try not to wet my entire car, Miss Granger." He turned the engine on and the massive car roared to life.

"Sorry," I whispered under my breath and tried to keep as still as possible, even though my body was shaking from the cold.

I heard another long sigh. His hand shot out and fiddled with the air conditioning, then he pointed all the vents in my direction and a blast of hot air hit my body. The relief was instant.

"Thanks," I whispered.

"Don't mention it," he said dismissively as he focused on the road ahead of us.

We drove in total, awkward silence after that. I looked around the car. A sign hanging from the rear-view mirror caught my attention. It was a disabled sign and I wondered if he was one of those dickheads who used it just so he could get a good parking spot?

"Turn left into this road," I said when we approached West Parks. I had no idea why it was called West Parks; there wasn't a park or a tree in sight. Some weeds growing through the cracks in the pavement were the extent of the greenery in this area, not to mention that black mossy stuff that grew on the ceiling of my bathroom.

This place was a concrete jungle of old, ugly and cheap apartment housing. Most of the apartments were falling apart and a few local drug dealers had taken up residence on the streets below them. I was always very polite to them and turned down their kind offers of drugs with a sweet smile and a "maybe another day, but thanks so much for offering!" The last thing I wanted to do was offend the local dealers.

"There." I pointed at my building.

"You live here?" He stopped the car and looked around nervously.

"Yes. But don't worry, I doubt they'll come out to steal your car in the rain." I said it in jest, although I was being somewhat serious.

"What?" He shot me a look that told me he was totally out of his depth in this environment. He clearly was.

"Well, thanks for the lift." I didn't look at him but reached for the door handle, when another loud sigh filled the car and stopped me dead in my tracks. What was with this guy and all his sighing?

"Can you answer a phone?" he asked reluctantly.

"Yes!" I swung around. "I can. I swear I'm good at answering phones . . . *Hello, Mr. Stark's office how can I help you . . . I'm sorry, he's not in, but I'd be pleased to take a message!*" I hung up the fake phone receiver I'd just made with my fingers and looked at him as confidently as possible.

He shook his head. "Computer literate?" he asked.

I rolled my eyes. "Of course."

"I don't tolerate lateness," he said sternly.

"Never." I jumped in. "I'm always on time." That was a total lie.

"And no crying in the office."

"Absolutely not." (I hoped not anyway.)

"You can start work on Monday. Be in the office at seven a.m. sharp. Don't be late," he mumbled.

I was so overjoyed that, without thinking about it, I threw my arms around him and pulled him into a hug. I realized that I'd done the wrong thing immediately when he wriggled out of my grip and brushed the water droplets off his suit.

"And absolutely no hugging," he quickly added. "Ever."

"Sorry." I smiled from ear to ear. "I won't let you down, I promise." I jumped out of the warm car into the cold rain and scuttled across the muddy ground to my apartment block.

CHAPTER SIX

~

Ryan

He sat in his car and watched the strange, wet creature running away from him. This place was a total dump. The road was full of mud-filled potholes, and every now and then she would stand in one and an explosion of brown mud shot up her leg. By the time she'd gotten to the building, both her legs were completely covered.

He watched her struggle to open the door and then . . .

"What the hell?" He was shocked to see her give the door a firm roundhouse kick before it popped open. *Who was this woman?* And then she disappeared into the terrible-looking building. He glanced up at it; its tiny, jail-like windows were covered in bars. *Were the bars there to keep people in, or out?* He couldn't imagine living here, and for a second he felt a stab of guilt when he thought about the house he was returning to. He turned on his ignition once more and pulled away; a dodgy-looking guy came out of the shadows and glared at his car as he passed. *Shit!* He sped away quickly. This really wasn't a safe area to live in and his thoughts suddenly drifted to Doris's safety. He drove for a few more minutes before it dawned on him . . .

WTF had he just done!?

Had he really just given the job to the least qualified, and certainly the strangest person who'd applied for it? What had he been thinking? Clearly, he hadn't been thinking, because if he had, he would never, ever, have done that! And on top of that, had he actually invited her into his car? That was completely inappropriate on so many levels. He did *not* mix his business and personal life—ever. And having her in his car, his personal space, felt like it was crossing a line. He never wanted to cross that line again.

"Shit!" he mumbled to himself and slapped the steering wheel. He'd never done anything so impulsive and emotional in his entire life. The thought unnerved him. He would just have to make her quit on Monday. There was no way she would make it through the day anyway, especially when he gave her the special Ryan Stark treatment that usually had them bursting into tears and running for the door before lunchtime. And she seemed like a crier.

He drove for a while before the environment started changing. Broken pavements and potholes gave way to rolling lawns and mansions on the hill. He arrived at his house and drove up the long steep driveway that wound its way up to his modernist mansion. He parked his car and climbed out, but paused before going inside. He always did this. He'd done this for the last two years, ever since his twin sister Rachel's death. On her deathbed, he'd promised to take care of his niece, Emmy. To care for her and raise her like his own. The only problem was, he had no idea how to be a father, let alone a father to a teenage girl. The first year she had been fine, but since turning thirteen, everything had changed.

She seemed so angry and emotional all the time, and nothing he did was right. They fought constantly and he felt like he was failing her. He hated failing. He was good at everything—except raising a teenager, it would seem. And normally when he wanted advice or needed someone to talk to, he would call Rachel.

"Emmy," he called out when he'd gathered himself enough to walk inside and face whatever was waiting for him. "Emmy?" he called again when he didn't get an answer.

"You're late," a sulky voice returned from the other room. He walked in and she turned. His heart skipped a beat. She looked so much like his sister that sometimes it unnerved him. Like seeing a ghost.

"Sorry." He tried to smile at her, but she didn't reciprocate.

"You promised we'd have dinner together." She stood up angrily.

He looked at his watch. "It's not too late to eat now."

"Whatever. It's not like I care anyway, and I've already eaten." And with that, she marched across the room and up the stairs.

He stared after her, trying to think of something to say to make this better. But before he could, she disappeared into her bedroom.

He shook his head. Raising a teenager was totally above his pay grade, and he feared that if his sister were here to see what he was doing, she would be very disappointed. He'd tried to make Emmy happy, but everything he seemed to do was wrong. Like the time he'd come home with a Barbie for her. She'd looked at it and almost burst into tears, asking if he thought she was still a baby?

He shook his head and made a mental note to google what thirteen year olds were playing with these days.

CHAPTER SEVEN

‿

Poppy

By the time I saw the big, silver skyscraper on Monday morning, I was already dripping with sweat—despite the cool weather. I had grazes on my knees and elbows, a ripped skirt that I was holding together with a hairpin that I'd pulled out from under my wig, and I was wheeling a broken bicycle with me.

I'd borrowed the bike from one of my neighbors since I was no longer in possession of a car—or any mode of transport, for that matter. In retrospect, it hadn't been a good idea. In fact, it had been a monumentally bad idea, since I didn't even know how to ride a bike. It's not like I'd had a father to teach me that kind of thing. To my credit, I'd almost gotten the hang of it a mile or two into the ride, but the sudden honking of a car horn had caused me to tumble dramatically to the pavement. The bike fell hard, as did I, breaking the already dodgy-looking wheel as it crashed into the concrete pavement.

All in all, not a good morning. Everything that could potentially go wrong had gone wrong, and now I was almost running late for my first day at work. I ran the last few blocks; it was challenging dragging the heavy bike with me. But I couldn't be late. I chained the bike to the only thing I could see outside the office—a small fever tree. A mere sapling growing out of the concrete box it had been planted in. I was surprised the great Ryan Stark would have allowed such a thing outside his building. Wouldn't want the place to look human, after all. I ran for the door once I'd locked the bike up, but before I went in, I stopped and looked at myself in the reflective building.

I stared. I was trying to figure out which part of me looked worse? The top half of me, with the windblown wig, broken glasses and blood-stained elbows. Or the bottom half . . . ripped skirt and bloody, grazed knees. At least I hadn't fallen on my face, thank God for small mercies.

I straightened myself as best I could, but it wasn't working. No amount of straightening would make me look any better today. I still looked like I'd been dragged through a muddy swamp and then thrown into a thorn bush, with a bad wig on.

"Assume the character and act," I said to myself as I pushed the doors open. I rushed across the floor to the elevator, shouting a quick "hello" to the receptionist I'd met on Friday. I didn't have time for pleasantries because I was due at my desk in precisely seven minutes. And I bet *he* was counting the seconds.

"Hey!" the receptionist screamed after me. "Where do you think you're going?"

"To the office," I shouted over my shoulder as I arrived at the elevator.

"I don't think so!" I heard the sudden scurry of feet behind me. "Stop right there!" she said.

"Huh?" I turned around and came face-to-face with her.

"Don't move or I'll have to call security." She was swaying from side to side like she was getting ready to run if need be. But why?

I burst out laughing. "Oh . . . you didn't get the memo from Mr. Stark. I work here now. As of today." I gave her a friendly smile and turned back to the elevator. I reached out and was just about to press the button when . . .

"Hold it! Stop right where you are!" She shouted this time, and it made me jump.

"What's going on?" I asked. She was pointing a pen at me now, as if it was a weapon.

"Mr. Stark told me to remove you from the building if I saw you in here again."

"What?" My stomach twisted. "He said that?"

"Oh yes." She was circling me now. "He's concerned about your mental state, and quite frankly, so am I, just looking at you." Her eyes scanned me, top-to-toe, and I was mortified.

"Oh, this," I said. "My car was towed and I tried to ride a bike here but I fell. I don't usually look like this." I tried to laugh and make light of it. But clearly, it wasn't working.

"You're not welcome here," she hissed.

My mouth fell open. Wait, had he been tricking me? Playing some cruel joke on me by getting my hopes up? Was he really that much of a bastard? I was determined to ask him myself.

"Well," I squared off in front of crazy pen lady. "I want him to say that to my face!" I reached behind me and pressed the button firmly, but as I did, the pen-wielding psycho let out a yell.

"Security!" She screamed so loudly that it echoed through the large reception area.

Security, security, security the building screamed back at me.

The sound of feet hitting the marble floor made me look to my left. A frightening-looking security guard rushed towards me.

"Escort this woman out of the building. Immediately," she said.

But before I could object, before I could explain that this was obviously some kind of dreadful mistake, I felt the painful grip of fingers around my already sore elbow.

"Wait. Wait . . ." I tried to break free, but the man marched me all the way to the door and pushed me out of the building without so much as a word.

My heart raced. It beat against my chest like a bird trying to break free of its cage. Humiliation flooded me. And then anger. I'd never been treated like this in my entire life, I'd never been more embarrassed and more, more . . . more . . .

The tears burst out of me like water bursting through a crack in a dam. This was the second time I'd found myself crying outside this building. This was a sign! I shouldn't work here. And I clearly wasn't welcome here either. I walked up to the small green-stemmed tree where I'd locked the bike. I was barely able to see through the salty, wet veil of tears that coated my face. I reached into my pocket and pulled out the key that the neighbor had given me for the bicycle chain and tried to slip it into the hole.

"Fuck it!" I cursed loudly when the thing wouldn't fit. I wiped my tears and tried again. But still, it wasn't working. I pulled my stupid prop glasses off, which were making me blinder than I needed to be, and raised the key to my eyes. It was the key for my apartment. Not the key for the bicycle chain. I must have swapped them by accident!

"I hate this day," I yelled loudly and didn't care who the hell was looking. I stood up and looked at the small tree. I knew these things were surprisingly bendable, a gale-force wind wouldn't snap them. So, with one hand I began to lift the bike up while bending the stem with my other hand so that it could slip over the top. And it almost worked when . . .

"HEY!" A voice screamed at me and then, out of nowhere, the wetness came. A strong, long, cold rush of water made me fall backward onto the hard floor.

"What the hell do you think you're doing?" I finally saw where the water and voice were coming from. An angry, hosepipe-wielding gardener was moving in my direction. "I planted that last week. What the hell are you trying to do? Kill it?"

"I would never kill a plant," I said quickly. But my words clearly fell on deaf ears.

"Get out of here now before I call the police and report you for property damage."

"But my bike?" I struggled back up to my feet, dripping with water.

"NOW!" The man bellowed and pointed the hosepipe in my direction again.

I took that as my cue to leave. I turned and ran as fast as I could.

When I was a decent way away, I stopped and looked back at the intimidating silver building once more. This had to be, without a doubt, one of the worst mornings of my life, top five at least, and I'd had a few pretty damn shitty ones before. But this one took the cake and all the icing too! If the cake came with those decorative fondant flowers on top, it would take those things as well. Fuck it, this morning took the entire bakery!

I turned and started the long, wet, cold, painful, walk back home.

CHAPTER EIGHT

~

Ryan

*H*e was nursing a strange feeling in the pit of his stomach as he drove to work that morning. He hadn't been able to stop thinking about *her* all weekend.

He'd decided yesterday that he was going to force Doris to quit today. He estimated that she wouldn't even last until lunch, but today he was having second thoughts. In fact, thoughts of her were all he was having.

Strange Doris with the bad hair, cracked glasses and terrible clothes who had hugged him and left her scent on him. He'd been able to smell her all Friday evening. It wasn't the greatest smell, by any stretch of the imagination. In fact, it smelt more like cheap drugstore perfume or scented deodorant than anything else. It was only after his extra-long hot shower that he'd managed to wash her smell away.

"For fuck's sake." He shook his head and tapped a tune on his steering wheel in an attempt to dislodge her from his thoughts. He pulled into his parking lot just as he'd made another rather uncharacteristic decision. Instead of treating her like shit today and driving her off, he would simply tell her, very gently, that he'd found someone else who was more qualified for the position. He'd even give her a full week's salary and send her on her way. He hated the idea of seeing her cry again, so perhaps a more gentle, direct approach would work better with her?

But when he got to his office, it was empty! He stared angrily at the empty desk, willing her to magically fill it, but she didn't. *So much for a gentle approach!* He marched into his office and slammed the door, ringing straight down to reception.

"Has Miss Granger come in yet?" he asked.

"Yes, she did." The response came back immediately.

"Well, where the hell is she? She's five minutes late!"

"Uh . . . sir, Mr. Stark, you told me to throw her out of the building if she came back again."

"I certainly did NOT!" he huffed down the phone.

"Uh, sorry, but you did . . . remember? After her interview on Friday?" Ayanda stuttered and sounded nervous, and suddenly he remembered saying it. But that was before he'd decided to stupidly hire her.

"Sorry. I did. But that was a mistake. I hired her," he admitted.

"Oh God, I'm so sorry . . . I had no idea. She came and security threw her out and . . . I wish I'd known. I'm very sorry, Mr. Stark, I—"

"It's fine," he cut her off. He couldn't bear her wordy apology a second longer, it was making his head throb. "Where is she now?"

"I don't know," the voice returned.

Ryan slammed the phone down, walked over to the window of his office and looked down at the street below. No sign of her. It was probably better this way anyway, then he wouldn't have to get rid of her. In fact, it was all working out perfectly . . .

But then why did he have a desire to go and find her?

He pushed the thought from his mind, sat down at his desk and took out his laptop. He pressed some keys meaninglessly, all the while wondering where the hell she was.

"For heaven's sake!" He got up from his desk and strode out of his office.

* * *

It didn't take him long to find her. He could make her out in the distance struggling to walk up the steep hill. She looked a total wreck from behind, and he wondered what she looked like from the front. He put on his hazard lights and slowed all the way down. He came up next to her and opened his window.

"Miss Granger," he called. She turned and, oh God, she *did* look like a wreck. She was dripping with sweat, had a twig stuck in her hair, her skirt looked like it had been ripped, not to mention those stains on her shirt and . . . was she bleeding? "Are you okay?"

"Does it look like I'm okay?" she shouted over her shoulder and sped up. He easily matched her speed.

"Do you need medical attention?" he asked, feeling strangely concerned for her physical well-being.

She stopped momentarily and looked down at her grazed knees. "I'm sure my legs won't fall off, if that's what you mean?" Her tone was snappy and sarcastic, and she started walking again.

"Where're you going?" He was having to shout over the sounds of traffic flying past him.

"Home," she yelled over her shoulder without looking at him.

"There was a misunderstanding this morning. I forgot to tell Ayanda at reception that you were coming in."

She finally stopped walking and swiveled round. The movement caused her shirt to pull tightly across her chest, her buttons straining against her breasts. He quickly looked away.

"You know she had security drag me out?" she asked.

"I apologize for that. She didn't realize that I'd hired you. It was my mistake." *Mistake?* What the hell was he saying? Had he just admitted to making a mistake? He never made mistakes.

She glared at him through those silly broken glasses. "What did she say again? Something about you thinking I was mentally unstable?" She shook her head and then tried to march up the hill as fast as she could. He sped up and she glanced back at him angrily, and then started jogging. Ryan smiled to himself; he was finding this somewhat amusing.

"Miss Granger." He tried to hold back his smile and sound serious. "Just get in the car and come back to the office."

"NO!" She tried to sprint but looked like she was about to collapse.

"This is ridiculous. Just get in my car, and we'll go back to the office together."

"Your office?" She burst out laughing, sounding somewhat manic. "But I'm sure you don't want to hire a mad, crazy woman like me. You never know what I might do." She turned and made some bizarre gestures with her hands and then tried to start sprinting again.

A small chuckle escaped his lips. She was dramatic, he'd give her that! "You know, my car's top speed is well over 170 miles an hour." He bit back a smile again as he watched her power-march to the other side of the road in an attempt to get away from him. He crossed the road quickly and was right back at her side again. He opened his other window to continue their conversation.

"Where are you going in such a hurry?" he called out.

"I told you. Home."

"You're going to walk all the way home?"

"Yes!" she snapped breathily before finally coming to a stop. "Oh God, it hurts!" She moaned loudly and dropped down at her waist, totally out of breath.

"You can't walk all the way home. It's way too far." He stopped his car now. "Besides, it doesn't look like you're going to make it in the state you're in." That seemed to get her attention. Her head snapped up and she gave him another death stare.

"I don't need you telling me what I can and can't do!" She sounded genuinely pissed off and started walking again. He started his car once more and continued his slow crawl after her.

"It's not safe for you to walk alone like this." He tried a different tactic now.

"I've been in worse situations than this, trust me." She was picking up her pace again.

"Miss Granger. This is insane, you can't walk all the way home."

"Watch me!" she yelled, and started jogging again.

This was ridiculous!

"Well, if you insist, I'll just have to follow you all the way home." He closed his window and settled into his seat, fully prepared to crawl along at this speed right behind her as she walked home.

She turned and looked at him, her face contorted into an

expression of clear confusion. Then she shook her head, rolled her eyes so wildly that he thought they might pop out of her face onto the floor, and started walking again. He continued to follow her.

Why the hell was he doing this? He had work to do. He had calls to make and people to see. But for some reason, he couldn't leave her alone like this. This was partly his fault, after all. He called Ayanda again.

"Hi. Yes, Mr. Stark," she answered immediately.

"If anyone calls for me, please give them my mobile number. I'm just in the middle of something and probably won't be in the office for the next hour." The voice on the other end of the phone sounded shocked. He didn't blame her. *He* was shocked!

CHAPTER NINE

⟲

Poppy

I could feel his presence the entire time. The big black car crawled next to me as if it was stalking me. I tried not to look back, but every now and then I couldn't help but steal a glance in his direction. And every time I did, he looked like he was busy talking away on his phone.

Truthfully, I wished I was in the car. I was exhausted, I was in pain, I was sweating, and my legs felt somewhat jellyfish-like. I'd almost given up a few times, thinking about that oh-so-comfortable seat, but I wasn't about to give him that satisfaction! I was going to walk all the way home, come hell or high water. After all, I was a total nutter, wasn't I?

I finally rounded the last corner before my house. I'd been walking for over an hour already, and I'd never been so happy to see my crappy, dirty apartment building before.

"I'm home!" I stopped walking and turned to look at the black car that was only a few feet away from me. "You can go now!" I gestured for him to leave. But he didn't. Instead, the window came down and I found myself looking at him once more.

God, he was hot. Hot, but frightening as hell. It was an odd combination. Unnatural even. Like a cute snake that you're just dying to reach out and pat. Something you would never do. It was venomous and would surely bite, much like this man in front of me.

"So, I'll see you in the office tomorrow then?" He turned the engine off and leaned out the window.

"Huh? What are you talking about?" I asked, dumbfounded.

"We'll write off today because of the misunderstanding, but I'll see you tomorrow."

I couldn't believe what he was saying. He expected me to work for him after he'd had me thrown out of the building—by security, no less? Clearly, *he* was the insane one. Not me.

"No thanks." I dismissed him and started walking away again. But this time, I heard a door slam behind me. I whipped around. He was standing right behind me and his sudden proximity gave me a fright. I stumbled backward and an arm shot out and grabbed me.

"Uh . . . thanks." I looked down at his hand. It was wrapped tightly around my arm. His hand was so big that it almost covered my entire forearm. And he didn't seem to be letting go. I continued to look at his hand, wondering if his fingers were ever going to loosen.

"Sorry," I thought I heard him mumble as he finally let go and plunged his hand into his pocket. "So tomorrow, be there at seven again." He started walking away from me.

"Look," I called out. "I should never have taken this job in the first place. It was stupid of me. I have no way of getting to work. I don't have a car anymore, and as it turns out, I'm not very good at riding a bike and even worse at chaining it up."

"You rode a bike to work this morning?" He turned around, looking stunned.

"Well, I had an accident midway, which isn't surprising since I don't actually know how to ride one, and then I had to—"

"Wait!" he cut me off. "You don't know how to ride a bike?"

"No," I stated.

"You borrowed a bike and yet you don't know how to ride one?" He looked at me strangely. Tilting his head to the left, and then to the right. *Why the hell was he tilting his head like that?* It made me want to snap it off his neck.

"Yes," I said matter-of-factly. "I borrowed a bike when I knew I couldn't ride one."

"Well, that wasn't a very well thought out plan, was it?" he said.

At that, any iota of patience, politeness, sanity . . . left me.

I pointed at him. "Listen, you—"

"You?" A slight smile played on his lips. It pissed me off.

"Yes, *you.* I am sore, I am tired, I am sweaty, and my stockings have a hole in them that is running all the way up to my ass. I just want to go home and shower and wash this terrible day away. Bottom line . . . I just can't work for you. Thanks, but no thanks." I started walking away. He didn't follow me this time, and I was finally free of him. Forever. I managed to make it all the way to the door of the building when I thought I heard him say something.

"I'll fetch you at six thirty sharp. Don't be late. Only until you get your car back."

When I realized what he'd said, I opened my mouth to protest. But it was too late. He was already in his car pulling away.

I stood there and watched his big, black car as it drove off into the distance and then finally disappeared. *He was picking me up tomorrow? For work?*

I wasn't sure if I was supposed to be happy about this, or absolutely terrified.

CHAPTER TEN

⌒

Ryan

*W*hy *the hell had he just agreed to pick her up for work? Was he mad?*

That hadn't been his intention, at all. The intention had been for her *not* to work for him. But as she'd walked, he'd realized just how determined she was. He admired that quality. She could have easily buckled and climbed into his car at any point during the hour, but she hadn't. He could use someone with her sheer stubborn determination around the office. Maybe that attitude would also translate into her work? Besides, if he was honest with himself, she fascinated him, and he wanted to see her again, just out of curiosity. Nothing more.

Work was frenzied that day; his hour out of the office had meant that things had piled up. It was amazing how much everyone here relied on him. Sometimes the pressure felt too much to bear; it felt like everything would fall apart if he wasn't there, and that scared him. He felt like he always had a million balls in the air and he was getting to the stage where juggling them was getting harder and harder.

He'd barely thought about Doris all day, that is until he'd gotten back into his car and started driving home. Then she became all he could think about. The way she'd tried to jog up the hill to get away from him in that silly skirt that she kept having to pull down. Towards the end of the walk, she'd taken off her shoes and had carried them in her hands. He'd been trying to talk on the phone but had become so preoccupied with watching the ground in front of her, in case she walked over some broken glass or stood on something that could hurt her. He'd almost honked his horn when he'd seen a branch obstructing her path, but she'd jumped over it.

It had been a long day at work, and he wasn't really looking forward to going home either. Not after the unpleasant incident he'd had with Emmy this morning. He'd only asked her to hurry up, they were going to be late for school. And then he'd simply suggested that it probably wasn't necessary to spend *that* much time in the bathroom doing her hair, since it still looked terribly messy anyway.

"It's a messy bun! It's supposed to look messy!" she'd said before stomping off, throwing a "Don't you know anything?" at him. How was he meant to know that looking like you'd just rolled out of bed was a thing? And how the hell did it take a full forty minutes to achieve that look? After that, things had just gotten worse when she'd made him park two blocks away from school so she could walk the rest of the way. And when he'd insisted on driving behind her, to make sure she was safe, she'd thrown another one of her favorite phrases around: "I'm not a child anymore."

When he arrived home, there was no sign of Emmy, and her bedroom door was closed. She seemed to spend an unnatural amount of time in her room and it hadn't gone down well when he'd suggested that she get out more, or she might start looking like a vampire.

"Emmy." He knocked on the door and waited for a response. And when he didn't get one, he knocked again. Still no response. He reached out and opened the door, and there she was. Sitting on her bed ignoring him. He walked all the way up to her and she jumped.

"Oh my God, don't you knock?" she shouted, going red in the face.

"I did knock," he said. "Why are you ignoring me?"

"I'm listening to music!" She pulled the earbuds out of her ears and waved them in front of him.

He looked around the room. *Why did she need the door closed when she was just listening to music anyway?*

"What are you doing?" she asked.

"Why do you need to close your door?" he asked.

"What? Can't I even get some privacy around here? Or is that also not something I'm allowed either?" She walked across the room in a huff.

"Are we back to talking about that party again?" He folded his arms and gave her a stern look.

"I don't know why I can't go." She folded her arms too. She was stubborn—in fact, she definitely reminded him of someone he knew all too well.

"Your mother would never have let you go to a party like that, and you know it."

"God, Ryan. I'm thirteen now! Mom was alive when I was

eleven. You can't expect me to sit at home all the time." She looked furious.

Where the hell had this all gone so wrong? This used to be the girl who bounced on his knee when she was small. Who called him "best uncle Byran", who—

"Why are you still standing there?" she asked angrily. "I am entitled to privacy, Ryan. This is my room, you can't just come inside whenever you want to."

He started backing away from her. "Fine. I'll leave."

He walked out and closed the door behind him. Well, this evening wasn't turning out as he'd planned. He'd hoped to have a nice dinner with her, do some work in his study and then go to bed. That was his usual routine when he was home; he liked routines. But since dinner looked like it was off the cards, he headed straight to his study.

He did a good four hours of work that night before finally climbing into bed and falling into yet another restless sleep. He dreamed about his sister again that night. He hated waking up after a dream of her, because for a blissful moment when he opened his eyes she was still alive. But then, as consciousness kicked in, he realized with a painful stab that she wasn't. It was like losing her, again and again.

* * *

When he arrived outside Doris's apartment, next morning, he was officially running ten minutes late for work, thanks to Emmy. They'd had a disagreement again this morning. She'd walked downstairs and announced to him and his housekeeper, Tamlin, that she no longer wanted to eat a cooked breakfast because she was going vegan. When he'd pointed out to her that Tamlin had already gone to the effort of making her breakfast—and that just because all the celebrities were vegan these days, it didn't mean she needed to go vegan too just to try and be cool—she'd gotten upset and asked him if he even cared about animals and their suffering? Apparently, he still didn't "*get it.*" Well, he hoped he got whatever it was that he was meant to get soon, because life at home was feeling rather unbearable.

Doris was already sitting on the pavement waiting for him. He scanned his surroundings again. This place looked even worse in the morning. The sunlight was very unforgiving, illuminating all of its unsightly blemishes, and there were many. There was a sad, lonely-looking jungle gym on a dusty patch of what had probably once been grass. He sincerely hoped that children didn't climb it. A rusty abandoned tumble dryer looked like it was now being used by a family of birds. An old car tire lying on the ground completed the "eclectic" look. Doris jumped up as soon as she saw him and awkwardly raced around to the other side and climbed in. Her face was slightly red, as if she'd gotten sunburned from the long walk yesterday. She probably had.

She climbed in silently, and he had no idea what to say to her, at all. A part of him—*a very large part*—couldn't believe she was still working for him and, more than that, he was fetching her for work. He'd never had an employee in his car before . . . well, that wasn't entirely true. But he knew how badly that had ended, and he wasn't prepared to make that same mistake twice.

"Hi," she said softly, wringing her hands together in her lap as if she was nervous.

"Hi," he replied awkwardly. He felt strangely tongue-tied. He was never tongue-tied.

Silence. A long one. An awkward one that seemed to drag on between them painfully. He tapped his hands against the steering wheel and it was the only sound in the car.

"Better weather," she finally spoke.

"Not raining," he replied.

"Yes!" she said, and they fell into another strange silence. God, she needed to get her car back. Asap. He usually enjoyed his drive to work, it gave him a moment alone to regroup and focus before the chaos of the day descended. But this was positively painful.

"A little bit windy, though." She spoke again, after a long pause, and for a moment, he wasn't sure what she was talking about.

"What is?" he asked.

"The weather. Not rainy, but windy." She was really fiddling with her hands now, and it was driving him mad. He hated fidgeting. It was repetitive and distracting.

He shot her a sideways glance and looked down at her hands. They stopped moving immediately. The silence resumed, and he had to break it by turning on the radio. A song by some pop star that Emmy probably listened to burst through the speakers. At least they weren't sitting in silence anymore.

He was relieved when he finally pulled into the parking lot of his office. He heard a terrible sound next to him and looked over at Doris. She was humming away to the song.

He watched her for a moment or two before turning the engine off. The music cut out immediately, but her humming continued for a few seconds before she realized that she was doing it.

"Sorry. I sing when I'm nervous!" She slapped her hand over her mouth quickly and then climbed out of the car and ran into the building.

She was as bad at humming as she was at riding a bike. But for some reason, he found himself smiling.

CHAPTER ELEVEN

～

Poppy

Not rainy, but windy?

Had I really said that? The second the words were out of my mouth, I realized what a total idiot I sounded. And his reaction had said it all. Well, it wasn't so much what this man said, it was rather what he *didn't* say. Those stern sideways glances, those steely, flat responses . . . it was clear he didn't like me one little bit. *So why give me this job?*

But what really had me wound up by the time I got to the office, was his smell. The second I'd climbed into the car, I'd been inundated by that warm, spicy, soapy, heavenly, manly—*I could go on forever*—smell! It was intoxicating and now, as I sat at my strange new desk, all I could smell was him. His scent had vel-croed itself onto me and was lingering. When he wasn't looking, I grabbed some deodorant from my bag and tried to neutralize it with a few squirts—but it didn't work. His scent was officially here to stay.

The second we'd arrived he'd gone straight into his office and shut the door. I had no idea what I was meant to do, or if he was ever going to tell me. His office was only a few feet away and made of glass. This, unfortunately, meant that he could glare at me all day, which he did. Because every now and then he would look up and eyeball me suspiciously, as if he was trying to catch me out.

I looked down at my desk. Cold hard thing with no character. I opened my drawer and took stock of what was inside. I turned on the computer in front of me and wondered if it had games on it and whether I should dare access my Facebook page; he probably monitored his staff's computer activities, though. In fact, he was clearly such a control freak that I bet he had listening devices and security cameras secretly placed throughout the office so he could spy on his staff. I looked up at the ceiling and scanned it for devices. *None.* That didn't mean they weren't there, though. I looked into the open-plan section of the office where everyone else was. They all had that same, somewhat somber look about them as they sat in their little cubicles with their heads down. What did they even do here? These sad-looking worker ants that came to this cold steel building at 7 a.m. and worked all day. There was certainly no joy in this place, no life.

With nothing to do and no instructions, I adjusted my chair a few times and sharpened some pencils. And just then, the phone rang. It was so loud and unexpected that it made me jump. I looked over at Mr. Stark's office; he'd looked up in my direction again and was now glaring at me. I smiled at him and looked back down at the phone. *Oh my God, why did it have so many buttons?* One of them was flashing, usually a sign to press it. So I did and raised the receiver to my ear tentatively.

"Good day. Mr. Stark's office, how may I direct your call or be of assistance?" Thank God for that telenovela right now, because all I was doing was reciting lines from the show. Maybe I could do this after all?

"I'd like to speak to Mr. Stark. It's urgent." The voice sounded angry.

"Of course, please wait a moment while I put you through." FUCK! I looked down at the buttons. How exactly did I direct a call? I looked up at his office; he was still staring at me in a way that made my blood run cold.

I looked back down at the phone and started pressing buttons randomly. Crap! I was screwing up, and he knew it. The way he was shooting deadly laser beams out of his eyes at me right now made me want to burst into tears. I looked down at the phone cord, it was long, and without a second thought, I jumped up and started pulling it into his office. Maybe it would reach him? But it stopped *just* short of the door. I looked at the cord attached to the receiver, the curled part, and without thinking I threw the receiver over my shoulder and started stretching out the tightly wound cord, careful not to break it. Finally, after what felt like hours of bloody pulling and stretching, the phone reached him by mere centimeters.

"Here we go . . ." I quickly passed him the receiver and then almost tripped over the phone cord on the way back out of his office. It was stretched to capacity and any sudden movements would probably send it flying across the room, like a bungee rope. I sat back down at my desk. I was shaking and he was watching me with an expression that I couldn't read. But it scared me. And then he started talking and finally looked away.

I bit my bottom lip as I felt the tears well up. The last thing I needed to do now was cry, so I got up and raced to the bathroom in an attempt to get a grip on my now very turbulent emotions. I didn't know how long I'd been in the bathroom, but the second I came out, I knew it had been too long. He was now standing in his office doorway, eyes fixed on my empty desk.

"Sorry, I just needed to . . ." I didn't finish the sentence as I ran back to my desk and sat down.

"Please keep your restroom visits as short as possible. I don't want you to miss any important calls—which is all of them, by the way."

"Of course." I nodded and tried not to fiddle with my hands, I still remembered the look of disdain he'd given me over that. God, this man was a dragon. All he needed to do now was breathe bloody fire and the picture would be complete.

"You put calls through like this." He walked over to my desk and pressed some buttons. "And if you need me, please don't knock on my door or come into my office, dial 124, that's my extension."

I nodded. "Of course. I'll do that." I forced myself to look up at him. "Uh, um, I would really like to know, if you have time, of course, I know you are a very, very busy man with all the important things you do, uh, but I would really like to, uh, uh . . ."

"Stop stuttering, Miss Granger!" His harsh tone made me shudder. "If you have something to ask me, come out and say it."

"Okay. What exactly are my responsibilities here?" The words shot out of my mouth.

"I'm glad you asked. Come into my office in ten minutes. Bring a notepad." He walked back to his office but paused before going in. "And please, go easy on the perfume. I can barely breathe in here!"

I nodded at him and forced a smile. Working for this man was clearly going to be hell on earth! Mind you, I had worked for worse. When Santiago's evil twin, Ignacio, had come back from the Amazon rainforest and taken over as CEO, he'd killed me.

Oh dear Lord, I hope this man wasn't capable of such things? But who knew with Ryan Stark? A few of his staff had looked up when he'd walked out of the office and looked back down quickly, as if they were all genuinely frightened of him.

I got that. *I* was frightened of him.

CHAPTER TWELVE

⌣

Ryan

*H*e'd had to look away after she'd brought the phone into his office, or she would have seen him smile, which would have been very unfortunate. It was common practice *not* to tell his new employees what to do. He liked watching them suffer and squirm and seeing how they would react to situations—you can tell a lot about a person when you throw them into the deep end. Sink or swim. And he always looked forward to the first call and the confusion and panic that followed. But today he'd been surprised.

No one had ever thought to get out of their chair and bring the phone directly to him. Most of them sat pressing buttons randomly until it drove him nuts. Others crept into his office and asked him what to do, and some buckled under his death stare and burst into tears when they couldn't put the call through. But not her. She'd come up with a unique solution. Not one he ever wanted to see repeated, but nonetheless, it had been unique, even though the phone cord was now permanently damaged and stretched.

He watched his clock like a hawk to see if she was also

punctual. He watched the second hand as it ticked its way up to ten minutes and just as the second hand reached 9 minutes 55 seconds, she knocked on the door.

"Come in," he barked loudly. He looked up at her hands to see what she'd brought to write on. There were no notebooks in the office, another little one of his tests. He hated it when they came into his office with scraps of paper and once, one of them had even written on her hand. It had washed off when she went to the bathroom, and she'd forgotten absolutely everything he'd told her. He'd had to fire her. But not Doris Granger. She was carrying a small bunch of papers that she'd stapled together on the side. On the front, he could clearly read that she'd written "Notebook."

"Sit." He gestured. "You were asking what your responsibilities were." He watched her as she laid the makeshift notebook on his table and took out a very sharpened pencil, letting it hover just above the page.

"Yes." She looked up at him through her cracked glasses. They irritated the hell out of him. How could she even see through them? Maybe she should get new glasses altogether because these big, purple-framed things that she was currently wearing looked like they'd been fished out of a box at a garage sale. Not to mention that they totally obscured her entire face, they were that big.

"Ready," she said, sounding confident, even though he could see her hand was shaking.

In his experience, it was always better for his staff to be scared of him: that way no friendships—or other things—developed. It was safer that way. Many years ago he'd made the terrible mistake of mixing business with pleasure, and that had ended very badly for him. He'd walked away with a broken heart and a seriously tarnished reputation, and she had walked away with his business partner. Office romances, friendships even, never worked. He had proof of that. Never cross that professional line.

"Right," he said, turning his attention back to the strange woman sitting in front of him. "You need to answer all my calls, obviously. I have a diary, you have access to it on your computer, and you need to keep it up to date with all my meetings. Do you have any idea how important my meetings are, Miss Granger?"

"Um . . . very?" she replied.

"Very is an understatement. If I don't attend certain meetings, this company could lose millions. And I would hate to have to deduct that from your salary."

Her eyes widened at that. "No. Millions. Of course. I understand." She looked back down at her notepad and wrote:

Meetings = millions + NB CAN'T MISS!!!!!!!!!!!! + NB EVER!!!!! (or broke for the rest of my life 😵)

She circled that three times and then raised her head and looked at him expectantly.

"I need you to deal with any scheduling clashes, for meetings and travel. You'll need to also take notes at meetings and then type them up afterward. A copy needs to be emailed to me and all the people who were in the meeting. I hate 'misunderstandings,'" he gestured air quotes, "which often happen when money is on the line, so be precise." She was writing frantically now and he continued, giving her no break. "Booking travel when need be, and arranging transport to and from the airport when flying. Booking hotels and transport for any important guests or board members coming to meetings here if traveling from out of town.

Seeing to their needs and making sure they are comfortable and well treated. You will be the buffer between me and the other staff. All queries and requests for meetings and phone calls go through you—I do not want any of them knocking on my door. That is very important. No one is to disturb me during the day. I need you to bring me lunch—a brown bread chicken sandwich, no mayonnaise—from the cafeteria downstairs and a strong cup of coffee—no milk, no sugar—at exactly 1:10 p.m. Then you may take lunch from 1:10 to 1:57. But be back at your desk at 1:57 exactly to start work at 2. Then I need you to collect my suits from the laundry once a week; they are situated only a block away, you can walk, since you don't have a car. And I expect you to leave when I leave, in case anything comes up. Working hours can be long."

He watched her scribble. Her tongue had wandered out of her mouth and it was flicking about as she concentrated. He hoped she didn't do that in meetings. Her hand moved fast and she nodded as she went, repeating the odd word here and there—he also hoped she didn't do that in meetings. She finally finished and looked up at him.

"You can charge for overtime, obviously," he quickly added.

"On that note, money, uh . . . well . . . I was . . ."

"Stop stuttering." He hated it when she stuttered.

"Sorry!" She sat up straight. "Money. I was wondering what my salary is and when I would be paid? The advert said ten to fifteen thousand, negotiable. Depending on experience."

He sat back in his chair and observed her. She looked very uncomfortable talking about money. "How much do you think you're worth?" he asked.

"Sorry, what?" she asked.

"Simple question. How much do you deserve to be paid? The higher end, or the lower end? I mean, you don't have that much experience, do you? But perhaps you think you can bring something extra to this job, another skill you have that I'm not aware of? Perhaps if I ever do business in a Spanish-speaking company, for example, you might be able to translate?" At that her face went white. She was no more fluent in Spanish than she was ever going to win a "best dressed" contest. It was clear that she had lied about that one.

"Uh . . . um, uh . . ." Her hands flew up to her mouth. "Sorry, didn't meant to stutter." Her brow wrinkled and the corners of her mouth twitched. And that was when, for the first time, he noticed her lips. They were full and stained a pastel-pink color which made them look like cotton candy . . . He quickly pulled his eyes away from them.

"So," he pressed, "what are you worth?"

"I don't know," she finally said.

"Everyone should know what they're worth, Miss Granger."

She wriggled in her seat, looking anxious and uncomfortable.

"What do you think I'm worth?" she finally asked, looking him directly in the eye.

His body stiffened and something shot through him, but he quickly composed himself.

"I have no idea. I hardly know you. I have no idea whether you can even do this job. I mean, in the ten minutes that you've worked for me you've already damaged a telephone beyond repair, so . . ." He tapered off when he saw the look on her face.

She looked deflated.

"You have until the end of the day to tell me what you're worth, Miss Granger. Dismissed," he said quickly and then looked back down at his desk, wondering why he now felt guilty for saying that to her.

She stood up and started walking away.

"Miss Granger?" he called after her, and she turned. "I have a meeting with Mr. Grey today in an hour. I believe you just spoke to him on the phone. The man irritates the hell out of me and I really have better things to do than listen to him drone on and on. Ten minutes into the meeting please walk into my office and tell me I have something important to attend to, so I can end the meeting. Otherwise I'll be trapped with him for two hours longer than I should, like last time."

She looked confused. "Uh . . . sure. What should I say?"

He shrugged. "I don't know. I'm sure you'll work it out."

She looked thoughtful for a moment. "I guess I could say you had an—"

He cut her off. "Miss Granger, I don't care what you say or do. Just make sure you end my meeting."

"Why can't you just tell him the meeting is over?" she asked.

He looked at her and sighed. "Because he needs to feel he is special and that I have time for him, even though I don't. It's all part of these manipulations and corporate games we play with each other every day." He didn't want to add that Mr. Grey had been a friend of his father's and, other than Ryan, held the most shares in the company. As a result, his opinion held a lot of weight; in fact, he'd been the primary reason for a business decision Ryan had made recently that he was really starting to regret. But he'd felt strong-armed into making it. It had been very clear in the last meeting that Mr. Grey had been working and influencing the other shareholders and board members behind his back—except for Mr. Rautenbach, who remained unswayed still.

"Sounds terrible," she said, snapping him out of his thoughts. She turned and walked away.

He watched her exit. Something about her fascinated him, but irritated the hell out of him too.

CHAPTER THIRTEEN

~

Poppy

$\mathcal{H}$e wanted me to walk into a meeting and stop it!

How was I meant to do that? I'd waited with bated breath for the arrival of this Mr. Grey fellow, and when he finally did arrive, he wasn't anything like the film version of Mr. Grey. In fact, the short, portly man with the bright red cheeks and orange comb-over hair looked more like a horizontal version of the American president than a man who had the power to stir the loins of women everywhere. His name was very misleading, since it conjured up all kinds of images.

I'd sat there nervously waiting for the ten-minute mark, waiting for the moment I was meant to go in there and put an end to the meeting. But I was still trying to figure out how on earth I was going to do that. The last thing I wanted to do was walk back into his office, it filled me with terror and fear. At that moment someone walked past my desk and then stopped.

"Shit, it's Mr. Grey," she said.

I looked up at the woman standing by my desk; I'd seen her walk in this morning.

"I better let the others know," she said quickly and then put some papers down on my desk. "Quarterly financial reports, he'll want to see those today." She started walking away, and I stopped her.

"Why do you have to tell the others that Mr. Grey is here?" I asked.

She turned around and looked nervous. She leaned in and lowered her voice. "Mr. Stark hates him. He's always in an extra-terrible mood after meetings with him. We dread it when he comes into the office."

"Oh, I see," I mumbled, looking over at the office. You didn't need to be a body language expert to see that he was irritated with the man. In fact, he wasn't doing a very good job at hiding the way he felt about him or the meeting, and at one point he actually rolled his eyes and sighed. God, this man had no behavioral etiquette whatsoever. Most people worked hard to hide things like that. He did not. In fact, he seemed to go out of his way to show his displeasure with everything.

"I'm Juniper, by the way. I work in accounts." She extended her hand for me to shake.

"Po—" I cut myself off quickly, almost forgetting my character's name for a moment there. "Doris," I replied, taking her hand. God, this was the ultimate method acting, being in character all the time like this.

"If you ever need to know anything, by the way, you can always ask me. I've been here for five years—that's four years and eleven months longer than I should have been." She rolled her eyes and I smiled at her. I knew what she meant. I had already been here for—I looked up at the clock—three hours and forty minutes more than I needed to be too.

"Thanks for the offer," I said as she walked back to her desk. I looked at the clock again; I needed to be in there in one minute and put an end to the meeting. This was confirmed when Mr. Stark glared at me. I stood up nervously and walked over to the office. I could do this. I was an actress. I knocked on the door.

"What?" he said, sounding irritated by the disturbance. Clearly playing along. I walked in.

"Sorry to disturb you, Mr. Stark, but you have a call."

Mr. Grey turned and looked at me. "A call?" He sounded dubious.

I nodded. "Mmm, a very important one," I quickly added, upping the stakes and feeling rather pleased with myself for thinking of that.

Mr. Grey stared at me blankly and I smiled at him. Doris was a smiler. I'd decided that smiling should be one of her character traits. You can't be mad at a person who smiles a lot, can you? Mr. Grey looked unmoved, though, and then Ryan started blinking at me. Rapidly.

"Do you have something in your eye?" I asked innocently.

His eyes widened, his face reddened and now he just looked angry. I smiled even more and decided I would need to improvise. I cleared my throat and then dropped the smile.

"Yes!" My voice was high and borderline frantic. "In fact, I think you better take the call right now, Mr. Stark, sir. Immediately. It seems very urgent. Very urgent indeed. The voice on the other end was very—"

"Urgent?" The portly old man cut me off. He leaned over his

chair and eyed me suspiciously. "I didn't hear the phone ring," he said sarcastically, and suddenly I got the feeling that Mr. Stark had tried this on him before. He was onto us.

"It was on silent," I said quickly. I could see he didn't believe me.

The man slowly looked over at my office desk and then back up at me again. "Interesting," he said. "I didn't see you answer any call either."

"Well, that's because you had your back to me," I retorted.

"I can see you in the reflection of the glass." He pointed at the window in front of him and, lo and behold, my desk was reflected in it.

"It was an SMS," I said.

"An SMS?" He sounded very doubtful and I started to panic. "Yes. On my phone. An urgent SMS. And let me tell you . . . they used a lot of very, very urgent-looking emojis, you know." I put my hands up to my face and opened my mouth. "Screaming ghost face emoji. Aaaahhhhhh," I said and immediately regretted it when I saw the look on Mr. Stark's face. My heart started beating in my throat as the panic grew. Without thinking, I opened my mouth and said, "Should I put the call through or would you like to take it somewhere else?" The second the words were out of my mouth I realized the mistake I'd just made.

"I thought you said it was an SMS?" Mr. Grey jumped in, not letting that golden opportunity to play sleuth slip him by.

"Uh . . . uh . . ." I stuttered, not sure how to salvage this.

"Miss Granger is new here," Ryan finally said. "I think she's confused. Aren't you confused, Miss Granger?" He looked at me and I started nodding.

"I'm confused," I said. "So, so confused." I did something

stupid with my face and hands and then regretfully said, "Confused face emoji," before I slipped out of the office as quickly as I could. I sat back down at my desk and held my head in my hands. That hadn't gone well at all. In fact—

My phone beeped and I looked down at it. It was from Ryan.

Ryan: I said END THE MEETING!

How the hell was he typing a message to me and Mr. Grey hadn't noticed? I looked at him and realized that although he was still talking, his one hand was under his desk discreetly sending a message. God, the man had serious phone skills. He obviously did this a lot. My phone beeped again and I looked down.

Ryan: NOW!

I stood up out of my seat and looked around. I thought back to the telenovela and searched my mind for a scene I could play out. And then it hit me. The evacuation scene, when the mutated, infected rats which were being used as biological weapons were released into the building. I walked down the corridor to where I'd seen it earlier. And in three, two, one, I activated the fire alarm. The alarm blared. It was so loud that I had to cover my ears. I ran straight for his office and, this time, I threw myself into it. I did a perfectly rehearsed forward roll and then jumped to my feet.

"What the hell, Miss Granger?" Ryan said when he saw me.

But I didn't say a word. Instead, I looked at them both with perfectly rehearsed horror plastered across my face.

"What?" Mr. Grey asked, looking nervous. *Was he really buying this?* Maybe I was a better actress than I thought? I dialed it up a notch.

I shook my head. Bit my lip and then raised my hands to my head and started shaking it from side to side, just as Ramona had done.

"What?" Mr. Grey shot out of his seat now. *And the Oscar goes to . . . me!*

"It's bad," I said, my voice shaking and quivering.

Ryan shot up out of his seat too. "What?" he asked. Even he was buying this performance of mine.

And that's when I did it. It was perfect and brilliant and . . . tears of fear welled up in my eyes. "It's the containment field," I said, looking behind me as if I was terrified of something. Mr. Grey looked behind me too.

"Containment what?" Ryan asked.

"It's a disaster. It's been breached," I suddenly screeched. They both jumped.

"We have to get out of here. NOW!" I grabbed my chest in panic and then, just as Ramona González had done, I stared off into an imaginary camera and narrowed my eyes like Melania. In fact, the First Lady had been a great inspiration for many of Ramona González's facial expressions. Mostly those of distress and confusion.

Mr. Grey suddenly bolted out of the office. I quickly stopped my dramatic stare and then gave Ryan a smiley thumbs up followed by a wink. I expected him to smile back. But he didn't. In fact, he looked very displeased. He shook his head at me in blatant disapproval and stormed out of his office.

CHAPTER FOURTEEN

⟨⟨

Ryan

*O*ne whole hour. Sixty goddamn minutes and they were all still standing outside the building in the emergency parking lot assembly point. One hour was what he'd hoped to avoid when ending the meeting, but Doris had failed at that miserably. And even though this had been a very false alarm—*what the fuck was a containment field anyway?*—it was company policy that when the alarm went off, the building needed to be swept by firemen and given the all clear before people could go back in.

He walked over to Doris; she had been avoiding him for the past hour. Every time he walked in her direction, she'd ducked behind someone in the 300-strong crowd of staff members who were all clumped together. Finally, he caught up to her.

"A whole hour," he hissed into her ear so the others wouldn't hear him. "That is how long we have been standing outside and approximately how long I was hoping to avoid with Mr. Grey."

She turned and looked at him, taking a small step back. She

looked terrified. "You said to end the meeting. You used capital letters!"

"I meant pull me out, not set off an alarm so the whole building needed to be evacuated."

"I tried to pull you out, remember?" she said.

"Not very well," he replied snippily.

"Well, it's not my fault that you've probably done this to him so many times before that he was onto me the second I walked in."

"Maybe he was onto you because you weren't very convincing. Don't quit your day job and become an actress," he said.

And at that, she burst out laughing. Her laughter was so loud that a few people turned around and looked at them.

"This is not funny," he whispered. "Oh God, this whole thing, all of it, is ridiculous. I can't believe you did that. And why on earth would you do a forward roll into my office?"

"It was for added dramatic impact," she said and then looked at him angrily. "You told me you didn't care how I did it or what I did. You told me to end the meeting, and that's all."

He paused. He had said that. But who in their right mind went from "please end a meeting" to setting off a false alarm and dramatically babbling about containment fields and doing acrobatic moves in the office?

"But look." She spoke again, her tone changed now. "Look how happy and relaxed everyone is."

"What?" he asked.

"The staff. Look around."

He looked around and she was right. Everyone had smiles on their faces. Everyone was talking and laughing and they all looked like they were enjoying their break in the sun. This pissed him off. Work was not meant to be enjoyable and social.

"I think a fire break is good for office morale," she said, looking pleased with herself. "A break outside in the fresh air always helps destress."

The firemen finally exited the building and gave him the all clear. A collective disappointed sigh rose up from everyone, and this *really* pissed him off.

"We'll see about that," he grunted. He walked up to a small wall and climbed onto it. "Everyone," he said. "You will all be staying for an extra hour after work to make up for this." He climbed down and walked straight back inside.

CHAPTER FIFTEEN

Ryan

*B*y the time he'd finished his last call for the day, it was well after 11 p.m. He put the phone down and stood up, stretching out his back which was really starting to kill him. He reached into his drawer and took out an aspirin, he could feel a headache coming on.

He packed up his things and walked out of his office, only to see her there. *Her.* He'd almost forgotten about her. He'd forgotten about Doris Granger who worked for him and had been the cause of all that drama today and was now slumped over her desk fast asleep and making little squeaking noises with each out breath.

He walked over to her desk quietly and stood over her. She was an odd one. She'd surprised him today with the telephone but then in the next breath had completely fucked up with the evacuation. He was just about to wake her up when she let out a little moan followed by a breathy sigh as if she was dreaming about something pleasant. He couldn't remember the last time his dreams had been happy ones. He stood above her, fascinated by the little noises she was making and by the way her nose crinkled when she breathed. She'd pushed her glasses onto her head and he was curious to know what she looked like without the cumbersome things.

"WHAT?!" She suddenly shot up as if she knew he'd been standing over her. "Who? Where am ... Oh God, did I fall asleep? What's the time ... What?" She looked around frantically, as if she had no idea where she was for a moment or two, and then tilted her head up and her sleepy eyes locked with his and ... and ...

Without the glasses on, he could finally see her face properly. And he was stunned. Her eyes were startling. They were big, round and an unusual amber color. In this light, they looked golden. Her cheekbones were high and defined, and her face was dotted with small freckles. He tried to open his mouth and say something to her, but couldn't. She quickly pulled her glasses back on, and her perfect features disappeared.

"Sorry, I didn't mean to fall asleep." She shot out of her seat like a firecracker had been lit underneath her and grabbed her bag. "I'm ready to go," she said, but then followed it with a massive yawn. She slapped her hand over her mouth and tried to act as if it hadn't happened. He smiled this time—completely forgetting that he was trying *not* to smile at her.

"Let's go!" He quickly wiped the smile off his face and strode towards the elevator. Down to the ground floor, through the empty reception area and out into the parking lot he walked. He turned around and could see Doris was struggling to keep up. She was walking on her tiptoes as if she was in some kind of circus act. He looked down at her feet and then ran his eyes up her legs.

"What happened?" He pointed at them.

"Uh, the knees and shins are from my incident with the bike, and I think I walked over some thorns yesterday too." She was walking very strangely now. Balancing on her toes and then rolling back onto the sides of her feet, as if avoiding her heels.

"Did you disinfect them?" he asked.

She stopped walking and gave him a puzzled look.

"Like with an antibacterial lotion, or Dettol or something like that?" he clarified. He hated repeating himself.

"If you mean, did I wash them with soap and water, then yes!"

He sighed. "Clearly, you *want* to get an infection then!" He found it highly irritating that she was walking around with legs that could get infected at any moment. Who did that?

"They're just grazes." She continued walking, and it was utterly ridiculous. She looked like some ludicrous cross between a flamingo and a kangaroo, balancing and hopping and kind of dragging too.

"I take it you didn't manage to get all the thorns out either?" He pointed at her tiny feet as they shuffled strangely across the parking lot.

"Some were too fiddly, and I couldn't reach a few of them. But don't worry, I'm sure they'll come out on their own."

"Thorns don't just come out on their own!" He huffed loudly and turned to open his car. He could hear the little, pathetic foot sounds on the paving and he couldn't take it a second longer. He opened the back door and pointed at the seat. "Get into the back seat! Now."

"What?" She stopped shuffling and stared at the back seat. She looked panicked.

"Oh, for God's sake, I'm not trying to get you into the back seat for sex or something like that!" he said matter-of-factly.

Her head whipped around, her jaw slackened and her golden-colored eyes were as wide as saucers. "Then what?" she asked.

He shook his head. He hated explaining himself. Especially to employees. And he usually didn't have to. People never questioned him. Except her.

"Just get in." He pointed at the seat and then walked around to the passenger side of the car. He kept a very extensive medical kit in the cubbyhole. When his sister had been ill, she'd scraped her leg once when they'd been out. Her body had been so run-down that a bad infection had set in quickly. Had he had something on hand to disinfect the cut right there and then, perhaps it wouldn't have gotten so bad so quickly. After that, he'd always made sure to travel with a fully stocked medical kit for any kind of emergency—he just never thought it would be this kind of emergency.

He grabbed the kit and walked back to her. She'd climbed into the back seat and her legs were hanging out the side of the car. She looked up at him anxiously, and for some reason, he found the look to be both irritating and endearing. The look of shock that had washed over her face when he'd said the word "sex" had amused him. God, he couldn't remember the last time he'd had sex, let alone thought about it. Sex was always so messy, and not just physically. When emotions were involved, things seemed to get messy and ugly, quickly. He liked things in his life to be neat and ordered. He'd had a brief encounter with some nameless woman at a conference a year ago, but it had been highly unsatisfying and had only momentarily (partially) scratched an itch. But since then . . . nothing. He hadn't missed it either. He was far too busy to worry about something as trivial as sex.

"Sit back and stretch your legs out on the seat." He waved his arm at her.

"Sorry, what?" She looked at him and blinked like a deer in the headlights.

"Well, those knees aren't going to disinfect themselves, are they?" He gestured for her to move. Slowly and tentatively she moved back, stretching her legs out as she went. He unzipped the medical bag and pulled out the tube of cream he was looking for. He took the lid off and squeezed some out onto a cotton wool bud. He was just about to put it on her knees when he stopped. Her skirt had crept up her thighs and she was clearly unaware that, at this angle, he could see all the way up it to her pretty pink panties. His breath hitched in his throat and he looked away quickly. But it was too late. Because suddenly, just like that, after all this time, he was thinking about sex . . .

Chapter Sixteen

~

Poppy

*S*omething in the air changed. Something strange and inexplicable was happening, and I wasn't entirely sure what the hell it was. He stared at my knees with the most focused, intense look on his face, as if they were all he could see. As if he was too afraid to look anywhere else but there. His previously blue eyes were dark, or maybe it was just the light? His jaw clenched, and his entire body tensed. My stomach tightened and a warm shiver ran through me. *What was going on?*

I swallowed hard, as if something was stuck in my throat, and looked down at his hand. He was holding a cotton wool bud in his fingers and it was hovering just above my knee. I had a sudden image of him dropping it and bringing his hand down on my knee. Clasping my knee in his big hand and then running it up my thigh, digging his fingers into my flesh and running it higher, and higher and . . .

God, I felt like such a perv right now. But truthfully, I was as sexually frustrated as hell. I hadn't had sex in ages—not since my last boyfriend anyway. And he certainly hadn't been much to write anywhere about. I wasn't exactly lucky in love, or lust, for that matter. I had this uncanny ability to attract total, idiotic losers who never seemed to be any good in the sack, or anywhere else. Sometimes I thought I was doomed to a life of mediocre sex with men who earned less money than I did—and that was saying a lot.

But the hand didn't do anything of the sort. Instead, the sudden sting of fiery disinfectant coming into contact with the broken skin of my knee made me wince.

"Ow!" I tensed up as the sting intensified.

"Keep still or it will hurt more," the stern voice fired back at me, and any semblance of lust I'd been feeling a few seconds ago was gone. I tried to keep as still as possible as he dabbed cream on my knees and then stuck two massive Band-Aids over them.

"Take off your shoes!" he suddenly commanded in a tone that made me shiver.

"Why?"

"The thorns in your foot. Or would you like to leave them in and see if they get gangrenous?"

"Uh . . . you're not going to . . . ? Um . . ." I watched in horror as he pulled out a needle and a pair of tweezers from the bag.

"I'm going to try," he said, waving his free hand at my shoes once more. "If you'll take off your shoes so we can get this over and done with. I'd like to get home before the sun comes up. Wouldn't you?"

"It's okay." I pulled my feet towards myself. "You don't have to do it. It's fine."

He glared at me for a moment or two as if he was irritated, and then his face seemed to soften slightly. "Here. Take this." He put the tweezers and needle back into the bag and passed it to me. "Maybe you could get someone to assist you with that?" The tone of his voice made his question seemed very loaded. "Maybe someone you live with?" he asked.

"Live with?" I took the bag from him.

"It's a very simple question, Miss Granger, you either do, or do not have someone at home who can help you get the thorns out of your foot?"

I nodded and had no idea why, but I lied (I seemed to lie a lot around him). "I do. Yes, I have someone at home to help me." I looked at him and saw his shoulders slump slightly, and for some reason, I felt compelled to quickly correct myself. "No. I don't. No one lives with me. I live all alone," I said.

He raised an eyebrow at me. "You're not very good at answering questions with a straight answer, are you?"

"I am," I defended myself.

"No, you're not. I ask you why I should employ you, and you have nothing to say. I ask you how much you're worth, and you have no idea. Then I ask you if you have someone to help you and, at first, you do, and then you don't."

"Mmmm," I mumbled to myself. He had a point.

"So?" he asked again.

"No. I have no one who can help me get the thorns out of my feet, unless I ask my dodgy neighbor who is permanently on crack, or meth, or E, or cocaine or . . . shit, I have no idea what drugs the guy does. But trust me, he does them. Then there's the other neighbor who I'm currently avoiding because I never brought his bike back and I'm just hoping he's not going to kill me or steal my TV for retribution, because I'm living in some strange gangsters' paradise, or something like that." I stopped talking, thrust the bag back at him and started taking my shoes off. "Fine. Do it." I pushed my feet in his direction and hoped to hell they didn't smell.

He watched me for a few seconds and then looked down at my feet and started picking at them with the tweezers. I sighed. I couldn't figure out whether this was the weirdest thing that had ever happened to me—letting my new boss pick thorns from my feet—or whether this might actually be the nicest thing that anyone had done for me in a while.

What was I thinking . . . it was weird. *Fucking weird.* But then again, lying on my CV, changing my name, assuming a character and dressing up in disguise to get a job I had no idea how to do, was weird . . . so what the hell had I been expecting?

"I'm done," he suddenly said.

I reached down and ran my hand over the soles of my feet, and they felt completely smooth. "Thanks." I was actually very grateful to have those tiny thorns out, they'd been getting more and more painful as the day had progressed.

He walked around to the front of the car and climbed in. He turned and scowled at me. "This isn't a taxi."

"Right!" I climbed over the armrest in the middle to get to the passenger seat.

"The back does have doors, you know."

"Sorry," I said. The car started and we drove off in total silence until we finally arrived at my place.

"Thanks for the lift." I reached for the door handle.

"Wait. I better come with you. It doesn't look safe out there."

I chuckled under my breath. "I think I'll be okay walking to my door, it's only a few meters away."

"What about all your dodgy neighbors?" he asked.

"Uh . . ." I turned and looked at him curiously. "Are you being serious?"

"Yes. When a staff member says a neighbor is possibly trying to kill them, or steal their TV, I take it seriously." His tone was dead-pan and I couldn't work out if he was joking, or had really taken me seriously. Not that he shouldn't, I mean, there was a slight possibility that "Little Mike" could come looking for his bike in a very bad mood.

"Okay. Fine." I opened the door and climbed out. "Personally, I would be more afraid of leaving my expensive car here unattended, but hey, that's just me." I walked towards the building, fully expecting him to leave. Poor rich guy wouldn't want his big, beautiful Porsche to get stolen. But he didn't leave. Instead, he jumped out of the car and followed me all the way up to the door.

I took my keys out and started fiddling with the lock. There was a trick to opening the door; sometimes it involved kicking it. Luckily for me, Ramona González had been trained in martial arts. Finally, the door flew open and his face fell as he looked inside.

"How long have you lived here?" He looked into the dark hall with its solitary flickering light. The light had been flickering for months now, and no one had bothered to fix it.

I shrugged. "Too long." The move here was meant to be temporary. I was only going to live here for a short time, while I saved some money to get a better place. But that hadn't really worked out. I guess I should have known that; my life was dotted with many examples of things just not quite working out the way I'd planned. But things had become particularly tough after my mother died. When she'd gotten sick she hadn't been able to work for a while. Her bills had piled up, including the medical bills, and since I was the next of kin, legally those bills fell on me to pay. I'd managed to settle a fair amount of them when I'd been working on the show, but since being unemployed, I hadn't managed to keep up with the regular payments, and now the bank was phoning me more often than I would like. That was why I needed this job so badly.

Suddenly, unexpectedly, he took a step towards me and stared. The look on his face stole my breath. "I asked you what you were worth?" He pointed into the dark corridor behind me. "I think it's got to be a bit more than this, don't you think?"

"Um . . . uh . . ." I stumbled on my words. Completely shocked.

He gave me one last strange look and then he turned and walked away. "I'll see you in the morning," he said over his shoulder, before climbing into his car and driving off.

I stood there staring at him with the strangest feeling I couldn't quite pinpoint.

CHAPTER SEVENTEEN

～

Ryan

*B*y the time he got home the house was completely silent. To be honest, he was grateful that Emmy was asleep, especially considering what was happening between them at the moment. Every single time they were in the same room, something bad inevitably transpired. Or more to the point, he seemed to do something that would anger/upset/irritate/infuriate (take your pick) her. He didn't know how much of that was teenage hormones, or how much of that was because of her mother's death.

It had been almost two years since his twin sister, Rachel, had passed away. Motor neurone disease; he hadn't even known what it was until her shocking diagnosis. It had taken only eighteen months from the time the doctors had told them to the day she passed away. He'd been sad that day, obviously, but the overall feeling had been one of total relief. Believe it or not, there are worse things than death. He'd watched her muscles waste away until she was wheelchair bound, unable to feed herself, swallow and even talk. She and Emmy had moved in with him soon after the diagnosis. He'd hired the best nursing care possible for her, but even with all the money in the world for the best doctors and nurses, she'd still gone. Money can buy you many things, but it cannot buy life. Sometimes he didn't know what was worse: seeing your sister die, or watching your sister suffer like she had. In many ways, it would have been easier if it was a sudden death. One moment she was there, and then the next she was gone. But it hadn't been like that. Because she was already gone, before she was dead. That had been one of the hardest things to deal with. She had physically been there, sitting in her wheelchair, but the Rachel he knew was long gone. The cruel truth of the disease is that, in some cases, like his sister's, once it's finished stealing your muscles, it steals your mind too.

He walked up the stairs and passed Emmy's room. He stopped momentarily and put his ear to the door. Her lights were on but he had no idea what she was doing. He placed his knuckles on the door, about to knock, but stopped himself. He wanted to reach out to her, but honestly, she felt so far away from him right now that he didn't know how to. So he kept on walking into his room and closed the door behind him too. He peeled his clothes off and looked at himself in the mirror. He hadn't been to the gym in a while and could see his middle section wasn't looking as good as it used to. In fact, he was definitely filling out in a few places. He ran his hands up his arm and over his tattoo. He smiled to himself. He and Rachel had gone to Thailand after school for a holiday. They'd been young and wild and spontaneous and had drunk too much and landed up at crazy island parties where they'd gotten matching tattoos. It had been fun. But now, that life seemed to belong to a totally different person. He didn't even know that guy anymore. Because soon after coming back from that holiday, he'd gone to business school like his father had wanted, and then began running the company, also like his father had wanted. It had been expected of him, since his name was on the building, his father had always said. Truthfully, if he had done what he'd wanted with his life, he probably wouldn't be running the company at all. Not that he knew what he wanted to do, but still. Rachel had never done what their father had wanted, though. He'd always admired that about her, and been envious too. She was a much stronger person than him. She did things differently. She moved to the beat of her own damn drum. He climbed into his bed, and his thoughts immediately drifted towards Doris. He'd come so close to letting go tonight.

Too close.

There'd been a moment with her when all he'd wanted to do was be wild and spontaneous again. Where he'd wanted to rip her ugly clothes and glasses off. There was something about her that was getting under his skin. Clearly, she was dangerous for him. Which was very surprising, since she'd pissed him off no end today when she had single-handedly disrupted the entire working day of 300 staff members and forced them all out of the building.

He looked up at his ceiling and suddenly found himself wondering what her ceiling looked like? Judging from that corridor in her building, it probably didn't look like his. That bothered him. It bothered him more than he could explain.

Fucking hell, he needed to sleep, but Doris bloody Granger was running through his mind, shuffling on her stupid thorn-infested feet. Every time he thought of something else, he came straight back to her. Doris with those stupid glasses. Doris with those hideous clothes and irritating stutter and those grazed knees. Doris who had a terrible habit of sticking her tongue out of her mouth when she wrote and had a nose that made squeaking noises when she slept and did forward rolls into his office. She was absolutely everything that irritated him, and more.

So why was he thinking about her?

CHAPTER EIGHTEEN

⌒

Poppy

I paced around my tiny apartment. I felt strange and unsettled. In fact, I hadn't felt this damn odd in a long time. I pulled my stupid wig off and threw it to the floor. It had been making my head itch all day and I was mentally kicking myself, at least every few minutes, for deciding to wear the stupid thing in the first place! I released my long auburn hair from the tight braid that I'd put it in this morning and scratched my scalp. It was so itchy that I was sure I was going to scratch bits of my head off. But taking the wig off still hadn't made me feel any better.

"How much do you think you're worth?"

Something about that question had cut me to the quick. It did something deep inside that felt fundamentally uncomfortable. My stomach twisted itself into knots as memories and moments and phrases from my past started running through my head . . .

"I never wanted a fucking kid in the first place!" The words I'd heard my father say the night he'd walked out of the house for good. They'd played in my head over and over again through the

years, and I'd always wondered what I could have done differently to make him want me.

"*She'll never amount to anything*," one of my teachers had said after I'd failed a test. I'd never been good at school. I was far too much of a dreamer to be present in the classroom, and as a result, I'd barely made it through high school. Academic learning had never been my strong point.

Sports hadn't been my forte either. The only time I'd attempted to play tennis, I'd been knocked in the face with a racquet and rushed to the hospital with a broken nose . . . I'd hit myself while trying to serve. I'd joined the chess club, but realized I didn't have the patience or the skills to think strategically. I'd tried to play a musical instrument, but blowing into a flute had just made me feel dizzy. I'd never quite been pretty and confident enough to be one of the popular kids, growing up, and had never been ambitious or smart enough for college and a big fancy career in a designer suit. The only time I could ever remember standing out at anything was when I'd acted in the school play, and everyone had laughed loudly and clapped for me. That was the one moment when I'd felt like I was worth something, or had been good at anything.

The only person who'd had faith in me had been my mother. But now she was dead. *Cancer!* I still couldn't wrap my head around the idea that someone so nice and good should get sick like that. Surely, only bad people should get dreaded diseases, not kind ones who made a difference and lit up the world with their smiles. Life was unfair, wasn't it? At least I'd had time with her, and she had been there for me growing up.

My childhood had been a happy one, my mother had made

sure of that, even though we didn't have as much as others. My mother had been a florist, and we'd lived in the flat above her flower shop. Correction, she was so much more than *just* a florist. My mother had been an artist and flowers were her medium. I'd loved living above a flower shop, there were so many flowers and plants downstairs that they often made their way upstairs into our small flat. When I was younger, I'd thought I lived in a jungle, like in the picture books I read. I used to have so many adventures behind the big ferns and pot plants that covered almost all the surfaces at home. And when I was older, I would work in the flower shop over the weekends, helping my mom make the most beautiful arrangements for clients. She once landed a huge celebrity wedding and the two of us had worked for days making the most spectacular arrangements of sweet-smelling lilies together. We'd stayed up all night making the bouquets, listening to old Janis Joplin records and drinking sweet hot chocolate with marshmallows in. And then the next day when it was time to go to school, she'd called in sick and the two of us had sat on the couch watching soap operas together. Another one of her favorite things. I just wish she'd lived long enough to see me get a role on a soapie—even though it had been so short-lived, she would have been so proud. I'm not so sure how proud she would be now, though, considering the blatant liar that I currently was.

I marched over to the fridge and opened it. Nothing to eat other than some peanut butter; I'd finished the last of the stale crackers this morning. I pulled the jar out and stuck a spoon into it. I scooped it out and shoved it into my mouth. I know keeping peanut butter in the fridge seems odd, but with windows that don't open and no aircon, a summer's day here soon turns the small apartment into a sauna, and let me tell you, runny peanut butter oil is a very hard thing to get out of the carpet.

I walked over to the tap, poured some water into my watering can and started watering all my plants. When my mother had died, I'd taken possession of every single one of her pot plants. There were far too many of them, and they filled my entire apartment— even more so than my childhood home. But I refused to get rid of any; my mother had loved them, and I intended to honor her memory by keeping them alive. I got to the pot of daises and looked at them carefully. My mother had loved daisies, and poppies, hence my name. Bright like a daisy and bewitching like a poppy, she always used to say. One of the daisies was drooping. I plucked the flower and held it in my hands. My thoughts drifted off to Ryan Stark again and that poor plant that was busy dying in his office. I had to do something about it. I couldn't sit there and let it die, my mother wouldn't do that either. I was about to throw the daisy away when a thought hit me. I took one of the petals between my fingers and . . .

"He hates me, he hates me not. He hates me, he hates me not . . ." I said out loud as I plucked the petals out. I continued to do it until I came to the last one. I burst out laughing when it ended on a "he hates me not."

"As if," I mumbled to myself just as I heard a loud scream. I looked up at my ceiling. The light was swinging again, which meant that the upstairs neighbors were fighting, again. This meant that the police would probably be here soon, which meant that all the drug dealers would start running up and down the stairs hiding their stash as the sound of sirens came closer. *Great!* Just another night in paradise. I really needed to get out of this place. It was a bloody miracle I hadn't been mugged yet, or worse. I went into my small, pokey bathroom and started brushing my teeth. I looked at the bills that I'd stuck on the grimy bathroom window. Not because I needed reminding of them, but because I'd once caught my creepy neighbor leaning over his balcony, trying to look at me. I didn't have curtains, so I'd used the only other thing I could, the stack of bills that the bank and medical aid kept sending me. At least they were good for one thing. I spat and gargled and then gave my hair a quick brush.

I walked over to my mirror and pulled my clothes off. I looked at myself. My pink cotton panties certainly didn't match my bra, but I'd never been one of those people that believed in matching underwear. I ran my hand down my stomach and pulled my underwear down slightly, exposing the ill-fated tattoo on my hip. It read "on." I sighed. Not my finest moment. In high school I'd thought I was very in love with my boyfriend Leon. We'd rushed off to get matching name tattoos, only to break up three weeks later. I'd tried to get it removed, but it had been so damn painful that I'd only made it through the "L" and the "e". And now I looked like I had an instruction tattooed on my hip bone. Some guy had once suggested that I put the word "turned" in front of it. His comment had turned me off so much that I had sent him packing.

I walked across the room and climbed into bed. My apartment was so tiny that the lounge, dining room and bedroom were one small "open plan" space. There was a tiny shelf with a microwave on and a bar fridge underneath it that constituted the kitchen, and then a tiny bathroom with a shower that had no water pressure whatsoever.

I tried to get comfortable on my small, squeaky bed. But it wasn't easy, because now I was suddenly thinking about that look Ryan had in his eye just before he'd put the cream on my knee . . .

I knew that look. But the guys that usually gave me that look were the kind you picked up at dive bars, or at a flea markets, and still lived in their mothers' basements. A guy like Ryan Stark had never, ever, given me that kind of look before.

I chuckled to myself. I was probably imagining it. The guy basically hated me. *Or not?* I couldn't work it out. Bandaging knees and extracting thorns was almost kind, but then he followed it up with that stern grumpiness, and I was just plain confused. I looked over at the clock on my wall. I better get some sleep, because boss man would be here in a few hours to pick me up.

CHAPTER NINETEEN

~

Ryan

*H*e felt uncharacteristically nervous as he drove to fetch Doris. That may have had something to do with the fact that he'd woken up at 4:30 after having a terribly graphic and detailed sex dream about her. He couldn't remember the last time he'd had a sex dream—maybe not even since he was a teenager. But there you have it! He'd had one, and it had been very inconvenient and terribly inappropriate and, and . . .

Hot!

His nervousness peaked when he pulled up to her apartment and found her sitting on the pavement waiting for him. She was a vision of particularly ugly clothing today. She was wearing some strange purple ruffled blouse which was, he was sorry to say . . . *hideous*. Just awful. One of the worst items of clothing he'd seen in a long time. His mother had worn something similar in the eighties, when they were still perming their hair. At the time it had been considered very "chic," but now, here, like this . . . no. *Just no!*

She stood up when she saw his car approaching. The look was completed by another pencil skirt that sat around her knees, and the cherry on top was the cracked pair of cat's eye glasses. He sighed. How the hell was he supposed to take *that* with him to a meeting? And he had a very important meeting with the shareholders and board today. He did have a dress code at his office. It was corporate, *not eighties fondue party*. It's not like he was expecting a YSL corporate dress suit, he just wasn't expecting purple . . . *and were those shoulder pads?*

"Hi!" She climbed into the car and his body involuntarily stiffened in response to her presence.

"Hi," he mumbled back while pulling away from the kerb. And then they sat in silence again. It was not a comfortable one. They seemed to fall into these silences rather often. But of course they would, it's not like they had anything in common to discuss. In fact, Doris Granger was about as common to him as an exotic bird of paradise. She didn't fit into his life at all, and yet here she was, in his car. But as they reached the last block before his office the silence was broken with a loud,

"*STOP THE CAR!!*"

Ryan jumped with fright and slammed on the brakes. For what, he didn't even know. As soon as the car had come to a stop, she jumped out and ran onto the pavement. He stared at her in total confusion. As if this person couldn't get any stranger, she was now jumping out of moving vehicles.

"What the hell?" he muttered to himself. He put his hazard lights on and climbed out. He seemed to put his hazard lights on a lot when he was with her. Maybe that was a sign? *This woman was a hazard.*

As he got closer he finally saw what she was looking at. There, on the side of the road, was a wounded pigeon. Its wing was outstretched, as if it couldn't retract it, and his first thought was that it had been hit by a car, and his next thought was that playing with wounded pigeons on the side of the road was going to make him late for work. And then, to his horror, she picked it up.

"Uh . . ." He took a step back. "You have heard of bird flu, right? Put that bird down immediately."

"It's injured, though," she said.

"Well, that's life, isn't it? Just leave it there and let nature take its course."

"Nature take its course?" she repeated, slowly and deliberately, with a clear smattering of anger in her voice.

"Yes," he said, pointing back down at the pavement. "Put it down."

"To die?" She was glaring at him.

"Well, what do you think you're going to do with it?"

"Take it to the vet." She looked determined. Clearly, she wasn't joking.

"You don't take injured pigeons to the vet!"

"Who says?"

"Um . . ." Who *did* say? "I don't know, but I'm sure you don't run around taking every injured bird you find to the vet."

She glared at him with a look that could kill.

He sighed. "It's the cycle of life, or something like that."

But his words looked like they were doing nothing to change her mind. He clearly wasn't going to win this. She looked so determined right now, so single-mindedly focused.

"Fine. But you can't put it in the front of the car. Put it in the back. There's a shoebox in there. Take the shoes out," he conceded, very much against his will.

She smiled at him, and he felt another involuntary feeling; a slight flutter in his stomach. He quickly shut that feeling down. Immediately.

"But if I do this for you, there's something I need you to do for me later." He walked to the back of his car and opened the trunk.

"What do you need?" she asked.

"I'll tell you later. But you have to promise to agree to it now."

"How can I agree if I don't know what it is?"

"You just have to." God, he wasn't used to people arguing with him.

"That sounds suspicious." She eyed him peculiarly.

"Just agree to it so we can get to the vet and then get to work before lunchtime."

She studied him for a moment, and then nodded tentatively. "But it better not be something . . . you know, like, something . . . bad."

"Bad?" His mind immediately plummeted into the gutter.

"I watched a program about this guy that was laundering money for a drug cartel. He also worked in an office and dressed in an expensive suit like you . . . so you never know, these days."

He blinked a few times—this was the last thing he'd expected to hear—and then he burst out laughing. "You think I launder money for drug dealers?"

"No." She bit her lip. "I'm just saying that I don't want to do anything dodgy."

"You think I'm dodgy?" He was amused.

"You're twisting my words." She sounded frustrated.

"I don't think so. You were very clear."

She opened her mouth to say something but closed it again and shook her head as if she'd changed her mind.

"Just agree already. We don't have all day," he said.

"Fine, fine."

"See, was that so hard?" He walked to the front of the car and got in. He glanced in his rear-view mirror and watched her fiddling around in the trunk trying to make the pigeon comfortable.

She was totally, utterly and insanely exasperating!

So why the hell was he trying to hide his smile?

CHAPTER TWENTY

Poppy

$\mathcal{I}$ took the expensive, shiny-looking shoes out of the box so I could put the pigeon in it. I momentarily thought about putting the pigeon on top of the shoes and letting it shit on them as punishment for even thinking that we should leave it on the side of the road. And then something caught my eye . . .

I stretched out my arm and reached further into the trunk to fetch it. I held it between my hands and stared at the thing.

A hairpin. A women's hairpin. In the back of his car. In the trunk. How did that even get here? Unless . . .

I quickly put it back down where I found it. It hadn't crossed my mind, not once, not for a second, that Ryan Stark would have a wife or girlfriend. He didn't wear a wedding band and I'd just assumed that a grumpy, mean workaholic like him wouldn't really have a life outside of the steel and glass Stark building.

But now I had proof that he had another life. I also had proof that he wasn't nearly as mean as he liked everyone to think he was. This trip to the vet was proof of this. One minute I got the impression that he was cold on the inside, that ice ran through his veins, but then in the next moment I got a glimpse of something else, something that might actually be a heart.

I did have some reservations about what the hell I had agreed to do later for him, though.

* * *

"NO! Absolutely no! Never. No, and not on my watch." I glared at the vet.

She looked at me empathetically. "I didn't become a vet to put animals down, but a pigeon with a broken wing is never going to survive in the wild again. It would be cruel to release it. It will be eaten by the next dog or cat, or run over."

"Well, then it won't go back to the wild," I said firmly.

"Huh?" Ryan looked confused.

"I'll take him home. I'll look after him."

"A pet pigeon?" He gave me a kind of deadpan look.

"Yes. Does someone also say you can't have pet pigeons either?" I asked.

The vet and Ryan exchanged a brief look that, quite frankly, pissed me off a little.

"If your wife wants to take the pigeon home, then I have no objection," the vet said, picking the bird up and passing it over to me.

"*She's not my . . . wife!*"

"*He's not my . . . husband!*"

We both said it at the same time, and so emphatically that the vet looked at us with a wide-eyed surprised look.

"Okay," the vet said, slowly and deliberately, and then changed the subject. "Do you have a cage?" she asked.

"Oh, I wouldn't want to keep him in a cage," I quickly added. "So cruel."

"Are you just going to let it wander around your apartment?" Ryan shot me another look.

"Why not? It's not a Great Dane. It's a pigeon."

"It will mess," Ryan said.

"I'll put newspaper down."

"In your whole flat?"

"Why not?"

"You'll cover your whole place in newspaper?"

"What's the problem?"

"No problem. That just seems a bit ridiculous."

"It's not your place," I quickly added.

We both stopped and turned when we heard a small chuckle from the vet. "For a *not* married couple you certainly argue like one." She smiled at us and I felt my cheeks go hot and red.

"We're running very late for work!" Ryan quickly broke the moment that was starting to feel very awkward. "Don't you need seed or something?" He looked over at the vet, and she nodded. He pulled his wallet out and handed her a credit card.

"You can deduct it from my salary," I said.

He shrugged. "It's a pigeon. Not a Great Dane. I'm sure I'll be okay."

And with that, he strode out of the building as quickly as possible. I ran after him, clutching my new pet, and climbed into the front seat of his car.

He looked over at me and let out a peculiar moan-cum-sigh. "It's not coming to work with us."

He looked at the bird, and as if it knew what he was saying, it raised its head and cocked it to the side.

"Okay, take me home and I'll leave it there."

Ryan looked at his watch. "Can't. We need to get to work. You'll have to bring it, but I swear if it starts walking on desks and disrupting work, I'll personally put it back on the side of the road."

"He'll behave, I promise." I smiled at Ryan.

Our eyes locked for a brief moment and something rose inside me again. Something seemed to flicker on, ever so tentatively. And then he scrunched his face up in that disapproving manner, and it was gone. He started the ignition and drove off.

"And now there's something you need to do for me," he said, as he sped towards the office.

"Yes?" I said nervously; I had no idea where he was going with this.

"We have a meeting later with my board members and the shareholders, and, as my assistant, you'll be there taking notes. But I can't have you wearing purple ruffles. At lunch you'll go to the shop and get yourself something corporate-looking. Get at least two outfits."

"Is that what you want me to do?" This was the last thing I'd expected him to say. But truthfully, I didn't blame him. The top was hideous, and if I wasn't trying to disguise myself as someone else, I would not have chosen to wear something like this. Not in a million years. But Doris seemed like the kind of character that didn't care much about fashion. Besides, the clothes were from the telenovela, so they'd been free.

"Yes. Very much." He sounded gruff and businesslike again, and I couldn't help but wonder if this was how he treated his partner. Told her what to wear. Told her what pets she could have, told her not to stutter and fidget and put newspaper down on *her* floor.

"Okay. Sure," I conceded.

He pulled the credit card out again and passed it to me. I paused before taking it. This felt weird.

"It's not a gift, Miss Granger. I'll take it out of your salary at the end of the month, along with pigeon stuff—that is . . ." He paused and looked at me pointedly. "When you decide to tell me what you think you're worth."

I took the card, slipped it into my bag, and the two of us fell into another bone-crunchingly awkward silence. *What was with these silences?* They weren't normal silences. These silences had a sound that wrapped around us and filled the car. A buzzing, scratching, prickly sound that made the hairs on the back of my neck stand up. Persistent white-static silences that seemed to be filled with some kind of strange, silent subtext.

What was it? I didn't know.

CHAPTER TWENTY-ONE

He was babysitting a pigeon. In his office.

He looked down at the thing. It stared up at him as if it was trying to tell him something. Doris hadn't wanted to go to the shops unless he watched it! *Watched a fucking pigeon.* He tried to work, but the sound of its claws walking across the cardboard box was driving him crazy and making his skin crawl.

"Shut up." He looked down at it again and it glared back at him, as if it were judging him. "Yeah, yeah, buddy! I'm the reason you're still alive so stop looking at me like that, okay!?"

"You know you're talking to a pigeon, right?" Doris's amused voice wafted into his office and he froze, embarrassed to have been caught like this.

He cleared his throat uncomfortably. "We were just renegotiating the terms of this babysitting arrangement. That's all." He looked up at her, and when he did . . . *crap!* He knew he hadn't been able to hide the look that must have flashed across his face. He knew this, because her cheeks flushed a pretty shade of pink.

"That looks better." He forced his eyes back down to his desk before the look on his face gave too much away. He heard her approach and then saw the credit card on his desk. He reached for it and, without looking back at her, put it into his drawer.

"Thanks," she said softly.

"It's not a gift," he said, allowing himself one quick look up at her. She looked stunning. She was wearing a simple knee-length black dress that was cinched in at the waist, showing off her petite figure.

"Please take this bird now!" he said.

"Sure. Thanks for watching him."

"It wasn't my pleasure," he grunted. She bent down to pick up the box and that's when he noticed the label sticking out of her dress.

"You haven't taken off the label." He pointed at her neck.

She stood up, stuck her hand behind her back and began trying to pull the label off. She was struggling, bending her arms into strange positions as she tried to get a better grip on it. He couldn't take it anymore. He opened his desk drawer and pulled out a pair of scissors.

"Turn around," he barked, waving the scissors at her. For a second she looked like she didn't trust him, but she finally turned. Like this, he could appreciate the back of her dress. The way it clung to her body, the long zip accentuating her curves as it ran the length of her back and stopped just above her bottom. His hand physically twitched as he imagined dropping the scissors and taking the zip between his fingers instead. She glanced over her shoulder at him, as if wondering why he hadn't started yet.

He stepped closer and took the label between his fingers. He could smell her again now. That powdery, floral scent that had been so hard to wash off the other night. He snipped the label off carefully, not wanting to damage the dress. He looked at the back of her neck; she had a very distinctive mole just below her hairline and, at this angle, it looked like the African continent. It fascinated him for some reason.

"Thanks." She turned around slowly and, for a moment, their eyes locked. *Like pools of molten gold*, he thought, as the overhead lights in the office accentuated the luminous color of her eyes. He quickly looked away and walked back to his desk.

"Meeting in an hour. You need to take notes," he said over his shoulder. "And get that pigeon out of my office, please."

"No problem, Mr. Stark," she said, sounding upbeat.

* * *

He was trying to talk with confidence and sound intelligent, but she was very distracting. She was sitting in the corner taking notes, but her tongue kept wandering out of her mouth every time she wrote. And he couldn't have any distractions now. This meeting was important. Tensions were flying high. Tensions were always high.

"I still think this is a bad idea." Brian Rautenbach interrupted Ryan again.

There were eye rolls all round, and sighs filled the room.

"Oh come on, Brian. We've been down this road before. We have been going down this road with you for the last six months.

You were outvoted, the construction continues. It's what is best for the company," Charles Grey piped up.

"Well, I disagree," Brian countered. "This is not in line with the vision of the company. It is not in line with what Ryan Senior would have wanted either."

"Ryan Senior wasn't trying to weather a recession," Charles shot back. "When he was alive, the financial climate was very different."

"This is a mistake." Brian folded his arms, and Charles glared at him.

"Okay, okay," Ryan interjected. "We really can't talk about this issue anymore. We have to move on."

Brian turned and looked at him. "Ryan, you know this is a mistake. There was another solution."

Brian was glaring at him now and he felt his stomach tighten. He was starting to think Brian was right. He looked around the room. The other twenty board members and shareholders shook their heads at him, and he felt himself falter.

"Okay, let's just move on," he said, feeling his confidence waning a bit.

"Fine. But let the record show that I disagree," Brian said and turned his attention to Doris. "Hi there," he said to her. She didn't respond. "In the corner, what's her name?"

"Miss Granger," Ryan said, and she looked up at him.

"Mmm?" she asked, looking directly at him.

Brian looked over at her. "I want you to write that down, Miss Granger. I disagree and am against this project."

Doris nodded and then scribbled in her notebook. "Noted," she said.

"Right." Ryan looked down at his watch. At this rate they would be here all day. "Let's move on. We have a lot to cover."

At that, everyone in the room settled back down. For the next ten minutes, things went smoothly until a noise from the corner made them all turn and look.

Doris had opened a can of Coke with a loud, long fizzing sound. "Sorry," she said, looking at everyone. "Thirsty."

One of his shareholders, Adam Sharp, who was probably the youngest in the room, other than him—which made him at least fifty—smiled at her and jumped out of his seat.

"Let me get a glass for that." He reached across the table and grabbed one. "Ice cubes?" he asked, looking over at Doris.

Ryan rolled his eyes.

"Thanks," she said sweetly, in a sing-song voice.

Wait, was she flirting with him?

He straightened up and looked at the two of them closely. Adam was definitely being flirty. He was a straight-up asshole under normal circumstances, never a knight in shining armor who fetched ice cubes for damsels in distress.

"Here we go, allow me. Please." Adam flashed Doris a big, white, toothy smile and then took the Coke from her and poured it into a glass.

What an asshole! Flirting shamelessly with *his* personal assistant.

"Perhaps you should consider investing in a restaurant next," Ryan said, without thinking.

A few of the others looked amused, and one or two chuckled. Adam did not; instead he turned around and stared at Ryan. This didn't bother him. He raised a disapproving eyebrow at Adam, letting him know that he knew what the hell he was up to—and how it was *not* appropriate for boardroom meetings. Adam sat back down and Ryan was just about to start talking again when the fucking pigeon walked in and made a loud cooing noise.

He was going to kill that bird!

CHAPTER TWENTY-TWO

~

Poppy

I felt his stare of blatant disapproval. Like darts into a bulls-eye. I didn't need to look at his face to know what he was thinking. He was giving off silent, but very violent vibes. I jumped up and made a move for the pigeon, but it was fast and trotted across the room. It disappeared under the desk.

"Sorry," I said, getting down on all fours and scuttling after it.

"Oh, for heaven's sake," I heard Ryan say as I crawled after the bird. "Sorry about this," he said to the others, clearly embarrassed.

"Come here, birdy, birdy, birdy." I reached out and tried to grab him, but he made a run for it. It was as if he was doing this on purpose, enjoying the commotion he was causing. I bumped into a few legs and feet as I shuffled under the desk and popped out on the other side. I made another mad grab for him, but the feathery little bastard hopped up on a chair and then, to my horror, onto the boardroom table.

"Oh no, you don't!" I threw myself at the table and lost my footing as I went. And then suddenly, unexpectedly ... *I was gliding.* Like a figure-skater across the smooth ice, I slid across the very polished boardroom table. The pigeon was in my sights, I was almost there, but then the momentum from the polished surface was lost and I stopped with a long, loud *squeeeeek*. The pigeon turned and looked at me indignantly. It let out a long, loud coo and then . . .

"Shit," I hissed under my breath as I watched in jaw-dropping horror.

As if it were happening in slow motion, the moist splatter of whiteness shot out of its bottom and landed on the table with a loud splat!

I was so getting fired for this.

CHAPTER TWENTY-THREE

Poppy

After wiping the mess off the table, I exited with my pigeon. "And this is the thanks I get for saving your life," I said as I put him inside his box and closed the lid. I sat at my desk and chewed the end of my pen, wondering how he was going to fire me? I hoped it would be quick, and I hoped I wouldn't cry. And sure enough, when the meeting was over, and everyone had left, I was summoned to his office. I walked in and stood waiting for him to speak.

"Sit." He didn't look up at me.

"I'm sorry about the pigeon," I blurted out.

"You should be." He finally looked up at me. "That bird better not come back to this office tomorrow."

"Tomorrow?" I was confused.

"Yes. Tomorrow. Do you have a problem with that, Miss Granger?" He sat back in his chair and folded his arms; his shirt tugged against his chest. Unbeknownst to him, one of his buttons had popped open and, *oh my God*, was that a tattoo on his chest?

Suddenly a whole bunch of "other" feelings flooded me. This man was so damn hot it was criminal. Honestly, someone should arrest him for looking like that and throw the key away. I mean, I knew he was hot, *but really*, could he get any better looking? But he did. And every time I looked at him I noticed something else. Something new. That small dimple in his cheek, that freckle below his left eye, that small scar he had on the back of his hand.

"Well?" he asked.

"Well, what?" I asked, caught somewhere between this reality and another one where he was busy unbuttoning his other buttons and showing me what his tattoo looked like.

"Miss Granger," he snapped, and I jumped, straight back into this reality. The one where he was glaring angrily at me and I was frightened of him.

"What?" I asked nervously.

"Do you have a problem with tomorrow?" he asked. His voice slow, firm and deliberate.

"No! No problem with that, and no pigeon. I promise," I quickly stammered.

"By the way," he pointed at my face, "You have a . . . a . . . thing, there."

"Huh?" I looked around. *What was he pointing at?*

"Your mouth. The corner." He wagged his finger about. "And your face."

I raised my hand to my mouth and touched it.

"Other side," he said, waving his hand at me some more.

I moved my fingers across my lips.

He sighed. "The corner, Miss Granger. The corner."

I ran my fingers over the corner of my mouth and pulled them away to look at whatever had caught his attention. A blue substance stained them. It took me a few seconds to realize it was pen ink.

"I was chewing on my pen," I explained.

He looked at me with his usual disapproving look. And then he spoke again. His words came out in a staccato fashion, and they had a way of slicing through me like fine paper cuts.

"Probably not a good idea," he said.

"Probably not," I repeated softly. I'm sure he didn't want his assistant walking around with a blue mouth. How embarrassing that would be!

"You should wash it off. You might have gotten some in your mouth. It could be toxic." He looked at me.

Wait, what the hell was that? Was there something resembling concern flashing in his eyes?

"Uh . . . sure. I'll go wash it off," I said, feeling very taken aback by this sudden and strange concern for my well-being.

"Good." He continued to look at me.

I sat there waiting for him to speak again. But his stare seemed to go on forever, and I shuffled uncomfortably in my seat. He finally broke the silence.

"I need you to make me a reservation at Cappello's tonight. In Camps Bay," he said, finally breaking the silence.

"For how many?" I asked.

"Just two."

"Really, two?" I enquired and wanted to slap myself the moment the question was out of my mouth. Him and hairpin, no doubt.

"Yes. Two," he repeated.

"Okay. That's fine. I was just making sure of that." I smiled at him, trying to hide the fact that all I could think about now was him and some mystery woman having a romantic dinner.

He looked at me expectantly, as if he was waiting for me to talk this time. But I didn't. I widened my smile.

His face scrunched up. "You smile far too much, Miss Granger," he said.

"What?" I blurted out.

"It seems that whenever you don't know what to say, you smile," he said.

That wasn't entirely true. Doris was the big smiler, not Poppy. In fact, if Poppy were sitting here right now, she might want to tip that poor dying *Chlorophytum comosum* onto his desk. I wiped the smile off my face.

"For what time?" I asked, as professionally as possible.

"Six."

I nodded and then looked at the clock on the wall behind him. "But that's in an hour."

"Yes. Be ready to go soon." He looked back down at his computer. "Please type up those notes from the meeting today and send them through to everyone."

"Sure." I exited.

I sat back down at my desk and looked at him. He was leaving early today, for his special date at Cappello's that I had to book. I went online and searched for the contact details of the restaurant. I looked at the photos of the place. It seemed very romantic. Beachfront views, and tall cocktails. I dialed the number and didn't have to wait long for an answer.

"Mr. Stark, how are you?" The voice on the other end of the phone spoke.

"Uh . . . no, it's his assistant," I corrected, caught off guard that they'd recognized the number.

"Would you like your usual table?" the voice asked.

"I guess," I replied.

"See you at six again?"

"Yes," I said and then hung up. I looked over to his office. *So, a regular, romantic date night at Cappello's.* The pigeon in the box suddenly gave a loud coo and I looked down at it.

"I know," I said to him, "I wouldn't have guessed it either."

Fifteen minutes later, I found myself back in his car with my pigeon. This was starting to feel oddly familiar—him driving me around like this. But this time I was alone in the car.

I looked around, wondering where he'd gotten to and when he was coming back. And then suddenly, he appeared from behind the building and my heart skipped an actual beat.

CHAPTER TWENTY-FOUR

～

Ryan

*W*heeling the bike was difficult, what with the broken wheel, and he suddenly wondered if returning it in this state wouldn't get her into more trouble with her clearly unstable-sounding neighbor. He looked at his watch. *Shit!* Dinner was in fifty minutes. Did he have enough time to take this thing past a bike repair shop, put on a new wheel, take it to her house and get home with enough time to fetch Emmy for dinner? Probably not. But then he looked up at his car and straight into her face. She was in the front seat, and she was beaming at him. Her smile was different this time, not like those fake-looking smiles she gave him around the office. This smile was real—big, wide and warm—and because of it, he knew he had to do this for her, even if it meant pushing his dinner back by half an hour.

Mind you, Emmy probably wouldn't be upset. In fact, it wasn't like she seemed to care about or enjoy their regular monthly dinners anyway. When Rachel had been alive, they'd had a regular dinner together once a month, before she'd gotten sick. Since her death he'd felt the need to keep it going. But it wasn't like it used to be. The three of them used to laugh and talk together, but now it was full of sulky silences, a lot of moaning, and her eyes were usually just glued to her phone. But he was determined to keep the tradition alive; if he let it go, it felt like he would be letting another part of his sister go, and he wasn't ready for that. He dropped Emmy a message, informing her of the time change. She replied with an emoji he didn't understand.

The bike was heavy and cumbersome and a huge mission to get into the back of his car. But he managed, despite breaking out in a sweat. God, he was unfit. He needed to get back to the gym, not that he had time to do anything for himself. He couldn't remember the last time he'd done something just for himself. Gym was a luxury, not a necessity. He climbed into the front seat and took his jacket off. He'd normally never look this casual around an employee, but he seemed to be breaking a lot of his usual rules when it came to Doris.

"Where did you find it?" she asked, turning in her seat.

"The gardener had it locked in the shed around the back of the building." He started the engine and pulled out.

"Thanks so much." She sounded genuinely happy. "I've been avoiding my neighbor for days."

"We need to take it past a bike repair shop to fix the wheel," he quickly added, as he drove off in the direction of town. He'd already googled the closest one, and luckily it was conveniently situated.

"No, you don't have to do that, I'm sure he'll understand . . ."

She tapered off. "Okay. He'll be angry, but I'm sure he won't kill me . . ." She tapered off again. "Okay, maybe he'll try and kill me, but I'm sure I can fight him off, or—"

He cut her off quickly. "Do you know how ridiculous that all sounds?" He was angry now. She shouldn't be living in a place where the neighbors could potentially inflict bodily harm on her. "You really shouldn't be living there," he concluded.

"It's not like I can move right now." The cheer in her voice was gone; instead, it was replaced with something that sounded a little mournful. "It's all I can afford."

"Well, when you calculate what your salary needs to be, make sure the number is sufficient for you to afford a place in a less murderous part of town."

"Huh?" She sounded surprised, and quite frankly he was a little surprised too.

Why was he doing this?

"It's simply a matter of employee wellness. I would be concerned if any one of my other staff members were living in a place that seemed detrimental to their health." He quickly covered, although that wasn't true, at all. He didn't know where any of his other employees lived, or gave a shit where they lived for that matter. But for some reason that he didn't like, Doris's living arrangements were really starting to irk him. He let out an involuntary sigh that he wasn't even aware he'd made until she pointed it out.

"You sigh a lot," she suddenly said.

"Mmm, it's a recent development," he muttered, half under his breath.

"What's caused it?" she asked innocently. Clearly, she was unaware that she was in fact the cause of it.

He shrugged, and was grateful that the bike shop came into view. This was not a conversation he felt like having with her.

* * *

They stood in the shop waiting for the man to put a new wheel on. He looked around at the bikes and felt his stomach contort. There was a cute pink bike with ribbons hanging off the handlebars. He remembered his sister having one exactly like that when she was younger. They used to insist on getting the same birthday presents, and that year she'd gotten a pink bike, and he'd gotten a blue one. They'd thought they were so cool, riding up and down the street all day, late into the evening, until their mother called them in for dinner. Riding his bike with his twin was definitely one of his favorite childhood memories.

He felt a salty sting in his eyes and quickly looked away, turning his back on Doris. *Shit, what was happening to him?* It was coming up to the anniversary of Rachel's death and he'd been thinking and dreaming about her more than usual. And he'd definitely been feeling more emotional lately. He took a deep breath and tried to steady himself; he didn't know why seeing the bikes had affected him so badly. He clenched his jaw and tightened his fists at his side.

"Are you okay?" Doris's voice made him jump. He hadn't realized that she'd noticed anything.

"Fine!" He turned around quickly. He pulled himself together in seconds and assumed his usual upright pose. He was used to stuffing his emotions down. One of his biggest fears was that one day they would all come out and he wouldn't be able to contain them.

"You sure?" She looked at him curiously.

"I think I can tell whether I'm okay or not, Miss Granger," he snapped angrily at her, hoping to deflect what he was feeling.

It worked. Her face immediately dropped.

"Sorry, I just thought . . ." She stopped talking and looked away. His stomach tightened even more.

When the wheel was finally fixed, they got back into the car in total silence and drove to her house. They hadn't said a word since he'd snapped at her. They pulled up to her place and climbed out. He took the bike out of the trunk and started wheeling it in the direction of the building. Doris placed her hands on the handle-bars and stopped him.

"It's okay, I've got it," she said, trying to pull the bike away from him.

"It's fine. It's heavy and hard to wheel." He pulled the bike back.

"You have dinner," she said, exerting more pressure on the bike.

"I insist. OKAY!" he snapped again and jerked it away from her.

"Fine," she said. "But it's a long walk up those stairs."

He looked up at the building and suddenly realized what he'd just insisted on doing. No doubt he'd be drenched in sweat and almost dead by the end of it. But he was determined not to give in. He couldn't now, since he'd been so adamant about doing it. They walked for a while and then Doris stopped and turned to him.

"It's your lucky day," she said.

"What?" He looked at her. She was pointing at someone.

"It's *his* bike," she said, walking towards him.

His mouth fell open. She'd borrowed a bike from *that* . . .

The man stood well over six feet tall. He also looked like he was about 600 pounds of pure, bulging muscle. His neck looked weighted down by all the gold chains he was wearing. *How the hell did he even keep his head up?* And when he smiled, Ryan thought he might be blinded by the reflection of the light bouncing off his golden grille. Doris walked all the way up to him and Ryan ran to keep up. He didn't like the idea of her standing alone with this man who was clearly *not* an upstanding citizen who paid his taxes.

"I've got your bike." She gestured to it and the man took a step forward.

How did he even ride a bike like this? For someone his size, surely it was impossible. The man, whose name was "Little Mike", flashed them both a golden grin and then took the bike from Ryan. He hated to admit it, because nothing intimidated him, but this man chilled him to the bone.

"Thanks for bringing it back," Little Mike said, casting his attention back on Doris. Ryan didn't like the way he was looking at her. And then, the man slowly extended his hand towards her. "The bike rental?"

"Huh?" Doris looked panicked. "I didn't know I had to pay rental for it, uh . . . I don't have any money for you, sorry . . . I didn't know."

"Nothing is free in this world." Little Mike sounded intimidating. "But maybe there's another way you can pay me back?" His voice took on a sly, creepy tone.

"How?" she asked. God, was she that naive?

"Well, I need someone to clean my flat, maybe you could come by and wash my dishes tomorrow night." The man smiled again, and Ryan knew that washing dishes was definitely code for something else.

"No, she won't be cleaning anyone's dishes," Ryan said firmly. "How much is the rental?' he asked, turning his attention to the man in front of him. The man had a bright mop of white hair and the most piercing blue eyes, which only seemed to add to his intimidating appearance.

"You don't have to do—" Doris objected, but he ignored her.

"How much is the rental?" he asked, louder this time.

The man eyed him up and down. "Two hundred," he said.

"Fine," Ryan reached into his wallet. He had a lot more than R200 in it. He paused and looked back up at the man. "Two hundred for the rental, and I'll give you an extra hundred because it came back late." He pulled the money out and held it out for Mike.

The man took a step closer, and he swore he could feel the ground shake beneath them. He reached out his hand and took the money. *God, it was like a fucking bear's paw.*

"I hope that gets her out of any domestic duties," he said, using his firmest tone. It wasn't a question, though.

The man smiled at him. "Of course."

Ryan met his eye and tried to convey a message to him, but he had no idea if it was sinking in. He walked back over to Doris, grabbed her by the elbow and marched her inside.

"You didn't have to do that," she immediately said, sounding somewhat angry.

"Oh yes I did." He looked around again; this place stank too.

"I can take care of myself, you know," she continued, but he ignored her again.

"I have to go now. Will you be okay?"

"Yes," she said. "I'll be fine. I'm always fine."

"Good night," he said and started walking away.

She called after him. "Enjoy your dinner tonight with . . . *your wife?*"

He stopped walking and turned around. "I don't have a wife," he said.

"Sorry. Enjoy your dinner with your girlfriend, then."

"I don't have one of those either."

"Sorry. Enjoy your dinner with your . . . ?" She looked at him with questioning eyes.

He paused for a moment, wondering if he should tell her, but that was definitely crossing a line.

"That's none of your business actually." He turned around and stormed off, knowing that he'd probably left a very shocked and confused Doris behind him.

CHAPTER TWENTY-FIVE

Ryan

*H*e was running late for work again, but this time it hadn't been because of Emmy. He hadn't been able to find his wallet. He was sure he'd put it on the table in the entrance hall, like he always did. But it wasn't there and it had taken him ten minutes to locate it. So by the time he reached Doris's apartment he was running ten minutes late. But when he saw a police van outside and Doris nowhere in sight, a bolt of panic shot through him. His immediate thoughts drifted to Little Mike. He looked around nervously for a moment and then jumped out of his car and ran into her building.

He pushed his way through a dodgy-looking group of guys loitering outside who, he was sure, had just offered him some weed—clearly, they were unperturbed by the cops. He walked into the dimly lit hallway and looked at the wall to see if there were any names and address on post boxes, anything to tell him where Doris lived. But there was nothing. He walked over to the elevator. It was obviously broken. A single orange cone was all that warned you *not* to take a step and plummet down the shaft below. He made a move for the staircase, and on his first step had to climb over an old pizza box and an empty bottle of Mountain Dew. Delightful!

He walked up the first flight and looked down the corridor. It was empty. The only clue that people actually lived there was the overflowing garbage can that stank to high hell. He held his nose and continued up the stairs.

Up the next flight, and the next and the next . . . he had no idea where he was going, or how he was going to find her, but he knew he needed to try. When he reached the sixth floor, he heard the sound of loud chatter and the *beep, beep* of police radios going off. He followed the noises and, as he got closer, he could see the police and hear her voice.

She sounded angry. "I'm late for work, okay!" He heard her stamp her foot. "I don't have time for this. Do you know that my boss is a very, very important man, and if I'm not at work on time, I will be in serious trouble. Serious trouble."

He smiled and decided to hang back in order to hear more.

"We just need a statement from you, then you can go," one of the officers said.

He heard a long sigh. "It was the usual. She probably threw a chair at him when he came home late. He probably threw one back. Then they screamed, as usual. Stamped and jumped up and down, and that's when some of my ceiling fell down, and then there was a loud crash and that's probably when someone decided to call you guys."

"Did you hear what they were saying?" the officer asked.

Another sigh. "You cheating asshole this, you bitch that, mother fucker et cetera, and cu—"

"Okay. You can stop there. I think we get the picture," one of the officers said.

Ryan smiled again. He couldn't have imagined that string of words coming out of Doris's mouth. But there it was. He walked up to her door and stopped a few feet away.

"Morning, officers. Is everything okay here?" he asked casually.

One of the officers looked at him as Doris's head popped round the corner of her door. She was dressed, but had a large towel wrapped around her head as if she'd just gotten out of the shower. She wasn't wearing her glasses either, and it had the same effect on him as the other night. He stared. He tried not to. But he couldn't help it.

"Sorry, who are you?" one of the officers asked.

"Oh, sorry." He tore his eyes away from her. "Ryan Stark. Big important boss." He smiled and out of the corner of his eye, he saw her cheeks flush a bright shade of red.

"Okay, I think we're done here." The officer turned to her. "If it happens again, here's my card." He handed her a card and she took it in her tiny hands. "And if you think of anything more, Miss Peterson, don't hesitate to call."

Suddenly, she burst out laughing. A strange high-pitched laugh. "Granger-Peterson. Granger-Peterson! It's double-barreled, but I usually just go with Granger. I sometimes even forget there's a Peterson attached to it. Some days I even forget about the Granger too." She looked confused for a moment or two and then pushed the policeman away with her arm. "Thanks for being so efficient!" she called after them as the officers walked away.

When the police left, he turned his attention to Doris

Granger-Peterson once more. "Everything alright here?" he asked, trying to look into her flat. She deliberately blocked his line of sight.

"All good." She flashed him a massive smile, one of those fake ones. "And I'm so sorry about this, I was just about to leave when they came, and I couldn't get rid of them." She gave him an apologetic look.

He shook his head. "It's fine. I'm just glad you're okay . . . are you?" He stepped closer to her and looked over her shoulder, this time seeing into her apartment. "You said something about your ceiling . . ." He was using it as an excuse to get inside. He was curious to know what her home looked like and he pushed past her without an invitation.

"Wait!" she called, but it was too late, he was already standing in the middle of her apartment.

He was shocked. He looked up at her ceiling; her light bulb had come loose and was hanging by a wire. He looked down at his feet where grey bits of concrete had fallen onto the old carpet. His eyes moved around the room, trying to find one single redeeming feature, but there were none. And to top it off, the place was crammed with plants. Plants on tables, plants on windowsills, plants on floors . . . *everywhere*. This place was like a jungle. He'd never seen so many plants in one place in his entire life. And then he saw the beady eye staring up at him from behind one of the pots. She'd put newspaper down on the floor and the bird looked like he'd made himself right at home.

"It's not much. But I call it home." Her small voice had a fun, playful tone to it. He didn't see the humor in it at all. "I need to . . . uh . . . get ready," she said.

He turned and looked at her. She looked so out of place here with her perfect doll-like features and those eyes that were even brighter now that the early morning sun was shining through the window onto her face.

"Of course," he said quickly.

She walked into the bathroom and closed the small door behind her. He looked around again.

God, she really didn't belong here.

CHAPTER TWENTY-SIX

Poppy

I could see he was irritated. It was painted across his face, and he wasn't even trying to hide it. I was in his office taking notes, but I could feel his disapproving eyes staring at me the entire time. It made me nervous, and I wanted to look up and scream . . .

WHAT?! What the fuck are you looking at? But Doris wouldn't do that. Well, Poppy probably wouldn't do it either—this man was too damn intimidating.

This man blew hot and cold, boiling and freezing all at once, so fast, it made my head spin. The drive to work had been okay, we'd said a few more words to each other today, and we hadn't discussed the weather, which was an improvement. I'd commented on how pretty the view over the city was at this time of the morning, and he'd told me that he used to live in a penthouse in the tallest building in the city and this time of day had been his favorite. The comment had caught me off guard—such a comment and you would almost think this man was a normal human being. But he wasn't. Because I was starting to disintegrate under the intensity of his gaze.

"Is there something I can do for you?" I asked politely.

"What?" he asked innocently, as if he bloody didn't know what he was doing wrong.

"Have I done something wrong?" I asked. "Am I not writing fast enough? Writing too fast? Don't you like the way my pencil sounds on the paper? Am I wearing too much perfume, too little . . . what?"

"Isn't that crack in your glasses irritating you?"

I shook my head. "No."

"It's not driving you absolutely mad that you're seeing the world through a cracked lens that is probably distorting everything around you?"

"No." I shook my head again. What did this have to do with anything?

"Well," he leaned back in his chair. "It's driving me mad. I can't look at it anymore. Because every time I do, it makes me wonder what everything must look like, and when you're going to misread something important because your vision is obscured."

"Oh," I replied flatly. What was I meant to say to that? Sorry, Your Highness, that the crack in *my* lens is making *your* day so bloody miserable.

"You need to go to an optometrist at lunch and have the lens fixed, or get a new pair of glasses."

At that, I laughed. Too loudly, probably. This stupid disguise was really coming back to bite me.

"What's so funny?" he asked.

"A new pair of glasses isn't really very high up on my priority list!"

"I can't have my personal assistant going to meetings with a giant crack in her glasses. It looks ridiculous. And it's distracting."

"Fine, then I won't wear them anymore." I pulled them off my face and closed my palm over them, feeling very relieved that they were finally off my face.

He shook his head at me and tutted loudly. Clearly, this wasn't the right answer. "I'm sure there's a good reason you're wearing glasses. You wouldn't want to mess your eyes up just because you're being stubborn."

"Stubborn?" I shook my head at him. "I'm being poor. Not stubborn."

His eyes narrowed and traveled over the features of my face, as if he was trying to take me all in. His mind seemed to be ticking away; I could almost hear it. *Tick, tick, tick.* What went on in that head of his?

"Come!" Suddenly, he rose up out of his chair like a massive tidal wave.

"Where?"

"To an optometrist."

"But . . . I . . . I . . ." I tried to protest.

"Stop stuttering and come. As an employee, you have medical cover. I'm sure a trip to the optometrist is covered. And hopefully a new pair of glasses too." He strode out of the room and I ran after him.

He wasn't serious, was he?

Oh, but he was. He was *very* serious. Because ten minutes later, after a rather awkward, silent drive (not that I should have expected anything else by now), we arrived at an optometrist. He'd demanded an immediate appointment. He'd declared it an emergency, and so that's how I now found myself sitting in the chair looking through all the fancy machines and pointing when I saw the dots of light. I'd tried to object several times, but he'd insisted. And now he was sitting outside in the waiting room; I could hear him talking on the phone.

"Well, your eyesight is perfect, Miss Granger," the optometrist finally said when it was all done. "No need for any glasses."

At that, a chill ran up my spine. If I walked out without a bloody prescription, even if it was for the mildest of eye issues, he would know that I'd been wearing fake glasses this entire time. I laughed nervously and followed him out of the room, back to where Ryan was waiting. As soon as he saw me, he put his phone down and looked up.

"Well?" he asked.

"It's a miracle," I said, throwing my hands in the air. "I don't need glasses anymore." I smiled nervously at him and he looked from me to the optometrist, and back again.

"Her eyesight is absolutely perfect," the old optometrist said.

"WELL," I quickly cut him off, "not perfect, perfect . . . *per se*. It's OKAY. You know, not perfect."

"No, it's pretty perfect," the optometrist continued, and I wanted to kick him.

My grumpy boss was staring at me strangely again, and I shrugged. "Like I said. It's a miracle."

"Well," the optometrist butted in again, and now I *really* wanted to kick him. "It would be very unusual for a problem to *simply* rectify itself all on its own. What did you say you were again? Short-sighted, far-sighted?"

"Yes. Those!" I said quickly.

The optometrist looked confused but nodded at me slowly. "Yes, like I said, it would be unusual for that to correct naturally," he added again. He wasn't letting this go! And every time he opened his mouth, he was digging me deeper and deeper into a hole.

"But nothing is impossible." I turned to the optometrist and glared at him in a way that screamed "play along!" A poster of a woman looking up at the moon with glasses on caught my eye. "Think about it. Do you think primitive man would ever have expected us to walk on the moon?" A poster of someone looking at $e=mc^2$ on a chalk board through a pair of glasses also caught my attention. "And what about the Internet? Imagine what Einstein would have thought about an email." I looked from poster to poster and continued with my rather clever (well, I thought so) analogies until I came to the last poster. "And what about Ryan Gosling—" I blurted but quickly stopped myself.

Wait, why did he have a poster of Ryan Gosling on the wall? I stared at *my* Ryan blankly.

"What about Ryan Gosling?" he asked. Clearly confused.

"Well . . ." I looked around for an answer. "Um, he's very, well, he's a funny actor, obviously and, well, you are not an actor, obviously, but you know . . . and you have the same name." *Oh God, this was making no sense.* But I couldn't stop myself because they were both staring at me now, waiting for answers. "Not that that makes you the same. I'm not saying you are similar, because you're not alike. Sure you're both hot but that's a given—" I slapped my hands over my mouth. Had I just said that? *Shit!* "Right!" I jumped, changing the subject. "Let's go!" I rushed out through the door, past the confused-looking optometrist, and headed straight for the car. At least I didn't have to wear those stupid glasses anymore.

I waited at the passenger side for him, mortified that I'd just called him hot. I heard the beep of the immobilizer, climbed in and put my seat belt on. I really, *really* needed to get my car back, this lift club was becoming weird. We drove in silence once more, and I kept wondering if he'd figured out that my glasses had been fake—or if he'd bought my little miracle. Probably not, he was far too smart to be fooled like that. And I was starting to wonder when he was going to ask me about them.

He suddenly spoke. "When you get back, I need you to type up the notes from the meeting yesterday and email them through to me and the others. You have their email addresses?"

"Yes." I nodded. "I'll get onto that immediately."

"Good. I need that sent off before the end of the day."

"Absolutely," I replied and looked out the window at the passing traffic. I hoped I could type fast enough.

We fell into another awkward silence and didn't say a word to each other until we pulled into the parking lot. I went to take my seat belt off but, for some reason, couldn't. I struggled with it a few times.

"Sometimes it sticks, I need to get it fixed," I heard him say, and then, before I could move my hands out of the way, he reached over and grabbed the seat belt. It felt like it happened in slow motion . . . the way his fingers brushed against mine, the way my fingers swept across his open palm, the way our fingertips touched and seemed to stay there for a second longer than they needed to. I flinched and pulled my hand away quickly when I felt the shock. He flinched too as the bolt of electricity took us both by surprise.

"Static," he quickly mumbled as he went to work on the seat belt and finally unclipped it.

"Static," I agreed, even though it had felt like something more than that.

I reached for the door and started climbing out when his voice stopped me. It was soft. Almost inaudible. But I definitely heard it.

"You look nice without glasses."

I swung around to look at him, but he was already gone. Out the door and striding towards the building.

CHAPTER TWENTY-SEVEN

⤳

Ryan

*H*e was trying not to look up at her, but he couldn't help it. And, no, it wasn't because she looked good—*which he should never have fucking said to her*—it was because her typing was appalling. He'd known she was highly under-qualified when he'd hired her, but surely not this unqualified? She was typing with two fingers, for heaven's sake, and it was clear she was never going to get her work finished.

And to top it all off, she'd let two staff members slip by her today and both had come walking into his office unannounced and uninvited. It had pissed him off. She'd also left the mayonnaise on his sandwich, had missed two calls and put one through to the wrong extension. And all the while, she'd been scratching her head like she had lice. It made him want to scratch his head too.

But then she'd also called him "hot" and had been seductively nibbling the end of her pencil all day and licking her lips while concentrating. She never stopped fidgeting either, which had caused her to drop her pencil twice, meaning that he'd watched her crawl under her desk on her hands and knees far too many times today. At one stage, when she'd been down there, he'd fantasized about things he knew he shouldn't! God. She was seriously bad news for him. She was making him crazy. He put his head back down and tried to work, but another interruption made him look up. This time it was his phone. He didn't recognize the number, but answered immediately.

"Hello, is this Mr. Stark?" a woman's voice asked.

"Yes. And who are you?" He didn't recognize the voice and hoped it wasn't going to be some telemarketer selling him insurance. Because that would piss him off even more.

"It's Madeline Brown, headmistress at Holy Trinity."

He sat up straight. "Uh . . . what can I do for you?"

"I'm very sorry to have to tell you this, but Emmy didn't come to class after recess, and one of the teachers said they saw her climbing into a taxi and driving away from the school property."

"What?" he screamed down the phone.

"I'm so sorry," the headmistress said.

His heart plummeted to his feet and a cold sweat prickled on his forehead. "Where was she going?" he asked, his mouth feeling dry as panic set in.

"I don't know," she replied, sounding solemn.

"I can't believe you could let this happen!" he snapped back at her as panic now gave way to a more familiar feeling—anger. "I pay a lot of money to send her to one of the best schools in the country and you can't even make sure my niece stays on the property! I mean how on earth do you lose a student?"

The headmistresses changed her tune and he could hear she

was panicking now. "I'm very sorry, Mr. Stark, this has never happened before, and we will be reviewing our security policy after this. We are not sure how a taxi even managed to get into the property, as we have very strict security at the main gate—"

"Well, obviously not!" he grunted angrily.

"What can we do to help find her?" the woman asked.

"Nothing. You've done enough!" He slammed the phone down, caught somewhere between anger and utter panic. The two feelings were fighting each other for control, and he felt totally off kilter. *How the hell had she even paid for a taxi?* And then, like an icy wind moving through him, he remembered his wallet this morning. He reached for it quickly and opened it. It was almost empty.

"Fuck!" She'd stolen money out of his wallet. His mind raced . . . drugs, alcohol, taxi rides to where? What the hell did a teenage girl need R1,000 for? His sister would be frantic right now if she was alive to see this. She had tasked him with looking after her most precious possession, and he couldn't even keep track of her. He had no idea what to do. Did he call the police? Did he mount a search party, but where would a teenage girl even go? Was she running away from him? Was she punishing him for not allowing her to go to that party? He felt an urgent need to do something, but what?

He walked over to the window and looked out over the city. Cape Town was a big place and with R1,000, she could be anywhere. But he needed to find her. He grabbed his car keys and walked out of his office. But he had no idea where to go. This time, he didn't have a plan.

Doris looked up from her desk.

"Miss Granger?" he asked quickly.

She shot out of her seat and stood up. "Yes?"

"You were a teenage girl once?" he asked.

"Uh . . . yes . . ." Her brow wrinkled up as she answered.

He really didn't want to ask her this. He liked to keep his personal and professional lives totally separate, but he had no choice. "Did you ever bunk off school?" he asked her.

"Why?"

"Please! Just answer the question." His voice sounded a little too desperate for his liking, and he could see that his tone had caught her off guard.

"Yes," she quickly said. "I hated school. Sometimes I would sneak out and go watch a film at the mall. The guy there used to let me sit in the projector room with him and we used to eat stale popcorn together and talk about movies all day. I was in so much trouble when my mom found out—"

"The mall?" he cut her off.

"Yes. Well, it wasn't like the fancy big ones nowadays that have every shop you can imagine inside. It was a small, crappy strip mall and the theatre was next to a funeral parlor, which I always thought was a bit weird, and the guy used to say that it was for those movies that made people die of boredom—"

"The mall?" he asked again, thinking about the location of all the local malls.

"Yeah," she repeated.

"The mall!" He clicked his fingers when the thought hit him. Only a few blocks away from the school there was a mall. They'd gone there recently together, to buy Emmy some clothes. She'd disappeared for ages in the shop and when he'd asked her where she'd gone, he could tell she'd been keeping something from him.

He ran. Straight down the corridor and didn't even bother with the elevator.

CHAPTER TWENTY-EIGHT

⁓

Ryan

*H*e didn't stick to the speed limit, and he hoped there weren't any traffic cops out today. He weaved through the traffic as quickly as he could and put his foot down flat when the lights turned amber. He made it there in just over twelve minutes, although the GPS had said eighteen. The parking lot was full and he would waste precious time looking for a space, so he did the only thing he could think of doing. He pulled into the closest wheelchair bay, and before jumping out of the car turned the disabled sign around that was still hanging from his rear-view mirror. The sign had been for his sister. It had been almost two years and he hadn't taken the sign down. He'd tried once, but just couldn't. Something had stopped him. That sign was his last link to her in this car, and he wasn't able to let it go just yet.

He jumped out of the car and was ready to race into the mall and comb through it, shop by shop if he had to, when he stopped. There she was. Right there. Sitting on the edge of the fountain outside the main entrance, her arms folded tightly and her head hanging down. He watched her for a moment while catching his breath. A warm feeling of relief washed over him but was quickly replaced by another feeling altogether.

"Emmy?" He shouted her name so loudly that people stopped and looked at him. Her head snapped up and he watched as horror washed over her face. She looked so guilty and he wanted to know why.

"What the hell are you doing here?" He raced over to her. A few more people stopped what they were doing to look.

Emmy sprang to her feet and started walking away from him. He raced up to her and took her by the elbow, stopping her in her tracks.

"What the hell?" His voice was loud and he didn't care who overheard them.

"Just leave me alone," she said loudly.

"I will not. What the hell did you think you were doing, bunking off school and coming to the mall like this? Not to mention stealing money from my wallet. What are you up to?" More people had stopped and a few were shaking their heads in disapproval as his story unfolded in this rather public manner. Something he hated to do, but he couldn't help it right now.

Emmy looked around at the growing crowd and then threw her hands over her eyes and went a bright shade of red. "This is so embarrassing."

"No, what's embarrassing is having your headmistress call me in the middle of a work day to tell me that my niece was seen climbing into a taxi and leaving the school property."

"Oh, I'm sorry, did I interrupt your work?" Her head snapped up and he could see she was trying to be tough, even though tears had started running down her cheeks.

"Yes, you did, as a matter of fact," he spat back. "And I demand to know why. Why would you take money out of my wallet and cut school to come to the mall?" He took a step closer to her and lowered his voice. "Are you on drugs?" he asked. "Are you seeing someone? Your mother would not approve of that, you know. Are you—"

"No!" she almost yelled. "It's not that."

"Then what?" he asked.

Emmy looked around and her eyes widened.

"Oh, for God's sake," he shouted at the people who had blatantly stopped to look at the spectacle. "This has nothing to do with any of you!"

"Oh my God, this is so embarrassing," he heard her groan again next to him.

"Car. Now!" He pointed at his car and she seemed only too happy to listen to him, *this time*. They climbed in and he slammed his door shut, feeling all sorts of emotions right now that he wasn't sure he could name. Relief, anger, guilt . . .

"I can't believe you did this." He heard his voice come out loudly.

"Stop shouting at me. Stop shouting at me, just stop—" the feeble voice next to him said, and then she burst into tears. Loud, uncontrollable sobs. *More guilt*. He looked over at her and felt his heart break. She looked so sad, vulnerable and lost right now, but he didn't know how to comfort her. He took a deep breath, trying to steady himself. Trying to calm down. He closed his eyes and counted to ten in his head, and then slowly turned in his seat and faced her.

"Emmy, please tell me what is going on?" He spoke softly this time. She was still crying and he sat patiently waiting for her sobs to slow down and finally stop.

"I . . . I . . . can't tell you," she finally whimpered.

"What the hell do you—" he stopped immediately. "I'm sorry," he corrected himself in a softer voice. "I didn't mean to shout again, I was just . . ." He paused. He wasn't good at expressing these kinds of emotions, but . . . "I was worried," he said, his voice even softer this time. "I was really worried."

His niece looked up at him with those blue eyes that were shining from the tears. It made his chest hurt to see her like this. "Please tell me," he implored her, leaning forward.

She turned and looked away. Stared out the window as if she couldn't look him in the eye anymore. As if she was embarrassed. She mumbled something so softly that he didn't hear her.

"I couldn't hear what you said." He leaned in even closer.

"I need a bra." She finally turned, but still didn't look at him.

"A what?" He was caught off guard. "Why would you need a—" He stopped himself when he saw her pull her jumper across her chest self-consciously. "Oh," he said flatly. This conversation was making him feel very uncomfortable. This was his little niece. He still remembered the day she was born, he still remembered her as a chubby, curly-haired toddler crawling around at his feet. *How could she need a bra already?* Where had the time gone, and what was he meant to do about it? This was so far above his pay grade, so out of his comfort zone, and he wished his sister was here right now. She would know what to do.

"Here." She dug in her pocket and pulled out the wad of stolen notes. She thrust them towards him. "I tried to look for one the other day when we were here, but I didn't know what to buy and I was too embarrassed to tell you so I just . . . just . . ."

She burst into tears again and this time he reached across the car and pulled her into his arms. She didn't fight him but laid her head on his shoulder. He placed his hand on her back; it was heaving up and down as she whimpered. God, he loved her. He really did, he just wasn't sure how he was meant to express all these emotions. His sister had been the emotional one, the heart to his head. That's why they'd worked so well. She'd always known what he was feeling, he never needed to say it out loud.

"I wish Mom was here," she mumbled into his shoulder.

"Me too," he replied, and then they sat in silence together for a while until she pulled away and wiped her tears.

"Did you not get one?" he asked slowly, looking down at the money in his hand.

She shook her head. "It was too confusing, and the shop attendant wanted to measure me and I . . ." She pulled her jersey around herself again.

He nodded. Of course she didn't get one. How could she buy a bra with a total stranger like that, all alone without anyone to help her? This was the kind of thing that a young girl needed to do with her mother, or another female relative at least. He cleared his throat. "Do you want me to call Grandma and—"

"No. No!" she quickly said. "Are you kidding? She still calls them 'brassieres' and you know her, she makes such a big deal about everything, she'll just turn it into this big embarrassing scene! I mean, the other day she was so shocked when she saw my G-string. She didn't even know what it was, and she was freaking out."

"You have a G-string?" he asked suddenly.

She made a tutting sound. "Have you ever tried to wear full briefs with a pair of skinny jeans?"

"No," he smiled at her, "I can't say I have. But if I do ever want to wear skinny jeans, I'll take that into account."

They looked at each other and shared a small smile. His heart felt like it was swelling and about to explode out of his chest. He hadn't shared a moment like this with her in a while.

"Uh . . ." he started talking tentatively. "Do you want me to—"

"NO!" she quickly cut him off. "No. I don't want you to . . . eeew, gross. How could you even think I would want that?"

"Uh . . . sorry, I was just—"

"I want to go home." She cut him off and suddenly her attitude changed completely again as she sat back in her seat and buckled her belt.

Clearly, he'd said the wrong thing. Once again. But he was somewhat relieved. He didn't really want to go bra shopping with her either. Obviously, the feeling was very mutual. He turned the engine on and drove off. They didn't say another word to each other on the drive home, and the second they got home, she ran into the bedroom and closed the door.

He sighed. What the hell was he meant to do now? There were no rule books or guides for raising a teenage girl, and he desperately needed one. He pulled his phone out, opened Google and started typing.

"Types of bras." The screen filled with pictures of bras and he started reading. Training bra, sports bra, balcony bra, push-up, plunge, T-shirt bra, bra-fucking-lette, soft cup, underwire, mini-mizer, triangle?

"What the hell?" he mumbled loudly as he scrolled through the pictures. No wonder she didn't know what to get. He pock-eted his phone. He needed to get back to the office.

"Goodbye, Emmy. I'll see you later," he called up. He waited for a response, but didn't get one.

CHAPTER TWENTY-NINE

⌒

Poppy

*H*e was still gone, forty minutes later. I looked at his office and then looked back at the elevator. I tapped my foot nervously. It was now or never. I reached into my handbag and pulled the sachet of plant food out. I'd been carrying it around for days now, hoping I could get a moment alone with that poor *Chlorophytum comosum*. But until now, it hadn't happened.

I stood up slowly and looked back at the elevator. If he caught me in his office he'd probably lose his shit! But I didn't know when I was going to get another chance like this. I picked the glass of water up from my desk and looked around to make sure no one was watching. And then I made a quick run for it. But just as I was about to disappear into his office, Juniper looked up. Her eyes widened and I quickly put my finger to my lips and gave a "shhhhh." I bolted inside and closed the door behind me. Not that it helped, since the whole thing was glass. I took a deep breath. The office smelt like him. Woody, citrusy, spicy and sexy as hell . . .

How could a man who smelt so delicious strike such fear into my heart? It didn't seem right.

But I couldn't get distracted now, I had a job to do. I walked over to the windowsill and picked up the poor *Chlorophytum comosum*. Its leaves were wilted and covered in dust. I slowly tipped half the glass of water onto the dry, cracked soil and watched as the soil soaked it up like a thirsty sponge. I opened the sachet of plant food and sprinkled the little white pellets onto the soil and then poured the rest of the water over them.

I put the plant back, moving it out of the full sun. I looked around for something to wipe the dust off the leaves, and when I couldn't see anything I looked over at the elevator once more and then reached into his top drawer, hoping to find a tissue. But I didn't. In fact, it was totally empty, except for one thing. A silver photo frame, face down. *Shit!* I knew I shouldn't be doing this. I should *not* be doing this, but it was *sooo* tempting. Like a cupcake on day three of your diet. Don't do it, Poppy. Do not . . . *but I did*. Of course I did. Slowly, nervously, I turned the photo over and gasped when I saw it.

It was him. Only it wasn't him at all. It was some cool, laid-back, happy-looking version of him. Him with a messy mop of hair, him with black stubble across his jaw, a T-shirt on, a beer in his hand and his other arm draped around the shoulders of a stunning woman with eyes just like his. I stared at the photo, trying to reconcile *this* man—with the huge smile and happy disposition— with the man I knew and worked for. There was such a difference between the two people that I wondered if they were even the same man. And if they were, what had happened to make him so different now? I heard a "ting" and dropped the frame back into the drawer. I looked up and saw the tip of a shoe coming out of the elevator, and I knew. It was him.

"Shit!" I dropped to my hands and knees and crawled under his desk as quickly as possible.

"Where the hell is Miss Granger?" I heard him bark before he pushed his office door open.

My heart raced in my chest and I was mentally cursing myself for doing this. I should have just left the plant to die and then I wouldn't find myself sitting under his desk. I closed my eyes tightly as he pulled the chair out and sat down. He adjusted his seat, sliding it closer to the desk. I looked up, his knees were coming towards my face, closer . . . closer . . . closer. And then they parted and— *OMG*—he stopped, his crotch mere centimeters from my nose.

I watched in horror as he reached down and adjusted the guys, before giving his tight pants a little pull . . . *Dear Lord, how much space did the man need in there?* I tried not to look, but it was all I could see. It was so in my face, literally.

"Where the hell is she?" he muttered to himself and then barked loudly. "Miss Paul?"

I heard the nervous scuttle of feet and then a tentative, "Yes, Mr. Stark?" It was Juniper. Shit!

"Have you seen my assistant?" he asked in that voice that I knew was intimidating the hell out of her.

"Mmm-mmm, no!" she said. Thank God.

There was a pause. "Really?" he asked. "Then why does it look like you're lying?"

I heard a nervous giggle. "Noooo," she said. It was not convincing.

"You know how I feel about honest employees I can rely on," he said. It sounded like a threat.

There was another pause and then, "She's in your office!" She almost yelled that part and I heard her rush away.

I held my head in my hands. How was I going to wriggle my way out of this? I looked around. Perhaps I could crawl to the other side of the desk, which would mean some maneuvering over the wooden divider.

"What the hell?" I heard him say as I watched his chair swivel around.

This was my chance. I turned around in the tiny space and then, on hands and knees, tried to shuffle my way across to the other side. But as I turned, I felt my bum come into contact with something. *Please let that be the desk and not his leg!* But it wasn't. That much I was sure of when I heard him say, "What the hell are you doing here, Miss Granger?"

I froze, hoping that by some magic I might turn invisible. But I didn't.

"I said, what the hell are you doing her . . . eeee . . . eh . . . ?" His voice tapered off.

I slowly looked back over my shoulder and that's when I realized the full extent of this thing. There he was, behind me. Me on all fours as if this was the doggy position and he was about to reach out and grab me by the hips and . . .

Goodness, had the temperature just risen suddenly?

CHAPTER THIRTY

~

Ryan

*H*e couldn't speak. Because when he looked down under his desk and saw what he saw, all words and coherent thoughts seemed to leave him in an instant.

There she was. On all fours. Ass only centimeters from his, *well*, let's just say that he'd been in this position with women before, and when he had been, they'd usually been naked and covered in a layer of sweat. She looked at him over her shoulder, much like other women had in this very same position. Suddenly the room felt way hotter than it usually was, *or was it him?*

"Uh . . . I . . . um . . ." she stuttered at him.

Damn, it was fucking hot. In fact, everything about this moment was hot, totally inappropriate, but nonetheless, it was downright, doggy-style hot. He tried to swallow. But his throat was too dry. He tried to open his mouth and talk, but nothing came out. His hands tingled. They wanted to reach out and grab her, pull her towards him, pull her into his lap, onto his lap.

"I . . . think I'm stuck," she whispered breathily, her face going a bright red color.

"Stuck?" he mumbled back at her.

"Stuck," she repeated.

But he didn't really want her to move—in fact, he could quite happily stay here like this, with her "stuck" in this position, for a while longer.

"I need to . . ." she said and then, to his surprise, started reversing.

Her ass was getting closer and closer and closer to him and then, it connected with his knees. She didn't move it away, and neither did he. For a moment they stayed there like that, looking at each other. His hand started to travel down his leg towards his knee, towards her. She saw the movement and looked at it. They both did. They watched in total silence as his fingers crept closer and closer. He heard her inhale sharply as his hand came to rest mere millimeters away from her. But he kept it there. He didn't dare move his fingers anymore.

Silence. You could have heard a pin drop as the whole room went still and silent. All that existed in that moment was him, her and his itching fingertips. They stayed like that, in the awkward screaming silence until it felt like it was becoming unbearable. Until it felt like he was going to explode. Until it felt like he had one of two options. One, touch her and open up a world of trouble, a can of worms so big that it could never be closed again. Or two, get as far away from her as possible. He thought back to that terrible mistake he'd made many years ago with one of his employees, Sasha. He thought back to how it had ended, how it had almost cost him the company. He thought back to what his father had said to him the day he'd found out . . .

So he did the only sensible thing. He pushed his chair back and stood up as quickly as he possibly could. He flipped the switch. The internal switch that he had become so good at flipping.

"For God's sake, Miss Granger, will you get the hell up from the floor!" His voice cut through the silence like a knife.

Her eyes widened and her jaw slackened.

"I . . . uh . . . YES!" She shuffled backward and finally popped out. She stood up, adjusting the skirt that had crept up her thighs. She looked at him. He could see she was confused.

"I don't want you coming into my office when I'm not here!" he said.

"Sorry, I was—"

"I don't care what you were doing," he cut her off. "My office is strictly off limits when I'm not here."

"Of course," she said, sounding timid. "It won't happen again."

"No! No, it won't," he said. "And don't you have minutes to type up and send to people?"

She blinked at him a few times and then looked away. "I'll get onto that right away." She walked out of his office and back to her desk.

His fingers were still tingling, and he rubbed them on the side of his pants.

CHAPTER THIRTY-ONE

Ryan

*H*e'd been trying to work for hours, but it was proving very difficult. He felt compelled to look up at her far too many times, and when he did, she was either typing clumsily, or looking straight back up at him. This went on all afternoon until he heard a loud "ping" on his computer and looked down. It was well after five, and most of his staff had already gone home.

His email lit up and he opened it.

Assistant@starkleisuregroup.com

He looked over at her desk. She was rubbing her hands together as if they hurt. She made round circles with her wrists, as if she was stretching them. Her face was flushed a pink color, and she looked frazzled. He looked at the email and started reading it. The little note to everyone was way too cheerful and informal. He shook his head as he read it, and wondered what everyone was going to think about it.

Hi all,

Please find attached the minutes from the great meeting you all had yesterday. I thought it was very constructive, thank you for all taking time out of your very busy day to attend it. I hope you have a lovely evening. If you have any questions, please don't hesitate to email, or call me.

Keep well.

Yours sincerely,

Doris Granger

Executive Administrative Assistant to the CEO Ryan Stark

He shook his head again. Anyone who had *any* corporate experience whatsoever would never have written an email with such a casual, chatty tone. He looked up; she was massaging her fingers one by one now. Obviously, she hadn't typed this much in her entire life. He opened the attachment, picked up his cup of now cold coffee and started reading it.

"What the fuck?!" he gasped and almost choked on his coffee. He looked up at her, and her head snapped up.

"Miss Granger . . . get in here, immediately!"

CHAPTER THIRTY-TWO

⌒

Poppy

"*S*EX million rand!" He was fuming as he read it out to me. "You sent this email to my board and the shareholders."

"Uh . . . um . . . I . . ." I felt my cheeks flush a bright red color and my stomach plummeted.

"Yes. Now would be an appropriate time to stutter." He looked furious, or panicked, or terrified, or all of the above.

He continued to read my email. "The orgasming—I suppose you meant 'organizing'—of the contract will be done through independently elected attorneys—" He looked up at me and I wanted to turn and run from the room.

"Let's see what else we have here . . ." he continued, scanning the email.

My heart started beating double time. Fuck! I couldn't believe I'd written that—well, actually I kind of could believe it, because most of my afternoon had been spent trying *not* to think of that moment under his desk. Trying not to play the moment out with a different ending, one where his hands *had* touched me. Where his hands had slithered up my skirt and pulled my panties down. Where they had gripped my hips and brought me closer to him. Ripped my clothes off, pushed all the stationery off his desk and thrown me onto it. Yes, most of my afternoon had been spent trying *not* to imagine what kissing him would feel like. Oh God, I hoped I hadn't made any more Freudian slips . . .

"Shit!' he cursed loudly, and I guessed I had.

"What is this word?" He slowly turned the computer screen around, and my breath caught in my throat.

"Uh . . . breast." I stumbled. This was bad. So, so bad.

"And what should it say?" He was glaring at me now.

"Uh . . . best."

"Exactly." He sat back in his chair and scowled at me.

I wriggled in my seat under his gaze. My skin felt like it was on fire, and my head itched like hell. I reached for it.

"And stop scratching your head, for God's sake!" he snapped and then held his own head in his hands and shook it slowly.

I pulled my hand away from my head and dropped it into my lap as fast as I could.

"Do you know what it's like being in my position when you're only thirty-seven, Miss Granger? Do you know what it means?"

I shook my head.

"It means that I have to work twice as hard as everyone else to prove myself. I'm sure you noticed that the average age in that room was fifty plus. It took me years to earn their respect and for them to stop seeing me as a child. As my father's child who'd inherited a company just because he had the same name."

I nodded.

"So when my assistant sends off an email like this, like we're at some frat party, do you think it makes me look good?"

I shook my head again. I could feel the tears welling up inside me. He was so angry with me. I don't think I'd ever seen him this angry.

"NO!" he almost yelled. "It makes me look like an idiot. It undermines me, it makes me look incompetent because I'm unable to hire the right person to do the job!" The words flew out of his mouth like venomous bullets and I wasn't going to hold back the waterworks much longer.

"I mean, it looks like a horny SEXteen-year-old boy wrote this pile of pornographic crap."

I felt my lip quiver and quickly bit it.

"Are you?" he asked.

"What?"

"A horny SEXteen year old?"

I felt the first tear escape my eyes and trickle down my cheek.

"Oh God, please don't cry!" he said.

But he was staring at me in a way that made it impossible *not* to cry. More tears came, and no matter how hard I tried, they weren't stopping. I buried my face in my hands and shook my head, wishing I could magic myself out of there.

"Seriously, Miss Granger, what the hell were you thinking about when you wrote this?"

I was totally getting fired for this! And frankly, I didn't care anymore. I was so over this job. I was over the way he treated me. One minute he seemed kind, the next minute he looked at me the way he had when I was under the desk, and then the next minute he was shouting at me. This emotional roller coaster was getting way too nauseating to ride. I didn't know if I was coming or going, if I was up or down. I didn't know, from minute to minute even, what I felt about this man. One minute I wanted him to touch me, and the next I wanted to be as far away from him as possible.

"Well, what?" he pressed angrily.

This was it. I no longer cared about any of it. I threw my hands in the air. "Sex!" My voice was shrill. "Isn't it obvious? I was clearly thinking about sex. Okay? Happy now?"

I stood up out of my chair and started walking to the door.

"Where are you going?"

"Home," I declared loudly. "Home to think about sex some more. In fact, I think I'll think about sex all night long since I'm so damn horny."

"Wait!" He stood up quickly.

"Wait what?" I glared at him. "I'm sure you're dying to get rid of me anyway, so here is your chance. Fire me, so I can go home and think about sex! Isn't that what you've been wanting to do since I started working for you—fire me?

He stood dead still and didn't move. I locked eyes with him and waited for him to open his mouth and say something, while my heart thumped against my chest.

But he didn't.

"Oh, come on. What are you waiting for? Fire the mad sex deviant. Fire the woman who evacuates the office, screws up the emails, lets a pigeon loose in your boardroom, goes into your office when you're not there." I put my hands on my hips. "Do it." I was egging him on now, and I didn't care.

"I . . . I . . ." he stuttered.

"AH-HA!" I pointed at him. "Now look who's stuttering," I said smugly, relishing the fact I could call him out for it.

"Fine. YOU'RE FIRED!" His words came out so loudly that they made me jump.

And suddenly, all my bravado and confidence and sex talk melted away in an instant. I turned and tried to make a run for it, but . . . BANG! I walked straight into the glass wall of his office. I reached up and grabbed my forehead.

"Shit!" I muttered through my tears and rubbed the bump that was starting to form.

"Are you okay?" I felt a comforting arm on my shoulder and turned around, coming face-to-face with him.

He was so close now that I could feel his breath on my face and smell the coffee that was lingering on it. His hand tightened on my shoulder and my heart rate quickened.

"Doris, are you okay?" he asked again.

I nodded. The tears had stopped now, and my gaze drifted up to his lips. His hand loosened and traveled down my arm, slowly, and stopped by my elbow. I inhaled sharply as the warmth of his hand came into contact with my bare skin. I lifted my head up and looked straight into his eyes. The blue was almost completely gone and had been replaced by a stormy black.

Shit, what the hell was happening here?

CHAPTER THIRTY-THREE

Ryan

"*W*hy were you thinking about sex all afternoon?" he finally asked, ending the long silence that had dragged on between them.

She looked at him and blinked those big, amber eyes. They always looked like they held a secret. Maybe that's why he was like this around her? Because there was something about this woman he couldn't put his finger on. She intrigued him. Beguiled him. He wasn't proud of it, but that was the truth.

Her mouth opened slightly, as if she was going to say the words. God, he wanted to hear them. He wanted to hear her say that she'd been thinking about him as much as he had been thinking about her all afternoon. She'd been thinking about it so much that she'd written the world's worst email. And when she'd written the word "breast" instead of "best," she'd been imagining his hands and mouth on them.

"That's just something I said. I didn't mean it," she said. Her voice was breathy, and her pupils were dilating.

"I don't believe you." He took a step closer.

"I'm telling the truth," she whispered, leaning in.

"Then why don't I believe you?" He matched her pose. Their faces and lips were only centimeters apart now. He heard her swallow, but she didn't pull away. He could smell and feel her breath on his lips, and he wanted to kiss her like he'd never wanted to kiss anyone before. *Don't kiss her, Ryan . . . Kiss her, goddammit! Don't kiss her, Ryan . . . Kiss her, goddammit!* A war raged in his head right now.

"You know what I think . . . ?" He leaned in even closer, turning the centimeters into mere millimeters. *Don't kiss her, Ryan.*

"No?" she whispered back at him.

"I think—" *Kiss her, goddammit!*

RING, RING.

The loud phone made them both jump apart as if they'd just been caught doing something that they shouldn't have.

"Fuck!" She half shouted the word and then looked at him in utter horror. She slapped her hand over her mouth, as if she'd only just realized what had been happening between them. As if she'd been under some kind of spell that she'd just snapped out of now. He stood and watched her, ignoring the incessant ringing that was echoing around the empty office. He couldn't tear his eyes away from hers.

What was she thinking?

"Doris . . ." He stepped forward, and she jumped back, as if she was trying to get away from him. The sound of the phone seemed to be getting louder and louder, even though he knew that wasn't possible.

"Just . . . wait . . ." He held his hand up. "I have to take this, but wait . . . I want to talk to you." He moved over to his desk and turned away from her momentarily. "Give me a min—"

But she ran out of his office before he could continue.

Chapter Thirty-Four

Poppy

*B*ut I didn't wait for him. I raced out of the office, into the elevator and made my way down to the reception. "Dammit!" I cursed loudly when I saw it was raining again. Why was it that whenever I needed to make a fast escape, the heavens opened and made my life even more difficult? The rain wasn't coming down too hard, and I considered walking in it. That is, until a massive bolt of lightning cut through the black, stormy sky. I jumped.

"I know, it looks bad out there." I looked up when I heard the voice.

"Ayanda, you're still here?" I asked.

She shrugged. "I had a few extra things to do. I was going to leave soon."

I looked at her, and hoped she couldn't see that I'd been crying. But clearly she could, because her face softened.

"That kind of day, hey?" she asked sympathetically.

I nodded at her.

"He can be very hard to work for sometimes. You never know

what kind of mood he's in," she said, although I was sure she didn't really know what was going on.

"Do you need a ride home?" she asked sweetly.

"Please," I said with a sense of relief.

"Give me five minutes?" She smiled at me and I smiled back. I suddenly felt like crying all over again at her kindness.

"Thanks, really. That's very kind of you." I walked over to the chairs that I'd sat on before my interview.

"It's the least I can do after the mix-up the other morning," she said in a soft apologetic voice. "Which I haven't really apologized for yet."

I shook my head at her. "No need to, but I appreciate it. Thanks." I sat down in The World's Most Uncomfortable Chair (that should be its trademark). They should patent this design, because it must have really taken some work to make it *this* uncomfortable. I should have taken the chair as a sign of things to come on the first day—a total pain in the ass. I waited patiently, watching the storm outside through the huge glass windows. It was beautiful; in the distance there was still a small patch of blue sky, but it was being eclipsed and swallowed up by the growing black clouds . . . kind of like what *his* eyes had done a few moments ago when he'd looked at me, his hand holding my elbow. I squirmed at the thought.

Had that really happened, or had I imagined it? He'd fired me one minute, and the next minute was looking at me as if he was about to . . . I could barely think it. Had he wanted to kiss me? My lips tingled and I touched them. The sound of the elevator doors opening and heavy footsteps crossing the marble floor made me look up. It was him. He walked all the way up to me and then stopped.

"Miss Granger?" His voice sounded tentative.

"Mmm?" I mumbled, not daring to look up at him.

"What happened in my offi—"

"I'm waiting for a lift home. Ayanda is going to take me." I cut him off quickly, hoping to put a massive full stop to this conversation. I didn't want Ayanda to hear anything.

"Oh. She is, is she?" He sounded put out, but I couldn't understand why. Surely it would be a relief that someone else was taking me home. That he didn't need to be inconvenienced by me anymore.

He took a step closer to me. "I'd really like to talk to you, though." He whispered that part.

I stiffened in response to his proximity. "Nothing to talk about," I said back, looking up to make sure Ayanda wasn't listening.

"Oh, I think there is," he said, slightly louder this time. "And that's why I'll take you home."

At that my head snapped up. "Ayanda is tak—" But before I could finish the sentence, he'd already jumped into action.

"Miss Ndaba . . ." His voice boomed through the open-plan space. "Don't worry about taking Miss Granger home, I'll do that. Thank you, though."

"Uh . . . um . . ." Ayanda stuttered. "It's not a problem, Mr. Stark, I don't mind, I really do—"

"I insist, but thank you." He cut her off again and then walked to the massive door. He stopped and turned around. "Miss Granger?" He held the door open for me.

I looked over at Ayanda, almost in panic. This was the last thing I wanted, especially given what had happened a few moments ago. Ayanda shrugged her shoulders. I'd been painted into an awkward corner and there was only one way out of it. So I stood up reluctantly and walked over to the door.

CHAPTER THIRTY-FIVE

Ryan

The drive back to her place was tense and awkward. She kept fidgeting in her seat, crossing and uncrossing her arms and legs and leaning as far away from him as possible. At one stage, her entire body seemed to be pressed up against the window. He kept opening his mouth, wanting to say something to her, but each time he did, he ended up closing it again. Because honestly, he had no idea what to say to her. How to explain what had just happened in his office? That he'd fired her one minute and almost kissed her the next. It was totally inappropriate and unprofessional and he didn't want her getting the wrong impression about him. This was not something he ever did!

Honestly, he was over that email already. His anger had come from the initial shock of it, the thought that the board and his shareholders would take him for a fool after reading it. He'd quickly sent them all a follow-up email with an explanation far too technologically advanced for their older minds to comprehend—something about a breach in the firewall and a virus, etc. But the longer they drove, the more tongue-tied he became. It's not like anything *had* physically happened between them. But it almost had. Twice.

They finally stopped outside her apartment. This place seemed to get worse every time he saw it; there was a broken lawn chair lying in the middle of the road now, and the remains of what looked like a rat were splattered across the road. A very big rat, or was it a cat? She reached for the door handle and climbed out, throwing a very dismissive "thanks" over her shoulder. He sat there and watched her walk away from him and a bolt of panic rushed through him. He didn't want her to walk away. He hadn't spoken to her yet about what had happened, and he didn't want to leave things the way they were. He climbed out of the car and ran after her.

She stopped walking and turned around. "What are you doing?" she asked.

"Walking you to your door."

"Why?" she asked.

He shrugged. He didn't know what to say. The rain was a light trickle now, and she was standing in it with her arms crossed. Droplets of water ran down her cheeks and pooled in the corners of her mouth. He so badly wanted to kiss them away.

"I've been walking myself to my door every day for the last five months. All on my own. You don't have to come and rescue me. I'm more than capable of doing this by myself, thank you," she said.

"Well, you shouldn't have to do it by yourself," he said. "It doesn't look safe here."

"Why the hell are you so concerned about my safety anyway?" she challenged him.

He shrugged again. "Honestly, I have no idea."

"That makes no sense." She threw her arms in the air.

"Tell me about it."

She shook her head and started walking again. But still, he followed her. When she reached the front of the building she turned again. "Cool. I'm at the door now. Goodbye." She began her fight with the door. It finally opened, and she started walking through it. He knew he needed to talk to her. Now or never.

"About what happened in my office," he suddenly said.

She stopped walking and stood with her back to him.

"What happened should not have happened and I want to apologize if you felt uncomfortable in any way and—"

"Nothing happened." She cut him off. "Other than you firing me."

"I did," he conceded. "But then you walked into the wall and . . ."

"My head is fine, if that's what you're worried about." She walked inside and he followed her again.

"What are you doing?" She spun around and glared at him.

"Walking you to your door."

"We're already through the door."

"I meant your other door." He pointed up.

She sighed. "Suit yourself," she said and started making her way up the stairs. When they finally reached her door, she opened it and stood in the doorway, giving him a very clear message; he was not welcome inside.

He looked at her door. It was an old, rickety-looking wooden thing. There was no security gate on it, no double locks . . . nothing.

"What does your locking system look like from the inside?" he asked, walking past her and into her flat.

"Excuse me! What are you doing?" she asked.

He didn't answer; instead he looked at the back of her door in horror. "One little lock? That's all? No deadbolt, no chains, nothing?"

"God," she huffed. "You even disapprove of the lock on my door!" She threw her bag down onto the tiny kitchen counter.

"I do actually! Anyone could break in."

"Oh please, there's nothing to steal." She bent down and pulled a jar of peanut butter out of the fridge. He watched in fascination as she stuck a spoon into it and then popped it into her mouth.

"Dinner?" She extended her spoon to him in a sarcastic manner. "I didn't think so," she snapped, and pulled the spoon back.

"Is that what you're eating for dinner?" he asked.

"Yes."

"Just from the jar like that?"

"Yup."

"Well, that's not very nutritious, is it?" He glared at the spoon as she stuck it in her mouth and sucked the creamy, brown spread off it.

"I'll have you know," she turned the jar over in her hands, "peanut butter is full of calcium, magnesium and is high in carbs and protein. It's practically a balanced meal."

He looked at her thoughtfully and then walked over to her fridge and peered in. It was empty. "Nothing?" he asked, straightening up again.

"Nope," she said casually. She was swinging her legs and her shoes fell to the floor with a thud. His eyes traveled down to her shoes, but lingered momentarily on her feet where one of her toes peeped out of a hole in her stockings. She wiggled it at him.

"What? Not going to criticize my apparel again?" she asked sarcastically. "No *'Why do you have a hole in your stockings? It's very irritating. Go get another pair!'*?" She was putting on a strange voice that he guessed was meant to be his.

Their eyes met again and he held her gaze. She had a defiant, challenging look in her eyes, as if she no longer cared what he thought. As if she didn't give a shit about him . . .

His stomach knotted. He straightened up and walked to the door. But stopped before leaving. "I'll see you at six thirty sharp," he said.

"What?" The word sounded slurred through a mouthful of peanut butter. "But you fired me!" she said.

"Consider yourself rehired." He turned around and looked at her.

"Huh?" Her mouth fell open and she gaped at him. "I don't understand."

He shook his head. "Trust me. Neither do I." He was about to walk out the door but stopped once more. "Is that really what you're eating for dinner? Peanut butter?"

She nodded.

"Not on bread?"

She shook her head. "No bread. But I am closing my eyes and imagining it's a pepperoni pizza."

He nodded. "I'll see you in the morning, Miss Granger."

And then he left.

CHAPTER THIRTY-SIX

~

Poppy

I watched him as he walked away. He stopped momentarily to look at the lock on my door again, and I rolled my eyes. What the hell had just happened? He'd fired me and then rehired me so quickly that my head was spinning. My pigeon, as if directed to, gave a loud coo, on cue.

I turned and looked over at him. "I agree. I agree."

I stood in the middle of my room and looked at my door. For a moment I considered running after him and demanding to know why he was so weird? Why he blew hot and cold? Why one minute he was firing me, the next he was almost kissing me—at least, I thought that's what had happened. Then he was walking me to my room, criticizing my food and rehiring me?

I walked over to my window and looked out. He was talking on his phone and striding to his car. That was the other thing about him, he didn't walk like other people did. There was such an urgency to his walk, as if he was always running late for something.

I continued to watch him as he climbed into his car and drove off. I watched until I could no longer see his lights.

"What the actual fuck?" I said out loud. I didn't even know if I wanted to work for him. In fact, I knew I didn't. I mean, screw him. Who did he think he was, hiring and firing me and then rehiring me like I was some kind of puppet that he could do what he wanted with?

I started getting ready for bed and was just about to climb in when a knock on the door made me jump. "Oh God," I moaned. The only person who knocked on my door was the landlord when the rent was late, which it was. I momentarily thought about pretending I wasn't here, but then I heard someone call out. It wasn't the landlord.

"Delivery for Miss Granger," the voice said.

"I didn't order anything." I moved closer to the door.

"It's from Ryan Stark."

At that I turned the handle and looked out.

"Pizza delivery for Doris Granger. Pepperoni," a young man said and pushed a pizza box towards me.

The smell wafted over to me and my mouth watered. I reached for the box, but then stopped.

"I don't have money, I can't . . ."

"It's been paid for," the pimply-faced delivery guy said and walked off.

Wow! If I thought Ryan Stark couldn't confuse me anymore, this pizza had just thrown me over the edge.

CHAPTER THIRTY-SEVEN

Ryan

Unraveled . . .

That was really the best word to describe this whole thing with her. He felt unraveled. She was unraveling him. Whenever he was near her, he felt all these strings and loose ends that he'd carefully tucked away inside himself being pulled at. Tugged on. By her! She was loosening him up, and a part of him wanted to let it all go, but another part of him, the logical part, was telling him to keep it together. These contradictory thoughts and feelings were making him feel dizzy.

At first he'd been genuinely confused by his attraction to her; she had bad hair, terrible glasses, bad clothes and a kind of ditsy, clumsy, ridiculous way of being in the world that infuriated him, but inevitably always brought a smile to his face. No matter how hard he tried to conceal it. At first he'd thought he was alone in this strange attraction to her, but then they'd had the meeting in the boardroom and he could see that he wasn't the only man in the room to find her strange ways completely beguiling.

He was approaching home and suddenly realized that thoughts of her had consumed his entire drive. He pulled into his driveway and stopped when he got to the top of it. New thoughts consumed him now. Emmy. He had no idea what kind of a mood she would be in, or whether she would even come out of her room for dinner. He climbed out of the car, walked over to his front door and slipped his key into the lock. Sudden images of Doris's door and her totally inadequate locking system plagued him. *Fuck it! Why couldn't he stop thinking about her?* He walked in and looked around. Emmy was nowhere to be seen, so he dropped his bag on the floor and walked into the kitchen. His housekeeper, Tamlin, was still there.

"Hi," he greeted her.

She looked at him and shook her head. Tamlin had worked for him for well over ten years now. She was amazing with Emmy and, outside of work, she was the only other person he spoke to on a regular basis.

"What?" he asked. But he already knew the answer.

"Emmy," she said softly. "I heard her crying in her room and she wouldn't come downstairs for dinner, even though I cooked her favorite."

He nodded at her. "Thanks. I'll see what I can do."

"It's at this age that a girl needs her mother the most," Tamlin said as she exited the kitchen.

"I know," he replied. But there was nothing he could do about that. He couldn't wave a magic wand and make everything better. If he could, he would. In fact, if he could have swapped places with Rachel, he would have. It was so unfair that she had been the one who'd gotten sick, especially since she hadn't exactly had the easiest life. Her downfall, in his opinion, had been her propensity to always lead with her heart. She had been all heart and never any head. That's what had caused her to think she was in love with that idiot from the video shop. To run off on that romantic, whirlwind trip and come back pregnant and all alone when she realized that Lance wasn't in it for the long haul. In fact, having a child at the age of twenty-two wasn't part of his plan and never would be. Their parents had been very disappointed with her, obviously. Having a daughter with a child out of wedlock wasn't part of their plan either. But Rachel had adapted and made Emmy her total focus. Emmy was her world, but life as a single mom hadn't always been easy. He'd helped out as much as he could, financially and emotionally, but it hadn't been a bed of roses, that's for sure. He sighed. He felt so lost in the world without his twin. As if a fundamental part of him had been severed.

He walked up the stairs to Emmy's room and this time he knocked on the door. But when she didn't answer, he pushed it open and peered inside. She was fast asleep. She looked like a perfect cherub lying like that, her dark hair tumbling over the pillow, with her long black lashes, her pink cheeks. He walked in slowly, careful not to wake her. As he got closer, he could see that she was holding a photo of her mother in her hands. Slowly, carefully he bent over and gave her a tiny kiss on her forehead. Her hair smelt sweet, like jasmine. He turned and walked back towards her door and then an open magazine on her desk caught his attention. He walked over to it; it was the teen magazine that she'd bought the other day. He took another step closer to the magazine and read the page . . .

"*What the hell!?*" He said it so loudly that Emmy shot out of bed.

"What . . . What . . ." she stuttered sleepily. "What are you doing here?"

He grabbed the magazine and held it up, reading the headline out loud. " 'The Science of Kissing; how to up your make-out game'."

"Oh my God, Ryan, what are you doing in my room?"

"I came to say good night and then I found . . . *this*!" He waved the magazine around.

"This is such an invasion of privacy!" She jumped out of the bed and tried to snatch the magazine away from him. He held it in the air above her head.

"Is this the kind of stuff you're doing now? Did you really want a bra, or did you bunk off school to 'up your make-out game'?" He gestured air quotes.

"I can't believe you think that. Don't you trust me?" Her lip quivered a little, and then her eyes started to tear up.

"Well, I'm not sure. Am I meant to trust the girl that steals money from my wallet and bunks off school?" His voice came out loudly. Too loudly.

Her face crumpled and a tear escaped her eye.

The guilt punched him in the gut. "I'm sorry, I didn't mean to shout," he said softly.

"You never mean to shout!" she said, the tears running down her cheeks in stripes. She turned her back on him and folded her arms.

Okay, he hadn't handled this well. He could see that now, but he'd gotten such a shock. Was she really at this age already?

"I do need a bra," she whimpered through soft sobs.

He shook his head. He'd really fucked up again. "I'm sorry, I just—"

"Please get out of my room," she cut him off.

He nodded. "Okay." He placed the magazine down on her desk again. "I'm sorry," he said again, although his apology was clearly not having any effect on her.

He walked out of her room and closed the door behind him. Could their relationship get any worse? And where the hell was the manual for this? He needed one. Desperately. He needed to know what to do before their relationship crumbled and disintegrated beyond repair.

He pulled his phone out and typed a message to his mother. He knew Emmy had said she didn't want to go shopping with her grandmother, but what other choice did he have?

CHAPTER THIRTY-EIGHT

Poppy

*W*hen he came to fetch me for work, it was clear he was already in a bad mood. I climbed into the car with a smile, ready to happily thank him for the pizza the night before, but when I saw that stern look etched onto his face, my stomach dropped. This look still filled me with such fear and nervousness. We drove in total silence for a while before I summoned the courage to break it.

"Thanks for the pizza," I finally said.

"Don't mention it," he said dismissively.

I continued. "It was very kind, you didn't have to—"

"I know I didn't have to." He cut me off in that gruff voice that had the ability to strike terror into my heart.

I kept quiet after that. We finally pulled into the parking lot and that's when he looked at me for the first time. I smiled at him.

"Miss Granger, please don't let anyone into my office today. You let someone slip past you yesterday and it was very inconvenient."

"I did?" I asked. I had no recollection of this happening. It must have happened when I was typing up that email. "Sorry," I said quickly. "It won't happen again."

"No! It won't," he said and then climbed out of the car and closed the door so loudly that it bordered on a slam.

What the hell?

The day pretty much deteriorated from that moment onwards. Maybe it was because I was nervous, maybe it was because he seemed angrier than usual, maybe it was because I overheard him shouting at someone about some kind of late report, maybe it was because I'd eaten too much pizza the night before and my stomach now felt crampy. But in the first two hours of the day I managed to miss a phone call, put another one through to the wrong extension and then accidentally mark something in his diary incorrectly. And by the time lunch came along, I was in such a bloody state that I couldn't remember if he liked mayo or not. Why couldn't I remember if he wanted his coffee black or white?

My mind raced as I looked at the foods and finally made my order. It was 50/50 that I'd gotten one of the choices wrong and would probably be crapped on from a dizzy height—*again*. Ayanda and Juniper sat at a table together talking, and a part of me wanted to join them. I didn't have many girlfriends; my mom and I had been best friends and I'd never really needed anyone but her. But now that she was gone, I felt alone in this world. There was no one I could just reach out to. Have coffee with. Pick up the phone for a chat.

"Hi, guys." I waved at them as I tapped my foot on the floor, waiting for the sandwich and the coffee to arrive.

They waved back at me and both smiled. "Bad day?" Ayanda asked as she lifted a cup of coffee to her lips and sipped.

"It will be if I don't get this back to his office asap." We all shared a look of understanding.

"He seems worse than usual today," Ayanda commented. "I heard he made Martha cry earlier."

I nodded. "He really laid into her. I could hear it from my desk."

She shook her head and tutted. "It's like working for Dr. Jekyll, you just never know who you're gonna get."

"Tell me about it," I said. I knew exactly what she meant.

"Some days it's hard to keep sane. That's why pay day drinks are so important."

"Pay day drinks?"

"Yup. A bunch of us usually go out on pay day for some drinks. Which is today. But we'll go out tomorrow, on Saturday night, since we're all so exhausted from the week. It's nothing fancy, want to come?" Juniper asked. "You can meet some of the others that work here."

"Sure," I nodded. "I'd love that. What time?"

"Sevenish," she said. "I'll text you the address if you give me your number."

"Sounds good." I walked over to them with my phone and we exchanged numbers. "I better get this stuff to him now," I said to them.

They nodded again and I raced back to his office, acutely aware that my conversation with them had officially cost me thirty seconds, and now I was running late. But when I got there, a disastrous moment was about to play out in front of my eyes. A man. A man in a dark suit carrying a big briefcase was making a beeline for Ryan's office.

"*Do not let anyone in my office today.*" His voice screamed inside my head.

I threw the food and coffee down on my desk and, as fast as I could, wedged myself between the determined-looking man and the door to Ryan's office.

"I'm sorry." I smiled at the man. "Mr. Stark doesn't take walk-ins. Unless you made an appointment with me?" I asked, knowing that no one had made any such appointment.

The man blinked at me as if I was mad. "I don't have an appointment, but he's expecting me."

"No, he isn't." I stretched my arms all the way across his closed door. This man would either have to climb under me, or pull me off with force.

"Yes, he is." The man looked pissed now.

"He does not take visitors during the day, and certainly not ones that I haven't cleared with him first."

"Look, I don't know who you are, but I always come here."

"I don't care if you come here every day, you cannot just walk into his office without an appointment. And all appointments need to go through me." I glanced behind me. Ryan was watching me now. He wanted to see if I would break. See if I would fail him again. Well, I wasn't going to give him that satisfaction, come hell or high water. This man, whoever he was, was not getting past me.

"Look, lady—"

"Lady?!" I quickly cut him off. "I am not your lady." I stamped my foot and stood my ground.

The man's eyes widened. "Mrs.—"

"Miss," I cut him off. "*Miss* Granger. Executive Administrative

Assistant to the CEO Ryan Stark, and you are not allowed in this office."

"Oh, for heaven's sake." The man made a very determined move towards the door. "Ryan? Ryan?" he called out loudly. But Ryan didn't budge. He was clearly testing me. Trying to see what I would do in this situation.

"Don't Ryan him," I said, trying to cling to the door as the man started to push past me. "*Noooo!*" I shouted as he pried me off the door and walked into the office.

"Don't you dare!" I threw myself through the air with a loud "*hi-yaaaa*" and attached myself to the man's back.

"What the!" The man swung around and flapped his arms.

But I clung on even tighter. This was starting to remind me of a scene from the telenovela. He tried to shake me off, and I tightened my grip.

"I know where you sleep at night, Señor," I slowly whispered into his ear.

"What?!" the man shouted, sounding scared.

I didn't blame him; when Ramona González used *that* voice, she meant business.

"Ryan, Ryan!" he called, somewhat frantically. "Please can you get this crazy woman off my back."

"Miss Granger . . ." Ryan stood up and walked over to me. He tapped me on the shoulder and I turned my head and looked at him.

"Yes, Mr. Stark?"

"Please will you dismount Mr. Mabuza."

Mr. Mabuza. That name sounded familiar. "But you said never to let anyone into your office."

"It's lunchtime. My private time. I can have whoever I like in my office during this hour."

"Uh . . ." I slowly loosened my grip and finally let go of the man, sliding down his back and onto the floor. "I see," I said softly. Well, this wasn't embarrassing. At all.

Ryan smiled at me. A small, slow, sly, skewed smile that lit up his blue eyes. It was the first smile I'd seen all day and it reminded me of that scene from *The Addams Family* when Wednesday Addams smiles and everyone gasps. "This is the lawyer that will be . . ." he leaned in closer to me and whispered, "orgasming the contract."

My cheeks flushed red with embarrassment. "Oh. Uh . . . sorry." I moved off and headed for the door but his voice stopped me.

"My lunch and coffee," he said.

"Of course." I turned and smiled sheepishly at the lawyer.

He was staring at me now, a strange look plastered across his face. He looked both confused and terrified.

"She's very dedicated to her job." Ryan leaned across the desk and spoke to Mr. Mabuza.

The lawyer ran his eyes up and down me curiously. "I can see. Very dedicated," he said flatly, still unimpressed.

"And can you get Mr. Mabuza a . . . ?" Ryan spoke again.

"Coffee. Strong. Black," he said, not tearing his eyes away from me.

What was up with this man? Had he never been tackled by anyone's assistant before?

"Coming right up." I gave him a smile and then ran from the office. Oh God, what a monumental screw-up. I made the coffee and grabbed Ryan's food from my desk, hoping to hell I'd remembered his mayo preference correctly. I walked back into the office and laid it all down for them.

"There we go," I said as sweetly as I could.

"It's *no* mayonnaise, Miss Granger. No mayonnaise."

"Sorry," I muttered as I walked out of the office. Oh my God, this day just couldn't get any worse, could it?

CHAPTER THIRTY-NINE

⌇

Ryan

*H*e had a meeting later that afternoon. It was a Friday afternoon meeting and, contrary to popular belief, he hated Friday afternoon meetings because he did like to go home and relax after a long week. He allowed himself this one small moment a week when he relaxed. Emmy's grandmother always fetched her from school on a Friday, and she spent the night with her; this meant that he had his own Friday night ritual. He got home, took his suit off, dropped it on the floor, or wherever he was, ordered greasy fast food, watched Netflix and then drank at least three single malt whiskeys before he climbed into bed early and slept the night away. He looked forward to Friday nights, the one day in which he unwound slightly.

He reached for his phone and pressed a few numbers. It immediately rang, and she jumped as if she'd gotten a fright and then answered.

"Miss Granger . . ." He spoke into the phone and looked at her through the glass wall. She made eye contact briefly and then looked away.

"We have a meeting this afternoon, you've seen it in the diary, no doubt?"

"I have," she said anxiously.

"We need to leave for it in one hour, and I need you to go to the laundry and fetch me another shirt," he said. "You might not be able to see it from your desk, but I have mayonnaise on my collar, which is why I don't like to eat sandwiches with mayonnaise on when I'm at work."

"Oh. Sorry." She sounded defeated.

"But I need you to make sure you ask Oliver for my clothes. That is important. Tell him they are for me, he knows who I am and washes them in a special way."

She nodded at him. "Sure."

He hung up and she continued to sit there. He watched for a while, before phoning back. She jumped again and answered. He shook his head. Why did she get a fright every time the phone rang? It was ridiculous. It was on her desk and it was a phone. Phones rang.

"Now," he said into the receiver. "We have to leave in fifty-eight minutes and counting."

She jumped out of her seat and made her way down the passage. He watched her go. There was nothing normal about her. About the way she moved around in the world. Her movements were all so big and dramatic—and then of course there'd been that incident when she'd attacked his lawyer. He smiled at the memory. He'd tried not to smile in the moment, but my God, watching

her cling to Mr. Mabuza's back had been a moment he wasn't sure
he would ever forget. He continued to watch her walk away, and
then she stopped. She seemed to be having a debate with herself.
She almost turned around and then stopped herself. She repeated
this movement a few times, before she finally turned around and
walked back to his office sheepishly. She peered around the door
tentatively, like a tortoise sticking its head out of the shell to sur-
vey its surroundings.

"Um . . . where is the laundromat, exactly?" she asked in a
small voice.

"Directly behind this building at the strip mall," he replied.

She nodded at him and walked away again, but then stopped
once more. Her head appeared again. "Do I need money?"

He sat back in his chair and crossed his arms. "I have an account
there," he said. She shot him a thumbs up and then walked away
again. He watched, waiting for her to turn and come back, but this
time she didn't. He felt slightly disappointed by that.

CHAPTER FORTY

～

Poppy

*W*hen I got back with his laundry, I was in desperate need of a cup of coffee. I was exhausted; hanging onto Mr. Mabuza had certainly depleted my energy, as had my very brisk walk to the laundromat. I grabbed a cup of coffee and started walking back to the elevator, when disaster struck.

"Oh shit!" I gasped when I saw what I'd done. I'd spilt some of my coffee onto the collar of his shirt. His crisp, new, shiny white shirt that I'd just gone to fetch. "Shit, shit, shit!" I grabbed the shirt and made a run for the women's bathroom. I had to get this stain out before he noticed.

I threw the door open and let it slam behind me. The loud sound echoed ominously through the bathroom as I turned the tap on and started carefully running a stream of warm water over the stain. I rubbed the fabric between my fingers, but to no bloody avail. It wasn't coming off. The stain stared up at me, all dark and coffee-like. "*Noooo*," I wailed. "Please no!" I grabbed hand soap and carefully started working it into the brown stain which I swear looked like an evil, laughing clown face now.

"No, *noooo, noooooo*," I moaned, so loudly that I didn't hear the bathroom door open. I jumped off the ground when I saw Juniper standing there. I put the shirt behind my back and tried to act natural.

"*Hiyyya*," I said, out of breath from my sudden jump.

She eyed me suspiciously. "Are you okay?" she asked.

And then I remembered what she'd said to me.

"No. No, I am not okay. I need your help. Please . . ." I pulled the shirt out from behind my back, and she gasped.

"Is that his?" she asked.

I nodded, and she shook her head furiously.

"Is that a—" She pointed at the shirt, her finger almost trembling.

I nodded again. "Coffee stain. I can't get it out, and he needs to wear it for his meeting."

"Oh my God!" Juniper looked horrified. "Jesus . . . Oh. My. God!" Her reaction, bordering on hysterical, only made my panic rise even more.

"Can you help me?" I beseeched her.

She seemed to pause for a moment or two and then looked me square in the face. "I believe I can, Doris, I believe I can."

"How?" I asked.

"I know where we can find some washing power," she said solemnly with a firm nod.

"You do?"

"Come!" She raced out of the bathroom and I followed behind her.

Five minutes later, and after some very careful massaging with a dash of washing powder, the stain was finally (almost) out. I was so relieved when I saw the last of the brown color disappear from the crisp white collar. As it turned out, Bradley from the accounts department was a legitimate germaphobe, not in the sense that someone who doesn't like having dirty hands is, but the kind that actually goes for—*what did he call it?*—"exposure therapy." Bradley is so obsessed with germs that he wears gloves to work, and in the trunk of his car he has every kind of washing detergent, disinfectant and cleanser, *just in case*.

Well, thanks to Bradley it looked like I might still have a job by the end of the day. I thanked Juniper profusely and promised I'd buy her a pay day drink. Now all I had to do was get this collar dry and it would be as if none of this had ever happened. Ryan Stark would put this shirt on and be none the wiser. I held the shirt under the hand dryer and watched the clock carefully. I had five minutes to get upstairs to his office and give him this shirt. And with exactly sixty seconds to go, it was finally dry.

I breathed a massive sigh of relief and headed up to his office again. Crisis averted! Nothing was going to go wrong now.

CHAPTER FORTY-ONE

Poppy

*T*en minutes later and wearing one crisp, white, fresh shirt, we sat in his car once again. I'd had a moment of absolute terror when I'd handed the shirt over to him, but he hadn't noticed, and in fact, he'd even said "thank you."

The drive was silent once again—we never spoke when he drove—but the silence was suddenly shattered by the ghastliest sound I'd heard in a while. I got a fright and turned to locate the source of it.

"GGHHAARRGGHH!"

What the hell was that? I looked over at Ryan, who looked as surprised as I was at the strange noise that had just come out of his mouth.

"Excuse me," he said, tapping his throat with his fingers. He seemed somewhat confused.

I turned and looked back at the road ahead of me, but a very sudden and violent movement made me turn and look at him again. He was scratching the side of his face, hard. I rolled my eyes quietly and turned away again. He hated me scratching and yet here he was, scratching away. Pot calling the old kettle, methinks. I looked out the window at the passing buildings until another horrific noise broke the silence in the car again and I turned once more.

"*GGHHAARRGGHH!*"

This time he seemed to be going a little red in the face. He tapped his throat a few times again and then . . .

"*GGHHAARRGGHH!*" The noise that came out of his throat was really disturbing, as if he was choking on something while simultaneously gargling.

"You okay? I asked as he started scratching the back of his neck.

"I'm fine." He sounded belligerent and turned to me.

"Oh my God. Your face, what's wrong with it?" I pointed.

His entire face had gone a strange shade of splotchy red.

"What do you mean?" He pulled the rear-view mirror down to look at himself, and when he did, he let out a strange moan.

"Are you okay?" I asked again. I was frightened by this uncharacteristically dramatic reaction of his.

He turned and looked at me; his big blue eyes were wide open and full of panic. My heart jumped into my throat. He opened his mouth to speak and . . .

"*GGHHAARRGGHH!*"

"Oh my God! Your eye is swelling." I pointed in horror as his lid suddenly looked ten times the size it normally was.

"Shit!" he hissed. "Are you sure you picked my laundry up from Oliver and no one else, and are you sure you said it was for me?" His voice had an urgent high-pitched quality to it, and it unsettled me greatly.

"Yes!" I replied quickly. *Panic!*

"Well, something must have gone wrong with this shirt then." He suddenly pulled over to the side of the road and put his hazard lights on. He reached for a bottle of water and then clicked his fingers at me frantically.

"First-aid kit! First-aid kit," he said.

I reached into the cubbyhole and passed it over to him. He dug in it and pulled out an antihistamine. I recognized it immediately. Despite my mother loving flowers, she had a terrible pollen allergy—ironic.

"I'm allergic to certain washing powders," he said suddenly. "The laundromat uses an organic one on my clothes, but something must have happened this time." He swallowed the pill and then washed it down with half the bottle of water.

"Oh shit!" I threw my hands over my mouth and stared at him in horror as his other eye started to swell.

"What? Miss Granger?" He looked at me suspiciously out of his one eyeball.

I shook my head, my hands still placed tightly over my mouth. I didn't want to have to utter the words. My heart was racing, and I'd broken out in a cold, panicky sweat.

"What have you done?" he asked again.

My heart thumped in my chest. "I am so, so, so sorry. I spilt some coffee on the collar. I tried to get it out and Juniper knew someone who had some washing powder and I used it and—"

"You what? *GGHHAARRGGHH!*" He made that terrible sound again. His face seemed to be going redder now and white spots had broken out across his neck.

Oh my God, was I going to kill him?

"Are you going to die?" I suddenly blurted out.

"Die?" He looked surprised at my question, albeit a little panicked. Seeing him like this was so unsettling that I felt I was losing my grip. He was usually so cool and calm and . . .

"I don't want you to die," I suddenly blurted out, and then burst into tears.

He grappled for the seat belt, unbuckled it and then climbed out of the car.

"What are you doing?" I asked, as he opened the passenger seat from the outside.

"You need to drive me to the hospital. Move over . . ." He started pushing me over to the driver's side.

"Shit! Shit!" I was in a total flap now. Just because I was used to getting myself into dramatic situations, it didn't mean I was any good at handling them. "I can't drive this car!" I howled loudly. But he ignored me and continued to push me. I climbed over the handbrake and my leg got stuck. Without thinking, I yanked at the handbrake and then . . .

"AAAAAHHH," I squealed as the car started rolling back. Ryan reached out and pulled the handbrake back up. The car stopped with a hard jolt.

"For God's sake, *GGHHAARRGGHH*, just how many ways do you want to *GGGGHHHHHAAAARRRGGGGG* . . . kill me today?"

"I don't want to kill you," I wailed, even though the thought had crossed my mind at least three times a day since I'd started working for him.

"Drive, drive," he commanded, tapping his hand loudly on the dashboard. The noise grated against my already shattered nerves.

"Okay, okay." I looked around at the complicated thing and then couldn't help it, but I burst into tears again.

"Why are you crying?" He sounded very displeased.

"I can't help it. I cry when I'm stressed and you are stressing me out—"

"*I* am stressing *you*?" He sounded indignant and then ended that sentence with another *GGGGHHHHHAAAARRRGGGGG*. "You are the one who has done this to me, I should be stressed with you."

I cried even louder and started wiping the tears away as I tried to figure out how to drive this beast of a car.

"It works like any other car in the fucking world . . . *GGGGH-HHHHAAAARRRGGGGG!*" He was shouting at me now. It wasn't helping.

"Silent night, holy night, all is calm, all is bright," I suddenly sang.

"What the hell are you doing?" he asked as I tried to pull out gently. But this sporty SUV was anything but gentle, and it jerked forward so fast I almost gave myself whiplash.

"I sing when I'm nervous, okay!" I yelled at him. "I sing and I cry, okay? So let me sing and goddamn cry!" I shouted back as I managed to pull into the traffic. The car was huge, like driving a fucking tank, and it was fast. In fact, the engine growled and screamed loudly at me as if it didn't want to be driven slowly. His car was just as disagreeable as he was. Trust him to drive a car that actually roared at you.

"You sing Christmas songs when you are nervous . . . *GGGGH-HHHHAAAARRRGGGGG*?" he asked, his throat sounding even worse now.

"YES!" I spat. "And sometimes I sing 'happy birthday to you, happy birthday to you, happy birthday . . .' Oh my God, why do you have to drive such a large car?" I was trying to keep it inside the lanes but the huge car seemed to want to spill all over the road and ram people out of the way. (Again, how typical that he would actually own a car like this!) I looked over at him again. "OH MY GOD! Your ear is huge!" I started crying even more and then sang another song. It was all I could do to stop myself from having a complete freak-out.

I was going to kill my boss! Then I would probably go to jail for the rest of my days for culpable homicide or something like that, and if he didn't die, he would most certainly fire me for this and then I would probably still go to jail for not paying back my bank loan!

"On the first day of Christmas my true love gave to meeeee—"

"Shut up! Please just stop *GGGGHHHHHAAAARRRGG-GGGGGG*!" He was scratching his face so hard that I was sure his skin would start peeling off.

"Stop scratching," I yelled at him, as I drove as fast as I could to the nearest hospital, which luckily, was just up the road. Unfortunately, I knew it well. Too well. And I didn't exactly like the idea of going back to it. I hadn't been to it in years, not since my mother.

"I can't," he yelled back at me.

"Sit on your hands," I barked at him.

He nodded and shoved them under his bum while grimacing as if not scratching the itch was sheer agony.

Finally, the sign for the hospital came into view and I pulled into the parking lot as quickly as I could, right into a long, static row of cars. I honked the horn, loudly. "Move, you idiots, move!"

I shouted. When no one jumped at my command I climbed out of the car and started waving and shouting at them all.

"Medical emergency, move, move, move, move, move!" The cars started moving, like I was Moses parting the Red Sea, or a conductor waving a baton. I climbed back into the car again, my forehead now glistening with a fine layer of sweat, and slammed my foot down on the accelerator. The massive beast lurched forward and with a loud and dramatic tire squeal I skidded up to the entrance of the ER. I jumped out and ran through the doors waving my arms.

"He's allergic to washing powder," I screamed at the top of my lungs.

Everyone in the room turned and looked at me, and I just burst into tears all over again.

God, this was just too much drama for one day. Even for me!

CHAPTER FORTY-TWO

_◡_

Poppy

"*T*his antihistamine might make him feel a little sleepy, but it will help with the swelling and itching. I'm also going to give him something to calm him," the doctor said as he stuck a needle into Ryan's arm.

"You don't say," I said as Ryan's usually tense face melted and drooped into something dopey and, dare I say it, cute-looking. He was lying in the hospital bed without his shirt on—the doctor had cut it off the moment he'd arrived—and I'd been trying not to stare at his big, hard chest and the tattoo that snaked over it onto his arm. Who would have thought . . . Ryan Stark, with a tattoo? He must have gotten that in his previous life, the life where he held beers in his hands and smiled and let his facial hair grow.

"I feel shfine," he said, his lips barely opening as the words oozed out of them.

I looked over at the doctor and we shared a brief smile.

"He's totally fine to take home, though. I'll ask someone to help you get him to the car if you want, Mrs. Stark?" the young doctor said.

"Oh, I'm not—we're not . . . married," I corrected. This had been the second time in a matter of days that someone had thought that we were married. The idea was just so ridiculous.

"Oooohh, noooooo," Ryan started slurring next to me. "Wes snot married, and if we were, I'd have to shdivorce you for shending me toos the hossssspital."

The doctor chuckled as Ryan's head lolled from side to side.

"I'll send a nurse and a wheelchair around now." The doctor smiled at me and turned to leave.

"Will he be okay?" I heard a hint of desperation in my voice.

The doctor looked at me, sympathetically. "He's fine. He just needs to sleep off the meds and he'll wake up feeling and looking like a new man. It wasn't a bad allergic reaction, despite what it looked like. So you don't need to worry about anything like anaphylactic shock or carrying an EpiPen. Just make sure you carry a stronger antihistamine around with you, and try and stay away from most commercial washing powders. But other than that, he's in good health as far as I can see. Just get him home and into bed, he needs some rest." He gave me one more smile and exited the room, pulling the curtain closed behind him.

"Yous hear that, Dorisssss," he hissed the "s" so long and loudly that I couldn't help but hear it.

"What?" I asked. He looked like a puddle of human jelly in the bed now. I'd never seen him looking so relaxed before. In fact, maybe I should slip one of these things into his morning coffee every day. I'm sure all the staff would be a lot happier for it. God, *I* would be a lot happier.

"I'm in gooooood healf," he slurred again stupidly.

I smiled to myself. Mr. Always In Control Freak would absolutely hate it if he knew what he was doing right now. In fact, I was tempted to film it and show it to him later. The nurse arrived with the wheelchair and it took a lot of maneuvering to get the rather floppy sack of human potatoes into the chair and then deposited onto the back seat of the car.

"Right," I said to myself as I adjusted all the mirrors.

"Did yous sphone to cancel my meeeeting?" he asked.

I couldn't believe he was thinking about work now! "Yes," I said.

"Whats did yous say?" he asked sleepily. "You can't say I went to hospital. They will shmell weaknessss."

I laughed. "You make them sound like the Mafia."

"Oh, they are. They arrr—" I heard a snore and looked back. He was fast asleep, his mouth open and his arm flung over the top of his head. Not the most graceful sleeping position, I'll give you that.

"Get him home, get him home," I said to myself, realizing that I had no idea where home was. In fact, I could barely imagine him having a home. I could picture him living in his office, in some secret room there, so he never had to leave it and was never late.

"Hey." I leaned into the back seat and tried to wake him. "Hey! Mr. Stark!" I said, a little louder this time. But he didn't budge. "HEY!" I slapped him on the shoulder and he opened his eyes and looked at me. His lids were less red now, but his blue eyes had a hooded, sexy, bedroom look to them. They locked onto mine and my heart quickened. *How damn inconvenient was it that*

I found him so adorably hot and cute right now! More so now that all that Ryan Stark bravado seemed to have melted away.

"Where do you live?" I asked him as his eyes started closing again.

"Whyyyy?" He smiled at me. "Want to come home with me, Doris?" he chuckled softly, and then his head flopped back again.

"HEY!" I whacked him a little harder this time. "Mr. Stark—"

"Call me Ryyyyaaan." He winked at me—at least I think that's what it was—and then followed it with an even bigger smile.

I gasped. *Who was this man and what had the medication done with him?* I'd seen more smiles from him in the past five minutes than I'd seen in days.

"Okay, Ryan," I said awkwardly. Saying his name out loud for the first time felt strange. Strange but . . . *good*.

"Yes, Doris," he said breathily. "Do you mind if I call you Doris?" he asked.

"Uh . . . sure," I said.

"Doris Day," he slurred again with another smile.

God, he had a nice smile. I wondered why he didn't use it more often.

"My mother luuureved Doris Day. I loved Doris too." He tried to sit up but slid back down again. "Oooops," he chuckled again.

"Ryan, I need you to listen to me," I said, softly and slowly.

"Mmmm," he muttered. "But you don't look like Doris Day, though, you're waaaaayyyy too pretty." His smile grew. It was sleepy and dopey and, again, so damn cute. "Do you mind if I say shthat?" he asked quickly.

"Say what?"

"That you're pretty?" He reached out a floppy hand. I guess

he was trying to touch my face, but it missed and crashed to the seat.

I smiled back at him. "No. It's nice to hear." Nice to hear. *Well, that was a bloody understatement* said the butterflies flapping about in my stomach.

"Okaaay," he slurred. "You're pretty. You're *soooo* pretty."

"Thanks," I said. It looked like he was about to close his eyes again.

"I'm shorry I'm so mean to you sometimess," he whispered.

"What?" I asked, wondering if I'd heard correctly. But he didn't respond. I really needed to get him home.

"What is your address?" I asked again, talking clearly, slowly and enunciating the words so carefully that I felt like I was talking to a kindergarten-aged child.

"Yous want to know where I liffff?" he asked.

"Yes."

"Mmmmmmmm, ish been a very, very, veeeery shlong time since a pretty woman came to my house." He opened his eyes and smiled at me again. "13 SEX Ocean Drive, Clifton. Doris." He suddenly burst out laughing. "Sex, six. Get it?" He was laughing even more now. "Yous so funny, Dorisss." He closed his eyes and put his head back down on the seat.

"Clifton. Fancy." I sat back up and started the car. I guess I was driving my doped-up boss, who was making very bad jokes now, home. Not to mention putting him to bed! *Could this day get any stranger?* Mind you, I had half killed him with washing powder. But on that note, who the hell is allergic to washing powder? Suddenly the sound of Ryan's phone ringing filled the car. I looked behind me as he started fiddling in his pocket for it.

"What are you doing?" I asked. "You cannot talk to anyone right now." God only knew what he would say to them in this state.

But clearly he wasn't listening; he started raising the phone to his ear. I quickly reached around and pulled it away from him and looked down at it.

"It's Mr. Grey." I put the phone on silent and dropped it on the passenger seat. "You can call him back later." *When you're not babbling incoherently*, I thought.

He moaned loudly. "He's probably shcalling to shout at me. I really dishlike that man. I dishlike him a lot, Doris."

I smiled to myself. I was sure the feeling was mutual.

He moaned again, even louder this time. "I reeeally dishlike my job." And then he sighed. Loudly. Sadly. I spun around and looked at him. His eyes were open and he was staring at the ceiling. He looked so far away and distant, I wasn't sure if that was the drugs, or something else.

"That's not nice. To dislike your job," I said.

He tried to sit up again, and this time he managed it. He put his chin on the passenger seat and looked over at me. Sleepy-looking blue eyes stared at me. His hair was ruffled and messy from lying down, and it dawned on me that this was what he must look like in the morning, before he put the big Ryan Stark suit on.

"Do youss like your job, Dorissss?" he asked.

"Uh . . . uh . . ." I stuttered. I didn't know what I was meant to say to him. I didn't want to offend him, even though there was a high probability he wasn't going to remember this conversation in the morning.

He sighed again. "I fink I made a mishtake," he suddenly said, tapping his hand on the back of my seat, as if he was trying to get my attention.

"Uh, I'm sorry to hear that." I wasn't sure what to say to him.

"I think Mr. Rautenbach is right." He sounded mournful.

"Oh, well, can't you fix the mistake?" I asked. I was curious to know what this big mistake was that everyone had been arguing about at the boardroom table the other day.

He slumped into the back seat again. "Ish a big one," he said.

"No mistake is too big to fix, is it?" I offered up happily.

"Shnot when ish a two-hundred-million-rand mistake," he mumbled to himself.

My head snapped up and I looked at him in the rear-view mirror and watched as he closed his eyes again and drifted off to sleep. I studied his face, and for the first time since meeting him I suddenly felt very sorry for him. I felt this huge rush of sympathy and had to stop myself from reaching into the back seat and putting my hand on his arm. Because that would just be ridiculous, wouldn't it?

CHAPTER FORTY-THREE

Ryan

*H*e woke up the next morning on the couch in his lounge wearing a suit jacket with no shirt on underneath. For a split second, he had no idea how he'd gotten there. And then it hit him all in one moment.

Washing powder . . . Doris . . . the hospital . . . *Shit!* He looked around the room; no one was there.

"Miss Granger?" he called out, but didn't get an answer. He walked over to the front door and looked out. His car was parked in the driveway, very badly. So, where was she? Had she taken a taxi home? He walked back into the lounge and then noticed the smell. The aroma of fresh coffee hung in the air. He walked into the kitchen and saw that a fresh pot had been brewed. The kitchen door was open and he walked out of it into the garden and looked around. Still no sign of her. But someone was here, unless a ghost had made the coffee. He turned and started walking back inside, and that's when he saw her.

She had her back to him, standing at the edge of the garden

where it dropped down like a sheer cliff to the sea below. The sky was dark and grey, making the sea below a turbulent black color. There was a strong wind and it was whipping the water around, forcing it to crash against the rocks below with such force that a massive spray shot up into the air every time it did. She was probably getting wet there.

He walked up to her and when his foot crunched down on a loose stone, she turned and looked at him. He was shocked by what he saw. Her face was covered in a thin layer of water that was shimmering in the muted light of the day. She had no make-up on and, like this, he could see how many freckles were scattered across her skin. Her skin was pale, and her cheeks and nose were flushed pink from the cold. She was holding a cup of coffee in her hands and had draped one of the sofa throws around her shoulders. She smiled at him and looked like an . . .

Angel?

"Ryan," she said.

He did some kind of auditory double take at the sound of his name coming out of her mouth. He wasn't quite sure how to respond at first but then . . .

"Doris," he said.

"How are you feeling today? You look better. I can see your eyes."

He touched his face and could feel that all the swelling had gone down. He hated to admit any kind of fear or weakness, but yesterday had scared him. "Thank you for helping me," he said softly.

She shook her head vigorously and took a step forward. "No, I'm so sorry. I didn't know about the washing powder and I was just trying to get the stain out. If I had known, I would never have—"

He smiled. "Really? If you had known you wouldn't have intentionally tried to poison me?"

"Well," she smiled back at him. "Maybe. But if I had tried to poison you, I can guarantee you would be dead by now."

"Really?" He heard himself laugh. "And what would you have used to poison me?"

"Mmmm . . ." She looked over the sea, as if she was really thinking about it. "Belladonna. It comes from the plant deadly nightshade. Almost untraceable in the blood." She flashed him a huge smile. It seemed to brighten up everything around her, including the grey light of the overcast day.

"I can see you've thought about this."

"Maybe once or twice." She turned away from him now and looked out over the sea. "You have such an amazing view. You must never want to spend time inside."

He walked over to her. Truthfully, he hadn't been out here in ages. He hardly ever came outside. Most of his time was spent in his study, which was the one room that didn't actually have a view.

"If I lived here, I would come outside to drink my morning coffee no matter what the weather was. Oh . . ." She quickly turned. "You don't mind, I made coffee this morning. I didn't get much sleep last night."

"Where did you sleep?" he asked.

"I kind of sat up all night watching TV, and you."

"You watched me?"

"Well, you were so out of it I was worried that you might stop breathing or something," she said.

A strange feeling shot through him. No one had cared that much about him in a while. "Thanks," he mumbled under his breath, not sure if he even wanted her to hear that. His pocket beeped and he jumped. He pulled his phone out and looked at it. It was a bank notification; it was the 25th of the month and his salary had been paid into his account. And then he noticed the time.

"It's already ten a.m." He looked up at Doris in shock. He hadn't slept until ten in, well, in forever maybe.

She shrugged. "I figured you needed the sleep."

"It was pay day yesterday," he said.

"I know." She nodded. "It's pay day drinks tonight."

"What's that?"

"Juniper and Ayanda and a few others always go out for drinks every pay day, it's a thing they do every month."

"They do that?" He couldn't imagine it. That his staff actually did things together, after working hours, was a strange concept—something that had never crossed his mind before.

"I'm planning on going with them too," she said quickly, a small smile gracing her lips.

"Oh, that sounds . . ." He stopped and couldn't think of the words. "Nice," he added, although he wasn't quite sure that was the word he would use.

"You could come with me, I guess," she said and then suddenly burst out laughing. Her face did something truly unique and special when she laughed. Her eyes sparkled, her cheeks dimpled and her nose crinkled up.

It was contagious and he laughed too. "No. I don't think they would want me there," he said.

"Probably not," she admitted playfully. "But they are really nice people, maybe you should get to know them better. They're not just people who work for you. They're more than that."

"Mmmm," he muttered. "That's not really how I conduct business. I don't like to mix my personal life with my professional life."

At that, she smiled. Broad, bright and full. "Well, I am at your house on a Saturday morning." She waved her arms around. "I'm even drinking coffee out of your mug." She held it up and looked at him over it.

"I've kind of noticed that," he said. It was true, he seemed to break a lot of his rules when it came to Doris, despite his resolve not to.

They looked at each other for a moment. The invisible gap between them seemed to be crying out to be filled with something. But what? He didn't know.

He decided to change the subject. "So, coming back to that pay day thing—"

"Ten thousand," she suddenly said.

"What?"

"That's what I'm worth. I know I'm not very experienced, but I am a hard worker and I do try my best and I did save your life last night—"

"After you almost killed me first." He cut her off with a smile.

"Irrelevant!" She smiled back at him. "Point is, I think that I—"

"Done," he said, raising his phone to his face. "You've worked for me for just over a week, so I'll pay you pro rata this month."

"Done?" she asked. "Just like that? You're not going to argue with me or negotiate me down?"

He shook his head. "No. In fact, since you aren't officially added to the payroll this month, I'll pay you myself, right now. I have your banking details."

"Oh. Oh! That's really nice of you, thanks," she said as he logged into his online banking and went into the business account.

"I'll even put a 'pay and clear' on the EFT so it clears immediately. You can enjoy pay day drinks with all the others tonight." He clicked a few buttons and sent her the money.

"Uh . . . thanks, that's . . ." Her voice trailed off and then her eyes widened. "Oh my God, I have great news for you then," she suddenly said, looking very excited.

"What?"

"I can get my car back now. You won't need to fetch and carry me anymore. Isn't that great news?" She gave a cute little squeal and something punched him in the gut. Hard.

"How exciting," he said. But it didn't feel exciting. In fact, it felt very wrong.

"Would you mind giving me just one more lift, though?" she asked.

A wind suddenly blew through the garden and it pulled at the throw around her shoulders. She reached out and grabbed it as it twirled about in the wind. She giggled as it tried to escape her, and then wrapped it around her shoulders again with a smile. He was so busy watching her that he was caught off guard when she asked again.

"Will that be okay?" she asked.

He snapped out of it. "What?"

"Would you mind giving me one more lift?" she asked again.

"Sure, of course. No problem," he said, trying to pull his eyes away from her.

"Thanks." She smiled again.

"Where do you need to go?" he asked.

"The pound. To get my car back." She looked so genuinely excited about this.

"Sure," he said, even though the idea didn't excite him at all.

CHAPTER FORTY-FOUR

～

Poppy

*M*y car and I were finally reunited! And although it was a total piece of shit, I must say I was really happy to see it again. I didn't like to rely on other people for things, and I'd been relying on Ryan for far too long already. Although, truth be told, I'd come to enjoy the trips, in some strange way—like the way one enjoys being bitten by a mosquito.

"So, this is me," I said as I stood there, keys in hand. "I mean, I know it's nothing to write home about, but it does get me from A to B." I slipped the keys into the door and opened it. The car smelt a bit stale and musty since it hadn't been driven in over a week.

"So, I guess this is . . . goodbye," he suddenly said.

I looked up at him and, for some reason, I felt sad.

"No more lift club then?" he said, but it sounded like a question, not a statement.

"Well, unless she breaks down," I said.

"Oh?" He seemed to perk up. "Does she break down often?"

I shook my head. "No, despite her looks, she's very reliable."

"Ahhh." He nodded, looking somewhat disappointed. "Can't judge a book by its cover, so they say."

"So they say." I climbed into my car.

Ryan took a step closer and put his hand on the open door.

"Okay. Right then," he said awkwardly. "So, I'll see you on Monday afternoon in the office."

"Afternoon?" I asked.

"I have a site meeting in the morning, I'll only be back later." He said that strangely.

"Okay," I replied. And then it dawned on me, I wouldn't see him for another forty-eight hours. "I'll see you then." I pulled the door towards me and he stopped it.

"Enjoy tonight." He bent down and looked at me.

His eyes met mine and I suddenly forgot myself.

"What's happening tonight again?" I asked.

"Pay day drinks."

"Oh. Yes. That. Thanks, I will."

"Drive carefully," he said.

"I will." I nodded at him. "Definitely."

"And make sure you lock your apartment doors tonight."

I smiled at him, he was so obsessed with my one pathetic lock. It probably bothered him that my household security wasn't done properly, or done to his standards. "I'll lock the door. I always do."

"Good." He nodded. "See you on Monday then." He closed my car door gently.

I looked at him through the window and gave him a little wave before I started the car. He waved back, put his hands in his pockets and then smiled at me. I reversed out of the parking spot but paused before driving away. I looked at him in my rear-view mirror. Why did this feel so hard? And sad?

I gave him a final wave and drove away.

CHAPTER FORTY-FIVE

Poppy

I couldn't remember the last time I'd gone out for drinks with friends. Not that they were my friends yet, but it was nice. We found ourselves at some trendy bar in Camps Bay that was way too fancy and cool for the likes of us. We'd taken a table at the back of the bar and the first round of shooters had already been ordered and downed. I was introduced to some of the other staff. They all felt sorry for me, and offered me their "deepest condolences"—apparently being Ryan's assistant was the least coveted job in the building. Extra drinks were bought for me because I "probably needed them more than anyone else." Everyone seemed very close.

"Working in a war zone really brings people together," Ayanda said.

I looked at everyone and suddenly felt gutted that they were talking about Ryan like this. It seemed such a pity, and so unnecessary that everyone should hate going to work because of him.

"Has he always been so . . ." I paused, thinking about what word to choose.

"Rude, asshole-ish, mean, douchebaggy?" Juniper asked.

I shrugged. "I mean, I wasn't going to choose those words, but—"

"Yes! He's always been this bad, although he did get worse about two years ago," Ayanda said.

"Oh, I remember that," Juniper said. "Didn't something bad happen to him?"

"Bad?" I asked, sitting up straighter.

Ayanda shrugged. "You know what he's like, he would never say, but I did overhear him talking about a funeral once."

"Shame. Who died?" I asked, feeling very concerned all of a sudden.

"Who knows?" Juniper said. "That man is a mystery. Probably one *not* worth solving, though."

"Did you hear that one rumor about him from before The Great Culling?" Ayanda said.

"The Great Culling?" I asked.

She nodded. "Mmm, that was about five years ago when he fired almost everyone and then retrenched the rest. I'm one of the ones who made it."

"Why?" I asked.

"Rumor was that he hooked up with someone from work and it ended badly—she cheated, or he did, or she betrayed him, or he did, or something."

"That's very vague," I said, trying to figure out if there was anything to this.

"She probably cheated," Juniper said. "I bet he doesn't even have sex. He's so bloody stiff and formal! That guy needs to loosen up. I bet he hasn't gotten laid in years. And if he does get laid, I bet he wears a suit while doing it." She and Ayanda burst out laughing and I watched, trying to force some laughter too but feeling uncomfortable. Ayanda stopped laughing and then raised her drink to her lips thoughtfully. "Unless he does have sex. Unless he's all freaky and Mr. Grey and shit in bed! Whips and paperclips and stuff like that."

Juniper burst out laughing again. "Well, he is totally hot. We'll give him that."

I quickly swallowed my drink. All this talk of Ryan and sex was making me feel a little strange. I didn't know if I wanted to participate in this conversation; in some strange way, I felt like I would be betraying him if I did.

My phone beeped in my pocket and I pulled it out. I did a double take when I saw the message. I almost spat my drink out of my mouth.

Ryan: How's drinks?

"What?" Ayanda asked. "You look like you've seen a ghost."

"Uh . . . I think I might have." I turned my phone around and they all looked at it.

"Oh my God!" Ayanda and Juniper gasped and leaned across the table.

Ayanda shook her head. "Don't tell him you're having fun, or he'll want to ruin it."

Juniper nodded in agreement. "He can probably sense you're having a good time and is swooping in to ruin it."

"Guys, he's not that bad," I said, taking another sip of my long pink cocktail.

"Do you know that he doesn't even come to the office Christmas party that we all have?" Ayanda said. "He doesn't even know why we have one. Old Scrooge McScroogy."

"And," Juniper chipped in, "he told us to stop bringing in cake for people's birthdays because it's messy and it takes up too much time! And he calls us all by our surnames. Who does that?"

"What should I say?" I asked them, waving my phone in the air.

"Tell him how much fun you're having. Tell him you are on your fifth cocktail and are about to hit the dancefloor with Bob from human resources." Juniper laughed stupidly. She was very pay day drunk, and I wasn't that far behind. "And then tell him after you've finished dancing you're going off to eat cake, plan the Christmas party and have sex!"

"Maybe not the last part," I giggled as I typed him a much more toned-down version of the message and pressed send.

I put the phone down on the bar counter and we all waited for a response. I sipped on my tasty pink cocktail as my phone beeped again. We all leaned in.

Ryan: I need you to come to the site meeting with me on Monday. I'll send you the address and time.

"Oh my God!" Juniper pointed at the phone. "I told you he was just trying to spoil your fun." She made a loud booing noise at the phone. A few trendy-looking hipsters turned around and looked at her disapprovingly.

Ayanda shook her head. "I think he's really trying to torture you. He never takes his assistants to site meetings."

"Really?" I looked up at them in horror. "You think?"

They both nodded at me. "But despite that," Ayanda said, "I wouldn't mind having your job."

"Why?" I asked.

"Because I've been working there longer than anyone else and I've never gotten any kind of a promotion. It's not my dream to be a receptionist," she said. "I'm thinking of leaving. I need to move up in the world so I can drink champagne on pay day, not this crap." She held her cider up and we all laughed. Without planning it, we all leaned in and clinked our glasses together.

"To champagne," Juniper said. "And lots of it."

I looked down at my phone again and wondered if they were right? Was he just trying to ruin my fun and torture me with this meeting on Monday? Juniper reached out and snatched my phone away.

"Let's put that thing away and dance." She jumped up and pulled us both towards the dancefloor. Ayanda followed us, laughing and tripping over our feet in that way that lets you know you've probably had a few too many drinks and need to slow down.

I slowed down pretty soon after that, when I caught an Uber home and climbed into bed at around eleven thirty. The others were all still there, drinking and dancing. I was just about to turn my light off when my phone beeped again. It was Ryan. He'd never messaged me this much before. Ever. And never at this time.

Ryan: Change of plans for Monday, meet at 8:30, not 8.

I messaged him back immediately. Did this man never sleep? Did he eat, breathe and dream work?

Me: Noted.

Ryan: Are you still out?

The question caught me off guard. What did that have to do with him anyway? This conversation was starting to irritate me. Maybe it was because I'd had a few drinks and all I wanted to do was climb into bed and sleep.

Me: No. Why?

There was a long pause before the message came back.

Ryan: Just wanted to make sure you would remember this and I didn't need to remind you on Monday morning again.

"What?" I hissed out loud, feeling somewhat insulted by this not so subtle insinuation of his. I typed a message back, hard.

Me: Excuse me! Are you implying that I'm drunk?

Ryan: Well, it is called pay day drinks, not pay day snacks.

I stared at the message. I didn't even know what to say back to that! My brain wasn't as sharp as I would have liked and I couldn't think of a snappy, quick comeback.

Me: I didn't drink that much. Not that it's any of your business btw.

I typed the message and pressed send, feeling the buzz of Dutch courage rushing through my veins.

Ryan: I should hope not, if you drove home. Because that would be irresponsible, not to mention illegal. I don't want to have to come and bail my assistant out of jail in the middle of the night.

And now I was just confused. I looked at his message and read it, over and over again. Did this man hate me? Did this man want to punish me? Or did he, in some strange, bizarre way, care? The kind of "care" that a madman holding someone hostage might exhibit when they tossed some stale breadcrumbs through the basement trapdoor. But before I could reply, a message came back to me.

Ryan: Well, did you? Drive home?

And now my irritation was back. This was not his business! Or was he such a control freak that he even wanted to have a say over how I conducted my weekend arrangements?

Me: I took an Uber home.

Ryan: That was at least sensible.

I paused. Huh? This conversation was getting weirder by the minute. I typed a message back to him and sent it.

Me: Thanks. I guess.

There was another long pause and I stared at the screen, waiting for another message from him. I could see he was typing. But every now and then the typing would stop, and then start again. I waited for ages, but the long message never came through—clearly he had deleted it.

Ryan: Good night.

Me: Night.

Ryan: Make sure you lock your door. I can't afford to lose my assistant.

My mouth fell open at that, and now I just wanted to rub him up the wrong way.

Me: Oh, I thought I might just leave my door completely open tonight.

Ryan: That's not funny.

Me: I'm not trying to be funny.

Ryan: Your neighbors are dangerous. Lock your door.

Me: I'll take that under advisement, Mr. Stark.

There was another long pause, but this time there was no typing. I wondered if I hadn't pushed him too far this time? My phone finally lit up and I looked at it.

Ryan: Good night.

I stared at the message, expecting more to come through. Something snarky and angry and sarcastic. But it didn't. I brought my fingers down to the keypad and let them hover over it. A part of me, the slightly alcohol-lubricated part, wanted to challenge him on all his strange behavior. I imagined typing a long message demanding to know why he was so Jekyll and Hyde. Why one minute he blew like a polar vortex and the next minute he seemed to, dare I say it, dare I even *think* it . . . *Care? Be a nice guy?* But I didn't say anything of the sort. Instead, I typed a measly good night back to him. I looked at my phone and waited for his response, but when it didn't come, I dropped my phone on my bedside table and rolled over.

I stared up at my ceiling and looked at the crack that ran the length of it. It divided the entire ceiling into two very distinct halves. I wasn't a structural engineer at all, but I was sure there shouldn't be a crack like that across the ceiling. I smiled to myself. I better not get crushed by my ceiling. Wouldn't want Ryan Stark to have to come over and pick his assistant out of the rubble, that would be very inconvenient for him.

CHAPTER FORTY-SIX

～

Poppy

*I*t was 10 a.m. and I was in the bathroom brushing my teeth when I heard the noise. I was cursing the fact that I'd woken up this early on a Sunday in the first place.

"What the hell?" I stuck my head out of the bathroom and looked at my front door. The noise was coming from behind it. I crept towards the noise tentatively and stared at the door. I could see the shadow of feet underneath it, and it was vibrating! My door was vibrating and shaking and a strange buzzing noise was coming from outside of it.

Crap! Someone was clearly trying to break in. I ran into my kitchen and grabbed the first knife I could find. I crept towards the door and the strange noise continued. My heart pounded in my chest and I remembered Ramona's karate training. I reached for the door handle and took a deep breath.

"In three, two, one . . ." I counted loudly and gave myself a small encouraging nod before turning the handle and swinging the door open.

"I'VE CAUGHT YOU, YOU FUCKER!!!" I screamed and waved the knife in the air, only to come face-to-face with Ryan. Ryan Stark was standing on the other side of my door with a drill in his hand.

A drill?

"What the hell are you doing here?" I blinked a few times in disbelief. "What are you . . . I mean, why are you . . . ?" I stuttered and stumbled over my words, looking down at his feet where a large tool box sat. I pointed at it. "Why you? With that?" I looked at my door again and noted that a big, brass lock was now attached to it. "You did this?" I pointed at the lock and then looked back at him.

What was wrong with him? He was staring at me. Jaw open, eyes about to pop out of his head, almost standing out on stalks like in those cartoons. He wasn't even blinking, for heaven's sake.

"Jesus! You gave me a fright, I thought someone was breaking into my house," I said, lowering my knife.

And then he finally blinked and a new look washed over his face. His jaw closed, his eyes narrowed and his forehead creased. "You thought someone was breaking in?" He sounded angry.

I was taken aback. "Yes."

"You thought someone was breaking in, and instead of doing something sensible like . . . oh, I don't know, CALL THE POLICE," his voice was loud and firm, "you opened the door and decided to attack the burglar?" He dropped the drill into the toolbox and took a large step forward.

"Uh . . . ? I guess." I stepped back, and he came marching in.

He closed the door behind him and glared at me. "You decided to attack the burglar with a butter knife?" He pointed to my hand. "*A butter knife???*"

I looked at the knife. "Oops, must have grabbed the wrong knife."

"What?" He spat the word out with absolute anger. "You grabbed the wrong knife? Are you kidding me! Are you looking to get injured? Are you looking to get attacked by one of your many, clearly unstable neighbors?"

"Huh?" I was floored. I had no idea what was going on.

"Has no one ever told you *not* to run towards danger?" I backed away from him and he took another stride towards me, throwing his arms in the air as if he was exasperated. "It's one thing living in a place like this. It's another thing living in a place like this without adequate locks on your door, but it's another thing entirely to live in a place like this and RUN TOWARDS DANGER WITH A BUTTER KNIFE IN YOUR HAND!" He was fuming, but I'd moved so far away from him that my back was pressed into the wall. I had nowhere to go.

"I . . . I . . ." I had no idea what to say to this.

Now he also disapproved of the way I handled myself in emergency situations! This had absolutely nothing to do with him, whatsoever. He came to a stop in front of me and stared straight into my eyes. His gaze was intense and, once more, I could feel myself crumbling underneath it. Then he reached out, took something between his fingers and looked at it. My stomach fell.

"Your hair?" He was looking at a strand of my *real* hair.

Shit! I'd opened the door without my stupid wig on.

"Have you been wearing a wig?" he asked.

"Uh . . ." My brain raced and raced and the only thing I could come up with was, "It's my sheitel." Oh God, I wanted to kick myself for saying that.

"Your what?"

"My sheitel. I'm Jewish, you see."

"Doris Granger-Peterson is Jewish?" He took a step closer to me and tangled the strand of hair around his finger.

"Grangerman-Petersonnerwitz," I whispered stupidly. I stared at his hand as he wrapped and unwrapped my long hair around his finger. "My grandmother was . . . um, I was . . . and we . . . uh . . ." I stopped dead. *What the hell was I trying to say? And why couldn't I just shut the hell up?*

"Your grandmother was—what?" He leaned in and whispered. It was low and husky and sexy as hell, and suddenly I felt myself being transported once more. Transported to that strange place where I seemed to (unintentionally) go with Ryan. Despite my best intentions *not* to go there.

"Uh, from . . . Germany and uh, after the war she married a . . . um . . ." I stumbled over my nonsensical words while staring at his lips. God, he had nice lips. And his lips got even nicer when a tiny, slow, seductive smile parted them ever so slightly.

"Married your Spanish uncle from Paraguay?" he asked.

Shit! He moved closer to me and I realized that I'd painted myself into such a damn corner with him. But I stubbornly tried to un-paint myself, once more.

"Yes. He was in exile, you see, so, you know . . . and did I mention the war?"

Suddenly, he dropped my hair and in a move that caught me totally off guard, a move that felt so intimate and strange and . . . nice . . . he placed his finger over my lips to keep me quiet.

"I can see I'm going to have to forcefully stop you from lying," he said.

CHAPTER FORTY-SEVEN

Ryan

"*L*ying?" she asked innocently, her eyes locked onto his as if she couldn't look away.

He nodded slowly, suddenly aware that he had his finger over her lips.

"Doris, it's pretty obvious that you're lying about who your family are. And I get it, I also like to keep my personal life separate."

She started to nod. Slowly. And with each move, her lips dragged up and down his finger. He couldn't tear his eyes away from her. Her long auburn hair brought out the amber color in her eyes, the small freckles that dotted her nose and the flushed pinky color of her cheeks. *Why on earth would she hide this?*

"So why are you *really* wearing a wig?" he asked, finally moving his fingers off her lips, but not without letting them trail slowly down her small, soft chin.

She swallowed hard. "I already told you—"

He cut her off. "You're Jewish? You're as bad at lying as you are at writing emails, Miss Granger. Did you really work as an assistant before this?" he asked.

She nodded again. "In a manner of speaking." Her voice was small and tentative and laden with something he wasn't totally sure he understood. She looked away, looked at her feet and in an almost inaudible voice said, "Why are you even here? It's Sunday."

Now that was a good question. *Why the hell was he here?* He'd asked himself the same thing at least a hundred times this morning. And he still didn't have a good enough answer. The only answer he could come up with was that he'd lain awake in bed for hours thinking about her stupid door lock and how someone could easily break in—especially after their irritating SMS exchange. And before that, he'd sat in his office, unable to work because all he could think about was her driving around at night going to God knows where for pay day drinks. He'd paced around his house thinking of a reason to contact her, to find out if she was alright and if she had gotten home safely. The only thing he could come up with was the lame site meeting thing, which had then led to the irritating SMS exchange. And on top of that, he and Emmy had had an explosive fight this morning—he'd not done the right thing when he'd asked his mother to take her bra shopping. He needed to get out of the house for a while until things simmered down, and so that was why he found himself here. Outside Doris's house on a Sunday morning with a drill in his hand.

He shrugged and shook his head, then shrugged some more. "I don't know."

She looked at him, with those stupidly beautiful eyes that were no longer concealed behind big glasses. *Wait, were those also fake?* This woman was strange and distracting and stubborn and clearly not telling him the whole truth. But she was also so damn fucking beautiful . . . He felt himself being pulled across the room towards her, even though his feet had not moved.

"That makes no sense," she whispered. "In fact, you make no sense. Do you know that?"

"Says the woman who's wearing a wig and I'm pretty sure was wearing fake glasses too," he said back. And then something happened to her face. A look flashed over it that he hadn't seen before: guilt? She shook her head as if trying to rid herself of the feeling, and then her demeanor completely changed. She stood upright, hands on hips, and glared at him.

"Do you know how little sense you make, Ryan?" She said his name pointedly. "Or is it Mr. Stark? I never know these days. I just can't keep up."

"Excuse me?" he said indignantly.

"Oh please, don't pretend you don't know what I'm talking about. One minute you're buying me pizza and fixing my bike wheel, and the next you're making my life a living hell when you scream at me at work, and fire me too. And suddenly you're also messaging me at night, insulting me because I went out for a drink, and now you're standing outside my door on a Sunday morning fixing a lock that I never asked you to fix."

She ran her hands through her hair; it shimmered in the light, and he was transfixed by how soft it looked.

"I can take care of myself, you know. If I wanted to fix my lock, I would have. I also know how to use a drill!"

At that, he scoffed. He doubted it very much.

"You don't believe me?" she asked.

He looked at her for a moment or two. And then, without

saying a word, he held the drill out. She took an indignant step towards him and then snatched the drill away. She looked up at him defiantly, and he couldn't help but smile.

"Well?" he asked.

She shook her head. Her cheeks were red, and she looked genuinely angry. "Oh, you'd like that, wouldn't you? You'd like me to fail at it so you can prove how right you are and how wrong I am? Because that's what you do, Mr. Stark." She folded her arms and looked like an impenetrable wall. "You deliberately didn't tell me how to answer calls and how to find a notebook on my first day. Didn't you? And you did that because you like to see people suffer, don't you? You like to watch people fail. Does it give you satisfaction?" She was getting more riled up and he could see this had been a terrible mistake.

What had he been thinking? He needed to put an end to this. And so, he did something uncharacteristic: he backed down.

He turned and walked out. He closed the door behind him and left without saying a word.

CHAPTER FORTY-EIGHT

Poppy

I could still feel his finger across my lips hours later. And every time I thought about him, my lips physically tingled. It had been so hard to lie to him this morning about my wig. The guilt had hit me so hard that I'd wanted to open my mouth and tell him the entire truth. But things had gone so far already, too far. It had become one of those lies that the longer you don't say, the harder it becomes. And lies beget more lies, and more, until you're a Jewish immigrant with a double-barreled surname who is fluent in Spanish! Besides, what would he think of me when he learned the truth? The idea that he would think less of me made me feel sick to my stomach. And so, I'd started a fight with him. I'd deflected in the only way I could think of. And I regretted it now.

I touched my lips. This was becoming complicated. I mean, where exactly did I think this was going to end? Was I going to be able to keep up this lie? Was I going to work for him forever? Honestly, I hadn't thought that far. All I'd thought of was that I'd needed money and I'd needed it now. But as each day passed, it was becoming harder and harder to keep the lie alive. We kept having these moments where he would look at me like *that*, and the truth was, he was looking at Doris. Not *me*. I wondered what he would think of Poppy when he met her? Mind you, it was clear he didn't think that much of Doris anymore either. The look he'd given me before walking out the door had been . . .

My phone beeped and my heart thumped when I saw the message.

Ryan: It was inappropriate to come and fix your lock. I shouldn't have done it. It won't happen again.

I typed a message back immediately.

Me: I shouldn't have said those things I did. It won't happen again either.

There was a long pause, and I wondered if he was finished messaging me. I decided to put my own full stop to this conversation.

Me: I'll see you tomorrow.

Ryan: Don't be late, Miss Granger.

Me: I won't, Mr. Stark.

* * *

I woke up on Monday morning to another sound at my door. This time it was a knock, and unless it was another pizza delivery guy, I knew who it was. I walked over to the door and called out just in case it was a dodgy neighbor, though.

"Hello?"

"Poppy?" I heard my name. My real name—and it suddenly

dawned on me that I hadn't heard anyone call me that in a while. God, it felt good. This Doris person was becoming such a burden to me.

I opened the door. "Hey, Mr. Reddy," I said and followed it with a sweet smile. Not that I was expecting a smile to soften him.

It didn't, and he launched straight into it.

"Do you know why I'm here?" he asked.

I nodded. I did.

"You paid rental short this month, and last month," he said.

I nodded. "I know. I just got a job and I could have paid in full this month, but I had to get my car back, otherwise I wouldn't have been able to work and earn money. I promise, I'll pay everything I owe at the end of this month. *Promise*."

He glared at me. Mr. Reddy wasn't exactly the most upstanding of landlords, he couldn't be, what with owning a building like this. I was also rather weary of his debt collection process; my suspicion was that it would involve some snapping of bones.

"You'll pay me back with interest," he said. "Twenty per cent."

"What? That's more than the bank."

"Well, then go get a loan from your bank and pay me with that," he said sarcastically. He was clearly betting on the fact that people who lived in this building weren't exactly the kind who were square with their banks.

"Fine," I conceded. "Twenty per cent. Next month." I closed the door.

Talk about bad timing! Just when it looked like my job really might be in jeopardy again.

* * *

I drove to the meeting in a state of nervous anxiety. I didn't know what Ryan would be like this morning. Especially after the lock incident yesterday. We pulled up next to each other and I didn't look at him. Instead, I sat in the car for a moment, trying to compose myself. I hadn't worn the stupid wig this morning, since the cat seemed fully out of the bag. A door slammed next to me and then he was at my window. I looked up at him.

A shaft of sunlight illuminated one side of his face, leaving the other side in shadow. The duality hit me as symbolic, because from what I'd experienced so far from my so-called boss, he was exactly this. Light and dark. Hot and cold. It was almost as if he hid in the shadows deliberately. Mind you, I guess I was hiding too. Except now my wig and glasses were finally gone.

His knuckles rapped against my window. "Are you coming, Miss Granger?"

"Coming!" I reached for the door and climbed out. I looked around, and something struck me.

"I thought this would be a hotel." I stared at the massive building site in front of me. It clearly wasn't a hotel.

"It's a shopping center," he said flatly.

"But I thought Stark built hotels?" I walked after him, struggling to keep up.

"So did I," he suddenly said. His voice had taken on that same mournful quality I'd heard in the car after the hospital. He stopped walking and looked around, putting his hands on his hips. I stopped walking and looked at him. He stood upright, like a soldier. It looked like he was surveying the area, looking for what?

"We did build hotels," he said slowly. "We *should* build hotels.

But in this recession, you have to try your hand at other things. Diversify, as Mr. Grey is always so bloody fond of saying. Funny thing is, people seem to shop more in a recession."

"Oh?" I asked, genuinely interested.

He turned around and looked at me. "The only recession-proof businesses are bottle stores, casinos, hair and nail salons, candy shops, tattoo parlors—and this shopping mall will have all of those." And then he paused and looked around again. "I hate fucking shopping malls," he said through a tightly clenched jaw. "And I think this one is going to be a giant mistake."

"They're okay," I said softly, trying to lighten the mood which had suddenly become very dark. I couldn't help but wonder if this was the big two-hundred-million-rand mistake he'd been talking about?

He continued to look at me, shaking his head from side to side as if he was trying to dislodge a bad thought. And then his eyes drifted down to my feet.

"You're wearing heels?" he asked flatly.

"So?" I asked.

"This is a site visit." He said it like I should know what the hell he was saying.

"And?" I still wasn't sure what was being implied.

"A building site!" he said firmly and slowly.

I shook my head at him.

"Oh, for God's sake, Miss Granger. Have you never been to a building site before?" He folded his arms.

"Not really," I admitted.

He looked me up and down again and then shrugged, as if he gave up. "I see you're not wearing your wig today," he said.

"What you see is what you get," I said, flipping my long hair over my shoulder playfully, hoping to defuse some of the awkwardness of this moment.

"So, you're no longer Jewish?" he asked in a smug tone.

"Um . . ." I faltered.

"Or have you converted suddenly?" he asked.

"I . . . I . . ." I stuttered.

"Your rabbi must be very disappointed." He was smug and sarcastic AF right now! I wanted to grab him and shake him. Clearly, he was toying with me. Playing a game. Waiting to see how long I could keep this up and when I would crack. We stared at each other for a while, like in those spaghetti westerns, each one of us waiting for the other to draw. He finally broke eye contact with a loud huff—clearly, he wasn't even trying to hide his feelings right now. He turned and walked away again.

"Just watch where you walk," he said over his shoulder. "Building sites are dangerous. Lots to trip over, lots of places to fall."

I looked down at the floor and knew exactly what he meant when I saw the gravel in front of me, not to mention the bricks and bits of steel and wires lying about. He was quite a way in front of me, and I called out to be heard.

"Mr. Stark, what exactly am I meant to be doing here?"

He turned and looked at me again and this time, for a brief moment, it seemed like he didn't have an answer. Then he cleared his throat and started rattling off a list.

"I need you to take notes of what is being said. Then type them up again and send them to me. If I make any suggestions, changes, et cetera, I might forget them. I want them written down." He started walking away again.

Forget? I doubted that very much. Ryan Stark didn't forget things, so why was I *really* here? I looked around. Places like this were not good for me. Give me an uneven surface and I was sure to trip. A steel pole sticking out of the ground, sure to impale myself. Wet concrete, yup, I was sure to fall in and drown. It was all part of my drama; things like these were just props in whatever ridiculous scene was about to unfold. *Mmmm* . . . I needed to be very careful. Very careful. Besides, I didn't want to give him the satisfaction of having something happen to me.

I was struggling to keep up as Ryan, Mr. Stark, Ryan Stark—oh God, whatever this man was called—stopped by a group of men. They all turned to watch my approach, and the moment soon turned painfully awkward. Their expectant eyes were on me and because of their intense waiting and watching and impatient foot-tapping, I suddenly forgot how to walk. And to make matters worse, I was trying to walk over gravel in high heels. There was silence. Except for my shoes . . .

CRUNCH, CCCRRUUUNNCCCHHH!

The sound of my soles grinding against the gravel was ear shattering. And it was made even worse when it echoed around the cavernous building site. It was just *soooo* loud. Every step I took . . . CRUNCH!!! The men were clearly getting impatient, Ryan certainly was. I must have looked like a real idiot too, because in order to keep from toppling over, I was flapping my arms at my sides, like a fucking pigeon.

Crunch. Flap, Flap. Crunch. Flap. It must have been painful to watch. I know it was embarrassingly painful to do. Finally, I reached them all.

"Congratulations, Miss Granger," Ryan mumbled sarcastically.

A few of the others smiled and one gave a not so subtle chuckle. Bloody chauvinists! Bloody male, superior assholes thinking how smart they were with their flat working shoes and big yellow hard hats. Thinking that a woman's place was probably in the kitchen and not on a building site. Well, I would show them all. Watch me as I nimbly skip across the gravel, step over the concrete walls, masterfully weave in and out of the steel poles sticking out of the grouooo—

"Ooooo," I squealed and flapped as I lost my footing and started to fall.

An arm shot out and grabbed me. It was Ryan. His firm grasp stopped my fall, and he pulled me up straight. I looked away, I didn't want to see the satisfaction in his eyes or hear his snide little comment, but instead I heard a small whisper.

"You okay?"

I turned to look at him. To verify that those words had actually come out of his mouth. But I couldn't figure it out, because he'd already started talking to the others. And then, as if confirming I had heard incorrectly, he looked over his shoulder and fired a quick, "*Now* would be the time to take notes, Miss Granger," at me in a tone that seemed totally incompatible with the tone I'd thought he'd used a few seconds ago. Yes, I'd probably imagined that.

And then suddenly, with no warning, Ryan placed a big yellow hard hat onto my head. The thing was so large that it covered the top half of my face. Great! So now I was also straining to see properly. And then slowly, ominously, Ryan turned to me with a strange smile.

"Oh, I'm sorry, I don't think I've introduced you yet," he said, looking way, *way* too pleased with himself.

I shook my head. The hat almost fell off. "No, I don't believe I've had the pleasure." I smiled sweetly at everyone.

"This is Mr. Matthews, the foreman. Mr. James, the project manager. And this is Mr. García, the architect. Of García and Fernández Architectural Firm." He said that last part with such a sly tone in his voice, but still, it took me a while to click.

"Mr. García is from . . ." He turned to the dark-haired man. "Where did you say you were born?" he asked.

My stomach plummeted. I broke out in a cold sweat.

"Brazil," the man replied.

Yes, I broke out in a very cold sweat.

"What a coincidence." Ryan eyeballed me with a look that I wanted to smack off his face. "Doris here spent some time in Paraguay. She's fluent in Spanish actually."

He was testing me. After the wig and the glasses, he was testing me on the other parts of my story too. I didn't blame him.

"Oh, wow," the García fellow said. And then he turned to me and my stomach crawled into my toes. "¿Cómo estás?" he asked.

I knew this! I knew this! I'd heard the director and the assistant director speaking Spanish to each other, and some of the lines we'd said on the show had been Spanish too.

"Bien, ¿y tú?" I replied, shooting Ryan a look.

"¿Cuánto tiempo llevas aquí?" he said to me.

I had no idea what the hell he was asking, but when I googled it later, it was something to the effect of how long had I been there?

What the fuck? I thought back to the show. Was there anything I could say back to this man so as not to give Ryan the satisfaction of catching me out? And so I said the first thing that jumped into my mind. A line I remembered from sitting in a very long edit while recording additional gargling sounds for my dying scene.

"¡He regresado de la jungla para vengarse la reputación de mi familia!" I said, and then quickly burst out laughing.

Mr. García looked at me strangely for a moment and then burst out laughing too. We laughed together for a while before Ryan quickly put an end to it.

I smiled to myself. It certainly wasn't every day you got to say, "I have returned from the jungle to avenge my family's name," to an architect on a building site.

I turned and shot Ryan a very-pleased-with-myself look.

He scowled back.

CHAPTER FORTY-NINE

～

Ryan

*H*e should have told her not to come, after what had happened yesterday. It had been awkward from the moment she'd climbed out of the car, and more so now that she was shuffling around on the gravel. It was very distracting, and as for that hard hat, she looked like a big yellow mushroom. An unbalanced mushroom, tottering around like a toddler learning to walk.

He really shouldn't have brought her, he really needed to concentrate, but every few minutes he felt himself looking back at her to make sure she was okay. He tried to shake her from his thoughts and focus on the important task at hand. And it *was* important. In fact, the future of his company rested on the success of this mall. "*We don't do malls.*" He could hear Mr. Rautenbach's favorite phrase repeating in his head, over and over again. When Mr. Grey had first proposed the idea of the mall, he'd initially been very much against it. They knew nothing about malls. But they needed to make money, and soon. His father would not just be rolling in his grave if he saw this mall, he would be cartwheeling in it.

Mr. Rautenbach had come up with a solution. Short weekend breaks were up by 20 per cent, he'd said. They needed to build a few smaller hotels, closer to the city, to cater for that. People were still going away for short breaks during the recession, but the huge Stark leisure resorts were too far away for people to go to for the weekend. But his idea had been scoffed at—a mall was "a sure money maker"—and now they had sunk everything into it.

He looked around at the empty building; they were currently standing in the proposed food court. "Didn't I say floor-to-ceiling windows?" he asked, pointing at the cavernous holes in the wall. But it wasn't really a question. "I *did* say floor-to-ceiling windows, so that people can look out over the city when eating, so that this place can have at least one redeeming feature to it." He raised his voice and turned to the architect, who quickly nodded at him.

"Miss Granger," he turned to her. "Please make a note that they must redo these windows here and make them floor to ceiling."

She nodded, but looked at him blankly. She took a small step forward and whispered. "I didn't know I needed to bring a notepad."

He sighed. "Can someone please give my assistant a pen and paper to write on?" He looked at the others, but none of them moved. "Don't tell me no one here has a pen and paper on him?" he asked, getting irritated.

The architect jumped. "I have some old plans she can use." He fetched a massive sheet of paper from a bench and passed it over to Doris. The paper was almost the same size as her. It dwarfed her . . . *and then she tried to fold it!* They all watched as she wrestled with the massive sheet, holding one side between her knees while she brawled with the top half, trying to bend it into shape.

When she realized that clearly wasn't going to work, she threw it ~~down on the ground and~~ climbed on top of it. Shuffling across it on her knees, she tried to fold the massive thing. And, adding to the spectacle, her yellow hard hat kept falling off her head. And it only got worse . . .

She turned, still on all fours, her ass now pointing in their direction (much like it had been under his desk), and crawled across the paper again. He could feel the mood around him change. He needed to put an end to this. Having them all look at her like this was, was . . .

His stomach tightened.

"Oh, for God's sake, Miss Granger." He stomped over to her and, without a moment's hesitation, pulled her back up onto her feet. She was so light. He picked up the massive sheet of paper and tore it in half, then in half again. He folded all the pieces together into a makeshift notebook of sorts and passed it over to her.

"Oh. That . . ." she mumbled, taking the paper in her hands.

"Right, now where were we?" He turned away from her and started talking again, acutely aware of the scribbling sound coming from behind him now. This woman was a bit like a noisy bulldozer. Everywhere she went, she seemed to leave a drama behind her, usually a loud one. I mean, in the last week she'd evacuated his entire building, attacked his lawyer and sent him to hospital. What was next?

And of course, all of this really did beg the big question, the billion-dollar one: why was he still employing her and why the hell could he not seem to get her out of his thoughts?

He sighed. He wished he had the answer to this wildly inconvenient question.

CHAPTER FIFTY

∽

Poppy

Fuckity, fuck.

Nothing was going my way here. I was barely able to walk, and now I was trying to take notes too. These two tasks might seem simple, but when you combine them in this environment, they were not! And they talked so fast. Throwing out words and phrases that I'd never heard of in my life . . .

Bifurcate. Programmatic adjacencies. Optimizing special adjacencies. What on earth did it all mean?

And of course, I dared not interrupt them and ask what something meant. It was clear I was already in the dog house with *him*. *Why do I need this job again?* I mentally asked myself. Oh yes, the landlord and the small rent issue—not to mention the small bank issue, lack of food issue . . . The list could go on.

The meeting seemed to last forever. Traipsing up escalators that weren't moving, which you know are hell to walk up, because your body expects them to move, but they don't, so your legs feel strange when you take steps. And then I came to a section I wasn't sure I would be able to manage. A ladder stood in front of me. It rose up to a hole in the roof. Everyone had already gone up it and now it was my turn. I rolled the papers up and was just about to shove them under my arm, when a hand came through the hole.

"I'll take the papers, it will make it easier." It was Ryan, and I was shocked. Now he was being helpful? But I was grateful for the offer, and gave him my notes.

"Be careful of the pole at the top," he said and then disappeared,

"Pole?" I asked, but he was already gone.

I gripped the sides of the ladder and carefully, slowly, took my first step. I immediately slipped.

"Crap," I hissed under my breath. This was ridiculous! I was scrambling up a ladder to join a man who clearly didn't even want me here in the first place. I was as welcome here as herpes. I was sure my time would be better served sitting in the car and twiddling my fingers. I took another step, trying to balance on the toes of my high heels, but I slipped again. "Crapping hell!" I took my shoes off; there was no way I was climbing a ladder in heels. I put one of the shoes under my arm, and reluctantly clamped the other one between my teeth. I needed to free up at least one hand to hold the bloody ladder.

This time, it was much easier and I managed to make it all the way to the top. But that's when I saw the pole. Jutting out of the concrete floor, making the space even smaller to climb through. I removed the shoe from between my teeth, and the taste of fake leather filled my mouth. I spat a few times, trying to rid myself of the ghastly flavor. I then carefully reached up and threw the shoe through the hole. But then disaster struck as I tried to get the other shoe out from under my arm . . .

I lost my balance.

I felt my body topple, wobble and then start to fall. "*Fuuuuck!*" I cried as I plummeted. But then, like magic, as if something had answered my scream for help, my body jerked back with a long, loud, spine-chilling tearing sound. I'd stopped falling. I was hanging. Suspended in the air like a puppet on strings, my arms and legs flapping from side to side.

What the hell was holding me up like this? And then I felt the hard, poking sensation in my back. The pole had pierced my shirt, and I was dangling from it.

"Oh. My. God!" How the hell was I supposed to get off this? And then . . .

Riiiiiiiiiiiip! My whole body fell a centimeter.

"Noooo," I wailed. This was not happening to me. How on earth had I managed to be the person hanging by a thread, literally, from a pole on a construction site?

And then my body fell another centimeter . . . another centimeter . . . and I knew my shirt wasn't going to hold me much longer. I had no other option but to call out for help, as much as it irked me. I didn't want to give *him* the satisfaction of having to save me from this situation, but what could I do?

"Hellooo!" I called. When I didn't get a response, I called again and again and again. No one was coming to my rescue, though. I'd have to handle this on my own. So, I prepared to swing my body like a dangling sack of potatoes and grab hold of the ladder. I took a deep breath and in three, two, one . . .

I swung. The ripping sound was terrible. I closed my eyes, grabbed the ladder and held on as tightly as possible. I kept my eyes tightly shut, until it felt safe to open them again. I was so happy to be alive, but then I looked down . . . *my shirt*. Torn and tattered, lying at the bottom of the ladder like a dead thing. One of my shoes was lying next to it, rather like a murder scene, with its snapped-off heel. I looked down at my chest and sighed. I was wearing nothing more than a bra now.

CHAPTER FIFTY-ONE

Ryan

Where the hell was she? He'd been talking for what seemed like at least ten minutes before he realized he no longer heard the irritating scribbling sounds. Not to mention the sound of her shuffling across the concrete.

"Miss Granger?" he called out and walked back to the ladder. Surely she wasn't still trying to climb up it?

"Here!" Her voice was high-pitched and strange-sounding.

He looked around to find the source of it, but couldn't. "Where?" he called out.

"Here," she replied.

He swung around and surveyed his surroundings just in time to see a head peer around one of the pillars. He did a double take.

"What on earth are you doing there?" he asked.

Her face scrunched up. "You know, just checking it all out. It's all very fascinating," she said. "The way it all comes together like this." Her hand appeared and she patted the pillar firmly. "It's very solid," she said.

"Okay," he said dismissively. "Just try and keep up with us." He turned and walked away but quickly turned around again when he heard the sound of fast, scurrying feet.

"Miss Granger?" he asked again when he couldn't see her anymore.

"Yes?" Her high-pitched voice came from a different direction now.

"Where are you?" he asked.

"Over here!" Her head popped out from behind another pillar.

"I can see that. But why?" Was she playing some sort of strange game? He let out a sigh and rolled his eyes. "Never mind. I don't want to know. Just keep up."

He turned and walked back to the others, who were now discussing the rainwater drainage system on the roof. He stood there listening to the conversation when he heard another scurrying noise, followed by a loud bang. This time they all turned around.

"Miss Granger?" he asked when, once again, she was nowhere to be seen.

"Yes." He heard her voice again.

"Where have you gotten to this time?"

"Here," the voice responded, but still no sign of her. And then a metal barrel moved slightly and they all looked at it. "Miss Granger, I know you're behind the barrel," he said.

And then slowly a forehead appeared, followed by a pair of eyes, a nose, a mouth and finally a chin. She smiled at them. She looked nervous.

"What is going on?" he asked.

And then she burst out laughing—or was that crying? Or was it a combination of both? God, this looked so unprofessional. "I'm so sorry about this." He turned to the others and apologized. "I'm not sure what she's doing."

"Miss Granger." He looked at the little face again. "Please can you stop hiding behind pillars and barrels and come out so we can continue with this site visit."

She shook her head and then bit her lip. "No," she said. "I can't come out."

"What do you mean you can't come out?"

"I mean, I can't come out," she repeated.

"Are you stuck?"

She shook her head. "Not really."

"Not really?" He repeated her words, trying to make sense of them as he went. "Then what?"

She stared at him with those big, round amber eyes of hers but didn't say another word.

He was totally exasperated now. "Please can you stand up so we can continue this tour? *Please*."

A strange look swept across her face. A look of resignation almost. She nodded her head and then started to stand up.

Everyone gasped. Including him.

CHAPTER FIFTY-TWO

~

Poppy

*N*othing left to do but face the music. I couldn't hide behind pillars and barrels any longer, and so I stood up. Slowly, tentatively and apprehensively. And the higher I seemed to get, the wider their eyeballs became.

I didn't know what else to do at this point but smile as sweetly as I could at them. There was a strange moment of silence as they stared at me, and then, as if someone had told them to, they turned their backs, looked down at the ground, and one of them even shaded his eyes. At least they were being gentlemen about this and not using it as an opportunity to gawk.

"I . . . I . . . had an accident," I said, looking over at Ryan, who was the only one who hadn't looked away. Instead, he was staring at me. His gaze was so intense that I could almost feel it, like fingers running up and down my skin. I was wearing a skirt and bra, but I felt completely naked under his stare.

And then he jumped. I'd never seen anyone pull a jacket off so quickly. Before I knew what was happening, it was wrapped around my shoulders and fastened in the front.

"Thanks," I said feebly. I felt like bursting into tears.

He looked over at the others. "It seems that Miss Granger has hurt herself." And then he got angry. "You really need to make sure this site is safe for people to visit. This is ridiculous. I think this meeting is over!" he snapped and then quickly pulled me away. He rushed so quickly that I couldn't keep up, what with trying to walk in only one shoe.

He stopped and looked down at my feet. "Where's your other shoe?"

"Broke it when I fell," I said.

"You fell?"

I couldn't work out if his tone was a concerned one, or an angry one.

I nodded. "Well, my shirt kind of stopped me from plummeting." I gave him a small smile. But, God, I was embarrassed.

"You can't walk barefoot, or we'll be pulling nails out of your feet next," he said.

"I guess not . . ." I lifted my shoeless foot and hopped.

He shook his head, gave me a very disapproving look, and then started to bend over at the waist.

"What? You want me to climb on your back? A piggyback?" I laughed. This was ridiculous.

He looked at me over his shoulder. "I'm open to other suggestions."

"Shit." There didn't seem to be anything else to do. I couldn't believe this was happening.

"Just get on with it, Miss Granger," he said.

"Fine, fine," I conceded. I hiked up my tight skirt and placed my hands on his back. It was big and solid, and he was so tall I wasn't sure I was even going to be able to climb onto him. I tried to jump onto his back, wrapping my arms around his neck and my legs around his waist. But I slipped. He tried to stop my fall by gripping my thighs, but it wasn't enough. The sound of his palms slipping down my now sweaty thighs was one I wish I'd never heard. We looked at each other awkwardly as the sound continued to echo around the vast concrete hall.

"Uh," he said, flexing his hand. "Shall we try that again?"

"Sure." My thighs felt like they were on fire now; it was as if his fingers had blazed a trail down them and now they were burning. He turned around and bent lower this time. I took a slight running jump and landed on his back. He grabbed me behind my knees and pulled me onto him. I wrapped my arms around his neck and then, God, I couldn't help it, but I laughed.

"What?" he asked.

I tried to speak through my laughter. "This," I said. "I'm on your back."

"It would seem so." I heard a small smile in his voice as we started walking.

"Hey!" A thought hit me. "How are we climbing down the ladder?"

"We'll take the long way down," he said.

And it was the long way. He walked . . . and walked . . . and walked. It seemed to go on forever. My laughter finally subsided and was replaced by something else. Being this close to him meant I could smell him. And I could feel how big and hard he was.

How strong he was, able to carry me like this, as if I was as light as a piece of paper. Slowly, very slowly, I brought my nose to his neck and inhaled quietly. At that moment, his head moved to the side, and my nose and then my mouth and then my chin came into contact with the side of his neck. It smelt salty and of sandal-wood all at the same time, and I didn't pull away immediately. In fact, I stayed there a second too long, breathing him in, letting my lips trail slightly across the side of his rough neck.

CHAPTER FIFTY-THREE

～

Ryan

*H*e sat there holding onto the steering wheel. The car was running but he hadn't pulled away yet. His eyes stared straight ahead, but he was acutely aware of her presence next to him, and even more acutely aware of her state of undress. He was also now very aware of how her lips felt on the side of his neck, how she smelt, how her upper thighs felt when he'd gripped them and how her breasts felt, pushing into his back and . . .

He cast a quick glance her way and ran his eyes over her before she noticed. His jacket was loose on her, exposing her breasts ever so slightly. They were full, and her chest was pale and soft-looking. A few freckles dotted her collarbones, running across them like a spray of small stars. Her bra was a soft pink color, blending almost perfectly with her skin, making her look naked . . . and then another thought flashed through his mind. An unwelcome thought that he sincerely hoped he had the common sense *not* to act on.

"Uh," he mumbled. *Stop it, Ryan! Fucking stop thinking it.*

"Uh." *Don't say it, don't say it*, he quickly repeated in his head. But before he could finish mentally warning himself, she jumped in.

"I know. I know how inappropriate that was and I'm sorry. I didn't mean to, I mean, of course I didn't mean to. It was an accident, and I know you told me to be careful and I tried, but I always seem to land myself in these—"

"Is that a balconette bra?" He went there and immediately regretted it.

"Excuse me?" she asked.

He didn't need to look at her to know how shocked she was by his question.

"I asked," he persisted, trying to sound perfectly normal, as if he was asking about the weather or telling her to send an email, "is that a balconette bra? Is that what you would call it?"

"Uh . . . uh . . ." she stuttered. "I guess so. Why?"

"You guess, or you know?" He turned and looked at her. As he did, a pretty pink color crept into her cheeks and she looked . . . *fuck*. She looked good. He tried to keep his eyes glued to her face and not let them drift down to where they wanted to go. God, this was inappropriate. Mind you, every single thing about the day had been inappropriate.

"Yes," she whispered, locking eyes with him. "It's a balconette bra."

"Is that a good kind to wear, I mean . . . is it comfortable and, uh . . . does it do its job?" he asked in a businesslike fashion.

"Its job?"

"Yes. Does it, you know . . . hold them in . . . uh, keep them in . . . uh . . . do they feel . . ." He was grappling to find the words. "Supported?" He finally found the right word and spat it out.

She gasped slightly. "You want to know if my breasts feel supported?"

"NO!" he quickly corrected. "I don't want to know anything of the sort. I'm not asking about your breasts—"

"Yes, you are," she cut him off.

He shook his head. "I'm asking a technical question about the clothing you are wearing—to be more specific, your bra. I am trying to ascertain whether or not it does its job? That is all, Miss Granger." This conversation had gone totally pear-shaped. He knew that, and unfortunately his question wasn't exactly one he could take back either. It was out there. No salvaging this.

"Uh . . ." She looked down at her breasts.

And this time he couldn't help it, but his eyes drifted there momentarily. God, they were beautiful. Small, but perfect-looking.

"I mean, it's fine. For the most part—although I do think I need a slightly smaller size, since I've lost a little weight, and I'm not looking as good in that department as I used to," she said in a small voice.

A thought jumped into his mind again. One that this time he was *not* going to act on. The sudden desire to tell her that she was in no way defective in that department. At all. In fact, that department was perfect. More than perfect. Spectacular even.

"So, you would recommend it then?" he asked.

"Depends on who wants to wear it."

He turned and looked at her again. "What do you mean?"

"Well, it depends on your shape and size, or what you want to get out of your bra."

"Get out of it? Doesn't a bra only do one thing?" He was intrigued now.

"Not at all. Some women need more lift than others. Some need less, or more support, some want a certain shape, some want underwire, some need them to look smaller, some want them to look bigger," she concluded.

"Really?" His mind raced. Up until this moment he'd had no idea bras were such complicated things. His only experience of them had been taking them off. And when you're doing that, you're not exactly paying attention to all those nuances. When taking a bra off, one isn't really thinking about *how* they work, but rather about how quickly one can get what they contain into your hands or mouth or . . .

He cleared his throat and looked away. He could feel the heat rising in his cheeks and he didn't want her to see what he was thinking. Because he shouldn't be thinking this! He knew that. Thoughts like these lead to dangerous places. A silence descended on them and he could feel she was waiting for him to speak again. His mind was racing. He started debating whether or not to do it? Should he ask her? How else was he meant to help Emmy? *Shit!* Right now, bloody Doris seemed like his best chance. And that didn't exactly fill him with confidence. It's not like she had the best track record when it came to following instructions or getting things right. But if not her, then who else?

"I . . . I need you to go bra shopping for me," he suddenly blurted out.

"Oh." She sounded confused. "I didn't know you were, uh . . ." She stopped.

He turned and looked at her again. "Were what?"

"It's totally okay if you are." She smiled at him. "I mean, I had a friend who used to cross dress too—"

"NO!" He cut her off quickly. "It's not for me. Well it is, but not personally. Indirectly for me . . . it's for my niece."

"Your niece?" She sounded shocked, as if the idea of him having a family, or a life outside of work, was hard to imagine.

He lowered his head and slumped his shoulders. "She's thirteen. She lost her mother. She bunked off school and stole money from my wallet and went to the mall to try and buy a bra."

"Oh no, shame." She said it with such sincerity and empathy in her voice that he looked up at her. "I lost my mother too," she said. "It's really hard."

"I didn't know that," he said quickly. "I'm . . . I'm sorry."

"You learn to live with it, I guess." She sounded so sad now, and his throat tightened. "So, tell me more about your niece and the bra situation?" she asked, turning in her seat. The movement tugged at the jacket and pulled it open even more, revealing what was inside it. He tried not to stare.

"Well, she's too embarrassed to let me take her shopping for one. Her grandmother tried, but that just ended badly. I think she needs someone younger to—"

"Say no more. I would be more than happy to take her bra shopping." She cut him off and then smiled so sweetly.

Something inside his chest seemed to respond directly to her smile. It was as if her lips were connected by invisible threads to something inside him, and when they moved, those threads tugged at his emotions.

He smiled back at her, as if his lips were also connected to her smile. "Maybe we should stop at your house first so you can . . ." His voice trailed off and he flicked his eyes around, trying not to look at her again.

"Oh. Yes. Get dressed." She quickly folded her arms across her chest as if she had forgotten she was semi-naked.

He put the car into drive and soon they were back on the road.

"I am really sorry about what happened back there," she suddenly said softly. "It was an accident, I swear. I really was trying to be careful."

He shook his head and chuckled without even realizing it. "It was terribly unprofessional."

"It was," she conceded.

"But on the other hand, I don't think I've ever seen Mr. James at a loss for words before. It really shut him up, which I was grateful for. That man can talk."

She giggled. "I know. It didn't look like he'd seen a woman in a bra since 1914. Looked like he'd forgotten what one even looked like."

Without thinking, it slipped out of his mouth. "I can relate," he quickly said, and then realized how that sounded. It made him sound a hundred years old. "I mean," he corrected, "of course I *have* seen . . . no, present tense, I see . . . That is to say that I—" He stopped talking and gave up. "It's been a long time for me, too," he said. It was the truth, after all. In fact, Doris was probably the only woman he'd seen in any kind of a state of undress for about a year now.

"Me too actually. If it makes you feel any better, it's been a long time for me too."

He turned and looked at her. "Oh. OH!" he said. "I didn't realize that you were . . . not that it matters of course."

"What?" She looked confused.

"Well, that you haven't seen someone in a *bra* for a while," he said. Honestly, it hadn't crossed his mind that Doris was anything other than straight. Not that he met people and wondered what their sexuality was, because it didn't matter, but—

"Me?" She burst out laughing. "No! No." Her laughter seemed to escalate. "I meant that I haven't seen a man in a br—No, I mean . . ." She was giggling even more now, and he heard himself chuckle. "I mean without a shirt on, or . . . *I'm* straight. Not that girls in nice bras aren't sexy, but I prefer men. Not in bras, though. Well . . ." She paused for a while, as if she was actually considering whether she liked men in bras. "Nope, I prefer my men without bras on. I definitely prefer my men all bare chested and—"

She quickly stopped talking as a strange tension filled the small, confined space of the car.

"Sorry," she said quickly.

He shook his head. "It's fine."

But it wasn't fine. Because all this talk of bras and bare chests had his mind racing off to places that it shouldn't go. Places where both of them were wearing much less than what they were wearing now. Places where they weren't driving in the *front* seat anymore. Places where her bra was hanging off his rear-view mirror and he wasn't caring about what kind it was, but rather caring about how her breasts felt in his hands.

He reached out and turned the aircon on.

God, it felt hot in here.

CHAPTER FIFTY-FOUR

Poppy

So, this wasn't strange and awkward at all. Talking about semi-nudity with my boss! I was glad he'd turned the aircon on, because it felt like the temperature had shot up by at least five degrees. Maybe even more. I crossed my arms over my chest and looked out the window, very glad that the glass was tinted. I'd already given enough people a show today, I didn't want pedestrians and passing motorists to get an eyeful as well. Perhaps I could now add "stripper" to my CV, although it had been unintentional. An unintentional stripper. Was that even a thing? I guess in my dramatic world, it was.

After what felt like a very long and silent drive, we finally pulled up to my place.

"I'll be five minutes," I said, looking back at him.

"Take your time," he said.

He looked strangely laid-back without his jacket on. He was wearing a blue shirt and a grey tie. The combination brought out the color in his eyes, which I was suddenly feeling very drawn to look at.

I climbed out of the car and started walking to my building. But I could feel him watching me. I could physically feel his eyes on me, and I suddenly became acutely aware of every single step I took. So aware that I became obsessed with walking and landed up tripping over a stone and falling to my knees. Why is it that when you concentrate too hard on one thing, it starts to feel foreign? Like repeating a word too much, until it feels like it doesn't belong in the English language. Try it. Say "moist" out loud ten times!

I stood up quickly, dusted my knees off and gave him a thumbs up to let him know I was fine. I managed to make it into my apartment without any other mishaps. I chose some more appropriate clothes before walking back to the car.

When I got there, he was leaning against it. He'd loosened his tie, his top button was undone, and he looked more casual than I'd ever seen him (seeing him topless in a hospital didn't really count). Our eyes locked and my feet stopped moving. I tried to look away, but couldn't. I felt stuck. Like someone had superglued our eyes together. Cue staring contest. I felt myself being sucked in. And when he smiled, I smiled too. He ran his hand through his hair and, for some strange reason, I felt compelled to touch mine too. He became my mirror; everything he did, I felt my body wanting to do too. This was all so . . . so *what*? What the hell was this? I finally managed to untangle my gaze from his and look away. He did too.

I climbed back into his car; he'd insisted that I leave mine at the site. I couldn't drive barefoot and half naked, he'd said. We fell into a silence again. But this time, it felt different. It wasn't awkward. It was the kind of silence that two friends shared. The kind that didn't need to be filled with a hundred words. We drove out of the

West Parks area. There was a stark difference the second you exited it. We drove towards town and started weaving through it, popping out on the other side underneath the great Table Mountain. It had been given that name hundreds of years ago when sailors had seen it from their ships for the first time. Completely flat on the top, it had looked like a great table rising up from the land, and even more so today. The famous "table cloth" of low-hanging white clouds was draped over it, the clouds oozing over the side of the mountain like a hanging cloth. It was the texture of cotton candy, and you just wanted to reach out and touch it.

We drove along the road that wound round the mountain range. It was spectacular. To our left the mountains, to our right the sea. The sky was a dark grey color, making the sea almost black. I hardly ever ventured into this part of Cape Town, where they probably charged you money just to breathe the air. It was *that* expensive here. I'd only been here once recently and that was to visit my so-called agent. The elusive creature who'd stopped taking my calls a few months ago. I saw her office coming up—"Susan O Management"—the bitch. She'd gotten a big fright the day I'd just rocked up and knocked on her door, demanding to know why she hadn't been taking my calls. She had some lame excuse about losing her phone, but I didn't believe her for a second. She'd taken my calls when I was working and she was getting her 15 per cent.

"What's wrong?" Ryan asked.

"Huh?" I asked.

"You look angry all of a sudden, like you're contemplating someone's demise." His voice had a playful, friendly quality to it. A total change to how it had been an hour ago. But I was used to this by now.

"I kind of *was* thinking of someone's demise," I said.

"Not mine, I hope?" he joked.

I shook my head. "Not this time."

He laughed and, God, it sounded nice. Warm and soft. Like a fluffy blanket in winter, wrapped around your shoulders.

"Remind me never to get on your bad side," he said.

"How do you know you're not already on it?" I asked.

He paused for a moment and then I heard a small, soft sigh. It wasn't like the ones he usually gave. Those long, desperate-sounding ones. "It wouldn't really surprise me if I was. I think most of my staff feel that way about me." I sensed a sadness in his voice and took the opportunity to broach the subject.

I turned in my seat. "And why is that?"

"Why is what?" he asked, as if he had no idea what I was even talking about.

"I think the great Ryan Stark has a secret," I said.

He turned and our eyes met. "Secret?"

"Yup, and God forbid anyone ever discovers it," I added.

"And what's my secret?"

"That Ryan Stark might actually be, on occasion—*shock, horror, gasp*—a nice guy," I said, feigning a shocked face.

He didn't turn and look at me this time, and the atmosphere in the car suddenly changed. Oh shit, had I crossed a line?

"I'm not very good at . . ." He spoke softly and slowly. An air of subtle vulnerability in his voice. "Not good at being nice. It doesn't come easily to me."

"Oh, I don't know about that. I don't know too many people that take pigeons to the vet, help fix broken bicycle wheels and door locks—even if I didn't ask—and give strangers a lift to and from work or carry them on their backs when they don't have shoes."

There was a silence. "Maybe being nice just comes a little easier with certain people," he said.

My fingers started to tingle. The tingle moved into my arms, shooting up them and into my shoulders, into my face and then into my lips.

"And what about you and all your secrets?" he asked.

"My secrets?" I tried to sound innocent.

"Are you a criminal?" he suddenly asked. His tone had changed.

I burst out laughing. "A what?"

"I'm asking because you've been wearing a wig. And I'm pretty sure those glasses weren't real either?"

I shook my head. "No. Not a criminal."

"In some kind of trouble with someone?" he asked.

"Nope," I said again. "Not that I'm aware of."

"So you're not in any danger?"

I shook my head again.

"Not in the witness protection program?" he asked.

"Nothing like that."

There was a long pause and then he spoke again. "Are your intentions malicious?" he asked. He sounded less playful and more serious now.

"What? NO!" I shook my head emphatically. "No, I have no malicious intentions. No!"

He studied me for a while and then nodded. "I believe you."

"It's nothing like that," I said, in a soft voice.

And then he smiled. "I would ask if you're a corporate spy, but I think I already know the answer to that."

"What's the answer to that?" I asked.

"Well, let's be honest. If you were a spy, you're not a very good one. And I think if someone were trying to spy on me or the company, they would send someone who was actually good at it." His smile grew, and I smiled back.

"Maybe that's part of the plan," I said. "Maybe I'm just throwing you off the scent by making you think I can't be a spy because I'm so bad, but actually I'm a spy."

He laughed and shook his head. "No, somehow I don't think you're a spy." And then his smile faltered for a moment and he looked at me seriously. "Is there something I should know about you? For example, does having you work for me put my company in some kind of danger? Like you're illegal in this country and I'm breaking the law by hiring you?"

I shook my head. "Nothing like that," I said.

He continued to look at me with such purpose and intensity. As if he was trying to look inside me. This was it. This was my moment to come clean and stop the lie. I opened my mouth but closed it again. It was obvious he knew I was hiding something, but what would he think if he knew everything?

"Are you going to fire me?" I asked suddenly.

At this he smiled again. "No. Unfortunately not." He looked back at the road.

"Unfortunately?" I repeated.

What the hell did that mean?

CHAPTER FIFTY-FIVE

~

Ryan

*S*he looked so vulnerable this time. Her usual smiles were gone and she sat in the seat in a way that made it look like it was swallowing her tiny body up. He knew she had secrets, that was obvious, but for some reason he didn't seem to care. But he knew he *should* care—he'd found himself in this situation before, an employee with secrets—well, she was more than an employee, wasn't she?

If he were an objective outsider looking in, he would tell himself that he was making the exact same mistake he'd made five years ago. Mixing business with pleasure, trusting someone with secrets, who'd only betrayed him in the end. But Doris was so different to his ex, who'd been calculating and ruthless in her lies and betrayal, whereas Doris wasn't. Maybe he was being naive? Maybe he was trying to convince himself because he felt so damn attracted to her, intrigued by her? And God, he wanted to kiss her so badly right now . . .

"Can I ask you something?" he blurted.

"Uh, depends what it is," she said.

"What do you mean?" he asked.

"Well, if it's very personal, I might not answer it."

He laughed. "Doris, I think we crossed that line an hour ago when we started discussing what bra you were wearing."

"True," she said. "So fire away, I guess." She turned in her seat again, pulling her legs up and making herself comfortable.

"Right." *Where to start?* he thought. He took a deep breath. "When you were thirteen, were you, uh, kissing?" he asked tentatively.

"What?" She laughed.

"I'm being serious. I saw an article in one of my niece's teen magazines on how to make out!"

At that, she laughed even more. "I'm sorry," she said. "I don't mean to laugh, it's just . . . I don't know. I guess I never imagined we would ever have a conversation like this."

"Trust me, neither did I," he said, feeling amused by it all now too.

"Well," she said thoughtfully. "At thirteen that's pretty much all you're thinking about. Boys, dating them, kissing them, what they think of you, your changing body, hanging out with friends."

He shook his head. "Shit. I just can't believe we're there already. I mean, I know they grow up, but this fast?"

"Were you kissing girls at thirteen?" she asked.

He cast his mind back to his teen years and sighed. "Yes. I guess I was."

"I bet you thought about that all the time?" she asked.

"Yes," he confessed. "Sandy Matthews. She was my first real kiss."

"Ooooh," Doris teased. "Sounds scandalous. And was there tongue?"

He burst out laughing at that. "Bad tongue."

"I know what you mean, my first kiss was with Arthur Gold-blum. He just shoved it all in and then flapped it about like a fish. It made this gross noise that I still remember to this day."

He laughed even more. He couldn't remember the last time he'd laughed like this.

"See," she said cheerfully. "She needs to have this."

"What?" he asked.

"This. This conversation—one day, with someone—about how bad their first kiss was."

He stopped and thought about it for a while. But first kisses lead to other things, which lead to . . . he didn't even want to think about it. He swallowed.

"And . . . sex?" he asked tentatively. "I just don't want her to . . . you know. How do I talk to her about that? When do I? Fuck, I don't know what I'm doing half the time."

Suddenly, he felt it. A reassuring hand on his shoulder. She squeezed and it felt, it felt . . . *God, it felt good*. He hadn't had a reassuring hand on his shoulder in so long, not since his sister. The traffic light turned red and he stopped the car; this gave them a moment. He turned in his seat and looked at her. He wanted to reach up and place his hand over hers, but . . . *should he?*

"I think the fact that you even worry about these kinds of things means you are doing a good job." She smiled. Her voice was soft and soothing, and he felt reassured.

"Thanks," he said.

"And for the rest of it, there is always Google." She smiled at

him. "I bet you there are single dad blogs out there you could follow, I bet there are online groups on Facebook you could join."

He nodded. He hadn't thought about that. "Thanks, that's a
good idea." Her smile grew and so did his. "I really . . ." He
paused. He struggled with words like these. "I really appreciate
this, Doris. You talking to me about this, and agreeing to help. It
really, it means a lot. Thanks."

She squeezed his shoulder again and he slowly began raising
his hand, determined to place it on top of hers. But before he
could, the traffic lights turned green and someone was honking
at him.

CHAPTER FIFTY-SIX

~

Poppy

*W*e arrived at his house and he led me upstairs. He knocked on one of the doors tentatively. As if he was scared to go in. Well, I hoped he wasn't in the habit of just barging into his teenage niece's room. That would be a recipe for a huge argument. Maybe I needed to tell him about that.

"Emmy," he called out.

A small voice finally replied. "What?" She didn't sound happy, and I recognized that tone immediately.

"Can I come in?" he asked. He looked nervous.

"I suppose." She didn't sound extremely excited by the idea.

He slowly pushed the door open and stepped inside. I followed behind him cautiously. I didn't want to upset what seemed to be an already rather tense situation.

"Who's that?" she immediately asked upon seeing me. She looked a lot like him; her blue eyes were just as striking as his, and she had long black hair that cascaded over her shoulders.

"Uh, this is my assistant, Doris." He sounded so unsure of himself right now.

This was so unfamiliar. Ryan Stark never seemed uncertain. Never seemed at a loss for words, and certainly never sounded like this.

"I thought that . . . that . . ." He paused and took another step into the room. "Well, you know how you need to buy something?" he asked.

She stood up from her bed. She was tall—it must be a family trait. "Huh?" She looked confused.

"You know," he said. His voice had taken on a strange high-pitched tone and he was flicking his eyes around the room as if he was embarrassed.

"What?" she asked.

"That thing you wanted to buy but couldn't get that time because—" He persisted with this vague description and I rolled my eyes. We would be here all day if this continued.

"I think the word he's looking for, rather unsuccessfully, is a *bra*," I said with a smile and then winked at the teenager.

She looked at me blankly, as if she didn't quite know what to make of me. And then her face softened slightly and I saw a small smile grace her lips.

"Yes. That!" he suddenly said. "Thank you, Doris, for clearing that up." He sounded stiff and formal—*damn, it was cute*—and I smiled a little more. "I thought that maybe you and Doris could—"

Her eyes widened and her jaw fell open. "What? You want your assistant to take me bra shopping?" she mocked.

Oh God, now that she put it that way, it sounded bad.

"Well, I just thought that, since I can't do it and Grandma couldn't and since Doris is a woman, like you, well, she is somewhat older obviously, but she is younger than Grandma and although I'm sure it's been a while since she bought her first bra ... uh ... she is wearing a balconette bra at the moment, which I did google, by the way, but I thought that—" He stuttered and stumbled over his words and it only made the whole thing worse.

Emmy was red with embarrassment and if I didn't do something to salvage this situation, it was going to crash and burn.

"*Okaaaayyy!*" I jumped in front of Ryan and put my hand over his mouth. "That's enough," I said and then started pushing him out the door. "Out. Out." I managed to get him out and then, as soon as I had, I closed the door and looked at Emmy.

She stared at me in shock. "Did you actually just do that?" she asked.

I shrugged. "I think so."

"You just pushed my uncle out of the room?" She smiled again. "You shut him up with your hand!"

I nodded. "I guess I did."

"Oh my God, I hope you know you're *soooo* getting fired for that." She sat back down on her bed and her smile faded. "I'm not going bra shopping with you, by the way." She turned her back on me, shutting me out.

I stood and looked at her for a while. Her bravado was transparent. The angry teen act she had going on, much like her uncle actually, was just a mask she was hiding behind. It was so obvious.

"I lost my mom too," I said after a while.

She turned around and looked at me.

"A year ago," I continued. "It was the worst day of my life. I still remember it as if it were yesterday. I woke up that morning and had a mom, and then when I went to bed that night, I didn't. She was just gone. And I couldn't wrap my head around it, you know. How one minute she was there and the next she wasn't. People don't just disappear like that, well, they're not supposed to anyway. It wasn't right. It wasn't. But there was nothing I could do to bring her back."

Our eyes met. I could see hers were shimmering with tears. I walked over to the bed and sat down next to her, but not too close. "Look, if you don't want me to go bra shopping with you, I totally understand. I mean, trust me, this is as weird and awkward for me as it is for you. We don't even know each other. But, if you're cool with it, I'd be happy to go with you and try to help. I can't guarantee I'll be any good, but I'm sure I'd be better than Ryan, who can't even say the word bra."

There was a long silence and I could see she was considering this carefully. Slowly, after a while, a small nod started. "Okay," she said softly.

"Okay?" I repeated.

And then she turned and met my eyes again.

"How does my uncle know you're wearing a balconette bra?" she asked.

"It's a very long and rather dramatic story," I said quickly. "I'll tell you in the car."

We both stood up and walked towards the closed door. "Shall we?" I opened the door only to see Ryan scramble to the other side of the corridor.

Emmy walked past him and down the stairs. I started to follow her when I felt a hand on my shoulder. I turned and Ryan was smiling at me.

"I'm not going to fire you over that, by the way," he whispered.

"Unfortunately," I said, trotting down the staircase.

CHAPTER FIFTY-SEVEN

Poppy

"So, I'll meet you guys later," Ryan said awkwardly. "Here." He pulled his wallet out and handed me his card. "It's zero-eight-nine-zero. The code."

I reached for the card, but as I did, our fingers touched briefly and a shock ran through me. It was a tingle at first, just in my fingertips, and then it moved into my wrist and snaked up my arm, pebbling my skin as it went. I shivered and pulled away quickly. My arm was full of goosebumps, despite the climate-controlled inside of the mall.

"Okay, we better . . . uh," I said, taking a step backward.

He did too, and I wondered if he'd also felt it.

"I'll wait here for you," he said. "Take your time."

I nodded at him and we walked off in the direction of the lingerie shop.

* * *

About an hour later, after trying on at least six different types of bra, we finally found the right type that fitted perfectly and felt comfortable. We got a few of them in different colors and headed to the counter to pay.

"Thanks for doing this," Emmy said softly as I paid for everything.

"I hope I was helpful."

She nodded. "I did kind of always imagine doing this with my mom, but . . ."

"Yeah," I sighed. "I know. I always imagined that when I got married, if I got married, that my mom would help me choose my wedding dress, you know?"

We looked at each other and it was like looking into a mirror. All the thoughts and feelings that she had, I had them too. I got her. Understood what she was going through.

"Hey." She shrugged playfully, lightening the mood somewhat. "When you get married I'll come help you choose the dress," she said.

"I'd love that." We walked together in silence for a while. "How does it feel?" I asked, looking at her.

She tugged on the bra strap. "A bit weird, but it doesn't hurt when I walk now like it did before. They were like, I don't know, sensitive."

"I know, it's the worst. But don't worry, it gets better." I paused for a moment and thought carefully about how to word the next thing I was about to say. "Do you need some sanitary things yet, or not? Or do you have any questions about those kinds of things?" I said under my breath as we walked through the mall back to Ryan.

She looked at me and relief washed over her face. "Okay, so this girl at school says that when you get your period for the first time you don't know. There's no warning signs or anything. Like it just happens, whenever. Like in the middle of the night or at school even. And that there's a lot of blood. Like way more than she imagined there would be."

I nodded thoughtfully, trying to remember how I felt the first time I got my period. "The first time I got mine, I got such a fright. I went to the toilet and I thought I was dying. But just because there's a lot of blood, it doesn't mean you're going to bleed to death or anything, even though sometimes it looks like it."

She nodded, but I wasn't sure I had waylaid her fears and concerns at all. "You know what?" I said. "Let's go buy you some pads, and then you should start carrying one around in your school bag and have some at home. So you're prepared for whenever it happens."

She nodded and smiled at me. "Does it hurt?"

"Mmmm, sometimes. But it's nothing a Tylenol or a hot-water bottle can't fix. We'll get some of those too. And I'll give you my number and you can call me if that happens. I don't mind."

At that, out of the blue, she threw her arms around me and hugged me. It felt weird at first but then, slowly, it started to feel really nice. For some reason, I felt close to her, even though we hardly knew each other. I put my hand on her head and stroked her hair.

"This was pretty cool of my uncle to organize," she said, pulling away.

"He loves you a lot," I said.

"I know." She sounded sad. "We haven't really been getting on that well lately. We used to get on really well, even after Mom died, but now . . . I don't know. I feel so irritated all the time and stuff."

"That's perfectly normal. That's just all the hormones racing around. Sometimes you can feel a bit crazy, but that will also come right."

"I think he also thinks of me like I'm a baby still. When I'm not," she said. "I'm thirteen. I'm not three. And he needs to give me some space too. He's always crowding me. And sometimes I just want to be alone, you know?"

"I can talk to him, if you like?" I asked.

She looked up at me and started nodding. "Okay. He listens to you."

"Mmmmm, I wouldn't say that," I said.

"Are you kidding? You pushed him out of my room! Trust me, he listens to you. He doesn't listen to a lot of people."

"I've gathered that," I said playfully.

"Nah, I guess he's cool. Sometimes," she said and started walking again. "He and my mom were really close. They were twins, you know."

"I didn't know that," I said.

"Their dad used to work a lot, he wasn't around that much, and Gran used to travel a lot too, so when they were kids, they really only had each other—that's what Mom always said anyway."

I listened with great interest now, hoping to gain a better understanding of Ryan.

"Grandpa was very strict too. He used to shout at them if they didn't do well at school and stuff. If they didn't work hard, they weren't allowed friends to play. I think that's why Mom ran away."

"She did?" I asked.

"Only for a few days. I'm not supposed to know that, but I once heard my gran talking about it. She said my mom was going through her 'rebellious stage.' It's weird, I can't imagine my mom as a rebel." Emmy turned and smiled at me.

"Well, when my mom died, I went through a box of old photos and I found this pic of her from when she was seventeen. She had a massive purple Mohawk and a safety pin through her ear. She was a total punk, and if you met her, you would never have guessed it," I said.

Emmy laughed. "You know, my uncle used to have bleached blond hair and an earring. My mom showed me a picture of him from their prom, he looked so lame." She laughed.

"Really?" I said conspiratorially. "Well, at least I know something else about him."

"I'll tell you something else too, but you're not allowed to tell, it was a huge scandal."

At that, I turned around. "Promise."

"So, you know he was engaged once?" she asked.

"*Nooo*, really?"

Emmy nodded. "Her name was Sasha. I didn't really like her. She was a bit weird. She had short red hair and these piercing green eyes. Anyway, she worked with him, and Ryan and my grandpa had a huge fight about it one night. My grandpa said something about 'crapping where you eat.' I didn't really understand it, but he said he was disappointed in Ryan, that he'd given him a company to run and he wasn't running it the right way, or whatever . . ." Emmy talked and I leaned in. This story intrigued me. "And then, his fiancée like cheated on him with this other guy who also ran the company with him—he's a cousin of ours, no one talks to him anymore. But then he and Sasha stole a deal from the Stark company and set up their own business together. It was a really big deal and my mom used to say that Ryan wasn't really the same after that. She broke his heart and betrayed him."

"Really?" I said. This was interesting. This was very interesting indeed, and it certainly gave me some more insights into Ryan.

CHAPTER FIFTY-EIGHT

Ryan

"So?" He got up off the bench he'd been sitting on for over an hour. "Successful?" he asked, looking down at the packets that Emmy was carrying.

Doris nodded at him. "I think we got what we needed, didn't we?" She turned and gave a small smile, and Emmy reciprocated.

It was so good to see Emmy smile again. She hadn't smiled in a while. This was probably what she needed, a female energy in her life, not him all the time. Besides, Doris had this way about her, he was coming to see it. She had this bright and breezy, sometimes silly quality that made him smile. God, she even made him laugh on occasion.

"So, I guess we should all get going then. I still need to take Doris to her car." He looked over at Emmy, and her smile faltered.

"Can't we all do something now?" she asked unexpectedly.

"Something?" He looked at his watch. "It's a school night."

"I'm not six anymore, Ryan. I don't need to be in bed at seven o'clock."

He briefly looked over to Doris, who gave him the slightest nod.

"Okay, but just for a short time. I'm sure Doris doesn't want to spend all evening with us—"

"But I do!" Her voice cut him off and her statement was so firm, so matter-of-fact that it almost made him jump. His stomach lurched, and suddenly his heart was beating just a little bit faster. "What do you want to do?" he asked Emmy.

She shrugged. "I don't know, something fun."

"Fun?" He looked around.

"What about there?" Doris pointed to the big game arcade.

"Cool." Emmy started walking towards it.

He exchanged a quick look with Doris. "Cool," he said and walked after her. He hadn't seen Emmy this happy and relaxed in ages; clearly Doris had the same effect on her as she did on him. Even though he'd been trying really hard to resist it.

They walked into the loud, flashing games arcade and it felt like all of his senses were being assaulted at once. To one side, there was a bowling alley, and to the other side, arcade games were lined up like slot machines, waiting to steal children's money. Across from them was a climbing wall, an indoor ski slope that children were hurtling down in big inflatable tires, and next to that was a . . . a . . .

"Did you know that Doris doesn't know how to ride a bike?" he said, looking over at the indoor cycle track.

"What?" Emmy swung around and looked at her.

"No, don't!" Doris put her hands up over her face. "Don't you dare think about it!"

"Why not? It's the perfect opportunity." He smiled at her playfully.

"Ryan taught me to ride a bike when I was young, he's a really good teacher," Emmy said excitedly.

Doris shook her head and backed away from them both. "No! Not going to happen. I've already almost killed myself once today by falling off a ladder, I'm not in the mood to do that again."

"You won't." Emmy stepped closer to her. "We'll teach you."

Doris stared at Emmy for a while and then looked over at him again. "Fine, but I swear, if I fall, that's it."

He smiled, and then without thinking too much about it, walked up to her and slipped his arm through hers and Emmy's. "Don't worry," he said, "I'll be there to catch you if you fall."

CHAPTER FIFTY-NINE

~~

Poppy

"*I* want those," I said, pointing to the little girl's pink bike.

Emmy laughed. "You can't have fairy wheels!"

"Who says?" I asked a little desperately. "Why not?"

I looked over at Ryan. He seemed to be enjoying this way too much as he wheeled the bike over to me. Emmy was already on a bike, strapping the helmet to her head, ready to ride.

"Can I at least have a helmet?" I asked.

"Here," Ryan said, popping a helmet on my head and fastening the strap below my chin with great care. His fingers came into contact with my skin. For a moment, I let my eyes blink a little longer, just to block out all the sights so I could concentrate on the warm feel of his fingertips as they brushed across me. I opened my eyes. He was staring at me.

"Done," he said softly, almost breathily.

I nodded stupidly, unable to look away. I felt like I was slipping into the lagoon of his eyes. And I was sure that if I looked into them for a second longer, I might find myself drowning. I looked away quickly.

"So," I said, trying to change the mood. "Now what?"

"Well, I would suggest climbing onto the thing first," he said cheekily.

Emmy gave a small laugh.

"Ha, ha, guys. You both think you're so smart cos you can ride, don't ya?" I put my leg over the bike and slid my bum onto the uncomfortable seat. I was glad I was wearing jeans. It gave me a little more padding *there*. In that short minute I'd "successfully" managed to ride a bike the other day, I'd discovered that bike seats weren't exactly comfortable things. In fact, to be crass, they sandpapered your vagina like crazy and I wasn't aware that one could actually get bruises *there!* But one could, as I'd discovered the next day when I'd woken up. The discomfort was comparable to a night of wild sex—except the guy had missed and had repeatedly poked your upper thigh instead.

"Okay . . ." Ryan walked to the back of the bike and placed his hand on my seat. "I'll hold the seat and one of the handlebars, and all you need to do is put your feet up on the pedals and practice balancing."

"Balancing is not my strong point," I said, trying to lift my feet off the ground and onto the pedals.

"I've noticed," he said sarcastically.

"Oh my God," I squeaked when the bike began tipping to the left. "I don't like this one little bit. I don't like this at all."

At that, Emmy let out a laugh.

"What?" I shot her a playful, disapproving look.

"Nothing." She smiled.

"Just try again," Ryan said. "And then, when you've gotten your balance, start pedaling slowly."

"You won't let go, right?" I started to panic.

"I won't let go," he said.

"Promise?" I turned my head around and looked at him. His face was close to mine.

"Promise," he repeated.

"Because I know where you sleep and I know where to get nightshade from," I said, clinging on for dear life as the bike moved forward.

"Now, pedal slowly," he said behind me.

I shook my head and closed my eyes.

"You have to keep your eyes open," Emmy said loudly, in between peals of laughter.

"Pedal . . . you can do it!" he said again.

I started to pedal, slowly at first, trying to keep my balance. His hand was still on one of the handlebars, and I could feel him holding onto the seat. "I'm going to let go of you now," he said.

"NO! Don't." I clutched on tightly. "You said you wouldn't."

"You can do it," Emmy yelled and then gave a loud "*whoop, whoop!*"

And then, just like that, he let go. And, as if my body knew exactly what it was meant to do, I was pedaling. "Oh my God," I shouted excitedly as I felt myself gliding through the air. I was graceful and agile and speedy and athletic and balanced. "I'm doing it, I'm doing it," I gushed excitedly as I expertly took the first corner like the most coordinated person in the world. Step aside, Lance Armstrong, I was winning the Tour de France next year because I was grace and speed and agility and . . . and . . .

"SHIT!" I started to topple. "Oh, crap," I screeched as the bike leaned to the side. It teetered there for a second and then toppled over. I landed on the soft carpeted track and lay there for a while, bike between my legs, looking up at the ceiling. A familiar pair of legs blocked my view and I rolled onto my back and looked up.

Ryan was smiling down at me.

"I don't think I'm meant to ride a bike," I said to him.

He held his hands out for me to take. I did. His hands were so big that when they closed, my entire hand disappeared into his. He pulled me onto my feet with such ease, bringing me to stand in front of him.

"I would say that riding a bike is not your strong point," he said playfully.

"You have to try again." Emmy was next to me, dusting me off. "If at first you don't succeed," she said.

"Try, try and try again," I said. "My mother used to say that to me."

"Mine too," Emmy said with a small smile just as a young kid, without fairy wheels, whizzed past me.

We all turned and looked at him. I sighed.

"Fine, I'll try again." I walked my bike back to the start of the track.

CHAPTER SIXTY

～

Poppy

*W*e walked out of the shopping mall eating ice creams, despite the cold, wintry weather outside. I'd had a great evening; I couldn't remember the last time I'd had such fun. Granted, I hadn't gotten the whole bike riding thing right, and in the end had sat and watched Ryan and Emmy go around the track a few times. I cheered them on from the sidelines, that had been my contribution. We walked to the car and climbed in. I was expecting a comment about how I better not get ice cream all over the car, but Ryan didn't say a word.

"Ryan," Emmy spoke as soon as we'd started driving. "Can you drop me off at home first before fetching Doris's car? I've got a little bit of homework to do before bed."

"Sure." Ryan looked at her in the rear-view mirror. "Tamlin will be there, I'll just call her and let her know you're coming home and ask her to come inside."

"You know, I'm thirteen, I don't need a babysitter inside the house with me anymore. She'll be in the cottage if I need her. I know where she is."

I gave Ryan a little encouraging nod and he agreed. "Okay, fine. But keep the doors locked and don't answer them and—"

"I know what to do," she said, with a smile in her voice.

He smiled back at her in the rear-view mirror. "I know you do. I trust you," he said.

Her face instantly lit up. She sat back, looking happy. She looked like a different child to the one we'd picked up to take bra shopping a few hours ago.

* * *

"Thank you for doing what you did for Emmy tonight," Ryan said after we'd dropped her off at home.

"Please, don't mention it. It's part of my job."

"No, it's not," he said. "I've never done anything like this with any of my other assistants."

"Other assistants?" I asked. It sounded strange to hear him speak of his *other assistants*. "And just how many other assistants have there been?"

"A lot," he admitted.

"A lot? How many is a lot?" I asked.

He shrugged. "I mean, I don't know."

"More than five, but fewer than ten?" For some reason this conversation made me feel a little strange. What exactly was making my stomach churn? *Jealousy?*

He looked at me and shrugged sheepishly.

"More!" I exclaimed loudly. "You've had more than ten?"

He nodded, still sheepish.

"And were they all . . ." I started, but stopped. "Were they?"

"All what?" he asked.

I looked down at the floor and shuffled my foot across the carpet. "Were they all . . . better than me?" I didn't dare make eye contact, lest he see the strange look that was now firmly etched into my face.

"Mmm, not necessarily," he said. "Just different."

"Different?" I looked up at him. "Different how?"

"Well, the last two that I had together—"

"Wait!" I held my hand up to stop him. "You had two? At once?"

He shrugged again casually, as if this was an okay thing. "I hired the one and discovered she couldn't do her job, so hired another one to help her."

My jaw fell open and I stared at him.

"I was desperate," he said defensively.

"Two at once!" I gasped.

"It wasn't as good as I thought it would be . . ." He turned and smiled at me. It was playful and sexy.

I smiled back and then my body started to lean, all on its own. I had no control over it. My arm slid across the center console and rubbed against his elbow. Silence. A sweet, soft silence that seemed warm and familiar.

"She's really sweet, Emmy," I said as we approached our destination.

"She is," he said. "She's been through a lot."

"She has. It's going to be hard for her."

"That's what I'm afraid of, and I don't really know how to make it better."

"You can't make it better," I said sympathetically. "All you can do is be there for her when she needs you."

"I'm trying. But I don't think I'm getting it right."

"She's a teenage girl, Ryan. Most of the things you do are going to be wrong."

"Really?" He looked over at me.

"Yes. Trust me. I know. I was a teenage girl once. We're complicated things, you know."

"So I'm learning," he said.

"You're doing a great job with her," I said to him.

He shook his head. "I don't know. I thought I was, but this year things have changed, she seems angry or—"

"She's going through puberty. She's supposed to be angry. She just needs some space and time and she'll find herself."

He nodded. "Thanks for that. Raising a teenage girl as a single guy wasn't exactly part of my plan, and it's not like it comes with a rule book. I keep thinking that I'm going to mess her up in some way."

"It's a parent's job to mess their kids up in some way," I said. "It builds character."

"And how did your parents mess you up?" he asked.

"Mmmm," I thought about this for a while. "Well, my dad did disappear on my mom and me when I was younger. I'm sure that's affected me in some ways, it's probably the reason I date such losers and idiots."

He laughed. "Losers and idiots?"

"Totally. Put me in a room full of guys and I have this uncanny ability to pick out the one that is totally wrong for me. Rule of thumb, if I'm attracted to someone, it means they're probably bad for me."

"Oh. Really?" His voice had taken on a strange tone.

"Yup," I replied.

"I'm sure there are some exceptions to the rule?" he asked.

"I have yet to meet that exception," I replied. "And you?"

"Me what?"

"Do you also date losers and idiots?" I asked light-heartedly.

There was silence for a moment. "I seem to date dishonest people," he said, and suddenly my mouth went very dry. "People who are fundamentally trying to deceive me."

"That . . . that sounds . . . uh . . . terrible," I stuttered as a wave of guilt crashed through me. I was fundamentally deceiving him, and how the hell would he react when he found out the extent of it? We finally arrived at the construction site and climbed out of his car.

"Will you be okay to drive home alone?" he asked.

"I'll be fine. Thanks."

"Okay, well, I guess that's it. Thanks again for tonight," he said.

"Don't mention it, honestly, it was fun."

"It was." He chuckled. "I don't get to have that much fun these days."

"Well . . . maybe we should see what we can do to change that." I didn't mean to, but as I said it my eyes drifted down to his lips, giving my statement a very flirty feel. Or had that been intentional? *Wait . . . was I deliberately flirting with him?* Oh my God, I was flirting with him.

And he took it. Hook, line, sinker.

"And what would you suggest we do to have . . . fun?" He took a step closer to me.

My lips prickled and my face went hot. "I'm not sure I know you well enough yet to know what you'd be into."

There was a pause. A lull in the conversation. I stared at his lips, waiting for him to speak again. Anticipation growing. And then he finally did, and I wasn't disappointed.

"Well, maybe we can remedy that in some way." And then he walked away. Back to his car.

I climbed into mine and pulled out. I looked at him in the rear-view mirror, my heart thumping in my chest, and suddenly it dawned on me. No, it didn't dawn. Dawn implies something gentle and gradual. This was not gentle and not gradual. This was like a brick smashing into the stomach. I was crushing on my boss, Ryan Stark. I was crushing on him hard, because—surprise, damn surprise—I actually liked him.

Wow!

Breaking news. The big headline . . . *I liked Ryan Stark. A lot.*

CHAPTER SIXTY-ONE

Ryan

riving to work the next day without picking Doris up felt strange. And when he arrived, it felt even stranger to see her sitting there at her desk. But today he was in a good mood, and it was all her doing. He walked towards her desk and she looked up at him and beamed.

"Morning. Do you want me to bring you a cup of coffee?" she asked.

"Uh . . . no, it's okay." Suddenly, the idea of her bringing him a cup of coffee felt strange. "I'll get one myself," he said.

She looked at him and nodded her head; the movement made her hair flick from side to side, and he was mesmerized by it. She looked beautiful this morning. Her amber eyes were particularly gold-looking, and she wore something on her lips that made them shine. He'd thought about those lips all night and wondered why he hadn't just leaned in and kissed them last night when he'd had the perfect opportunity to do so. He wanted to kiss her so badly, but first, he needed to tell her something. He was just about to open his mouth when the phone rang and she answered it.

He walked into his office and sat down. He watched her talk on the phone with a smile, he watched her flick her hair over her shoulder when she hung up, he watched her put her fingers down on the keyboard and type, badly. It was bubbling up inside him, and he wasn't sure he would be able to contain it much longer. He needed to tell her something. He stood up and walked over to her desk just as someone walked past. He greeted them with a small nod and a smile. They did a double take and almost walked into the wall.

"Miss Granger," he said formally. He didn't want anyone to hear they were on first names basis.

She looked up at him. "Yes, Mr. Stark."

"Would you mind coming with me?" he asked.

"Where?"

"I . . . I thought that maybe I could show you how to file the hard copies of the financials." That didn't sound as convincing as he'd wanted it to sound.

"You want to show me how to file?" She looked confused.

He nodded. "Did you even know we had a filing room?" he asked.

She shook her head, "No. I didn't."

"Well, don't you think that's something you should know?" he asked. "As my assistant. Because you will need to file things in it."

"Uh . . . sure. I guess it would be good to know where it is." She stood up, straightening the creases in her shirt.

He couldn't help but be transfixed by her hands, as they ran over her curves, flattening the material against her waist.

"Okay, let's go," she said.

He was going to take her to the filing room alright . . . only, he had absolutely no intention of showing her how to file. He had every intention of showing her something else entirely . . .

CHAPTER SIXTY-TWO

Poppy

*T*he filing room was just that, a massive room filled, floor to ceiling, with rows and rows of files. I looked around and sighed; this definitely looked like something I would have no idea how to do.

"So what do you want me to do with these files, then?" I turned and asked, as he closed the door behind us.

"Nothing. I don't want you to do anything with the files." He stepped closer to me.

"Well, then why are we in the filing room?"

"I wanted to thank you," he said.

"For what?"

"Emmy went to school this morning without a fight—in fact, I haven't seen her in such a good mood in a while," he said.

"It's my pleasure." I smiled up at him.

And then, without warning, he took a step closer to me and, in one swift movement, pulled me into his arms. His arms were huge and I felt completely dwarfed by them. He pulled me in tightly and my head connected with his large, hard chest. I froze against it.

"You're hugging me?" My voice was muffled against his chest.

"Yes," he replied. His tone was soft.

"Didn't you say no hugging once?" I teased.

"I did," he said. "I said many things, once upon a time."

I breathed him in and he smelt good. Very good. He was warm, and the hug felt comforting. I turned my head and put my cheek to his chest. I could hear his heart beating; it sounded fast. I could feel his chest rising and falling gently every time he breathed, like small waves ebbing and flowing in the sea. I synced my breath with his and held onto him.

"So how long do we hug for?" I asked after what felt like hours of holding onto him.

I felt him shrug against my body. "I have absolutely no idea."

"You seem to not know a lot of things, these days," I said.

His arms loosened and drifted up to my shoulders. He pulled my body away slightly, so he could look in my eyes.

"You seem to have that effect on me." He brushed a strand of hair out of my face. "I seem to forget a lot of things when I'm around you."

"Is that a good or a bad thing?" His eyes had zoned in on mine and I felt something strange and new bubbling between us.

He shrugged again and smiled. "I have no idea yet."

"When will you know?" I asked, leaning in. I hoped he was going to kiss me this time. Hoped that he didn't leave me high and dry, like last night . . .

But as luck would have it, his cell phone rang and he answered it.

CHAPTER SIXTY-THREE

Ryan

*H*e walked out of the filing room and back into his office. He needed to have this conversation behind closed doors as it usually ended up becoming heated.

"Brian," he said into the phone when he saw who was calling.

"Hi, I just wanted to talk to you after that board meeting, alone. Without Charles interrupting," Brian Rautenbach said.

"Sure." Ryan sat down at his desk and waited for what was to come.

"Ryan, we don't build malls."

Ryan sighed. "I know."

"So why are we?" Brian asked.

They had been down this road so many times before. Ryan kept silent.

"I'll tell you why, because Charles Grey said so. Because he has an ulterior motive for doing it. Your dad started this company to give people holidays. That is what we know about. I proposed an alternative to the mall and I'm telling you, my idea about the short-stay holidays—closer to the city, weekend getaways—will work."

Ryan rubbed his forehead. "Maybe you're right, Brian. But it's too late now. We're building the mall."

"Not necessarily," Brian said.

At that, Ryan raised his head. "Oh?" he asked. His interest had been piqued.

"I spoke to Omnicor Developments, and they said they would be happy to take over the project. We would get our money back, and some more. They were looking to build a mall in that area anyway, and we've broken ground and done the grunt work."

"Omnicor said they would take it?"

"Yes."

Ryan looked around his office, deep in thought.

"Ryan, you know why I joined this company all those years ago?" Brian asked.

"Why?"

"It was your father's passion. He was all about delivering the best holiday memories to families. That was the heart of his business."

Ironic, Ryan thought, that he hadn't exactly delivered the best family memories to his own children when he was alive.

"I know he was a hard man, but he had a vision and a passion. God, I still have that, and I would hate to see this company building soulless malls when we could be, *should be*, doing something else."

There was a pause as Ryan took it all in. His father had been passionate, he'd give him that. Ryan, however, didn't have that same kind of passion for what his father had been doing—maybe that's why he'd let this mall happen.

"God, you should be running this company, you know that," he said.

"Think about it, okay? It's not too late. You know this isn't right." And with that, Brian hung up.

Ryan put the phone down on his desk and stared at it. *Do the right thing*. He hung his head; they had sunk all their money into this mall and if they could recoup that, maybe it was for the best. But Charles Grey was very convincing, he talked a good game and, to be honest, Ryan didn't really think he had the energy to fight him on this. And if he did fight him, he was sure Charles wouldn't hesitate to have him thrown out of the company and replace the name Stark with Grey. Just as he was thinking about him, an SMS lit up his screen. He stared at it. *How the hell did this man know?*

Charles Grey: Rumor has it that our friend talked to Omnicor.

He looked around the room quickly. This had actually been Charles Grey's office, once upon a time. Had the guy left cameras and bugs in it?

Ryan: I wouldn't know anything about that.

Charles Grey: Ryan, don't be sentimental about this. It's a business decision. Use your head this time.

Ryan: This time?

Charles Grey: I'm sure you don't need reminding of what happened last time you forgot your head and let your emotions get in the way.

The fucking asshole. Ryan was furious now. Just because this guy knew him from the time he was in diapers, it didn't give him any right to talk to him like this. Like his father had. He pulled himself together and typed a message back.

Ryan: Noted.

He put his phone down and his computer screen lit up this time. He was being bombarded by technology right now. He looked at his screen, where a Google Calendar reminder was blinking at him.

"Shit!" He stared at it. He'd totally forgotten about the charity function this evening. He loathed those events, where all the important business and society people gathered wearing fancy clothes and drinking champagne while acting like they actually gave a shit about anyone less fortunate than themselves, anyone who had some dreaded disease or disability, or who lived on the fringes of society. He could quite happily miss this event—except he couldn't. He'd accepted months ago. A knock on the door made him look up; she was standing there in the doorway. *She.*

"Sorry to interrupt," she said sweetly. "I just saw a reminder come up on your calendar for tonight. I don't know if you saw it?"

"I did," he said.

"Is there anything you need me to do for you for tonight?" she asked quietly.

"I really hate these things," he said, sitting back in his chair.

"Why?" she asked. "Isn't it nice to do things for others?"

"Trust me, this evening has less to do with charity and more to do with being seen out and about in the latest designer outfits, eating fancy food, drinking expensive champagne and socializing."

She shrugged. "Doesn't sound that bad." She smiled and started turning away.

A thought hit him.

"Miss Granger," he called after her. "Come in, please."

She walked up to his desk and sat down.

"What are you doing tonight, Doris?" He called her by her first name when they were out of earshot of everyone.

"Nothing. Waiting for you to finish work, I guess."

He cleared his throat nervously. "Uh . . . would you like to come with me tonight? As my assistant, it would be helpful to me." He tried not to smile, but he couldn't help it.

She smiled back at him. "Sure, if it would be helpful to you?" Her voice sounded light and flirty, like it had last night.

"It would be," he said. "Very."

"Should I bring a notepad this time, so I can take notes?" she asked.

"Maybe not a notepad, but you can wear high heels this time, if you want," he teased.

"High heels, I'll make a note of that. Anything else?"

"Yes, it's very formal, black tie, that kind of thing. Do you have something to wear?"

"Actually, I do," she said.

"It can't have shoulder pads and purple ruffles," he said quickly.

She laughed. God, her laugh was nice.

"It doesn't," she said.

"Okay, we'll stop at your place on the way so you can get ready," he suggested.

She nodded at him. "Is that all?"

"For now," he said.

"For now?" She looked at him and smiled. Sexy, flirty, cute.

"For now," he repeated slowly, not caring that his voice had taken on a low, husky tone and that his eyes were probably telling her exactly what he was thinking.

She blushed. "Okay, I better go. I have work to do, and I wouldn't want my boss to get angry if I don't finish."

"Wouldn't want that," he said.

She walked out of the room and closed the door behind her. As soon as she was gone, he felt her absence acutely, on a physical level. He was in trouble here. He knew it. He was in danger of liking Doris bloody Granger way more than he should like her. He felt he was on the verge of putting aside all the beliefs that he'd clung to for the last five years, for her. The beliefs that had been drummed into him by his father: *don't mix business with pleasure*. But there was still something inside him, a small voice telling him not to cross that line. The voice was getting softer by the day, but it was still there. Somewhere in the back of his mind, reminding him, stopping him every time he reached that point with her. He wondered how much longer he would be able to listen to it, though? Because it was getting harder by the second.

CHAPTER SIXTY-FOUR

~

Poppy

*T*here was something strangely sexy about being half naked with Ryan Stark only a few feet away. Sure, we were separated by my bathroom door, but still. I'd climbed out of my clothes and was standing in my underwear. I leaned against the door to see if I could hear him, and when I could, the desire to walk out like that, wearing almost nothing, was overwhelming. But I didn't.

I stepped into my dress; it was the only smart dress I owned, also a prop from the TV show. This one was at least decent, maybe the only decent thing I'd worn on the show. After my character had viciously been killed off, they'd decided to bring her back for one episode only, in which I'd come back as a ghost in a terrifying dream. The dress I'd worn in the ghostly dream sequence, where I had nearly choked at the amount of smoke and dry ice they had pumped into the air to make the atmosphere mysterious and terrifying, was a long, black dress. I think the wardrobe department had intended it to be scary, like something

Morticia Addams might have worn, but actually it was more sexy than scary. It was black, skin-tight and long, with a low, swooping neckline.

I turned my attention to my make-up. Since the show had been so low budget, they hadn't been able to afford a make-up artist, so the actors had done their own. I'd gotten quite good at it over the time. I picked up my cosmetic bag and started on my winged black eyeliner, and once that was done, I moved onto my red lipstick. I ran a brush through my long hair and let it fall naturally over my shoulders. My hair was thick and wavy and usually very badly behaved. If I tried to do things with it, it just rebelled like a defiant teenager.

I looked at myself in the mirror. I looked good, I just wondered if I looked good enough for a fancy charity event. I'd never been to such a thing in my life before. The whole idea was so foreign to me. And to make it worse, Ryan looked good tonight. Really, really good. I'd picked up a suit for him—no washing powder this time—and he looked amazing in it. I opened the bathroom door and walked out. Ryan sat on the edge of my bed and as soon as I walked out, he looked up. The look on his face stole my breath. I froze to the spot. He looked shocked, and I wasn't sure if this was a good thing, or a bad thing.

"Do I . . . uh, look okay?" I asked.

He started nodding his head. The silence was deafening.

"Is it bad?" I asked, pulling at my dress.

"No! No!" He stepped forward quickly and started shaking his head from side to side. "No."

"Uh . . . no, I do look okay, or no, I don't look okay?"

"No, you look good," he quickly said. "You look very good."

CHAPTER SIXTY-FIVE

~

Ryan

*G*ood. Was he joking?

She didn't look good. In fact, she looked nothing like *good*. Her look was so NOT good right now that he didn't think he knew what to do with himself. There was nothing good about any of this. At all.

She looked . . . *fuck*, she looked amazing. Sophisticated. Beautiful. Elegant. Everything about her right now was *not* good. Except for the feelings rushing through him, those felt good. Feelings that had been lying dormant for so long were suddenly stirring, like something waking up after a long, cold hibernation.

"You look . . . beautiful," he said. His voice was almost a whisper.

She smiled at him and blushed. "Thanks," she said quietly.

"No, you don't look beautiful. You look amazing," he continued, taking a step closer to her.

"You look amazing too," she said. Her eyes swept over his body.

"We should go." He extended his arm for her.

"Wait," she said quickly. "I have to water my plants."

"Can't you water them later?" He looked at his watch and realized they were almost running late.

"No!" she said. Her voice was fast and desperate-sounding.

He looked at her. This seemed very important to her. This looked like something that she needed to do. "Okay." He nodded.

She walked to the kitchen area and fetched a small watering can. He looked around her apartment again; they would be here all night if she watered them all. He started counting but gave up when he reached sixty.

"Let me help you," he offered.

"Uh, that's kind of you. But this is usually something I like to do alone. It's sort of a—" she shrugged, and suddenly looked like the saddest person in the world. He felt his heart break.

"They were my mom's," she said in a voice so small it was almost inaudible. "My mom was a florist. They're all I really have left of her."

He gave her a reassuring smile and sat back down on the bed. "I'll wait for you. Take as long as you need."

"Thanks," she said.

He watched as she moved from plant to plant, gently filling each one with just the right amount of water. As she went, she ran her hands over their leaves, dusting them or just touching them, almost with affection. Almost as if she knew each and every one of them, and was greeting them all. He watched, fascinated by the way she moved, the way she did it all with such care and thought and he no longer cared if they were going to be late. She bent down to smell one of the flowers and then stopped, turned around and smiled at him. Her auburn hair tumbled across her face and settled onto her shoulder.

"There's another watering can in the cupboard," she said softly.

He shot off the bed. She was letting him into her world and he liked the feeling. "Sure." He raced over to the cupboard and fetched the can. He filled it up with water and raced back to her.

"Just a little bit," she said. "Just so the soil looks moist. You can drown them, if you're not careful."

He nodded and tipped the can gently; he wanted to do this right. He wanted to do this perfectly, because this was important to her and, for that reason, it felt very important to him too. He started with the plants on her windowsill. He carefully splashed one, taking great care to give it just the right amount. There were so many that he had to walk back to the kitchen to fill the can again. Strangely, the simple repetition of the task felt somewhat soothing and relaxing. He felt content and, when it was over, enjoyed a small sense of accomplishment. They stood side-by-side looking at the room.

"Thanks," she said, nudging him with her shoulder playfully.

"Pleasure." He nudged her back, but instead of moving his arm away from hers, he kept it there, gently pressed against hers. They stood there for a while, looking out over the plants together, shoulders touching, and he felt something he hadn't felt in a while: *happiness*. But this sense of happiness was suddenly shattered when he heard a familiar sound. He spun around and looked behind him.

"Where the hell did he come from?" He looked down at the pigeon, who seemed to have appeared out of thin air.

"Oh, he does that sometimes, it's very strange," she admitted. "That's why I've named him Houdini."

He laughed. "Houdini the pigeon!"

"I contemplated naming him after you actually, since you saved his life." She smiled at him, and he found himself completely transfixed once again.

"I'm very glad you didn't name him after me," he said, extending his arm for her to take.

This time she took it and they walked out together.

CHAPTER SIXTY-SIX

∽

Poppy

*T*he banqueting hall at the fancy hotel was full of round tables draped in velvety white cloth. Huge, fragrant cascading floral centerpieces graced every table. Ivy, roses and hydrangeas arranged in tall crystal vases. Low-hanging chandeliers, waiters in black suits carrying silver platters of canapés, an orchestra playing classical music in the corner and . . . I was so out of my depth here. I looked at all the foreign-looking people, clad in the best clothes; shiny, happy, bejeweled. *I did not fit in here and, suddenly, I felt nervous.*

"Don't worry, I feel uncomfortable here too," I heard Ryan say next to me as we walked in, arm in arm. "We won't stay for long."

I turned and nodded at him. The soft light in the room was making his eyes seem even bluer tonight. Blue like those tropical lagoons. I kept looking, falling into the lagoon, trying to stop myself, but I couldn't. It was so warm in there. So inviting. I caught myself before I went under.

"So . . ." I looked away from him. "What's the agenda for tonight?"

"Well," he scoured the room. "We usually stand around talking while drinking some things. There will be some kind of auction where we'll buy more things—and we have to buy things, since there seems to be some invisible tally kept."

"What kind of things?" I asked.

"Mmmm, things you don't need. Things like fancy sets of golf clubs and artwork. The money will then go to some charity that no one here really cares about, and then after we've had our cocktails and done our chatting we'll all go home and that will be it," he said.

"Okay," I said, reaching for a glass of champagne as it floated past me on a silver tray. I grabbed one for Ryan too. "So, shall we drink to it then?" I asked, as I passed it over to him. He took it and looked at me over the glass.

"What are we drinking to?" he asked.

"Mmmm," I looked around the room. "To not going home with an unnecessary set of golf clubs." I held the champagne glass up and he laughed. A genuine laugh. The kind that takes over your whole face. I also laughed. *God, this was strange!* I'd come to work for this man over a week ago, during which, for the most part, he seemed to have hated me, but today we were hugging and going to charity events and looking at each other like *this . . .*

This . . .

His blue eyes melted into mine and I found myself transported. Transported to some place where time and gravity and noise and other people no longer existed. Where the entire world and all that was in it faded away until it was just us. Standing in an empty room. Standing opposite each other. Standing, but not on firm ground anymore. Floating just above the floor, being pulled together by some invisible force . . .

"Ryan!" An unwelcome voice cut through the haze we now found ourselves in.

For a moment, we didn't move. We still wanted to hold onto the surreal world that we were a part of.

"Ryan," the voice said again, and this time, the bubble popped.

He turned away from me and started talking to the man. A sudden, acute sense of loss stabbed me in the gut and twisted my insides into knots. It was such a physical feeling that I had to excuse myself and go to the bathroom. I needed a moment to decompress. Like deep sea divers do when they come back up to the surface. But it was too late for me, because I already had the bends. I had come to the surface too soon, and now my head was spinning.

CHAPTER SIXTY-SEVEN

✎

Poppy

*A*fter a few minutes in the bathroom, I started to feel somewhat normal. I walked out and scanned the crowd for Ryan. It didn't take long to find him, he was the best-looking man in the room, by a mile. He was talking to someone else this time. Two people. I looked at one of them and . . .

Short red hair. Green eyes that pierced right through you . . . *OMG*, I knew exactly who that was. I recognized her immediately from Emmy's description. It was his ex, Sasha—and judging by Ryan's body language, his stiffened shoulders, tight jaw, the way he was clenching and unclenching his fists at his sides, he did not want to be talking to her. And then, looking smug as fuck, she held her hand out and showed him a ring. She smiled and then kissed the man next to her. That had to be the cousin, the one who'd betrayed him. I stepped closer. I didn't want to be seen, but I wanted to hear what they were saying.

"Wedding planned for next year . . . Hawaii . . . honeymoon in the Maldives . . . blah, blah, blah," she gushed. It was highly irritating and, on Ryan's behalf, I wanted to punch her in the face. "Alone again . . . no date . . ." I heard. It was said with a savage tone to it. "All work and no play . . ." she started saying.

And that's when I knew what I could do to help him. I flipped my hair, thrust my head into the air and walked over to him. Improv 101, ladies and gentlemen.

"Darling," I said in a British accent, which I don't know why I'd chosen, but I just did. I slipped my arm around Ryan's back and pulled him closer. "Oh God, you would think the barman would know what a Clos de Griffier Vieux Cognac is, but I guess not. Remember, like the one we drank on the Sky Deck at the Burj Khalifa last month, except they served it with those monstrous beluga caviar hors d'oeuvres in the oyster shells, because you know what they're like in Dubai, they don't care about silly things like them being on the endangered species list. I mean, my brother-in-law bought my sister that white tiger for her birthday, for heaven's sake. It was quite sweet how he wrapped it in that Hermès scarf, though," I laughed. Well, my strange character laughed. "God, that was such a lovely getaway, although I don't think I'll be flying first class on Etihad again, I mean their in-flight entertainment system was terrible. I definitely think we should go Emirates next time. Also, the shopping at Abu Dhabi airport wasn't great—I mean they were selling last season's YSL there—but, I suppose, if you want to do good airport shopping, the only place to be is Zurich. But the weather is so terrible at this time of year . . ." I was talking and drawing from the telenovela. Especially from the lines that Esmée, the gold-digging wife of Ramona González's boss, had spoken after she'd jetted around the world having an affair with an Arab sheikh. I didn't even know what half the stuff meant. I hadn't been out of South Africa, let alone eaten caviar in the Burj Khalifa. But I continued, "I guess Hamad airport in Doha does have that lovely Cartier shop where you bought me that divine necklace. *Oh gosh*," I turned and gasped as I looked at them, acting as if I hadn't even seen them standing there. "Oh God," I gushed, "how embarrassing, I didn't even see you there. And here's me, going on a whole pow-wow. Darling," I turned to Ryan, "you must introduce me to these people."

Ryan looked at me, and his eyes widened. I could tell it was taking him a bit of time to catch onto what was going on. So I jumped in and did it myself.

"Beatrice Pemberton-Buckley," I said, extending my hand. I was almost bursting with laughter at the sheer skill with which I'd chosen that ridiculous name. But it did sound aristocratic. And that was the point.

"Uh . . . Sasha." The redhead took my hand and shook it. "And this is my fiancé, Murray. We just got engaged."

"Oh, how divine." I turned her hand over in mine. "And look at that darling little diamond. Isn't it cute?"

Sasha looked at me and her eyes widened, as if she had no idea what to say. That was the point, though. Beatrice Pemberton-Buckley was a bulldozer of upper-crustiness. "Where are you getting married?" I asked, even though I already knew the answer to that.

"Hawaii,'" she said.

"Oooh," I winced. "Do people still go there?"

She looked at me blankly.

"I mean, hasn't it become a bit pedestrian these days? What

with all those loud Americans flocking to it? Doesn't it have a Disneyland there? A friend of ours just got married on the Amalfi coast in Italy. What a little slice of heaven that was, although I do still think I prefer the Riviera." I laughed and leaned in. "Call me a traditionalist, I guess." I leaned towards Ryan. "I mean, if I got married, I've always loved the idea of a winter wedding, you know? Like in Verbier, or St. Moritz—mind you, I'm such a klutz on a ski slope. Last year when I was in Aspen I broke my ankle on the first day!" I laughed again. God, I was irritating, and smug. Shit, this was fun. "I just spent the rest of my holiday in the spa with one of those Kardashian sisters. God, what was her name? I get them all so confused, they all look the same, don't they?"

Sasha and Murray blinked at me. Rapidly. They looked utterly speechless, like the cat had gotten their tongues and run far, far away with them. *Well, let's give them something to fucking talk about.* And so I leaned in, and kissed him. I had meant it to be a peck on the lips, but the second our lips touched, something happened. *Everything happened.*

Everything around us dissolved. It blurred. And like condensation slipping down the edge of a glass, we melted. We slipped. We fell over the edge and down into the abyss as our lips touched. Cold and hot and fuzzy around the edges. His lips and the warm breath coming out of them were all I could feel in the entire world. I felt dizzy, swaying on my feet as if the floor had spun away from us. Our kiss was soft at first. Lips dancing across each other's, just a warm, gentle breeze to begin with. But then his lips pushed into mine, harder. The force of them ignited a fire, a heat that exploded in my face and traveled down my body into my legs and toes. This was the kind of kiss that caused earthquakes. That caused the very foundations to rock and shake and crumble. I parted my lips, waiting for the warm wetness of his tongue. Waiting for it to caress mine. It did. And it stole my breath. It stole everything. My pulse raced, my heart exploded and I wanted to drink him in, to consume him, every centimeter of him. In the back of my head somewhere, I knew we were still in a room full of people. But I didn't care. All I cared about was his tongue, his lips and his hand on my lower back. His fingers splayed, kneading and digging into my flesh through the thin material of my dress. But it was too little, I wanted more, and I could feel he wanted it too.

We broke away and stared into each other's eyes, and then I nodded at him.

"Yes," I whispered.

He nodded back and took me by the hand, weaving through the crowd, pushing open a door, walking into a reception, pulling out a credit card. "Any room," he said, digging his fingers into my palm with urgency. "One night . . . checking in now . . ." he said.

And then he pulled me across the room again, pressing elevator buttons, the doors opening with a ping and closing, and then . . . we were alone.

Alone for the first time since the start of our kiss.

CHAPTER SIXTY-EIGHT

～

Ryan

That voice in the back of his head had finally shut the hell up.

Her lips were hot. They tasted of lipstick and champagne and salt, and he wanted more of them. The elevator doors had closed, he looked up at the lights of the floors. Floor six. He estimated they had only a few seconds, but he was going to make the most of them.

He grabbed her face between his hands and pressed her lips to his. This kiss had been years in the making, or so it felt. His hand traveled around the back of her head, he laced his fingers into the soft hair at the base of her neck. His fingers tightened in her hair and she gasped against his mouth, opening hers slightly, giving him a chance to push the tip of his tongue between her lips. He let the tip tease her for a second, while she shivered in his arms, and then he tilted her head to the side and pushed her mouth open. Their tongues slid over each other, as if they belonged together. Soft, wet, warm. The feeling ignited a million sensations that had been dormant until now. He gripped the back of her neck, driving deeper into her mouth and then . . .

Ting!

He pulled away quickly as the elevator doors opened. He looked at her. Out of breath. Her red lipstick was smeared across her face. He touched his lips and pulled his fingers away; they were also stained red from her lipstick. She'd left her mark on him. They stared into each other's eyes, chests rising and falling together, even though they were apart. Without hesitation, he grabbed her by the hand and led her down the passage. They had barely said a word to each other since the kiss in the banqueting hall. They didn't need to. Her eyes told him that she wanted him as much as he wanted her. And the way she kissed him, the way her lips felt against his, told him that she needed him as urgently as he needed her. He struggled with the key card in the door, mainly because his hands were sticky with sweat. Finally, he pushed the door open. He grabbed her around the waist and pushed her in. Not wanting his hands to be anywhere else but on her body, he kicked the door shut with his foot. It slammed, loudly. But the sound of her breathing, coming out fast and furious as he gripped her waist and walked her into the wall, was even louder.

A frenzied energy built up inside him as he kissed her and started pulling up her dress.

"Hurry," she said breathily.

And he obeyed her; as soon as he could, he put his hand on the bare skin of her legs, splaying his fingers, digging them into her flesh. He'd wanted to touch her like this since that night he'd taken the thorns out of her foot. And now, he was getting the chance to and he wasn't going to waste it. Her skin was hot to the touch as he trailed his hand up her thigh and helped her out of her panties. His lips left her mouth, his tongue moved down her neck, over her collarbones, stopping momentarily to kiss the indentation between them, and then down to the plunging neckline of her dress. He took the material between his teeth and pulled it down even further, exposing the tops of her breasts. His hand left her face as he slid his fingers under the strap of her dress and pulled it down until the left side of her dress slipped open. He quickly went to work on her bra strap, pulling it down in the same way as the dress, until her naked breast was exposed. He stopped and looked at it. Looked at her. She was beautiful. Even more beautiful than he'd imagined she would be.

She arched her back towards him, thrusting her breast towards his face. It was a clear invitation. He lowered his head, placed it on her chest and breathed in her scent. Sweet. Sticky. Floral and salty. He kissed her there. He licked off the fine mist of perspiration that coated her skin. But he didn't pull his tongue away. He left it there, connected to her skin, and dragged it across her. Dragged it up the side of her breast, dragged it underneath, where her breast ended and her ribcage began. He teased her like this for a while, dragging his tongue closer and closer to her nipple, but never touching it. Grazing it. Sweeping past it until her panting told him she couldn't take much more of the teasing. He took her in his mouth, and at the same time, he slipped his hand under her panties.

She let out a tiny yelp. Pleasure, not pain, as he skillfully worked her with his hand, and with his mouth. He opened his eyes and looked up at her face. Her head was back, her eyes were closed and her mouth was open, gasping for air, as if she was a fish that had been taken out of water. She raised her hands above her head, clawed the wall with her nails, as if she was looking for something to hold onto. She rocked her hips back and forth in circular motions as he increased the speed and flicked his tongue across her nipple.

Suddenly, she cried out and her whole body stiffened. She froze, dead still, and didn't make a sound. He could see the physical waves traveling through her. Starting at his fingertips, sweeping into her belly, causing her ribs to tighten, her breasts to harden and heave, her neck and jaw to clench and a flush of redness to light up her cheeks. Then he felt her body soften, crumple. He grabbed her as she started slipping down the wall.

But he didn't want her like this, up against a wall. He took her by the hand and led her to the bed. He wanted them both naked, so he pulled his jacket off and tossed it to the floor. He started unbuttoning his shirt and she watched with anticipation, until it was off. He stared at her dress, willing her to take it off. She gave him a tiny nod and then pulled the other strap off her shoulder; the dress fell with a soft thud, pooled on the floor at her feet. She stepped out of it, then kicked her high heels across the floor. His eyes drifted down to her panties. They'd been pushed to the side, exposing just a little bit of her.

He grappled with his belt buckle and removed it in one swift movement. He tugged at his trousers and let them fall. They stood there in their underwear, looking at each other, waiting with anticipation for what would come next.

CHAPTER SIXTY-NINE

~

Poppy

I was so hot I was melting. My cheeks burned and tingled and a knot tightened and throbbed in my stomach.

God, he was good. And God he looked good in his underwear. And he wanted me. I could see it in his eyes. I could feel it in his tongue, his hands, his mouth and the way he'd made me come.

He stepped closer to me. His eyes locked with mine but he said nothing. He didn't need to. I reached around and unclipped my bra, letting it fall on the floor. I put my hands on his waist and then moved them down to his underwear, the piece of material that stood between us. As I started slipping them down, he reached out and did the same to mine. They fell at the same time and then, we were completely naked. Nothing now stood in the way of our two bodies coming together.

He leaned in. Put his thumb over my lips and ran it over them. His lips came back down on mine. This time, he pulled my lip into his mouth, sucked on it, then bit it gently. Letting go, his tongue moved to my neck; down, and then up. He pulled my ear lobe into his mouth, and I giggled at the sensation. He chuckled into my ear, the low tone of the chuckle and the hot breath playing on my skin, causing a tingle to sweep through me, head to toe.

He ran his hands through my hair, pulling strands between his fingers and letting them fall back onto my shoulders. The feeling of hands in my hair felt so intimate. I closed my eyes and savored the feeling. And then, without warning, he tugged my hair back, exposing my neck once more. He brought his lips back down to my bare shoulders, nuzzled his face into the crook of my neck, kissed and blew on it until I couldn't take the anticipation anymore. I wrapped my hands around the back of his head, laced my fingers through his hair and guided his head down towards my breasts again. The power that he wielded over me, right now, in this moment, was like nothing I'd ever experienced before.

He walked me backward towards the bed and pushed. I fell onto it, totally naked, completely exposed. Laid out bare in front of him. I looked up at him; it was the first time I'd seen him naked. My eyes swept over his body. I took him all in, every single detail of him. And then he climbed onto the bed and crawled on top of me. Neither of us had said a word yet since leaving the banqueting hall. But then he spoke.

"On?" He was looking at my tattoo, a confused expression plastered on his face.

"Shit!" I covered my face with my hands. "Long story. Embarrassing story. Involving a boy . . . I was young . . . it was . . ." I shook my head.

"Cute," he said with a smile, and then kissed me again.

This time it was uncontrollable, so animalistic that we lost ourselves in the frenzy.

"I want you so badly," he rasped against my mouth, in between his breaths.

I pulled away and looked him in the eye. I didn't think I needed to say anything back to him, the heat in my cheeks, the lust in my eyes, I was sure my intentions were being communicated very clearly. I parted my legs and he slipped between them. His body was hard and heavy and crushed me into the mattress. An overwhelming burning sensation churned and bubbled deep inside me and I knew there was only one way to satisfy it. I wanted to feel him. I lifted my hips, inviting him in. He accepted the invitation.

I closed my eyes and let the sensations rush through me. The dizzying, mind-numbing feelings that pulsed and throbbed inside me. They were intoxicating and as powerful as any drug. He was slow at first, tentative even, as if he was exploring a new place. But once he'd familiarized himself with it, with *me*, he picked up pace until we were both rocking together in perfect unison. His breathing was getting faster, mine was getting erratic, and I was struggling to get air into my lungs with his weight pressed down on me. I felt confined, but free. Our movements escalated, became wild and uninhibited, and my grasp on reality seemed to slip away. We were no longer on a bed, in a hotel room—we were elsewhere. In our own magical world, where no one else existed but us.

Suddenly, my whole body jerked and, before I knew it, he'd hoisted me onto his lap. I opened my eyes and looked at him. We were nose to nose, mouth to mouth, and because I was looking into his eyes, I could see the exact moment when he tipped. His blue eyes glazed over and his pupils dilated. He looked so vulnerable, so penetrable, and in that moment, all his defenses were down. He was laying himself bare in front of me. This was the most intimate moment of my life, being able to watch him in this way and knowing that I had taken him there. Moments later, I felt it too. My whole body exploded.

Every single muscle in my body tensed up as I experienced a release like I'd never experienced before. I closed my eyes and everything in my head and behind my eyes went white and fuzzy. I felt myself losing control, I heard myself saying his name.

He gripped me tightly and held on as he moaned long and loud in my ear. And when it was all over, we stayed there like that. Covered in sweat, my hair sticking to his face, my legs locked around his waist, him still inside me. And in that moment, I felt like I didn't want this to end.

CHAPTER SEVENTY

～

Poppy

*W*e lay on the bed together looking up at the ceiling. We'd turned on the fan to cool ourselves down and we watched in silence as the blades spun around and around. The sheets were tussled like they are in the movies after the couple has just had wild sex. Strewn half on the bed, half on the floor, stained with sweat and red lipstick and smelling of lust. I heard him stir next to me and I looked over at him.

"So, what was that earlier, with Sasha and Murray?" he asked me as I lay there naked in the bed.

I rolled over onto my side and looked at him. "Do you think they bought it?"

He raised himself onto his elbow and looked at me. "NO! I don't. I don't think they bought a single syllable of it."

"What? Why?" I sat up.

He laughed. "It was ridiculous! In fact, I think they suspect that I might be dating a mad person right now."

"You're wrong," I argued playfully. "That was good improv there."

He laughed again. "Good? Um . . . sure, like the shopping in which airport?"

"Zurich," I quickly added. I smiled at him. "You really think they didn't buy it?"

He shook his head. "Not a single word, but the sentiment was very . . ." He stopped talking and looked at me.

"Very what?"

"Sweet. It was very sweet that you wanted to rush in there and . . ." It looked like he was searching for the word.

"Protect you from their douchiness?" I offered.

He nodded. "Their douchiness . . ." He said the word as if he was thinking about it. "So, I'm assuming then that you know who they are, if you felt it necessary to run in and protect me?"

"Um . . . a little birdie may have told me the story," I said.

He nodded at me. "The little birdie should have known that that was a private story," he mumbled thoughtfully.

"So, you guys were engaged?" I asked, my fingers threading through his. I looked down at his hands—he had such good hands. Strong. Perfect. Smooth. And they felt really good on my naked body.

"It was a long time ago and clearly it was a mistake," he said. There was a pause as he looked at me seriously. "And you. You ever been engaged?"

I laughed. "Nope. Not me. Haven't even come close. Longest relationship was probably six months—"

He pushed the sheet down and I shivered as cool air rushed over me. His fingertips traced a line down my stomach and then stopped and circled my tattoo. "Was that the relationship that ended in this tragic piece of tattoo art?"

I giggled. "No! That was my high school boyfriend for all of five minutes. His name was Leon. I tried to get it removed, but, God, it is sore. I mean, really, really sore."

He laughed. "So now you just have the word 'on' tattooed on your hip?"

"Basically," I said, raising my head and looking down at it.

"You could tattoo the word 'off' here." He ran his fingers from one of my hip bones to the other and drew circles around my tattoo. I gasped. My stomach muscles tightened and I raised my hips off the bed just a little.

"And become a human plug point?" I asked playfully. "Turn me on, turn me off?"

He lowered his lips to my hip and kissed it. "Are you on or off right now?" he asked.

"Mmmm," I mumbled, "I think I might be on." The sensation of his tongue across my stomach was ticklish and sexy all at the same time.

"Again?" he whispered against my stomach. But then he stopped, put his head on my stomach and sighed. "As much as I would like to flip the switch again, I'm afraid I really do need to get back home. I haven't spent a night away from Emmy before—"

"Sure! Of course, I totally understand," I said, raising my body off the bed.

He sat up slowly and then suddenly looked like he was disengaging from me.

"What?" I asked.

"I come with baggage, you know. And if you didn't want to, I mean, if that seems too much for you, I would get it."

"I like your baggage," I said quickly.

He turned. "I think my baggage likes you too."

"She's likeable baggage," I said. "Well, I guess we shouldn't really be calling her baggage."

"No!" He turned quickly. "She's not. She's a gift."

I smiled at him and we fell into another silence. Our eyes locked. A question seemed to hang in the air between us.

"So?' I finally asked.

"So, what?"

"Is this . . . are we . . . is this a thing, like a one-time thing, or is this a thing that you think you might want to carry on with?" I felt embarrassed by the question. Exposed and vulnerable.

He shook his head, as if unsure of himself. "Look, I usually don't do this, well, I did it once and it didn't end well, mixing business with my personal life. In fact, it nearly cost me the business once. Sasha and Murray, they didn't only betray me personally, but professionally too. They stole one of Stark's ideas and ran off and started their own business with it. I nearly lost my position in the company over that. If we did this, we would have to keep it a secret at work. I wouldn't want anyone, especially not Mr. Grey, to know what was happening, I think he's looking for a reason to kick me out of my own company and—"

My heart plummeted and I cut him off quickly. "No, you're right. It's probably not a good idea—I mean, I work for you, and sex just makes things messy. You're right, better that this is a one-off thing."

"I didn't say that. Unless that's what you want? Do you want that?" he asked.

"Do *you* want that?" I asked back.

"This was really nice. More than nice. This was amazing," he said. "And I would be cool if it happened again." He looked like he blushed when he said it.

I tried to conceal the giddy schoolgirl smile, but it wasn't working.

"I would be cool if it happened again too," I said.

"So, we're both cool?" he asked.

I leaned in and kissed him softly on the lips. "We're cool."

And then he looked at me seriously. "I thought you said that all the guys you were attracted to turned out to be bad for you."

I smiled at him. "Maybe you are? Bad for me."

"Maybe I'm not. Maybe I'm the exception to the rule," he said playfully.

"Well, we'll just have to wait and see," I said.

CHAPTER SEVENTY-ONE

~

Poppy

*W*e arrived at my place after driving back from the hotel. He parked his car and we sat there in silence, staring at each other and smiling.

"Well, thanks for that," I said teasingly.

"For what exactly?" He leaned in.

"Mmm, well, probably for that thing that happened in the hotel room. I mean, I don't know," I said.

"Thing?" he asked. "Just *one* thing. Not three? Or was it four?"

I smiled at him. "But who's counting, hey?"

"I am," he said with a low chuckle.

I laughed. I felt giddy. Like a teenage girl with a crush . . . *no, more*. This was more than a crush. And then a stab. I still hadn't told him the full truth. He'd just had sex with Doris Granger, not me. This was so complicated now, but I had to say it. I knew that.

"What?" he asked, obviously sensing the change in my mood.

I shook my head. "Just thinking."

"About what?"

"Things," I said. "Things that haven't been said out loud."

"Yeah, I know all about those kinds of things," he said.

But I was sure he didn't know what I was talking about. In fact, I wondered what he would think of me when he knew exactly who I was? We climbed out of the car together for the umpteenth time. It had all started in this car really. We walked up the dark staircase together and when we got to my door, we stopped and looked at each other. And that's when it happened, again.

His eyes drifted down to my lips, and mine to his. He came closer, our faces only centimeters away from each other. Perhaps we would be turning back "on" again, after all. My knees felt like they were getting somewhat weak and shaky, and I leaned back against the door as his lips came closer to me. I braced myself for their impact, as the anticipation bubbled inside me. Like a soda can that had been shaken, someone was pulling back the tab and all the liquid was about to fly out and . . .

"What the . . . ?" I turned around and stared at my door as my back pushed it open. "I . . . I locked it." I reached towards it.

"Wait!" He grabbed my hand and pushed me behind him protectively.

Fuck! I knew that big shiny lock on the outside of my door had been a mistake—it just made it look like I had stuff in my apartment worth stealing. Someone had broken in! It would have been easy. I reckoned that 90 per cent of the population here knew how to pick locks, and worse.

"Stay behind me," he said, as he pushed the door open and flicked on the lights. He stuck his head inside and looked around. "It's all clear."

I pushed my way inside and gasped. In a single moment, my

heart shattered. I looked around. The apartment had been totally ransacked. I didn't care about any of the drawers that had been tipped out, or the mattress that was turned over, all I cared about were the plants. Broken stems, cracked pottery and soil lay strewn across the floor.

"My mother's plants!" Tears welled up in my eyes and I ran into the room. I tried to pick them up and salvage the broken ones. I wanted to scream when I saw that one of the succulents had been stepped on. Smashed into the ground, bleeding green all over the floor.

I burst into tears. Uncontrollable sobs wracked my body and I couldn't stop them. Soil was falling from my fingers onto the floor, and tears were streaming down my face. I hadn't even bothered to look around my apartment to see what else was missing. I'd gone straight to the plants on the floor, because these were the only things of value that I owned.

CHAPTER SEVENTY-TWO

Ryan

"*I*t's okay," he said softly to her. "Most of them look fine."

"IT'S NOT OKAY!" she yelled through her crying. "You don't understand . . . I need to save them. I can't let them die. They cannot die!" She sounded desperate and he wracked his brain for a possible solution.

"I know! I have a huge garden. It's full of soil and pots and whatever you need. We can take these damaged ones back to my place now and fix them."

Her eyes immediately lit up. "You'd be okay with that?"

He crouched down next to her. "Yes. Let me help you pick them up."

She smiled at him. A smile that was so big and genuine and joyous. It was also completely contagious. He smiled back at her and then she leaned in and kissed him on the cheek. It was quick, *but it was everything*.

"Thanks. You don't know how much this means to me."

"It's a pleasure, I'm just glad I was here to help you, but . . ." he hesitated. "I don't think I can fit all of them in the car, just the damaged ones."

She nodded.

He could see she was loath to leave the others behind. And then a noise came from the corner of the room and they both turned. The bloody pigeon was hiding behind a plant. It poked its head out and he sighed. "I guess he can come too," he said.

He surveyed the crime scene. "I can call a removal truck in the morning to come and collect the rest of them, and I'll call an emergency locksmith too. But you should pack a bag with your clothes and anything else valuable that you want to ta—"

"Wait," she cut him off. "What are you talking about?"

"Well, you're not staying here tonight, that's for sure. Or ever."

She blinked a few times. "Where do you want me to stay? I have nowhere else to go."

"Yes, you do." He smiled at her. "I have a guest cottage that you can stay in."

She shook her head. "I couldn't. That's just . . . I mean, what would Emmy say? I can't come and stay with you—"

"I'm not asking you to move in with me, Doris. Just until we sort this out. Until we know you're safe here."

She held his gaze for the longest time, as if she was deciding what to do. And then finally, she nodded. "Okay, thank you," she said softly.

She didn't need to say thank you, because truthfully, right now, in this moment, he thought he would do anything for her. Move mountains, move plants, whatever.

He called the locksmith, who arrived as soon as they'd finished gathering all the damaged pot plants together. This was definitely going to take them a few trips up and down those stairs. His suit was completely ruined at this stage, but again, he didn't care. His priority lay in getting these plants to his house. Safe and sound.

They finished their last trip and started putting the plants into his car.

She hesitated. "They're going to make a mess all over your car."

"It's okay. It's just soil."

"Really? But you nearly died that first night when I splashed water all over it."

He sighed and looked at her. "That was before I got to know you."

"And now?" she asked, lowering the plants into the car.

"Now, you can mess up my car as much as you like."

She smiled and passed him one of the damaged pot plants. He looked down at it. The bright red flowers were drooping and he tried to lift one up. It flopped down immediately.

"It's beautiful," he said, placing it carefully in the car.

"It's a poppy." She said it in such a strange tone that he looked up at her.

"And this . . ." She passed him another pot. "This is a wild daisy."

He nodded and put the daisy in the car, next to the poppy.

"And that's my name," she said.

He looked up at her.

"What?" he asked.

"Poppy Daisy Peterson. That's my real name."

CHAPTER SEVENTY-THREE

～

Poppy

*T*he drive to his house was completely silent. He hadn't said a word since I'd told him my name. *My real name.* The only talking there'd been was the call he'd made to his housekeeper, asking if she wouldn't mind helping with the plants when we arrived. I had no way of knowing what he was thinking, and he was thinking something. I could see it on his face; he was sunk so deep in his thoughts that I could almost hear them churning about in his brain, as if they had been dumped into a washing machine. We finally arrived at his house and parked the car. I waited for him to say something, but he didn't. We climbed out and I couldn't take it any longer.

"I'm so sorry," I blurted out desperately. "It was wrong and deceptive and I'm not even sure I had the best reasons for doing it, now that I look back on it. My only excuse was that I was desperate, I needed a job so badly and—"

"I'm not stupid, Poppy." He said my name for the first time, *my real name,* and it felt so good. "I knew you weren't telling the truth about things when I hired you. It became more and more obvious as the days went by. I've suspected it since the moment I met you, but . . ." He paused and shrugged thoughtfully. "I let it go, because I didn't care. I let it go, because I wanted to see you again."

"I'm so sorry," I said again. This time there were tears in my eyes. I didn't want him to think badly of me, especially after everything that had happened between us. "I don't want you to think I am anything like that Sasha woman. I don't usually tell lies like this. I'm not a liar."

"You're nothing like her," he said. "She had a hidden agenda. A cruel one."

"I didn't have that. I swear. I just desperately needed a job."

He looked at me and shook his head. "Doris Granger," he smiled. "I suspected the name was fake from the moment I met you. It sounded made-up—and of course when I did a Facebook search for the name, only women who were in their eighties came up. And then I did some more research on the actual name and discovered that Doris was only a popular name between 1900 and 1930. So, it was pretty obvious."

"You really did your homework," I said nervously.

"Besides, you're clearly not very good at making up names, Beatrice whatever-whatever."

I smiled back at him. "So, you're not angry?" I asked.

He considered that carefully. "That depends on what else you've been lying about, I guess."

My stomach plummeted again.

"And now would probably be the right time to come clean about it, if there is anything else," he said.

I nodded. Fear and nausea and nerves gripped me. I opened my mouth and was just about to say it all when . . .

I heard a gasp and looked behind me. A woman stood there with a look of shock painted across her face. This must be Ryan's housekeeper.

"Ramona González!" she said, her mouth falling open. And then she rushed over to me excitedly. "I can't believe they killed you!"

Ryan looked at me. "Wait, who is Ramona González? And why is she dead?"

I opened my mouth to speak and was cut off again.

"Ramona is one of the characters from my favorite telenovela, *Venganza Ignacio*."

"Sorry, what?" he asked.

"*Ignacio's Revenge*," she clarified. "Anyway, she was the Executive Administrative Assistant to Santiago Alvarez, the CEO of the experimental, secretive government laboratory testing facility where they were conducting top-secret experiments. But Ramona wore these big glasses and her hair was short and brown because she was actually a spy, but that's only revealed much later. Anyway, she was having an affair with the CEO, but actually she was really sleeping with his evil twin brother, Ignacio, who everyone thought was dead, because of his plane crash in the Amazon rainforest. But actually he was alive and living with cannibals and then he killed Ramona with a poison dart that he made from the slime from the poisonous frogs in the jungle."

"So wait," Ryan said. "So *she* is Ramona González?" He pointed at me, and Tamlin nodded. "From a telenovela. That you watch?"

I felt the blood rush from my face and pool in my feet. I lowered my head and facepalmed, waiting for Ryan's response. This was going to be bad. But at least it was out in the open now. And then, I heard a small chuckle next to me.

"Executive Administrative Assistant to the CEO, with glasses and short brown hair, and having an affair with the CEO, you say. Very, very, *very* interesting."

I looked up. His eyes were fixed on me, and he was smiling. "This, he said, "*this* explains a lot. And I mean, a lot."

"She was such a good actress too. You should have seen her die! I actually cried!"

"An actress!" Ryan exclaimed.

I nodded at him. "Well, trying to be."

"Trying! Trying! You're so good, everyone loves you, haven't you seen your Facebook page?" she asked.

"What Facebook page, and how did you even see the show? It was only broadcast in Paraguay."

I heard another laugh. "In Paraguay. You don't say!"

"Don't you know?" Tamlin asked.

I shook my head. "Know what?"

"The show is huge in Nigeria. Everyone watches it. I never miss an episode. You can stream it online."

I blinked a few times. This was making no sense whatsoever.

"Look." She pulled her phone out, logged into Facebook and then held the screen up for me to see. I read it and almost choked on my spit.

"Bring back Ramona González. Over a hundred thousand followers! *WHAT*?" I screamed that last part.

"Someone started this page for you because they want your character to come back."

"How is this . . . wait . . . how could I be . . . I don't get this . . . uh . . ." I stuttered, staring at the comments on the page.

"You're famous," Tamlin said. "And you're standing in front of me."

"Let's see that." Ryan held his hand out and Tamlin passed the phone to him. He started reading.

". . . *show is not the same without her . . . She used to make me laugh so much . . . She was the best character . . . favorite scene was when she evacuated the entire building . . . my daughter and I used to watch her all the time, she's been inspired to take karate because of her . . . her dying scene should win her an award . . .*"

Ryan looked up at me and shook his head. "You're an actress?" he asked again as if he still needed some time to digest it all.

I nodded slowly and was just about to open my mouth and start apologizing when he shrugged and shook his head again.

"I guess I should be asking for your autograph next?"

CHAPTER SEVENTY-FOUR

~

Ryan

"*S*o, an actress?" he said, flattening the soil into one of the broken pots.

After that rather interesting and illuminating conversation with Tamlin, they'd come outside with the plants. First, they'd put the pigeon in the laundry room—it was the only place he could think of keeping it, for now. They'd dug up some soil from one of his flower beds, he'd found a few spare pots lying around, and they'd started repotting her flowers on the lawn together. It was freezing outside and the wind bit at his cheeks and hands as he went.

"Yup," she said, while concentrating hard on straightening one of the bent stems.

"Ramona González?"

"Yup," she said again. She didn't look up at him, instead focusing all her attention on the plant in her hand.

"Executive Administrative Assistant to . . . *what was it exactly?*"

She slammed the plant down on the ground and glared at him.

"To the CEO of an experimental, secretive government laboratory testing facility. OKAY! Alright!?! Happy now?"

Her anger caught him off guard. He was just about to open his mouth and speak, when she opened hers and the words started falling out.

"I know I lied. I'm a total liar." She hung her head. "God, my mom would be so disappointed in me. But I was desperate and broke and felt like a total loser with a jar of peanut butter in the fridge of the crummiest apartment on the African continent with neighbors plucked straight out of the Jerry Springer show. And I had this pile, an actual pile, of bills that I'd been ignoring because I just didn't have the money to pay them because I no longer had a job because I was killed." She shook her head and seemed more angry with herself than he was with her right now. He was going to stop her, but it looked like she needed to get this off her chest.

"They decided to kill my character—talk about a confidence booster! I'm not even good enough to be alive on a stupid telenovela with a plotline straight out of an episode of *Star Trek*. And then one day I was walking down the road, feeling like I wanted to disappear, or not exist, because I didn't know what to do and where to turn, and my agent wasn't taking my calls anymore, and this newspaper came out of nowhere and flew into my face and stuck to it, and when I pulled it away and looked, there it was. A job. Executive Administrative Assistant to the CEO of some company I hadn't heard of . . ." She paused for the tiniest moment and then looked up at him. "That's you, by the way, the CEO . . . and I just thought, *I have to.* I took it as a sign, even though I had no idea what the hell I was going to do when I got there. I didn't think that far, and the only way I felt vaguely okay with lying was if I wore that stupid disguise because, believe it or not, I'm actually not a natural liar. And if my mother was alive, she would be appalled that I lied because she taught me better than that. So I wore the stupid disguise and I lied to get the job and now the telenovela that I never wanted anyone to see is apparently huge in Nigeria and half of Africa has seen it and, and, and . . ." She took a massive breath like she was running out of steam, then finally stopped talking and sat there looking at him.

She looked so vulnerable and beautiful and in so much pain. His heart broke.

"You wanted to disappear?" he asked. Hearing her say that had cut him to the quick.

She shrugged. "Sort of. I don't know. I just didn't want to live the way I was anymore. I didn't want things to stay the same, and it felt like I had no way out." She shook her head. "FUCK IT!" She picked up a plant and examined it. "And now this plant is going to die . . . look at it."

There was something so sad about Poppy. Something slightly broken about her—but totally beautiful. And he wanted to fix it. He reached out and took the plant from her. "I'm sure with some water and sun, it will be fine." He tried to straighten the stem and leaves.

"Why are you being so nice to me after I lied to you?" Her big amber eyes met his. "You should be furious with me. You should be angry that you employed someone who lied on their CV. You should want me to leave immediately and get rid of me."

He looked at her. Truthfully, he couldn't be angry with her if he tried. He shuffled across the grass, right up to her. Her eyes widened as he put his face in front of hers and grazed her cold nose with his. He closed his eyes and breathed in her smell.

"Because," he opened his eyes and looked into hers, "no one makes me feel like this. No one makes me laugh the way you do— and trust me, I haven't laughed in a long time, and it feels so good. I feel awake when I'm with you, Poppy. You woke me up when I didn't even know I was sleeping."

"Really?" she asked.

"Remember when I asked you what you were worth and you couldn't tell me?" he said.

She nodded. Sweet, sad and vulnerable.

"Well, what you've done for me, that makes you invaluable."

CHAPTER SEVENTY-FIVE

~

Poppy

Invaluable!

The word repeated, over and over, in my head as I looked at him looking at me. The word seemed so foreign to me. I knew what it meant, but there was something about its meaning that seemed so far away, so removed from me.

"Invaluable?" I asked.

He nodded. "Invaluable . . ." He repeated the word, and yet it still didn't sound right. It just wasn't a word I would use to describe myself.

"I'm . . . not . . . I . . ." My words tapered off and I shook my head. "I mean . . ." I shrugged. "How can I be . . . ?" I pursed my lips together hard, trying to bite back the emotion that was welling up inside me, catching in the back of my throat.

"Why would you think that?" he asked. He held my gaze with such intensity that I thought I might capitulate under it.

"God." I shook my head. "Do you know how intimidating you can be sometimes?"

He smiled. "It's all an act."

"Really? It's a damn good one then. You're a better actor than I am." I forced a tiny smile. His thumb came up and touched my lip, which was cold and quivered under the warmth of his finger. I chewed on the corner of my lip, a mixture of nerves and excitement rushing through me.

"You're biting your lip," he said. His voice was low and husky and made me feel a little giddy.

"I do it sometimes when I'm nervous."

"Are you nervous?"

I nodded. "Yes."

His smiled faltered slightly. "I'm also nervous."

"YOU!?" I laughed. "The big Ryan Stark of Stark Leisure Group, in that big intimidating building with the purposely uncomfortable seats, is *nervous*?"

"I know. Hard to believe, isn't it?" He smiled playfully at me, and I wanted to kiss him again.

He was so stupidly gorgeous! Especially when he sat on the grass and helped me with my plants. I leaned in and was just about to kiss him when . . .

I heard Emmy calling his name.

"Ryan," her voice came from upstairs.

He turned and looked back at the house.

"Ryan!" she called louder.

"She sometimes has nightmares and wakes up in the middle of the night," he said.

"That's terrible." I could relate to Emmy; sometimes I had these dreams about my mother too. In them, she was alive and then suddenly she started disappearing and I couldn't stop her. I always woke with a start, drenched in sweat.

"Excuse me," he said. He stood up and dusted the soil off himself. "I'm coming!" he shouted.

I stood up and followed him, and it suddenly hit me that I would need to tell Emmy the truth about who I was too. I wondered what she would think of me for lying.

We reached the house and I hung back in the doorway as Ryan spoke to Emmy.

"What's wrong?" he asked softly.

She shook her head. "I don't know. I couldn't sleep. I couldn't find you in your study."

"Sorry, I was in the garden."

She looked at him strangely. "Doing what?"

"Uh . . . there's been a bit of a pot plant emergency," he said.

"What does that mean?"

Ryan stepped aside and revealed me standing in the doorway.

"Doris, what are you doing here?" she asked. She looked surprised and looked from Ryan to me and back again.

"Uh, what's going on here? Why do you both look so weird . . . like you want to tell me something?"

"Well, I kind of do want to tell you something," I said, stepping forward.

"What?" Emmy asked.

She looked at me with those big blue eyes of Ryan's, and I didn't know where to start.

"Maybe I should show you," I finally said.

CHAPTER SEVENTY-SIX

~~

Ryan

"*B*ut . . . but is the brother alive? I thought Ignacio died in the plane crash?" Emmy's eyes were glued to the computer screen. They all were.

"They all thought Ignacio died! But he didn't," Poppy said, stuffing a handful of popcorn into her mouth. "And watch this!" She spoke with her mouth full and pointed at the screen.

"Eeeewww! What's he doing with all those frogs?" Emmy cringed in her seat.

"He's harvesting the poison on their backs and using it to make poisonous darts!" Tamlin suddenly said.

Ryan burst out laughing "Who makes poisonous darts from the poison found on the backs of frogs?"

"He does!" Poppy turned and smiled up at him. She was sitting cross-legged on the floor and had kicked off her shoes. Her hair was messily piled up on the top of her head. She'd changed into a baggy, oversized tracksuit top and had pulled on a pair of comfortable-looking leggings. She looked so beautiful, he was struggling to keep his eyes off her and on the computer screen.

"And watch this part!" Tamlin sat up straight and pointed at the screen. "It's one of my favorite parts!"

Ryan leaned forward to look closer.

"Wait . . . who are they?" Emmy was transfixed, and Ryan looked over at her.

He smiled to himself. He liked seeing her like this.

"Those are the evil cannibals who took him in after the plane crash," Poppy quickly piped up. "They taught him to be evil."

"Very evil!" Tamlin quickly reiterated.

Ryan burst out laughing again. "He was looked after by cannibals in the Amazon rainforest? Why didn't they just eat him? This storyline makes no sense whatsoever."

"Because," Poppy turned around and looked at him as if she was going to make a long-winded point, "because . . ." She paused and looked like she was thinking. "Alright, you have a good point there, I have no idea why they didn't eat him!"

"Here comes Ramona, watch this part!" Tamlin pointed excitedly at the screen. "We have a celebrity in our house."

Ryan leaned in, curious to see her.

And then there she was. She looked exactly the same as the day she'd barged into his office. She filled the entire screen with the same intriguing energy she'd brought to his office.

Emmy burst out laughing. "Those glasses . . . how could anyone believe those were real? They look totally fake." She was laughing even more now.

"They *are* fake—she's actually a spy in disguise, but we don't know who she's working for yet. They killed her before we could get to that," Tamlin added.

Ryan felt a smile tug at his lips as Poppy turned around and looked at him with a knowing look.

"Shall I get the head of the army on the phone, sir?" Poppy's character suddenly said, looking panicked and flustered.

Damn, she looked fucking cute like that!

"Yes, Miss González," the man spoke. He was tall, with a chiseled jaw that looked almost cartoonish and big poofy hair that looked like it had been blow-dried.

"I'll tell him it's an emergency. I'll tell him it's a code red. I'll tell him there's been a breach in the radioactive containment field and the rats have mutated and are now very, very hungry."

"WAIT!" Ryan slapped his hand on the couch and laughed. "Mutated radioactive rats?"

"Shhhhh!!" Emmy and Tamlin simultaneously shushed him.

"Is there anything else I can do for you, sir?" Poppy's character said. Her big amber eyes widened and twinkled in the light.

"Yes!" The man with the massive jaw narrowed his eyes and then widened them again. "There is, Miss González." Then he launched himself across the room and grabbed Poppy in his arms dramatically. He dipped her and looked deep into her eyes.

"Whoa. Hang on a second there." Ryan sat up in his seat as a bolt of discomfort shot through him. He was watching Poppy being held in the arms of another man and—fuck it!—he didn't like it.

"I need to tell you something, Miss González. I've been wanting to say this to you since the moment I saw you walk into my office." The man pulled her glasses off and tossed them to the floor. He stared into Poppy's eyes with great drama.

"Yes, Santiago. What is it?" Poppy whispered, looking up at the man.

"I've fallen in love with you," the man said, and then for some unknown reason, he looked directly into the camera and narrowed his eyes before quickly looking back down at Poppy.

Ryan gripped the side of the couch and crossed his legs, trying to hide the fact he was feeling very, very uncomfortable with this scene.

"I . . . I . . . I'm in love with you too," Poppy's character spoke. Tears trickled down her cheeks. "But what will your wife say?" she whispered to him.

The man looked pained for a second. His face tensed up, his jaw clenched and his nostrils flared. "My wife is having an affair with Methat Ishmail, an Arab sheikh. She met him on her trip to Dubai at the top of the Burj Khalifa. I got a private investigator to follow them. They were drinking Clos de Griffier Vieux Cognac, it's our favorite drink, and eating our favorite food, beluga caviar." The man looked up at the camera again and then let out a long moaning sound. "I feel so betrayed."

Poppy's character gasped. "But isn't Methat Ishmail the man who's trying to steal all your company secrets?"

"Yes," the man blurted out. Then he flared his nostrils as if he was about to sneeze, only he didn't. "I think he and my wife are plotting to kill me and take over the company together."

"*Nooo.*" Poppy leaned in closer to the man, as if she was about to kiss him.

Ryan jumped up and pressed pause. "Okay, I think that's enough," he said.

"Ryan, I'm thirteen. I've seen millions of people kiss on TV before."

Ryan didn't want to admit it, but that wasn't what was bothering him.

"It's just a short kiss," Poppy said quickly.

"That is so gross, how do you just kiss people like that?" Emmy asked.

"It was so horrible! And he always stank of garlic. I used to hold my breath while it happened. I hope no one ever noticed."

Emmy laughed. "I could never do that."

"Of course you couldn't," Ryan said. "You're not ever going to be kissing boys, or making out, or whatever you call it."

"Whatever!" Emmy rolled her eyes. "Enough kissing talk, let's watch." Emmy turned her back on Ryan. "Press play."

"Yes, press play . . . this is when I get killed," Poppy said.

"Fine." Ryan pressed play, just as the actor's lips came down on Poppy's.

Emmy laughed. "I can see you're holding your breath."

Poppy laughed. Ryan felt slightly sick.

"Wait! What's that?" Emmy gasped at the cutaway to a man in a suit, tied up in a closet.

"That's her *real* boss," Tamlin piped up. "She's actually kissing the evil twin brother who is just pretending to be Santiago Alvarez."

"No!" Emmy gasped.

"¡He regresado de la jungla para vengarse la reputación de mi familia!" the man suddenly said and Ryan pressed pause again.

"WAIT! What does that even mean?" He looked at Poppy and she gave a small, somewhat embarrassed-looking smile.

" 'I have returned from the jungle to avenge my family's name,' " she said in a small voice.

Ryan burst out laughing. Now he knew why the architect had laughed so much.

"Press play," Tamlin said. "This is the best part."

He pressed play and Poppy's character suddenly winced in pain.

"My back," she said, grabbing it.

"He's stuck a poison dart in your back!" Emmy's eyes widened.

Poppy's character stood up straight and looked over at the man with the jaw. His eyes were broody and dark and evil-looking now.

"It's you! Ignatius!" She gasped and pointed at him. "But you're dead. Your plane crashed . . . it can't be!"

"But it is." The man with the jaw threw his head back and let out a loud, long evil laugh. "I'm back."

Ryan laughed. "Seriously? Do people still buy evil laughs like that?"

"Ssshhh," Emmy and Tamlin hushed him again.

Poppy turned and whispered, "You are going to miss my big dying scene now."

"It's the best dying scene ever," Tamlin said.

"What makes it so goo—" Ryan stopped talking and watched as Poppy threw herself on the carpet and wriggled across it in an attempt to remove the dart from her back. "Oh, I see."

"The director wanted to go for something very dramatic." Poppy looked over at him and rolled her eyes.

Everyone's eyes were glued to the screen as Poppy finally pulled the dart from her back and did a running forward roll out of the office. She looked around at the people working there and then pointed her finger back at the CEO's office. "He's returned," she yelled. "He's coming for us. RUN!"

"Wait," Ryan pressed pause again. "Why are you forward-rolling out of the room?" He remembered the one that she'd done in his office. And in fact, wasn't this the exact same line she'd used on him during her interview?

"Ramona is trained in martial arts, she's actually a spy who was sent by the Arab sheikh to gather information on the company," Poppy said.

"Is that who you're working for?" Tamlin gasped.

Poppy nodded. "But she was killed off before she could reveal that. And that she was also having a love affair with the sheikh. He gave her a baby tiger as a gift once."

"Okay, let's watch the rest of the scene," Emmy urged.

Ryan pressed play again.

Ramona came out of the forward roll and started running down the passage. She tripped and stumbled and then fell to the floor. But soon she was up again, running down the stairs. She burst through the door and ran into another passage, where she stopped.

"No! No!" she shouted as a massive rat—a very evil-looking, massive rat—came running out!

"That's the mutated rat!" Emmy gasped, transfixed.

"Wait!" Ryan paused the show again. "Why are they mutating rats?"

"Because," Tamlin said, "they're creating the ultimate biological weapons for the government."

"Okay." He nodded. He guessed it did make some sense—in this world anyway.

"Ryan, stop pressing pause!" Emmy clicked her fingers and he pressed play again.

Poppy's character screamed and ran in the opposite direction, only to stumble into the laboratory, fall onto the floor and roll in the glowing radioactive slime covering it. She got up again, covered in luminous green liquid, and tried to run.

"How long does it take for the poison to kick in?" Ryan asked, feeling somewhat amused.

"I'm telling you, they're going to bring your character back to life, that's why they made you fall into the radioactive slime," Tamlin suddenly said.

"That makes sense!" Emmy joined in. "You're going to come back mutated or something."

Ryan burst out laughing, trying to imagine a mutated version of Ramona González. "You probably won't need your glasses then. You'll miraculously have perfect vision again," he said.

Poppy turned and shot him a playful look, and he melted. She looked so good sitting on his carpet right now; she looked like she belonged there.

"Wait, it gets better." Poppy pointed to the screen again. "Keep watching."

Ryan watched as Poppy's character stumbled out of the laboratory and back down the corridor. Suddenly, someone jumped in front of her and pushed her to the ground.

"Who is that?" Emmy asked.

"That's Santiago Alvarez's wife, Esmée. She also wants to kill Ramona because she's just found out that her husband has changed his will and is leaving everything to her, including the company."

"I know what you're trying to do with my husband!" The woman bellowed. "I know the two of you are planning a secret romantic trip to the Amalfi coast—personally I prefer the Riviera."

"I love your husband," Poppy's character shouted.

"You just like his money, don't think I haven't noticed all those new handbags and jewels you're wearing. You could never afford a Cartier necklace on your own. I should strangle you with it now!" She made a grab for the necklace and Poppy jumped out of the way; she rolled across the floor and then, out of nowhere, she swung around and kicked Esmée. A perfect roundhouse kick like the one she'd used on her door.

"I'm a black belt," Poppy's character said suddenly.

Ryan burst out laughing.

"I'm going to kill you," the woman said, as she lay on the floor.

A dart suddenly flew through the air and hit her between the eyes.

Poppy's character gasped. "Seems like someone else is going to kill you first, Esmée."

Suddenly, Ignacio, the evil twin, stepped out of the shadows. "Hello, Esmée," he whispered.

"It's you," she gasped. "But I thought your plane crashed."

"Of course you did, since you were the one that sabotaged it and wanted me gone so you could have all the money and the company, you greedy witch."

Ryan burst out laughing again. "Another twist!"

"I'm dying," Poppy's character said and then started running again.

"You're running again, but you're dying!" Ryan said.

And then suddenly, out of nowhere, a massive explosion filled the air and the show ended.

"The entire laboratory exploded because of the radioactive breach in the containment field," Poppy explained quickly.

"Containment field? You don't say!" Ryan smiled down at her, and she smiled back.

"Wow! That was amazing." Emmy looked over at Poppy. "I mean, that was the coolest thing I have ever seen. That was so awesome. I can't believe you did that!"

"It's very popular in Nigeria. All my friends and family are watching it," Tamlin said.

Poppy burst out laughing. "I still can't believe that. It's so bad."

"I'd watch it if they brought you back," Ryan said.

"But I'm so bad in it. You saw me!"

"No, you're not," Tamlin and Emmy both said at the same time.

"You are brilliant, you're like so funny to watch," Emmy added.

Poppy looked at Ryan with a confused look on her face. He'd seen it before, that same look she'd given him when he'd asked her how much she was worth.

He smiled at her. "I agree. You have a gift. It's clear you were born to entertain and amuse people."

At that, her eyes lit up.

"God knows you've amused and entertained me from the second I met you, Poppy."

He couldn't stop looking and smiling at her. And out of the corner of his eye, he also couldn't help but notice the look that passed between Emmy and Tamlin.

CHAPTER SEVENTY-SEVEN

~

Poppy

*T*hey all sat in silence for a moment or two after the show had ended. The dramatic theme music filled the room. I'd heard it a million times before. But hearing it here, in Ryan's house, it felt strange. Strange but nice.

"Well, I better go back to bed now." Emmy suddenly shot bolt upright.

"Me too," Tamlin said, also standing up hurriedly. They both had a strange tone in their voice.

I jumped up too. "Emmy, can I walk you to your room? I'd like to talk to you."

"Sure."

We walked to her room together and, once we were out of earshot, I stopped her.

"I wanted to say sorry, for lying to you about who I was. You trusted me with a lot of things, and I wasn't being completely honest with you," I said.

She regarded me for a moment. "I can't believe you're an actress——" she started.

I nodded.

"And I actually can't believe you dressed up in a disguise and pretended to be an executive assistant . . . and worked for my uncle?"

I nodded. God, whenever I heard it repeated back to me, I knew how crazy it sounded. "I know. It sounds mad."

"Mad?" she said. "It's one of the craziest things I've ever heard. I mean, don't get me wrong, it's also one of the funniest things I've ever heard."

"Yeah, I guess I can be a little crazy like that," I said.

There was an awkward silence between us for a while.

"Did you lie about the other stuff too, about your mother?" Emmy asked.

I stepped closer to her and placed my hands on her shoulders. "No. Absolutely not. I would never do that. And I meant everything else I said to you too."

She nodded. "I didn't think you lied about that. You had that same sad look on your face that I do when I speak about my mom."

I sighed and shrugged.

"I wonder when that goes away?" she asked.

"I don't know," I said, trying to force a tiny smile. "Maybe it doesn't go away altogether. Maybe it's still there, but the gaps between the sadness just get longer and longer as you experience more and more happy moments."

"Maybe," she said and then smiled at me. "You have some serious guts, tricking my uncle like that."

"I would call it naivety. Had I known what he was like, I might have been too scared to do it."

And then she smiled at me again. Slow and strange, with a twinkle in her eye. "Well, he doesn't seem to mind that much, does he?"

"I know, it's surprising."

"Is it?" she asked.

"What do you mean?"

"Oh, come on, Poppy." She leaned in. "I might only be thirteen, but I know what a crush looks like when I see it. And right now, he is crushing on you big time—and it's super obvious you are too."

I felt myself blush.

"Yeah, I thought so," she said, looking at my cheeks. She winked at me and then walked off to her room. "I think it's really cool that you are an actor, by the way," she said over her shoulder. "I've never met anyone who's been on TV before."

"Thanks. It's not as glamorous as people think it is," I assured her.

"Good night, Poppy." She stopped at her door and looked me up and down. "That's also a much better name for you," she said. "Doris kind of sucked."

I laughed. "Good night, Emmy. Sweet dreams," I said as she disappeared into her bedroom and closed the door. I smiled to myself and walked back downstairs.

Ryan was on the couch waiting for me.

"I just wanted to apologize to her for lying like that," I said and sat down next to him.

"I'm pretty sure she forgives you. Did you see how into the show she was? I think she's blown away by the fact she knows a famous and brilliant actor."

"Famous and brilliant," I tutted. "Hardly."

"Stop putting yourself down like that," Ryan said, moving closer to me on the couch. "I don't like it when you do it. And it's not true."

"Thanks." I smiled.

"So, did she forgive you?" he asked.

"She did. And she also had some other interesting things to say." My heart fluttered.

"Oh, what?" Ryan moved closer to me.

"Well . . ." I twirled my hair in my fingers. "She said that you had a crush on me, and it was clear I had one on you too."

"Really?" He reached out and took the strand of hair away from me. He wrapped it around his finger and then tucked it behind my ear. He leaned in, put his lips to my ear and whispered. "Well, she's right. I have a serious crush on you."

I giggled. "You do?"

He kissed my neck. "I do," he said, bringing his lips to mine.

"I have a crush on you too." I opened my mouth and let him kiss me.

We kissed on the couch for ages. It felt naughty in some way, like we were teens sneaking a kiss while our parents were upstairs. We finally pulled away from each other.

"I guess I better get to bed at some point too. I wouldn't want to be too tired for work," I said. "My boss can be a bit of a slave driver."

"Really?"

I nodded playfully. "He can be a bit of a meanie sometimes."

He laughed. "Meanie? You want me to come in and have a few words with him?"

I stood up. "You could try, but I have to warn you, he's very stubborn, and scary sometimes."

"Does he scare you?" he asked.

"Mmmm." I thought about it. "He used to, but now I see that he's really just a teddy bear disguised as a tiger."

"Funny you should mention a disguise. I know someone who's really an actress disguised as an assistant." He stood up too.

"You don't say," I teased.

We stood there in silence smiling at each other again.

"So, your guest room?" I finally asked.

"It's outside," he said.

We walked across the room, through the kitchen and out the back door. It was freezing and I shivered immediately.

"Oh wow!" I grabbed my arms and hugged myself.

He wrapped his arm around my shoulders and we hurried across the garden to where the cottage was. He slipped the key in, opened the door and flicked on the lights.

"Wow. This place is bigger than my apartment," I said, looking around.

"Anything is bigger than your apartment," he said with a smile. He turned the heater on and soon a warm blast of air filled the room.

"There are extra blankets in the cupboard," he said.

"Thanks."

He walked up to me and placed his hands around my waist. "God, I would love to stay with you here tonight, but I don't think I can be away from the house, because of Emmy, and I'm not sure you should sleep in my bed."

"No!" I held my hand up. "Of course, you must sleep in your

own room. I get it. And I'm sure it would be a bit awkward if Emmy found me in your bed."

"Probably. Definitely," he said.

"So, I guess this is good night then?" I said.

"I guess it is." His hands ran down my waist, then onto my hips, and he pulled me towards him. "I'm happy I get to see you in a few hours for work."

"Work? And how on earth are we going to work with each other now, after everything that's happened between us? It's going to be very distracting."

"I'm very professional, Miss Granger. I'll be able to work. You won't distract me, I assure you." He said it like he meant it, but I wasn't sure. "And if you don't mind, can we keep this a secret until I work out how to play this so it doesn't backfire on me?"

"Play it? Backfire? You make this whole thing sound terrible."

"Sometimes it is," he said.

"Then why do you do it? Why do you work there if you hate your job?" I asked.

"I don't hate it," he said quickly. "I just don't like it."

I raised my hand and put it on the side of his face. "Well, that's really sad," I said softly.

"It is what it is, I guess." He slipped his hand over mine and leaned in and kissed me on the cheek. Soft and slow and sensual.

"Is there anything you like about it?" I asked.

He looked like he thought about this for a while. "I guess I enjoy the initial design phase of building. In another life I might have been an architect I guess," he said.

"You still can," I offered.

"I think it's a bit late for that." He smiled at me. Something about his smile was so sad. "Good night," he whispered, before turning and walking away.

I stood there and watched him walk across the garden. He pulled his phone out on the way and suddenly mine beeped. I reached for it and read the message.

Ryan: It's going to be hard going to sleep tonight alone, knowing that you're only a little way away.

I read the message and looked up. He'd stopped walking and was looking at me. The wind was blowing his hair around and ruffling his shirt. I looked at my phone and typed.

Me: I know. For me too. XXX Good night, Ryan.

He read the message and smiled at me. He gave me a small wave and then disappeared into the house. I walked over to the bed and sat down. It was soft and comfortable and I couldn't wait to climb in. My phone beeped again and I reached for it.

Ryan: Your fucking pigeon is on my bed! How the hell did he even get here?

CHAPTER SEVENTY-EIGHT

∽

Ryan

*P*oppy had been right. It wasn't just hard and distracting to work with her, it was fucking torture. And by noon, he couldn't take it any longer. He felt like he was going to explode. He strode out of the office. He'd been watching her all morning and she'd been driving him crazy. Physically he had something very inconvenient happening in his pants—and a meeting happening in an hour—and well, he needed to sort it out.

"Miss Granger," he said, standing by her desk.

She looked up at him, biting the end of her pencil seductively. On purpose. "Yes, Mr. Stark." His name oozed from her mouth like warm, delicious honey.

"Uh . . . may I have a word with you in the filing room?" He was holding a big file against himself, trying to hide that very inconvenient thing that was happening down below. She gazed at the file and her eyes widened.

"Why yes, Mr. Stark." She stood up slowly, deliberately flirtatious. "You may see me in the filing room."

She walked in front of him all the way to the room. He was transfixed by the way her skirt pulled across her ass with every step she took. They made it to the filing room and as soon as they did, he locked the door.

They reached for each other. Grabbed. Pulled each other into their arms and started kissing. Fast, hard, hungry and desperate. He had been desperate for her all morning and like an addict getting their hit, he was going to take as much of her as he could. All of her. Every last drop that she was willing to give. He would take it and savor it and devour it.

"God, I've been thinking about this all morning," Poppy whispered into his ear.

"Me too," he said, pushing her against the metal cabinet. The whole thing shook, and some files fell off and scattered across the floor.

"Shit." She looked at them.

"Fuck the files." He pulled at her shirt, opening the buttons and exposing her breasts in that bra—balconette, to be specific. He didn't bother with the strap at the back, instead he just pulled it down hard, exposing her soft breasts and nipples. They hardened immediately and he leaned in and took one between his lips. Pulling it into his mouth. She threw her head back and let out a long, loud moan. She grabbed him by the back of the head and held him in place as he devoured her. With his free hand, he reached into her skirt and, in one movement, tugged at her panties until they fell to the floor. She spread her legs for him, an invitation that he would gladly accept.

Her body shuddered as he ran his thumb over her, slowly at first, until he couldn't control himself any longer. She pulled his head up to her mouth and he kissed her deeply as he flicked and rubbed with his thumb until her muscles started to contract. He deepened the kiss even more as he felt her whole body start to shudder, and then go stiff. He held onto her as her body loosened again. She was like putty in his hands now and he was able to do what he wanted with her. To mold her and stretch her into any shape and position that he wanted. And he wanted her. He wanted her like this, face pressed into the filing cabinet, wrists held together by his strong hands, stretched above her head. Her skirt pulled up to her waist and him, inside her, as he thrust and breathed against the back of her neck.

With every thrust the cabinet shook. She shook. He let go of her wrists and then grabbed her hips, pulling her down on him, as if he needed to be deeper inside. But he also wanted to look at her and stare into those amber eyes that had bewitched him from the moment he'd met her. He pulled out and then flipped her around, making her gasp. He lifted her up, wrapped her legs around him and walked her over to the table in the middle of the floor. He laid her down and climbed on top of her. This time there was no speed or urgency. She moaned and he placed his elbows on the side of her face and stared into her eyes. His movements were slow and deliberate this time, not frenzied, not desperate.

She arched her back against the table, she wiggled her hips beneath him as he ground into her. He was going to lose it. Here at work, with her in the filing room. And he didn't care.

CHAPTER SEVENTY-NINE

～

Poppy

"*W*ell, that was ..." I lay on the desk panting. "Unexpected." I giggled as I buttoned up my shirt.

"Very," Ryan said. "And very bad to have done it at work like this."

"I know. I know." I covered my face with my hands. "*Soooo* bad."

Ryan rolled onto his side and looked at me. "Oh shit. You lost one of your buttons."

I sat up and gazed down at my shirt. I looked around the room, but it was nowhere to be seen.

Ryan sat up too, also looking around. "Sorry," he said.

"It's okay, I think I can hide it with a scarf. I have one in my drawer, I can g——" Suddenly a voice interrupted me.

"*I just don't understand why it's locked, it's never locked.*"

The voice came from outside and we both looked up in horror as the door handle started to shake. I stifled a gasp and looked over at Ryan. He was wide-eyed. And then we heard a loud clank. A metallic sounding clank as if ...

I gasped. A tool box, it sounded like a tool box. Ryan looked at me and shook his head. I could see he was full of fear right now.

"Maybe the lock got stuck on the inside," a male voice said. "I'll just open it from here."

"Please," the female voice said. "You know what Mr. Stark is like, if I don't get those files to him, he'll kill me."

"Tell me about it," the male voice returned. He was obviously the building handyman. "He's something special to work for. Once he made me stay after hours to work on the elevator because he was sure it was moving slower. It wasn't."

"It was," Ryan hissed under his breath.

I nudged him to keep quiet.

"Honestly, that man is a nightmare sometimes," the female voice returned.

"I think he needs to get laid," the handyman said, and then they burst out laughing.

I tried to smother my giggle but it quickly stopped when we heard the sound of the drill. We both panicked. We jumped off the table, I searched for my shoes, pulled my skirt down and tried to straighten my hair. My button! Where was my bloody button? Ryan jumped into his pants and pulled them up as quickly as he could.

"Almost got it," the handyman said.

"Good," the female voice said.

"*Shiiiiit!*" I was now running around in literal circles.

We scanned the room, but there was nowhere to hide. Ryan looked down at my missing button. This didn't look good, at all. And I couldn't help but think about what Ryan had said to me: Mr. Grey was looking for a reason to get rid of him. This could be that reason. I looked over at Ryan, I had never seen him look so panicked. And then suddenly, the door started opening. We froze and watched in stupefied horror as it started . . . and then stopped.

"There's something making it stick," the man said.

My eyes widened. No, not my button, not my—

"Oh, that's strange, it's a button." A hand shot out and took the button out from under the door. "What do you make of this?" he asked.

"Mmmm," a conspiratorial mumble. "Definitely off a woman's blouse. I wonder if the filing room is being used for other things too." A laugh.

"Fuck!" Ryan looked at me. I had never seen him looking so frightened before. "Shit, I'm in such trouble now," he whispered. His face was pale, as if all the blood had drained out of it.

And then the door opened.

CHAPTER EIGHTY

~

Ryan

There was this spine-chilling, bone-crunchingly awkward moment as Janice from IT and Jeff the handyman stared at them. Their eyes seemed to flick from him, to Poppy, and then back again. Their eyes were wide and he knew he'd been caught when Janice slowly lowered her head and looked at the button in her hand, and then back up at Poppy.

It was as if time had stopped and they were all suspended in a strange no-man's-land. Sitting in a silent waiting room, waiting for nothing in particular. There was no way out of this, really, and he felt sick to his stomach when he thought of the repercussions. This story would spread through the halls of the building and be whispered about over lunch and in the elevator too. This would seriously jeopardize his reputation as the boss and would not look good, at all. Not to mention that his board could have him removed over this—in fact, this was tantamount to a crime, having sex in the office. This had such far-reaching consequences that he couldn't believe he'd done it . . .

And then he turned when Poppy burst into tears. Loud sobs. Everyone looked at her.

"I can't believe you're firing me, over this!" she wailed loudly.

Ryan stared at her. *What the hell was going on?*

"So what if I came in here to take a private selfie of my boobs—"

"What?" Ryan half-yelled.

Jeff and Janice gasped.

"You know, I caught him—my very own partner—messaging the neighbor the other day, sending her all these cute kissy emojis. I just know he's going to have an affair with her," Poppy said and then wailed even louder.

What the hell was she doing?

And then she turned to Janice. "And I know it's because I haven't been in the mood latterly. It's the stress, you know. I'm tired when I get home from work, and then I still have to make supper for him and the kids."

He looked over at Janice; she was nodding at her now.

Poppy continued. "And I just thought that maybe if I sent him a picture, you know, something a little saucy, that maybe I could . . ." She covered her face in embarrassment and her sobs continued.

Damn, she was a good actress.

"I thought that maybe it would reignite the spark and that maybe he would stop flirting with the neighbor." She stumbled backward now, as if she was too emotional to even stand. And then she looked back up at Janice with a face that looked so pained and troubled. "I'm just trying to save my relationship!"

Janice nodded. "It's okay, sweetie, we all go through these ups and downs."

He looked over at Poppy. She was saving him, in the only way possible right now. She looked at him pointedly, as if urging him to play along. This was their only way out.

"Well, you can save your relationship outside of work hours, Miss Granger," he cleared his throat and said to her. "This is highly inappropriate," he added.

"She's only twenty . . . the neighbor. Can you believe it? She's like a child. She used to babysit our kids when they were little," Poppy said to Janice. "Our daughter, Skye, she thought she was so pretty and said that when she grew up . . ." Poppy whimpered loudly, "when she grew up, she wanted to look just like her."

Janice tutted and shook her head. "Disgusting."

Okay, wait! Now she was taking this a bit far. He tried to shoot her a look, but she looked so wrapped up in this character right now, he could see there was no stopping her.

Jeff nodded now too. "My wife left me for a younger man. I know how it feels. His name was Braxton. I mean, what kind of name is Braxton?"

Janice shook her head and so did Poppy. This was like a group commiseration in the filing room. Broken Hearts Anonymous. Poppy let out another long, loud moan. "I don't want him to leave me." She grabbed her chest as if in pain.

This was really taking it too far now.

Janice rushed up to her and draped an arm around her shoulder. "I'm sure he won't leave you," she said in a placating tone. "Why don't you have a seat?" She guided Poppy over to the table, the desk they'd just had mind-blowing sex on.

He cleared his throat again and straightened his tie. "Please will you clear your desk and leave the building, Miss Granger."

Janice gave him a disapproving look and then shook her head. *How was he the bad guy now?*

Poppy jumped up off the table and glared at him. "Fine!" she shouted. "Fine, if that's how you want it." She looked at him indignantly and then marched out of the filing room.

They followed her out, but when they walked into the open-plan section, everyone was staring at them. Poppy looked at everyone and then swung around dramatically and glared at Ryan. She had a captive audience now. He was almost scared of her.

"Do you hear that?" she called out angrily. "I'm getting fired. He's firing me!" She pointed a finger at him. "Fine. But I will see you in court," she spat and then marched through the desks, clutching her shirt closed with one hand.

Everyone stared. Flicking their eyes between her, and him.

At least this scene is over now, he thought. But it wasn't. Far from it.

"But you know what?" Poppy stopped walking and turned around again, as if she was a character in a play, taking their place centre stage to deliver the great monologue.

Everyone was totally captivated; they leaned in as if they were passing a bad car crash on the side of the road.

"Oh God," he whispered under his breath and rolled his eyes. He wished she would stop now.

"I knew you were allergic to washing powder when I put it on your shirt," she hissed in a strange voice.

"You did?" he asked. His stomach dropped.

"And I knew it was 'no mayonnaise' this whole time too," she continued.

It sounded like a few spectators tried to stifle their shocked gasps.

"And guess what else?" Her voice was getting louder and louder, more dramatic by the second. "The other day, it was a false fire alarm. I was the one who set it off because I couldn't bear to be in this building a second longer."

At that, Ryan heard a small clap and he looked around to see who'd made it.

"And that pigeon," she continued. "I let him into the boardroom deliberately. And I'm glad he took a shit on the table. I hope it stains."

And now there were gasps. No one was trying to hide it anymore.

She started walking again, and he breathed a sigh of relief. But then she stopped once more. "And guess what else?" she said.

Ryan hung his head and shook it. "What?" he asked flatly. Maybe if he played along, this could end sooner.

"You wear too much aftershave."

At that, he heard a few chuckles and then tried to smell himself subtly. *Did he?*

"Yes, you do!" Poppy spun back around, threw an "*Adios, hombre*" over her shoulder and then disappeared around the corner.

Everyone stared after her in absolute shock.

CHAPTER EIGHTY-ONE

⟋

Poppy

"*S*o?" I was standing in the parking lot with a box of things from my desk. "What did you think?" I asked excitedly into my phone.

"Think about what? About that thing you just did in my office?" Ryan asked.

"That thing? *Thing*. That was acting! That was brilliant acting, you should be so lucky that you have a famous actor at your beck and call," I teased.

"Did you really know I was allergic to washing powder?" he suddenly asked.

I burst out laughing. "Damn, I *am* a good actor. No, I didn't."

I heard a sigh of relief. "But you do wear too much aftershave sometimes," I quickly added.

"Thanks." He sounded sarcastic.

"Do you think they bought it?" I asked, getting serious. I knew from the look on his face in the room just how serious the whole thing would have been if they'd figured out what had happened.

"I don't know. Maybe," he said.

"I tried to be very dramatic and crazy, so they would focus on that! Give them something to talk about," I said.

"Well, that part definitely worked, because they're all talking about crazy Doris Granger." He chuckled softly, and then paused. "What you did for me in there . . . thank you. You got me out of a potentially very bad situation, I could have lost my position in the company even."

"Well, it was partly my fault," I said.

"Damn right it was your fault. You can't sit there at your desk looking so hot. It should be illegal."

"Well, I could say the same for you."

"But now you don't have a job," he said.

"Let's be honest, Ryan. I was never very good at it anyway. You should never have hired me in the first place."

"I'm glad I did, though," he said, and my stomach fluttered. "But I really do need an assistant."

"You know who you should get?" An idea popped into my head.

"Who?"

"Ayanda, at reception. You know, she's been working for you the longest out of all your staff there."

"Really?" he said.

"She's been waiting for a promotion for years, and she says she's going to leave if she doesn't get one soon. She's nice, she's clearly good at her job, or you would have fired her, and it's clear she can handle you, since she's worked for you for so long," I concluded.

"Handle me?"

"Well, you're not exactly easy to work for, Mr. Stark." I looked up at the building. He was standing by his window. "I can see you," I said. "Look down."

The figure at the window turned and, even though he was very far away, I imagined I could see him smiling. "You're still here?" He waved at me.

"You kicked me out, and I don't have a car," I said.

"Where's your . . . oh, we left it at your place last night."

"Wow, this is feeling very familiar. All we need is for it to rain," I said, waving up at him.

"Very familiar," he chuckled. "So, planning on walking home again?"

"I was considering it," I joked.

"Just wait there, I'll be down in a second."

"No shame, you're busy, I can catch an Uber. I have enough money in my bank account to do extravagant things like that now."

He laughed. "I'd never dream of it. I'll be down now." He hung up and I stood there looking up at the strange building.

I probably wouldn't be coming to it again. Barely two weeks ago, when I'd first seen it, it had struck fear into my heart. But now, it was doing something very different to my heart. Well, the man inside the building was anyway. Because I was completely falling in love with him.

CHAPTER EIGHTY-TWO

ⅽ

Ryan

*H*e walked back into the house after a long day at work. It had been a good day actually. He'd offered Ayanda the job and her face had lit up at the news. It had made him feel good. She'd also insisted that he call her by her first name, not her surname. He'd agreed. She'd tried to call him Ryan, instead of Mr. Stark, but he'd had to stop her. That was taking it too far.

He dropped his bag by the front door and headed into the lounge where he was assaulted by sounds and smells that he didn't recognize. He could hear voices. Two of them, chatting and laughing. He walked towards the sounds and stopped when he saw them. Emmy and Poppy were in the kitchen cooking together. It looked like a bomb had gone off in there; the contents of every single cupboard had been poured out onto the countertops.

They didn't see him, and he used the opportunity to watch them. Poppy's hair was loose, and unruly strands kept falling forward. She repeatedly tucked them behind her ears, but they kept on tumbling, over and over again. They were stubborn and beautiful and a little bit crazy, just like her. And Emmy looked happy, happier than he'd seen her in ages.

He called out to them. "Hey, guys!"

They both looked up at the same time and his heart skipped a beat. Seeing them like that, together, looking at him, made him feel . . . *feel what?* It was hard to understand exactly what it was. But it was big and warm and all-consuming. A feeling that was comforting, but also so overpowering that there was something about it that frightened him.

"What are you guys doing?" he asked.

"We're cooking dinner," Poppy said happily.

"We're trying to cook this thing we just saw on *MasterChef*," Emmy added excitedly.

"Oh?" He walked towards them.

"It's a braised chicken with something called a 'jus' and it has this puree made of this stuff called celeriac." She looked over at Poppy and they laughed. "We didn't even know what that was, but it kind of looked like onion, so we're making it out of onions." She smiled at him.

"Tamlin usually cooks supper, though," he said, running his eyes over the chaos on the countertop.

"We gave Tamlin the night off," Poppy said, licking something off her finger. God, he wanted to be her finger right now.

"And we felt like cooking," Emmy said, looking up at him.

'Since when do you feel like cooking?" he joked.

"Since I've been watching *MasterChef*," she replied.

"I see. And what's this music?"

"Oh, her name is Janis Joplin. I've never heard of her before, but she is so cool. Poppy was telling me all about her."

Poppy looked up at him. "My mom used to listen to her all the time. She loved her."

"Well, she's definitely better than One Direction," he said.

Emmy put her spoon down and glared at him. "Ryan, I haven't listened to One-D in like years, they don't even exist anymore. That was so four years ago. Seriously."

"Sorry," he teased, holding his hands up in mock defense. He leaned over the counter and propped himself up on his elbows. He looked up at Poppy, who was smiling at him.

"What did you say we were having again?" he asked.

"Braised chicken with a mushroom jus and onion puree. Oh, but we didn't have any mushrooms either, so we're using carrots," Emmy said.

"We're improvising," Poppy added.

"Mmmm, you seem to do that a lot," he joked.

"Well, I am an actress," she said with a smile. "Dinner will be ready in ten minutes, so do you want to go freshen up or something?"

"Why, because I'm wearing too much aftershave?"

"Ah, sometimes you do actually," Emmy said quickly.

"I do not," he objected.

Poppy stopped what she was doing and looked up at him seriously. "No, it's true. Sometimes you wear too much."

"Okay, I can take a hint. I'm going upstairs."

He walked away and started up the first stair, but then stopped. He looked back at them. His house was alive and buzzing with a kind of colorful chaos that filled it from floor to ceiling, the place was almost bursting with it. This wasn't something he was used to, but he liked it. A lot. And he especially liked having Poppy here. She brightened everything up, just like her namesake. The house had been very dark for a while now, and it felt like she was the ray of sunshine it desperately needed.

CHAPTER EIGHTY-THREE

~

Poppy

"Uh ..." I lifted the fork to my lips again. "Uh ... it's very ... um," I was searching for a word other than "shit."

"Interesting," Ryan offered up.

I nodded. "Yes, interesting. Good word. The chicken definitely explodes on your palate," I said, thinking about the lines from *MasterChef*. "I mean, you can tell that the onion is the hero of the dish and this 'jus' is definitely quite a symphony of flavors." I tried to take another bite, but it was very hard.

"A symphony of flavors," Ryan repeated. "Good term."

"Guys," Emmy said. "You can just come out and say that it tastes like crap."

"Hey. Language," Ryan said quickly, but then paused. "Okay. It tastes like crap."

"Absolute crap!" I put my fork down. "I'm sorry," I said quickly.

"No. No," Ryan jumped in. "I think it's very sweet you guys tried to cook dinner. Sure, it's a bit off—"

"A bit?" I said sarcastically.

"It's way, way off," Emmy said. "It's off AF."

"AF?" Ryan turned to her. "What does that stand for?"

Emmy smiled at him. "You say it when something is very bad, or very good." She gave me a little conspiratorial look and I raised my eyebrows at her.

I knew exactly what AF stood for, I wasn't that old.

Ryan leaned back in his seat and put his fork down. He was wearing a casual jersey that looked slightly old and worn. He'd just showered and his hair was damp. He looked so relaxed and casual and comfortable that I just wanted to crawl up onto his lap and hug him. Everything about this moment felt so normal and natural, as if I was meant to be here.

"Pizza?" he asked.

"Please," Emmy said quickly.

"I second that." I stood up and gathered the plates.

"What does everyone want?" He pulled his phone out and started dialing.

"Regina," Emmy shouted from the table.

I turned around and was just about to open my mouth when he smiled at me. "I know. Pepperoni."

I smiled back at him.

* * *

The pizzas arrived and we ate them on the couch while watching TV. It felt cozy, as if we were all in exactly the right place. As if I fitted here, perfectly. Like a key sliding into a lock, I was unlocking something so precious and special that I wanted to be a part of it.

"I think I'm going to go to bed," Emmy suddenly said, pushing the pizza box away and holding her stomach. "I am so full!" She stuck her stomach out even more.

"That pizza was good AF," Ryan said, and Emmy burst out laughing. "What?" He looked confused.

"Please, never try and use that in a sentence again," she said to him.

"Fine. Good night, love," Ryan leaned forward and planted a kiss on her forehead.

"Night," she looked at me, and I shot up.

"I better go to bed too. Before it gets too late and cold to walk out there and I freeze before I reach the guest room," I joked.

Emmy looked from me to Ryan, and back again. "I don't mind if you sleep inside. I mean, if you're worried that I might think . . ." She paused. "I get it if you want to move inside," she said.

"No, no!" I held my hand up. "It's not like that. I'm not moving in or anything, this is just temporary. Until it's okay to go home."

She smiled and shrugged at us. "Cool. Well, whatever. I'm just saying." She turned and walked upstairs.

I fiddled with my hair nervously; her words had caused a kind of awkward question to hang in the air, and now that she was gone, it felt like the question needed to be answered.

Ryan looked at me. "I wouldn't want to confuse Emmy," he suddenly said. "I wouldn't want to send her the wrong message with you sleeping upstairs if this thing between us wasn't—" He stopped talking and lowered his head. Put his hands into his pockets and shuffled his foot across the floor.

"Serious?" I asked.

He nodded. "Serious," he repeated slowly.

"And by serious, you mean?" I asked.

"That you and I, we're going to give this a go. Officially," he said softly.

I took a step towards him. "Are you asking me if I want to go steady with you, Mr. Stark?"

He fixed his blue eyes on me and his lips twitched into a smile. He looked so good like this. A casual version of himself. I realized how privileged I was to see him like this. I was pretty sure he didn't show this side to many people.

"Maybe I am, Miss Peterson." His smile grew. Cute and coy like a schoolboy.

I nodded. "Can I think about it?"

He looked confused for a moment. "You want to think about it?"

"There is a lot to think about," I said.

"Like what?" he asked.

"Well, I can't just move in here, for starters. That's not the intention. And I no longer have a job either, and quite frankly, I don't want to work as anyone's assistant ever again. I'm afraid the experience might have scarred me for life."

He chuckled. "Sorry about that."

"So, I don't really have a place to stay right now, I don't really have a job and it would be completely strange if I just went to sleep upstairs with you. Don't you think?"

"Well, what do you want to do?" he asked.

"Honestly, I don't know. Well, I do, but I'm not sure how to do it again."

"What do you want to do?" he asked.

I smiled. "I want to act. But my agent doesn't exactly take my calls anymore so I don't really know about any auditions going on at the moment."

"Get a new agent," he said. "You're big in Nigeria, after all."

I laughed. "I guess I could try and contact some."

"You should. It's your dream, it's what you want to do." He stepped forward and placed his hands on my shoulders. "I have an idea. Stay here, in the guest house, for a while and work on your dream. Besides, I like having you here. The house feels good with you in it."

I shook my head immediately. "No, that's crazy. I can't just move in with you."

"You're not moving in. You're simply temporarily staying in the guest house. Like a tenant might. And when you do get work, which you will, I can help you find a new apartment, if that's what you want."

"What about the apartment I have now?" I asked.

"You can't move back into that place, it's not safe there."

"I have to give a month's notice if I want to move out," I said, thinking about how great it would be if I never set foot in the place again.

"Well, give them notice."

"What about all my things in there?"

"We can move them out later, or do you want to go and get them now?" he asked.

I put my hands on my face and shook my head. "Are you being serious? This isn't a joke? You're just inviting me to come and live in your guest house?"

"Does it feel strange?" he asked.

"Strange?" I repeated, thinking about it. I shook my head. "No, it doesn't. But I know it probably should feel strange."

"Why?" he asked.

"Well, we've only known each other for two weeks, and I'm pretty sure you hated me for at least one of those."

He took a step closer to me. "I never hated you," he said softly, lifting his hand up to my chin. "I might have wanted to hate you, though." He smiled.

"And what about us then?" I asked.

"What about us?"

"Well, what does moving in here mean, for us?"

"Well," he leaned in and kissed me gently on the lips. "I can't speak for you, but I would really like to see where this goes."

"You would, would you?" I kissed him back.

"It feels good with you. *I* feel good when I'm with you." He let his lips linger on mine.

I nodded. My lips dragged against his. "I'd like to see where it goes too," I said softly.

We kissed. Long and slow and passionate, and it felt right. Like every kiss I'd ever had in my life before this one was only a rehearsal. Practice for this moment right here.

"So, are we dating then?" I asked.

He pulled me closer. "We are," he said.

My body shivered and I wanted to dissolve into his arms. "And are we taking it slow?" I asked breathily, as his hand slipped under my jersey and his fingers traced the curve of my lower back.

He pulled away momentarily and looked at me. "By slow, do you mean I can't do this . . . ?" His hand suddenly gripped my bum and he pulled me closer, rocking his hips into mine.

I shook my head. "It would be a tragedy if you couldn't do that anymore," I whispered breathily.

"A total tragedy."

Our eyes locked. His were dark and stormy and full of lust.

"It would be an even bigger tragedy if I couldn't do this . . ." He slipped his other hand down the front of my pants.

"What else would be a tragedy?" I asked breathily, closing my eyes as his fingers stroked me through the thin cotton fabric.

"How about this?" he asked, slipping his finger into my panties and straight inside me.

I opened my eyes and inhaled sharply.

"That would . . ." I moaned. "Def . . . ah, definitely . . . be . . ." I couldn't get the words out as he moved in and out of me. "Yes, a tragedy," I whispered. All I could do now was close my eyes and submit to the feelings rushing through my body. I held onto him, my legs getting softer and softer as he brought me nearer and nearer . . .

And then he stopped.

I opened my eyes with shock. Gasping. Panting. Feeling stunned by the sudden loss of him.

"But you know what would be an even bigger tragedy?" he asked, gripping my hips and walking me backward.

I shook my head as he guided me through the living room, towards the kitchen. "The real tragedy would be if I couldn't get you out of these clothes, right now, and have you naked, and underneath me."

I nodded. "That would be a great tragedy indeed."

"It would," he said, pushing me out the back door.

"Well, let's see if we can remedy that then." I took him by the hand and led him outside into the cold.

CHAPTER EIGHTY-FOUR

Ryan

*H*e climbed off the bed and searched for his clothes on the floor. He looked at his watch; it was already well after 1 a.m. "I should get some sleep tonight," he mumbled as he started picking his clothes up. "I've got a bunch of hectic meetings tomorrow, which I'm not looking forward to." He found his shirt by the door and slipped it over his head.

She sat on the bed watching him, her eyes following his every move until he was fully clothed. He sat on the chair and started lacing up his shoes. He could feel her eyes on him the entire time. He looked up; she was bundled in the warm jersey and scarf, sitting cross-legged on the bed.

"What?" he asked.

"I was just thinking about something you said after the hospital," she said.

He stopped lacing his shoes. "What did I say?"

"That you didn't like your job," she said softly, creeping to the edge of the bed to be closer to him.

He looked over at her. The fire that he'd lit in the room was casting a warm red glow across the side of her face. "On most days, I don't," he said, going back to his shoelaces.

"Then why do you do it?" she asked.

She watched him for a while and, honestly, he didn't really know what to say. He shrugged his shoulders.

She stood up and walked over to him. She sat on the floor, and suddenly she was lacing his other shoe for him. He watched her curiously, he couldn't remember the last time someone had tied his shoelace.

"Cross the bunny ears over each other, the bunny runs around the tree and it jumps into the hole and *voilà*," she said, pulling his laces tight.

He looked down at her and smiled. "Thanks."

"Do you know how long it took me to learn to do that?" She leaned back on her elbows. "My mom was so patient, though. She was a good teacher, except with bike riding. She tried to teach me that, but couldn't."

He uncrossed his legs and leaned forward in the chair, resting his elbows on his knees. "You said your dad walked out on you guys?" he asked.

"I was six," she said, looking down at the carpet. "I still remember exactly what I was wearing that day, isn't that weird?" She looked up at him. "I was wearing my favourite dress. It was pastel pink and had these embroidered teddy bears on it. God, I loved that dress so much. My dad had bought it for me a few months before. He'd told me I looked like a real lady in it." She looked back down at the carpet and paused. "I could never wear it after that."

He reached out and put his hands on her knees, giving

them both a firm squeeze. "That guy doesn't know what he missed out on."

Her face was still tilted down, and he could see she was trying to force a small smile. "Apparently, he has a whole other family now and lives in Texas of all places." Her voice sounded soft and breathy, and his heart tugged inside his chest.

"Emmy's dad is a DJ in Ibiza. After my sister Rachel died, he suggested that she come stay with him for a while. He hadn't seen her in over seven years."

She looked up at him and shook her head. "I can guess what your response to that was," she said, a small smile flickering across her lips.

"His DJ name is DJ Speed Ballz."

She let out a small chuckle. "Sounds like your sister shopped for boyfriends at the same place I used to."

"Yup, she could have done a lot better than him, but she always said she never regretted it and wouldn't change things for the world. Because of Emmy." Suddenly his throat tightened. An invisible punch to the gut and a kick in the chest. His heart pressed against his ribcage and that familiar feeling—the one he'd felt in the bicycle store—started rising up inside him again. His eyes started to sting and he quickly stood up.

"I . . . I better go." He marched towards the door. The emotions were bubbling up inside him and they felt like they were about to explode out of him. He needed to be alone. He didn't want her to see him like this. He didn't want anyone to see him like this.

"Wait, wait." Poppy chased after him and grabbed his arm as he tried to open the door. "Where are you going?" she asked.

"Into the house," he said, not making eye contact. He didn't want her to see the tears that were pooling in the corners of his eyes.

She put her hands on his face and pulled him towards her. "Ryan, it's okay to let go sometimes." Her voice was soft.

He shook his head, clenching his jaw as tightly as he could.

"Ryan, it's okay," she said again, running her hands down the sides of his face. "What are you afraid of?" she asked.

He finally looked at her as the first small tear escaped and trickled down his cheek. It pooled in the corner of his lips and he licked it off. "I'm afraid that if I start, I won't stop," he managed, even though his voice was quivering.

She smiled up at him. Her smile was so open and empathetic that, no matter how much he wanted to stop himself, he couldn't. Another tear slipped down his cheek; she wiped it away with her thumb.

"Some days," he whispered, "some days it all feels too much, I just have to push it all down."

She nodded. "But you can't push it down forever."

She took him by the hands and led him back towards the bed. She climbed on and pulled him next to her. She wrapped her arm around him and pulled his head down onto her chest. He lay there with his cheek pressed into her warm body; he could hear her heart beating and feel her breathing. She ran her fingers through his hair in such a gentle, caring way that he couldn't have stopped it if he'd wanted to.

He cried.

He cried for the first time since his sister had died. He hadn't even cried at her funeral, he'd been too busy trying to put on a brave face for Emmy and his mother.

"It's okay," she whispered into his ear as he held onto her and let it all out. "I've got you." She planted a soft kiss on the side of his face. "I'm here."

He'd never allowed himself to be like this with anyone before. So exposed and emotionally naked. And although this moment was so painfully raw, it strangled his throat and squeezed his stomach into knots, it felt good to finally let it all out. And to let it out with her. He'd never felt more vulnerable with anyone before, but also never so safe.

CHAPTER EIGHTY-FIVE

Ryan

It was Friday evening and he'd just dropped Emmy off at her friend's house for the night. He'd finally agreed to let her sleep over. Poppy had convinced him it was okay after she had befriended the mother at school and given her the third degree, and then gone home and stalked her on all the appropriate social media platforms to make sure she wasn't a psycho. He smiled to himself whenever he thought about her and as he drove something started to dawn on him.

Poppy had been living in the guest house for two weeks now. They'd made love every night; he'd sneak into the cottage after Emmy had gone to bed and then reluctantly sneak back into the house. They'd eaten dinner together every night, watched TV together, stayed up late talking for hours, they'd even built a small aviary in the garden with Emmy's help for the bloody pigeon. She'd fetched Emmy from school and taken her shopping and they'd all gone out to movies together. All of this, and he hadn't even taken her out on their first official date yet. He needed to remedy that, and he needed to do something rather spectacular to make up for it. And he knew just who to call to make it happen. Her name was Ayanda. Best damn assistant he'd ever had in his life. She was almost making his work life bearable—almost. Since Poppy had brought it up two weeks ago, he'd been thinking about it non-stop. He'd never wanted to run his father's company. That had never been his dream, not that he knew what his dream was. But it had been expected of him, so he'd done it. But with this mall, and all the tensions between the board and the shareholders, he was starting to fantasize about just walking away from it all. But what would he do?

At least Ayanda was relieving some of the pressure on him. He'd had to tell her the truth about Poppy—well, she'd figured it out—and now she too was a member of the "Bring Ramona González back" Facebook page.

He picked up his phone and called her. She answered immediately. "Ayanda, I need you to try and do something for me. It might be impossible, but I suspect if there's one person who can make it happen, it's probably you."

* * *

"Where are you taking me?" Poppy asked.

"I told you, I'm taking you on our first date." He turned and smiled at her. He loved to see her sitting in the passenger seat. In fact, whenever the car was empty, it felt wrong and he would always try to imagine her there.

"But where?" She pulled her legs up onto the seat and crossed them. She always sat like that; he found it funny that she had all this leg room, but preferred to cross her legs on the seat.

"You'll just have to wait and see," he said.

"But we've been driving for half an hour already, we've driven all the way out of the city," she pressed.

"Do you not like surprises or something?" he asked.

"No, not really."

"Well, you're going to have to get used to it. I am full of surprises," he said.

She burst out laughing. "No, you're not."

"What?"

"Oh, please. You eat the same thing for breakfast every morning, you go to work at the exact same time and read the paper in the exact same way—"

"Are you saying I'm boring?" he asked.

"Not boring. Predictable."

"Wow! Is that what you really think of me? That I am predictable?"

She laughed even harder now. "It's not a bad thing. It's cute. I think it's cute you only wear black and dark grey suits to work, with either blue or maroon ties. It's cute that you eat a bowl of Hi Fiber bran every single day of your life with one cup of almond milk and one spoon of sugar, and that you eat your lunch at precisely ten minutes past twelve, and that you have the same sandwich every single day, without mayonnaise, because you think it's messy."

He looked at her for a moment or two and then swerved off the road. "Predictable?" He turned the ignition off and unbuckled his seat belt. "Would someone who's predictable do this?" He undid her seat belt and then yanked her towards him.

She laughed. God, he loved that laugh. The sound of it, the way it made him feel.

"Would someone predictable do this?" He pushed his seat back and pulled her onto his lap.

She gasped and then giggled.

"And I'm guessing a predictable person wouldn't do this either?" He unbuckled his belt and pushed up her skirt.

She widened her eyes and looked out the window. "We're on the side of the road."

"I know," he said. "And guess what?"

"What?" she asked.

He pulled her panties aside as he managed to free himself. "I'm going to do this."

He guided himself inside her and they both moaned.

Chapter Eighty-Six

Poppy

"*B*utterfly world?" I asked, standing in the parking lot and looking up at the sign. "But it's closed." I read the operating hours.

He walked up behind me and wrapped his arms around me. We smelt of sex and sweat and unpredictability. "For you, I've opened it."

"What?"

"Well, technically Ayanda opened it. She promised that we'd give them a small donation."

"Told you Ayanda was good." I turned around and kissed him on the cheek.

"Yes, you did." He let me go and moved to the trunk of the car, where he pulled out a bag.

"What's that?" I asked.

"Picnic," he said, closing the trunk.

"What exactly is this place?" I asked. I'd never been here before.

"I came here with Emmy and my sister once, many years ago. And I wanted to bring you here because I know you're going to love it."

"Am I?" I asked.

"Let's go inside and find out, shall we?" He held his arm out and I took it.

It felt good, the way it slipped into his, and the way that when it did, we felt like we belonged like this. It had been a strange two weeks; I'd been staying in the guest house and we'd all fallen into a routine that, until now, I hadn't known I needed. But now that I had it, I didn't know how I was ever going to exist without it. We'd all eat breakfast together in the morning, and then he would go to work and Emmy would go to school. I'd spend the morning sending out my CV or going to meet agents or casting directors. In the afternoon, I'd fetch Emmy from school and we'd hang out until he got home and we would all eat dinner together. And the next day, we'd do it all over again. But I knew this wasn't permanent, this wasn't the answer to all my problems. I still had bills and no job and nowhere to stay, really—this was temporary.

We walked up to the entrance and someone opened up for us. We walked in and I couldn't believe it. We were inside a massive greenhouse. It was full of streams and tropical plants and the hot, moist air was full of colorful butterflies fluttering around us.

"It's . . . It's . . ." I was amazed. I had almost lost the words.

"It's all yours," said the woman who'd let us in, and then she walked out.

"I can't believe you did this." I turned to him and smiled. His blue eyes looked darker in the light that was reflected off the greenery around us.

"Don't you know by now, Poppy? I would do anything for you." He took a step closer to me.

"You would?" I asked, slipping under his spell.

"Come." He put his hand out, and I took it.

We walked through the greenhouse; the air was thick and heavy, and all the plants were covered in a warm, wet glow. Streams ran through the dense greenery, and the sound of rushing water and crickets made the place seem alive with a kind of natural magic. Huge ferns and Elephant's Ears and bright red Anthurium. Palm trees and candy-colored orchids and small rock pools filled with golden-colored koi. I walked down the path, touching the plants as I went.

"My mother would have loved it here." I leaned forward to inhale the intoxicating scent of sweet frangipani. A bright, aquamarine-colored butterfly landed on the flower in front of me.

"Come and look," I said to Ryan.

He moved closer to me.

"It's beautiful," I said.

"You're beautiful." He wrapped his arms around me and put his head on my shoulder.

"That was so smooth," I chuckled.

"Smooth, but effective?" He nuzzled into my neck.

I held my hand out towards the flower and the butterfly climbed on top of it.

"Look, look," I said excitedly.

Ryan lifted his head and looked at my hand. I brought it closer to us, slowly. The butterfly flexed its wings but didn't move off my hand. Its wings looked like they'd been doused in glitter, and they shimmered in the light. And then, suddenly, it flapped its wings and flew away. We both looked up and watched it disappear into the palm tree above our heads.

"I love it here." I tilted my head back and looked into Ryan's eyes.

"And I love you." His voice came out fast and shaky, and it made me feel as if every single butterfly was now inside me, fluttering its wings.

"You . . . you . . ."

"Love you," he said again. "In case you didn't hear me the first time."

"I heard you. I . . . I . . ." I stuttered as the butterflies were replaced by birds. I could barely breathe now.

"Um," he looked at me and raised a brow. "I'm kind of hoping you're trying to say it back to me?"

I nodded, fast. "I am. I am, I'm just . . . uh . . ."

"Stuttering?"

I nodded again, smiling. A smile so wide that it felt like my mouth would rip open.

"So?" he asked.

"Me too," I blurted out and wrapped my arms around him.

He pulled me into a hug.

"I love you too," I said.

Because I did. Somewhere along the way I'd fallen in love with this man. And now, I felt like I'd finally come home. I had a place I belonged. And that place was with him, and Emmy.

CHAPTER EIGHTY-SEVEN

ᴖ

Ryan

Three Weeks Later

*H*e drove home from work. In many ways, these last few weeks had been amazing. Every time he left work, he was in a good mood because he knew he was coming home to her and Emmy. Poppy being there made the house so much better. He'd been a much better boss too. He was a happier guy at work, and people had even started greeting him when he arrived.

But instead of going straight home, he made a quick stop at the locksmith. He'd been thinking about this for a while now and he'd decided to do it. And tonight would be the night. They'd already been sleeping in the same bed for weeks now—the guest room arrangement had somehow fallen away after that night in the greenhouse.

The locksmith passed him the keys. A key to his house and a remote for the gate. Until now, she'd been using the spare keys. But tonight he wanted to give her a set of her own and ask her, officially, if she wanted to move in with them. He knew it was fast—some would say impulsive and crazy—but now that she'd been there, in his home, eating dinner with them, watching TV on the couch together, feeling like part of the family, he never wanted her to leave again.

He looked at the keys in his hand and reached into his pocket. He pulled out a small box and slipped them inside.

He was even more excited to go home tonight.

CHAPTER EIGHTY-EIGHT

Poppy

"Oh my God, I've got great news!" I ran into the lounge and skidded across the tiles. Ryan was relaxing on the couch and turned around.

"Hey, I've been waiting for you." He smiled at me.

"Sorry I'm late, but something super exciting came up."

"What?" he asked, looking up at me with those blue eyes that I'd come to really like over the last few weeks. *That I'd come to love.*

"So," I flopped down on the couch next to him, "I spoke to my agent today—well, I didn't even know she was my agent anymore really, since she'd been avoiding my calls—and guess what?"

"Wait, didn't you get that other agent, the one who got you that shampoo commercial?"

"Well, I haven't signed anything official with him yet," I said.

He nodded, and I continued. "So anyway, she called me out of the blue to tell me that they want to bring Ramona González back. And more than that, they want to make me a main character. They're even changing the name of the show to *Venganza Ramona*. They want to sign me for the rest of the show, another twenty episodes."

"Really?" He pulled me into his arms. "That's amazing. I knew it would happen." He hoisted me onto his lap and cradled my face between his hands. "You're brilliant."

"I'm so excited. But I've got so much to plan. They want to start shooting next week, and they've actually moved the shoot down to Joburg into a proper big studio, since they have more budget now and—"

"Wait, they're shooting in Joburg?"

"I know! At this huge studio and, drum roll, I get my own dressing room. Like an actual room that I can dress in, just me. Not a room made with some hanging sheets that are pegged to a washing line that we all have to share." I climbed off his lap and flopped onto my back across the couch. "My own dressing room. I wonder if they'll put my name on the door? Maybe in some cheesy glittery star. *Rrramonaaa!*" I said, waving my hand in the air.

"In Joburg?" he said.

But I didn't really hear him. I was too busy imagining my name on the side of a trailer. "And, guess what . . . there is budget for hair and make-up now too, so I don't have to do that myself, and they're dropping Ramona's wig and glasses—something about my vision and hair improving during the mutation. Oh my God, Tamlin was right about how they're bringing me back!" I reached for my bag and pulled out the script and started reading. "Ramona González, back from the dead after gaining superpowers in a radioactive explosion, returns to take over the family business and avenge her murder." I laughed. "You hear that? Apparently, I have superpowers. I don't know what they are yet, but I hope it's something fun like invisibility, or telekinesis, or—"

"In Joburg," he said again.

This time I stopped talking. "Yes, I know, I don't love it there either, but it does have the best TV studios in the country. Cape Town is more film, you know. But Joburg—"

"Is in Joburg," he cut me off again. "As in Johannesburg, as in a city that is over thirteen hundred kilometers away?"

"Uh . . ." I looked at him and suddenly a cold, hard rock fell into the bottom of my stomach. "Yes," I said tentatively.

"I mean, I don't want to be the spoiler of dreams here, but what about us?" he asked.

I shook my head. "What do you mean, what about us?" I asked. And then it hit me. All at once. I'd been so excited about the news that I hadn't even thought about him and Emmy, in this house . . . in Cape Town.

"It's not forever," I said quickly.

"And how long does it take to shoot twenty episodes?" he asked.

I shrugged. "I don't know. A month or two maybe?"

"A month or two," he repeated. "And you'll be living in Joburg during those months?"

"I . . . I . . . guess. I hadn't really thought that far. I hadn't really thought about the logistics of the whole thing. I mean, I just heard the news twenty minutes ago, and I didn't really stop to consider—"

"Emmy and me? Didn't stop to consider us?"

"I mean, I guess. But let's talk about it now. It's not like I'm moving to another country, I'm only moving to—"

"So, you're just going?" he asked. "Just like that. One day you're here, and one day you're not." His face changed. It washed over with anger again.

I hadn't seen him like that in ages.

"This was such a fucking bad idea," he said. "I should have known this would happen."

"What was a bad idea?" I asked.

"Bringing you into our lives like this. I should never have done that," he said. "I knew I should have kept my business and personal lives separate."

"Bringing me?" I repeated. "Bringing me, like I am some kind of possession?"

He rolled his eyes. "You know what I mean."

"You were the one that said I should stay, remember?" My heart was thumping in my chest now.

"Well, maybe that was a mistake. Now that you've just suddenly decided to leave like this."

"I didn't say a thing about leaving. This is not me leaving!" I was frustrated now; he wasn't hearing me.

"I think the definition of leaving is when a person physically goes. And you are physically going." He looked at me.

I shook my head. Exasperated. "Yes, I am going for a while, but I'm not leaving. Well, not in that sense."

"How many different leaving senses can there be, Poppy? As far as I can see, there's only one. Either you are here, with us. Or you are gone. You've left."

He stood up and walked off. Walked into the center of the floor and looked around. And then he turned. His face looked so sad, so vulnerable. I wanted to stand up and hug him, but I knew

I couldn't. "We've just got used to having you here. I like having you here. It feels right. You bring this light into our home; I haven't had that for so long, neither has Emmy, and now you are just going to leave? Are we not important to you?" he asked. His eyes looked like they were watering now.

I stood up too. "You *are* important to me. You and Emmy are so important to me. And I love you," I said.

"I love you too. But then why does it feel like I'm losing you?"

"Who said anything about losing?" I asked. "I'm just—"

"Moving away from us for a couple of months," he said. He said it in a tone that was so sad and empty that I think I heard it for the first time. *I got it.* How would I feel if he and Emmy came to me, out of the blue, and said they were leaving?

I stopped. My heart felt like it was breaking now. "Are you asking me to choose between you and this job?" I asked shakily.

He hung his head. "When you put it that way, it sounds unfair."

"I honestly didn't think I would need to choose. You were the one who told me to follow my dream!"

"Yeah, I just didn't think that it would take you away from us."

"Neither did I," I said. "So what do you want?" I threw my arms in the air. "Should I say no to this job and go and take a job that I'm miserable in, like you? Should I take some job that I hate, that makes me unhappy and angry and irritable? Like you?"

"That's not fair," he said.

"But you hate what you do!" I said loudly. "You say it at least five times a day, every single day, and I don't want to be like you. Stuck in a job that is slowly killing me."

"Wait, I thought we were talking about *your* job, not mine?" he asked angrily.

"Maybe we should talk about your job?" I almost shouted that last part. In the time that we'd been together, it had become abundantly clear to me just how bad his work was for him. How stressed and angry it made him.

He shook his head furiously. "This isn't fair on Emmy," he finally said. "You've been here for her, and now you're going. I don't think she can handle more women that she cares about disappearing."

"Disappearing?"

There was a lull in the conversation, a pause that was so loud and painful that it screamed at us.

"Just go! Just go to Joburg and I guess we'll see you in a few months, or not. Whatever."

"I . . . I . . ." I stuttered again. I hadn't meant it to go like this. Not at all.

"Anyway, I guess you won't be needing this after all." He walked up to me and put a small box in my hand. I opened it slowly.

"What are they?"

"Keys. To the house. I was going to ask you to move in, but I guess that was . . ." He turned and looked at me again. "I think you should go now. Before Emmy comes home. I don't want her seeing this. I don't want her to have to say another painful goodbye."

"Wait, I . . ." I said in panic.

"Wait, what? Are you going, or aren't you going? Are you leaving us, or aren't you leaving us?"

"My things," I said. "My plants, the pigeon, my clothes, my—"

"Emmy is going to be home in ten minutes," he said, getting

angry now. "I want you gone. Go and pack a bag and take a few things. I'll make sure you get the rest."

"I am not leaving without my mother's plants!" I stepped forward angrily and almost shouted.

"Wow," he said, shaking his head.

"Wow, what?" I asked.

"Seems like some plants are more important than us."

"That is so fucking unfair," I said as the tears started.

"No, what's unfair is you leaving us—without any warning, I should add. That's fucking unfair, Poppy." He was fuming now and I started to cry.

"Jesus Christ! Please just get out before Emmy finds you here crying like this!" He spat the words at me so angrily, I felt my fucking heart break.

And so, I did. I turned and ran out the door.

CHAPTER EIGHTY-NINE

∿

Ryan

"*W*here's Poppy?" Emmy asked when she walked in.

She had called shortly after his fight with Poppy, to ask if she could spend the weekend at her new friend's house. He'd agreed. He didn't want Emmy seeing him like this anyway. But he hadn't really cooled down that much, and it had already been two days since the fight.

He cleared his throat anxiously. "She's . . . um, she's not here anymore."

"Oh," she said casually. "Where did she go?"

He shrugged. "I don't know," he admitted.

Emmy looked at him curiously. "Did you guys have a fight? Don't worry, I'm sure you'll sort it out soon." She smiled at him.

He shook his head. "No. She's gone."

"What do you mean?"

"She's probably in Joburg. They're bringing back her character, and she's going to shoot the rest of the show in Joburg."

"What?" Emmy's face lit up. "That's great news, she must be so stoked. That's awesome."

"Awesome?' he asked. "She's moving to Joburg to shoot it."

"Not permanently," Emmy said quickly. "Poppy would never just leave us like that, not permanently. Did she say permanently?"

"No," he shook his head. "She didn't."

"So, she's coming back then," Emmy said.

"Well, she didn't say that either."

"But did she actually say she *wasn't* coming back?" Emmy folded her arms and looked at him.

"No, she didn't say that either," he found himself repeating.

Emmy looked at him and raised her eyebrows. "So, what exactly did you fight about?"

He shook his head. "It's an adult thing. You wouldn't understand."

"An adult thing?" she asked. "Well, from where I'm standing, and from what you've told me, it doesn't sound very adult."

"What do you mean?"

"Well, you're standing here telling me all these things, making these assumptions about what she was thinking. And if you guys had had an adult discussion with each other, you would be telling me things very differently right now."

"What would I be telling you?" he asked.

"You'd be saying how excited you were for her. How it's only a two-hour flight away. How she can come back on weekends, or we can fly out there to see her sometimes. That it's only for a while, but it's cool because you love each other and she's pursuing her dream and you would hate to take that away from her because you love her."

He stared at her blankly. He hadn't even thought about this. He'd just seen her going, and that had been it. He'd reacted from a place of total fear about losing her. She was the best thing that had happened to him in a while, and he'd just freaked out.

"Please tell me you guys talked about that," she said.

He shook his head. "We didn't. I didn't really get to that, I just—"

"Lost it?"

"Yes, I kind of did."

"So, you let the one really good thing in your life just go, without trying to figure out how to make it work?"

He nodded. "I guess I did."

She shook her head. "Ryan, it's the twenty-first century. We have Skype, we have Facetime calls, we have these amazing things called airplanes that magically make you appear at another place within hours. I mean, Shelly's dad works in Joburg, he flies there on Monday morning and comes home on Friday afternoon. Shelly reckons it keeps the romance alive. She says it's pretty gross but she often hears them on Friday nights—"

"Okay, enough information."

"And it's not forever. It's not a soap opera; it doesn't go on for a hundred years like *Days of Our Lives*, it's going to end soon. And it's her dream. And she is so good at it—if she didn't do it, she would literally be depriving the world of her brilliance."

He sat there and clasped his hands together. "Okay, I might have overreacted a bit."

"So you guys basically fought about nothing," Emmy said.

"We did also fight about my work," he confessed.

"What about it?" she asked.

"She said she doesn't ever want to be like me, stuck in a job that I hate, that makes me angry—"

"And grumpy and irritable!" She cut him off, and he looked up at her. "She's right about that too. Your job sucks. Even Grandma said that."

"What did she say?" he asked. He was intrigued. He never really spoke to his mother about work.

"That guy came around to talk to her the one day when I was there," she said.

"What guy?" he asked.

"That one with the gray hair, Mr. Redbach, or—"

"Rautenbach," he said. "What did he want?"

"He wanted Grandma to talk to you about the mall or something. He said that the things you were doing were against everything Grandpa believed in for the company. And since Grandma also still has shares in the company, he wanted her to try and talk you out of it all."

Ryan listened to her speak, and his mind started racing. "God, do you know absolutely everything that goes on around here?" he finally asked when she had finished talking.

"Basically," she said with a smile.

"Shit." He hung his head and then shook it hopelessly. "Everything is falling apart."

"Language, Ryan," she joked, and it made him smile.

"I think I've made two huge mistakes," he finally said, after doing some more thinking.

"It happens. So, go and make them both right. Go and fix this work thing, and say sorry to Poppy."

He shook his head. "I think the things I said and did are way beyond a simple sorry."

"Nothing is beyond a sorry. You just have to make it a really, really, really good apology. Like in the Hollywood romcom movies. They are always doing these massive grand gestures at the end, after the guy has messed up and the girl has gone away."

He looked up. "And how do I do that?"

"Well, you know her. You know what's important to her, I'm sure you'll figure it out."

He sat and thought for a while.

"Maybe she hasn't left yet?" Emmy said. "Maybe she's gone back to her apartment? Perhaps you should go find her and talk to her, that's a good place to start."

"Her place?" He looked up. He'd almost forgotten they were still paying rent for it. The landlord hadn't allowed her to get out of her lease very easily and had made her give two months' notice. Some of her furniture was still there. Maybe that's where he would find her.

He looked up at his niece and smiled. "When the hell did you get so wise?"

She shrugged casually. "I'm thirteen, remember?"

"Fine, do you mind if I go quickly?"

"No. Go now!" She stood up and walked over to him. "You know what Mom would say if she was here?" she asked.

He nodded and chuckled. "Follow your heart. Stop thinking. Stop analyzing."

"And she would also tell you to stop being a total idiot, and don't let someone so perfect for you go." She put her hands on his shoulders and squeezed. "Seriously, she would be dragging you out the door by now."

He looked at Emmy, seeing the emotion in her blue eyes. She was so much like his sister. All heart. "You're so much like your mom, you know that? And she would be so proud of you. *I'm* so proud of you."

Emmy threw her arms around him and hugged him.

* * *

He ran up the stairs, taking them two at a time. He had no idea what he was going to say to her, but he knew he needed to try and make this right. He knocked on the door as soon as he got there, and when there was no answer immediately, he knocked again.

"Poppy!" he called out. "Please open the door, I really want to talk to you." He waited and finally heard the sound of feet shuffling across the floor. He heard the chain on the door being unlocked, saw the door handle move, and the anticipation grew as he watched the door handle going down and down and . . .

The door opened and a man stood there. "What do you want?" The man sounded irritated.

"I'm looking for Poppy. She lives here," he said.

"Well, she doesn't live here anymore, I moved in yesterday. Place is a total shithole, though, and looks nothing like the photos of it. And the landlord is charging a fortune to stay here. He's a total rip-off artist."

"Uh . . . I'm very sorry to hear th—" Ryan cut himself off. "You say you moved in yesterday?"

"Yeah." The guy put his hand up on the door. "Only good

thing about this place is the lock on the door. It will keep the bloody ex out." He laughed loudly.

"Well, okay, I won't keep you then," Ryan said and started walking away.

"The girl you're looking for, does she have long brownish hair?" the man asked.

He turned. "Yes."

"I saw her yesterday. She'd packed a bag, and it looked like she was in quite a hurry."

"I'm sure she was," Ryan said under his breath.

He hung his head and walked away. He couldn't rectify the mistake he'd made with Poppy right now, but he could rectify another one. He pulled his phone out of his pocket and started dialing the number.

CHAPTER NINETY

⌢

Poppy

It's night-time. The room is dark and Ignacio is sleeping peacefully. Thunder strikes and he wakes up. A massive puff of smoke fills the room, and out of it Ramona appears. Her hair is long and auburn, she no longer wears glasses, and she is glowing. Ignacio is terrified and scrambles to the other side of the room.

IGNACIO

You . . . (*trembling*) You, but you are dead. We found the
remains of your body after the explosion.

RAMONA

(*Lets out an evil laugh*) No, I am not dead. I am here,
and I have come back to avenge my name.
I have come back to take up my rightful position
as head of the company.

IGNACIO

(*Scrambles to his feet*) Never! It's my company now! Never, over my dead body.

RAMONA

(*Another evil laugh*) Dead body. Funny you should mention that. Because that is exactly what you're going to be soon.

Methat Ishmail bursts through the door. He is carrying a huge sword.

IGNACIO

What are you doing here?

METHAT

(*Also gives an evil laugh*) Ramona and I have been working together in secret for months. And tonight, we kill you and take the company and use it for our own agenda.

IGNACIO

Why?

At that, Methat reaches up and places a hand over his face, and then in one swift movement, he pulls his prosthetic face mask off and tosses it to the floor. Ignacio gasps.

IGNACIO

Who . . . Who are you?

MET HAT

Don't you recognize me? (*Taking out his contact lenses*)
It is I, your other brother.

Ignacio gasps and grabs his chest as if he is having a heart attack.

IGNACIO

But, but . . .

MET HAT

I know. You thought I was dead.
You thought I was lost at sea, didn't you?

IGNACIO

We . . . we all did.

MET HAT

(*Shaking his head*) I drifted for days, maybe weeks.
I drank rain water and ate fish. Finally, I washed up on shore,
in the Emirates, and was taken in by a group of nomadic
desert dwellers who raised me as their own.

IGNACIO

But why did you never contact us?

MET HAT

I had to keep my identity a secret until our father died.
Because it was he who tried to kill me.

Falling off our family yacht was not a mistake,
our father pushed me.

IGNACIO
Why?

METHAT
Because he just found out that our mother had had an affair
with his sworn enemy, Alessandro Iglesias, and I am his son.
I am the love child of our father's greatest sworn enemy,
and he hated me for it.

IGNACIO
(*His face softens*) Brother, you have returned to me.

RAMONA
Don't "brother" him. You tried to kill me. You killed your
other brother too. And for that, you must die.

*Ramona holds her hands out and shoots electricity
through her fingers. It shoots across the room and
shocks Ignacio. He grabs his chest as she laughs in an
evil way.*

IGNACIO
Don't kill me! I can tell you something.
A secret that is so great, so big,
that if you knew it, you would be
powerful beyond your wildest dreams.

Ignacio drops to the floor. Ramona and Methat look at each other and then run over to Ignacio. He is dying on the floor.

RAMONA

What? Tell us! Tell us this secret.

IGNACIO

When I . . . (*coughs*) . . . was living in the rain . . . (*coughs even more*) . . . forest . . .

He moans, in pain.

RAMONA

Tell us. (*Shaking him*)

IGNACIO

I buried something there, by the great rock. Something important . . . (*coughs*) . . . something that I had in the plane with me. Something that could change the world.

RAMONA

What is it?

IGNACIO

You must never let it fall into the wrong hands.

His coughing escalates as he clings onto life.

RAMONA

Tell us what it is?

IGNACIO

It's a . . . (*moans loudly*) . . . a . . . it's . . .

He dies. Methat and Ramona look at each other.

RAMONA

NOOOOO!

End of Scene 1

* * *

I walked to my dressing room; the day had gone better than I thought. I'd been treated like some kind of star, because my character now bore the name of the show. I could almost see my mother's face—she would be so happy for me. I wished I could call her and tell her. I wished I could call Emmy and tell her. I wished I could call Ryan . . . this was what I'd wanted for so long. *Then why did it feel so empty?* Why did it feel like I was missing something so huge in my life? But I knew the answer to that, of course I did: it was because Ryan and I were no longer together.

I walked through the studio lot to my trailer. It was small as far as trailers went, certainly not what Meryl would get, but I was grateful for the space. I noticed that my lights were on inside, but I was sure I'd switched them off. The warm glow of the light through the windows looked welcoming, after a long day on the set. I reached for the door handle, pushed it open and then . . .

"What the—?" I gasped.

The trailer was full of plants. Full. There was almost no space to move around. I looked a little closer; these were *my* plants, the plants that I'd left at Ryan's house. How the hell had these gotten here?

"They didn't all fit in."

I heard his voice and turned. "What are . . . I mean, how did you . . . ?"

"I'm sorry." The production assistant suddenly appeared from around the corner. "He said he was your boyfriend and he wanted to do something special for you for your first day back. I hope that's okay?" she asked, looking a little concerned.

I nodded. "It's okay," I said.

She smiled and walked off again.

"My boyfriend, eh?" I asked, raising an eyebrow at him.

He shrugged. "Well, it was either that or they might have thought I was a crazed fan or stalker, since you are so famous now."

I rolled my eyes. "I'm big in Japan," I said. "And by that, I mean Nigeria."

"You're still big," he said, taking a step closer to me. "The people love you. And more importantly, I love you." He looked at me meaningfully.

I shook my head. "You know, according to my daisy, '*you love me not*.'"

He shook his head, clearly confused. "You know . . ." I started miming the pulling of petals. "He loves me, he loves me not, he loves me, he loves me . . . *not*."

"That's not very scientific," he said.

"Well, it did kind of make sense. What with the things you said to me the last time we spoke."

He hung his head. "God, I was such an asshole. What I said and how I reacted . . . I was just scared."

"Of what?"

"Losing you. I was scared of losing you. It seems to me that the people I love, well, they tend to . . . go away. And you were going away." His eyes were tearing up.

"I wasn't going away. Well, physically I was, but emotionally, God, Ryan, don't you know you have my heart? You have it. And no matter where I am, you would still have it. I wasn't taking that away."

He nodded. "I see that now."

"And this is my dream, Ryan. You know that."

"And you deserve this. God, if there is one person in the world that deserves it, it's you. You deserve it all. Everything." He took another step closer.

"Do you really regret bringing me into your life?" I asked. That line had played over and over in my head.

"God, no!" He shook his head. "No. Not at all. That was a terrible thing to say, and I didn't mean it. I said it because I thought I was losing you, and I can't lose you . . ." He paused. "You've saved me. Don't you see that? Before you, I was empty, I was angry, I was lost. And now I'm none of those things, and it's because you've brought fucking flowers and pigeons and butterflies into my life. And now that I've had those things, I don't want to live without them anymore. I can't."

"How is Houdini anyway?" I asked.

"He misses you. We all miss you."

"I miss you all too," I admitted. I stepped closer to him. My heart wanted to explode out of my chest and right back into his hands. "Wait!" I suddenly said. "It's Tuesday, you have your board meeting every Tuesday afternoon. How are you even here?"

At that, he smiled at me. A strange, slow smile that I'd never seen before.

"What did you do?" I asked.

"I sold my shares in the company."

"*WHAT?* To who, not that Grey asshole?"

He shook his head. "No, I sold them to Mr. Rautenbach. I think I might have finally made my first good decision since taking that company over. I sold them to someone who is actually passionate about the company, someone who will actually do the right thing with it."

I looked at him and blinked stupidly. This was such a shock, I didn't know what to say.

"So, I am officially unemployed," he said. "For the first time in my adult life I don't have a job. And you know what? I have no idea what the hell I want to do with my life." He started laughing. "I'm thirty-seven and I have no idea what I want to do with my life."

"Is that a good laugh, or a nervous laugh?" I asked.

"A bit of both."

He looked at me and smiled, and I found myself smiling back at him.

"So what do you think?" He gestured to the plants. "I was going for a grand gesture. Emmy said it had to be a big, grand romantic gesture like in the movies. But I couldn't get all the plants in, and some are still in the van, but . . . I'm trying to say sorry, and I hope that you forgive me?"

I nodded. "And I'm sorry I just dropped the bombshell like that, about Joburg. Honestly, I hadn't really thought it through, and what it would mean for us."

He shook his head. "Your schedule is flexible—you're not even shooting every day—and next week, your last shoot day is on Thursday. I asked about your schedule. Sorry if that is a bit stalk-erish, but I did, and flights are only two hours. You could come home on weekends, and now that I am unemployed I have lots of time on my hands."

"Home?" A lump formed in my throat at the word. It seemed to have caught him off guard too.

"I mean . . ." He sounded unsure. "If you want it to be. I know I want it to be, and I know Emmy and Tamlin would love that too." Suddenly he looked vulnerable, unsure of himself. "Those keys are yours, if you still want them."

"Home." I repeated the word out loud to myself. "I . . . I . . . I just, I'm not sure. I mean, I don't know, this whole thing was so—"

"I believe in us." He cut me off. "I haven't believed in anything so much in a long time. I believe we're meant to be together and, as my sister would say, that the universe conspired to blow that news-paper into your face so you could see the job advert and come into my life. I believe in us so much that . . ." He looked around. His eyes widened, as if a realization had hit him. He walked up to me and took me by the hand. "Come." He pulled me into the trailer.

"I believe in us so much that I'm prepared to let the daisy speak for us." He plucked one of the flowers and held it up.

"What?"

He pulled the first petal out. "She loves me . . ." He dropped it. "She loves me not . . ." He dropped the next one.

I looked up at him and laughed. "You're not serious."

"Dead serious," he said.

"Okay." I folded my arms and waited.

"She loves me . . ." He dropped it again. "She loves me not . . ." He repeated this, over and over, until we got to the last petal.

My heart sank.

"She loves me . . . *not*."

The word "*not*" seemed to echo around the trailer. He dropped the yellow petal and it fell to the floor. We both stood there watching it. Finally, slowly, we looked up again at each other. Our eyes connected in a way that made it impossible to look away.

He shrugged. He looked defeated. He looked like he was going to open his mouth and say something. But he didn't. My heart started beating in my chest and in that moment, I knew. I knew I wanted him and Emmy to be my home. I knew I wanted to hand my heart right back to him.

"Fuck the flowers," I said. I took his face between my hands and pulled his lips to mine. "I love you."

EPILOGUE

~

Two years later

Mzansi Sun
Celebrity Wedding of the Year

Poppy Peterson, South Africa's favorite soap star, who plays the evil Delilah Winters in *The Obsession*, got married this weekend in what people are calling the celebrity wedding of the year. She rose to fame two years ago as Ramona González in *Venganza Ramona* for which she won Nigeria's most prestigious daytime TV award for Best Villain. She soon took on the role of Delilah Winters and has been lighting up our screens with her manipulations and machinations ever since, winning the award for Best Villain at the Strelitzia TV Awards this year.

But she was nothing like her murderous character this weekend when she walked down the aisle—or should we say the beautiful Clifton Beach—and married her partner of two years, Ryan Stark. A retired hotelier and now stay-at-home dad, she says of their unusual relationship: "It works for us. Ryan has worked so hard over the years that he wanted a total change of pace. And that change now involves running our fifteen-year-old adopted daughter Emmy to school and extramural activities. He's the soccer dad!"

Poppy wore a gorgeous custom-made gown by arguably South Africa's hottest designer at the moment, Sindiso Shabalala. The dusky rose, off-the-shoulder piece boasted a two-meter train covered in white silk flowers, and the bride looked ethereal in the sunset. Her daughter Emmy and best friend Ayanda were her bridesmaids. They both looked stunning in rose-gold, knee-length dresses, holding bouquets of white daisies. Her husband looked dashing in a white suit that perfectly matched the beach atmosphere of the wedding.

In an interview earlier this year with South African *Vogue*, the couple shared their hilarious story of how they met when Poppy took on a job at Ryan's company, dressed as Ramona González. In the article she spoke of the financial hardships that led her to take the job on, and the charity and shelter, Angel Haven, which she has since set up for women in need. "It's a safe place where any woman can go and receive help, whatever she is going through. We all have our struggles," Poppy has been quoted as saying. "And we should all be there for each other in any way we can. Life is hard and sometimes we just need a helping hand."

The couple said their "I do's" in front of family and friends and other well-known South African celebrities, including all the bride's co-stars, and in a moment that had the wedding party in stitches, her pet pigeon was carried up the aisle as a ring bearer. The couple then jetted off to the Amalfi coast for their honeymoon. When we asked Poppy what we could expect from Delilah moving forward, she assured us there would be some dramatic surprises coming up in the show.

We wish them many years of happiness. And when asked whether they would be adding to their family at some point, Poppy said perhaps in a few years. "Ryan is actually going back to university to study architecture at the tender age of thirty-nine," she told us. "It's something he's always enjoyed, but never gotten a chance to pursue. So maybe when my husband is no longer a student, we'll think about kids. But right now, we are very content with our family. Although Emmy is desperate for a baby sister."

Love funny, romantic stories?
You don't want to miss

Read on for a preview . . .

Chapter One

Bad Taste In Wigs

Don't ask me how the hell it happened . . .

I could blame it on the vodka.

Maybe I could blame it on JJ and Bruce. Maybe it was the strobing lights of the nightclub and the repetitive *doof doof* of the bass that triggered some kind of chemical reaction in my brain, causing me to go temporarily insane.

Maybe it was my outfit (NOTE: Never let a drag queen dress you for an evening out). I was wearing a sequined blue *thing* that could barely be described as a dress, and the famous "Marilyn wig" which they'd brought out especially for me, *God only knows why?* I looked like a crazed, transvestite prostitute with bad taste in wigs. Maybe that's why it happened?

But what are the chances?

To find a straight guy at a gay nightclub? Possibly the only one. And to find such a ridiculously hot one, who somehow knew my favorite drink and bought it for me all night long. Who kissed me like *that* on the dance floor and now had me pinned underneath him in the back seat of his car.

I *never* did this.

Someone else was half naked and sweating and moaning and grabbing at his tattooed shoulders. Someone else was licking Vodka Cranberry cocktails and sweat off his chest and having the best sex of her life—*deliciously dirty sex*—with possibly the hottest man that had ever walked the planet.

He'd made me feel like the sexiest woman alive, and that, coupled with the fact that I didn't know his name and would never see him again—*all that strong alcohol helped, too*—saw all my inhibitions fly right out the back window of his car. I did and said things I didn't even know I was capable of. With my face pressed into the seat, I told him how I wanted it. And he willingly gave it to me . . .

As well as several variations on the requested activity.

And when it was all over, he lay on top of me gasping for air and sweating beautiful glistening drops (God, even his sweat was sexy). It was easily the hottest experience of my entire life. But then he did something very odd, something that tipped me over the edge. He lifted his head and met my eyes with such intensity that everything around me went silent and blurry. He was looking at me like he knew me. Really, *really* knew me.

My mouth opened and an almost inaudible whisper came out, "Do I know you?"

He smiled at me. A naughty, skew, sexy smile. "Not yet." And then he kissed me. No one had kissed me like that before. It was the kind of kiss shared by long-lost lovers.

But when some nosey drag queens knocked on the car window

and made loud *oohing* noises and one of them mimed a comic blowjob gesture, I nearly died. I flung the door open and ran, leaving my Sex God shirtless and with his trousers still around his ankles. While I, the girl that never does stuff like this *(I reiterate)*, had to make an embarrassing run of shame across the now crowded parking lot. I could feel every single dramatically drawn, raised eyebrow watching me as I went.

Before I could get far, I was stopped by a distinctly masculine wolf whistle. Sex God clearly had NO inhibitions.

He was now leaning against his car, zipping up his jeans and doing it completely shirtless—*with a very appreciative audience, I might add*. He lit a cigarette, inhaled slowly and let the smoke curl out of his mouth.

He was like an advert for cool, in that *I-don't-give-a-flying-fuck-who-cares* kind of way. An advert for everything deplorable and lascivious, but downright filthy-sexy in a man. *Who the hell was he?*

I really had to go!

I climbed into my car and pulled out of the lot, allowing myself one last glance in his direction. The cigarette hung out of his mouth seductively; his wet hair clung to his face; he was leaning across the bonnet in such a way that he looked like a model from an X-rated Calvin Klein billboard. As I sped away, he blew me a kiss and shouted after me.

"I'm in love!"

CHAPTER TWO

I HEARD HE WAS RAISED
BY WOLVES . . .

*I*n my head-pounding, hungover daze, I rolled, slipped, and fell out of bed, feeling like someone had poured sand into my eyes and pushed me down a steep cliff. I got up and pulled the now very itchy sequin dress off and got the fright of my life when I realized I wasn't wearing any underwear. I knew I'd left the house with panties on last night. *Hadn't I?*

I was already running late for work—I had accidentally pressed the snooze button on my phone way too many times—but I couldn't rush to work looking like I was.

I grabbed some cotton wool, dunked it in make-up remover and attempted to wipe the thick, chalky layers of black smoky eye make-up off my face. My red lipstick was smudged and one of the false lashes was clinging on like a dry spider. The make-up was coming off, but the glitter was more stubborn. "A highlighter, babe. Fab," JJ had said as he'd emptied the entire jar onto my face. The glitter was sticking to my face like glue and some bits had even lodged themselves into my hairline. The wig was even worse.

The clips holding it in place had twisted so badly that everything was completely stuck—*no doubt from rubbing my head back and forth in the back seat of a total stranger's car.* Instant nausea rose as I started to think about it again. *Crap, what the hell had I been thinking!*

But the wig was my top priority right now, and I was left with no choice but to painfully rip it off. I yelped in pain as tufts of brown hair came out in chunks, then I cursed the wig and tossed it onto the floor. I couldn't believe I'd actually worn the thing—it looked like a dead Maltese puppy.

I dissed my usual middle part, scraping my hair back into a ponytail. Contact lenses out—after inventing some new yoga poses to pry them from my dried-out eyes—and glasses on. Black pantsuit, white-collar shirt and a pair of semi-high heels. Then one last mirror check before running out.

On my way to grab my laptop bag and a handful of headache pills, I passed JJ and Bruce's room, but before I could give them a vengeful wake-up knock, my passive-aggressive attempt at punishing them for their part in my early-morning state, I saw the note.

Sera,

　　You naughty, naughty girl! We heard you caused quite the parking lot spectacle. Dinner tonight, we want all the juicy details.

　　XX

　　J&B

I sighed and, as I went out to my car, my face went red-hot at the thought of telling them what had happened.

My twenty-year-old Toyota had been acting up lately. Another thing to add to the growing to-buy list, along with socks without holes, black pumps with non-peeling soles and now some new undies. But I just couldn't afford a new car right now—*or ever*—not between paying back loans and secretly sending money home to my sister Katie.

"*Please start, please start, please start,*" I pleaded with the hunk of metal junk.

My job was the most important thing in my life. Without it, I wouldn't be able to help Katie and she'd be at our dad's mercy. And there was no way I was going to let that happen. I simply couldn't afford to do anything that would jeopardize it especially since I was one of two interns vying for a permanent position at the company. Being late didn't exactly scream "hire me."

I also knew what being late meant. I would surely walk slap bang into an apocalyptic crisis lifted straight from the Book of Revelation. Working at an ad agency means going from one emergency to another. High stakes, lots of money on the line, demanding clients, demanding creatives and deadlines tighter than the skinny jeans they all wear.

My car finally started after a few smoky chugs and I threw a few thank-yous out into the universe. But as soon as I drove out of my apartment complex and turned onto the highway, I was assaulted by bumper-to-bumper Jo'burg traffic, made even worse by minibus taxis and their "creative" driving techniques. Currently I had one only centimeters from my bumper with a painted sign on his back window that read, "*What goes surround, Comes surround.*" At least something about this morning was vaguely humorous. But the static traffic gave me too much time to think and reflect . . .

What the hell had happened last night? Most of it was a blur, but every now and then an image flashed through my mind.

Vodka. Lots.

"Is this seat taken?" That smooth move and that husky voice . . .

Slowly grinding himself into me on the dance floor of Club Six, running his hands up my thighs, creeping way, way too high for public decency laws, until his hands were . . .

"You're so fucking beautiful," he'd whispered in my ear, his hands coming up and cupping my face.

"I want you so badly, Sera." Hang on, how had he known my name?

"I need you." That was the moment I melted completely and decided to walk outside with him . . .

Fumbling for his car keys . . .

On him . . .

Under him . . .

Windows steaming up . . .

"Fuck, you're amazing." More words that made me lose my mind as I writhed on his lap and totally forgot myself in the moment . . .

His tattoos . . . those dark piercing eyes . . .

"I could do this forever," he'd whispered in my ear seductively.

"Sera." He rasped as he came on top of me, the weight of his body crushing me into the seat.

Oh. My. God.

Had I really fallen for every lame jackass line in the book?

One night can change everything . . .

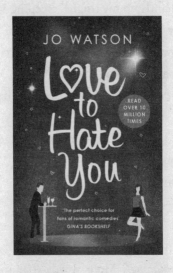

Love funny, romantic stories? You don't want to miss *Love to Hate You.*

Available now from

WARNING: Being jilted at the altar in front of 500 wedding guests can lead to irrational behaviour, such as going on your honeymoon to Thailand alone. Recovery will lead to partying the night away at Burning Moon festival – and falling in love with the person you least expect . . .

Don't miss *Burning Moon*, the first book in the Destination Love series.

Available now from

HEADLINE
ETERNAL

Newly single.

Holiday of a lifetime.

Bumping into 'the ex'.

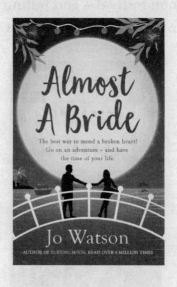

For more laugh-out-loud, swoon-worthy hijinks,
check out *Almost A Bride*, the second book
in the Destination Love series.

Available now from

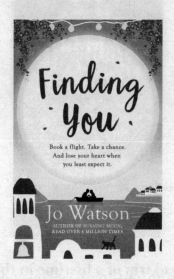

She believes in Fate.
He believes in logic.
But this unexpected journey could change everything...

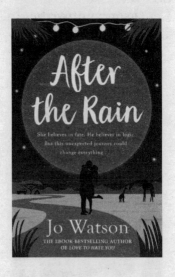

Take the road trip of a lifetime in this hilarious opposites-attract rom-com, as the bestselling Destination Love series continues with *After the Rain*!

Available now from

HEADLINE
ETERNAL

FIND YOUR HEART'S DESIRE...